THE WHALE ROAD

Robert Low has been a journalist and writer since the age of 17. At 19, he was in Vietnam covering aspects of the war and, after 18 months of it, swore he would never do anything as stupid ever again. Since then, he has earned his living as a writer safely in Scotland, with occasional lapses of judgement taking him to Sarajevo, Romania and Kosovo until common sense, age and the concerns of his wife and daughter prevailed.

To satisfy his craving for action and couple it to an obsession with ancient warfare, he took up riding, horse archery and, latterly – having moved to an area rich in Viking tradition – took up re-enactment, joining The Vikings. He now spends summers fighting furiously in helmet and mail in shieldwalls all over Britain and winters training hard. This is his first novel.

Visit www.AuthorTracker.co.uk for exclusive information on Robert Low and visit www.robert–low.com for his official website.

ROBERT LOW

The Whale Road

HarperCollins*Publishers*

HarperCollins*Publishers*
77–85 Fulham Palace Road,
Hammersmith, London W6 8JB

www.harpercollins.co.uk

Published by HarperCollins*Publishers* 2007
1

A catalogue record for this book
is available from the British Library

ISBN-13: 978 0 00 721529 4
ISBN-10: 0 00 721529 0

Set in Sabon by Palimpsest Book Production Limited,
Grangemouth, Stirlingshire

Printed and bound in Great Britain by
Clays Ltd, St Ives plc

This book is proudly printed on paper which contains wood
from well managed forests, certified in accordance with
the rules of the Forest Stewardship Council.
For more information about FSC,
please visit www.fsc.org

Mixed Sources
Product group from well-managed
forests and other controlled sources
www.fsc.org Cert no. TT-COC-2139
© 1996 Forest Stewardship Council
FSC

To my darling wife Katie, who makes sure my keel is straight and all my oars are in the water.

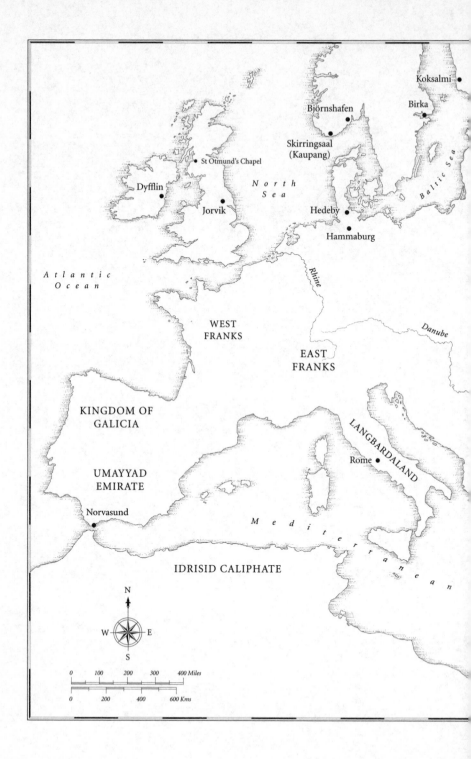

Aldeigjuborg
Holmgard

Voyages of the
OATHSWORN
965 AD

Dvina

GARDARIKI

Don

Volga

Konugard

Dnepr

Itil

KHAZAR
KHANATE

Caspian
Sea

Black Sea

Miklagard

Tigris

Euphrates

Serkland

Sea

Alexandria

Jorsalir

Nile

ONE

Runes are cut in ribbons, like the World Serpent eating his own tail. All sagas are snake-knots, for the story of a life does not always start with birth and end with death. My own truly begins with my return from the dead.

There was a beam, knotted and worn smooth where nets and sails hung, with a cold-killed spider hanging by the slenderest of threads, swaying in the breeze, swimming in my vision.

I knew that beam. It was the ridge beam of the *naust*, the boatshed at Bjornshafen, and I had swung on those hanging nets and sails. Swung and laughed and had no cares, a lifetime ago.

I lay on my back and looked up at it and could not understand why it was there, for I was surely dead. Yet my breath smoked in the chill of that place.

'He's awake.'

The voice was a growl and everything canted and swung when I tried to turn my head to it. I was not dead. I was on a pallet-bed and a face, jut-jawed and bearded like a hedge, floated in front of me. Others, too, peered round him, all strangers, all wavering, as if underwater.

'Get back, you ugly bollocks. Give the boy room to breathe. Finn Horsehead, you would frighten Hel herself, so

I am thinking you should bugger off out of it and fetch his father.'

The hedge-bearded face scowled and vanished. The owner of the voice had a face, too; this one neat-bearded and kind-eyed. 'I am Illugi, godi of the Oathsworn,' he said to me, then patted my shoulder. 'Your father is coming, boy. You are safe.'

Safe. A priest says I am safe, so it must be true. A moment's vision-flash, like something seen in the night when a storm flickers blue-white: the bear, crashing through the roof in a shower of snow and timbers, roaring and snake-necked, a great mountain of white . . .

'My . . . father?'

The voice didn't even sound like mine, but the kind-eyed stranger called Illugi nodded and smiled. Behind him, men moved like shadows, their voices ebbing and flowing in a tide of sound.

My father. So he had come for me after all. The thought of that stayed with me as Illugi's face faded to a pale orb; the others, too, dwindled like trailing bubbles as I slid away, down into the dark water of sleep.

But the priest lied. I was not safe. I would never be safe again.

By the time I could sit up and take broth, the story was round Bjornshafen: the story of Orm the slayer of the white bear.

Alone, when the White Bear, Rurik's Curse, came for revenge on the son – and then, presumably, the father – brave Orm, a mere boy becoming a man fought it over the headless body of Freydis the witch-woman. Fought it for a day and a night and had finally driven a spear into its head and a sword into its heart.

There was more of the same, of course, as my father told me when he came to me, hunkering by my bed and rubbing his grizzled chin and running his hand through his lank, once-gold hair.

2

My father, Rurik. The man who had fostered me on his brother Gudleif at Bjornshafen. He carried me there under his cloak when I was no more than fat knees and chubby fists, in the year Eirik Bloodaxe lost his throne in York and was cut down at Stainmore. I am not even sure if that was a true memory, or one patched back to the cloak of my life by Gudleif's wife, Halldis, who liked me above the other fostris who came and went, because I was blood kin.

She it was who taught me about sheep and chickens and growing things, who filled in the rents in my memory while she sat by the fire, the great hangings which portioned the hall stirring and flapping in the winds which thundered Bjornshafen's beams.

Patient and still, click-clicking her little bone squares as she wove strips of bright wool hemming, she would answer all my piped questions.

'Rurik came back only once, with a white bear cub,' she said. 'Said for Gudleif to keep it for him and that it was worth a fortune – and it was, too. But Rurik, of course, couldn't stop long enough to make it into one. Always off on the next tide, that one. Not the same man after your mother died.'

Now here he was, sprung like a breaching whale from the empty sea.

I saw a nut-brown face and, since folk said we looked alike, tried to see more handsome in it than, perhaps, there was. He was middling height, more silvered than fair now, his face roughened by wind and weather and his beard cropped short. His blue eyes laughed, though, from under hairy eyebrows like spiders' legs, even when he was being concerned.

And what did he see? A boy, tall for his age, with good shoulders and the scrawn of youth almost gone, with red-brown hair that fell in his eyes unless someone rough-cut it with shears. Halldis had done it while she lived but no one much bothered after the coughing sickness took her.

3

I looked at him with the same blue eyes, staring at his snub-nosed face. It came to me, with a sudden shock, that I would look like this when I was old.

'You are come after all, then,' I said, feeling foolish even as I spoke, for it was self-evident he had come – and not alone, either. Behind him, in Bjornshafen's boatshed, their temporary quarters, were the hard-faced crew of the ship he mastered. Gunnar Raudi had warned of these.

'Why would I not?' he answered with a grin.

We both knew the answer to that one, but I would have preferred it said aloud.

'When word comes that a man's son is in danger from his own kin . . . well, a father must act,' he went on, serious as stone.

'Just so,' I replied, thinking that he had taken his time about acting and that ten years was more than a pause for breath in the journey to his son. But I said nothing when I saw in his eyes how he was genuinely puzzled that I would think he wouldn't rush to my aid.

It only came to me later, when I had aged into life a little, that Rurik had done his task of raising me as well as any father and better than most – but looking at this new man, this rawboned hard man from a boatload of hard men and realising he was the one who had left me in the first place, with no word since and no prospect of one, I grew so angry and twisted with it that I could not speak at all.

He took that for something else – the moment of our meeting, the horror of what had gone before with the white bear and the snow journey – and nodded, smiling.

'Who'd have thought that bloody little bear cub would have caused such trouble,' he mused, rasping his chin with horned fingers. 'I bought it from a Gotland trader, who had it from a Finn, he told me. I thought to sell it in Ireland, to make a jarl's cloak, or even a pet, but that nithing Gudleif let it go. Arse. Just look at what happened – I nearly lost my son.'

4

Gudleif had cursed his brother, that bear and, in the end, the one he suspected of letting it go. It had grown too big for its original cage, so had to be tethered loose and fed mountains of good herring; the thrall had grown too afraid to go near it.

There had been about an eyeblink of cheering when everyone saw it had gone, then blind panic that such a monster was loose. Gudleif and Bjarni and Gunnar Raudi had hunted it all that year, but found nothing and lost a good dog besides.

The words were queued up in me, fighting like drunks trying to get out of a burning hall. My father was breathtaking . . . not one word about where he had been, or why I had been left so long, or what had been my life in the five years before he brought me here. Or even that the bloody bear had been his fault all along.

It was infuriating. My mouth gaped and shut like a fresh-caught cod and he saw it, put it down to the emotion of the moment, of seeing his long-lost father, and made manly of it. He clapped me on the shoulder and said, gruffly, 'Can you walk? Einar is in the hall and wants to see you.'

Fuck Einar, was what I wanted to say. Fuck you, too. Freydis is dead because of your bloody bear and the fact that you weren't around to decide what to do with it before someone got tired of it and let it escape. Where *were* you? And tell me of me, my mother, where I am from. I know *nothing*.

Instead, I nodded and weaved upright, while he helped me into breeks and shoes and kirtle and tunic, me leaning on him, feeling his wiry strength.

He smelled of old sweat and leather and wet wool and the hair grew up under the neck of his own tunic, all around, curling wads of it, grizzled and darker than that on his head and chin.

And all the while the thoughts in me wheeling and screaming like terns round a fresh catch. The years between us and the wyrd of that white bear. How long was it free? Six years? Eight, maybe?

Yet this winter it had sought me out somehow, tracked me down and brought my father back to me with its death, like an Odin sacrifice.

The wyrd of it made me shiver – those three Norn sisters, who weave the lives of every creature, had started on a strange tapestry for me.

Finally, as I fastened and looped a belt round my waist, my father straightened from doing up my leg-bindings and held out Bjarni's sword to me. It had been cleaned of all blood; cleaned better than it had been before, for there were fewer rot spots on it than when I had stolen it.

'It isn't mine,' I said, half-ashamed, half-defiant, and he cocked his head like a bird and I laid out the tale of it.

It was Bjarni's sword, he who had been Gudleif's oarmate of long standing. He and Gudleif had taught me the strokes of it, and then Gunnar Raudi, unable to watch any longer, had picked it up, spat between his feet and shown me how to use it in a real fight.

'When you stand in a shieldwall, boy,' he said, 'forget all the fancy strokes. Hit their fucking feet. Cut the ankles from them. Stab them up and under the shield and the hem of their mail, right into their balls. It's the only bits you can see or reach anyway.'

And then he showed me how to use the hilt, my shield, my knees and elbows and teeth, while Gudleif and Bjarni stayed quiet and still.

It was then I saw they were afraid of Gunnar Raudi and learned later – from Halldis, of course – that Gunnar stayed at Bjornshafen because he had got both Bjarni and Gudleif back from a raid to Dyfflin that went badly wrong. Everyone thought them dead and then, two seasons later, in they sailed with a stolen ship, captured thralls and tales of Gunnar's daring. They owed him their lives and a berth for as long as he breathed.

'I stole it from Gudleif,' I told my father, 'when it was clear he wanted me to die in the snow on the way to Freydis's hov.'

He rubbed his beard and frowned, nodding. 'Aye, so Gunnar said when he sent word.'

That had been the day Gunnar had cracked my world, a day that began with Gudleif sitting in his giftthrone with his ship prows on either side and himself swathed in furs, trying to be a great jarl and managing only to look like a bad-tempered cat.

Bjarni had died the previous year and Halldis the year before that. Now Gudleif complained of the cold and avoided going out much. He sat, hunched and glowering, with only old Caomh close to his elbow, the thrall who had come back as a slave from a Christ temple in Dyfflin.

Nearby, the equally old Helga shuttled a loom back and forth and grinned her two last teeth at me, while Gunnar Raudi, just visible in the smoking gloom, worked on a leather strap.

'I am not up to the journey to the high pasture this year,' Gudleif said to me. 'The herd needs to be brought down and some essentials taken to Freydis.'

It was an early winter, the snow curling off Snaefel, the colour leached from the land by cold, so that there were only black tree skeletons on grey under a grey sky. Even the sea was slate.

'It has already snowed,' I reminded him. 'It may be too deep to drive horses down now.' I refrained from reminding him that I had spoken of this weeks before, when it might have been easier to do.

There was no sound save for the clack-shuff of the loom and the sputter of a fire whose wood was too damp. Halldis would not have made it so.

Gudleif stirred and said to me, 'Perhaps. If so, you will over-winter there and bring them in spring. Freydis will have prepared.'

7

It was not an attractive proposition. Freydis was a strange one and, truth to tell, most people thought her a *volva*, a witch. I had never seen her, in all my fifteen years, though her hov was no more than a good day's walk up the lowest slopes. She tended Gudleif's best stallions and mares on the high pasture and was clever at it.

I thought of all this and the fact that, even if she had prepared well, there would not be enough fodder to keep the herd fed through the hard winter it promised to be. Or, perhaps, even the pair of us.

I said as much and Gudleif shrugged. I thought Gunnar Raudi was probably best to go and said that, too. Gudleif shrugged again and, when I looked at him, Gunnar Raudi was busy beside the hearthfire, too concerned with his strap of leather even to look up, it seemed to me.

So I prepared a pack and took the sturdiest of the ponies. I was considering what best to take Freydis when Gunnar Raudi came to the stable and there, in the warm, rustling twilight of it, tore everything apart with a simple phrase.

'He has sent for his sons.'

And there it was. Gudleif was dying. His sons, Bjorn and Steinkel, were coming back from their own fostering to claim their inheritance and I was . . . expendable. Perhaps he hoped I would die and solve all his problems.

Gunnar Raudi saw all that chase itself like cat and dog across my face. He said nothing for a while, still as a block of grindstone in the fetid dark. A horse whuffed and stamped; straw rustled and all I could think to say was: 'So that's where the *faering* went. I wondered.'

And Gunnar Raudi smiled a grim smile. 'No. He sent word by the next valley up. The faering is missing because I sent Krel and Big Nose to row it to Laugarsfel, there to send word to Rurik.'

I glanced at him anxiously. 'Does Gudleif know?'

He shook his head and shrugged. 'He knows nothing much

these days. Even if he finds out what can he do? Perhaps he might even have done it himself if it had been mentioned to him.' In the dim, his face was all shadowed planes, unreadable. But he went on: 'A trip through the snow isn't so bad. Better than here when Rurik arrives.'

'If you think so, you take the trip through the snow and I will stay here,' I answered bitterly and expected his wry chuckle and a growl of a reply. Instead, to my surprise – of both of us, it seemed to me after – he laid a hand on my shoulder.

'Best not, lad. What Rurik brings with him will be worse than a frozen nose.'

That was chilling and I had to ask. His eyes gleamed in the dark.

'Einar the Black and his crew,' he replied and the way he said it told me all I needed to know.

I laughed, but even to my own ears it was forced. 'If he comes.'

I looked him in the face and he looked right back and both of us knew the truth of it. I was like the white bear: someone else's property, unclaimed and in the way. My father might not get the news. Even if he did, he might not be bothered.

My father grunted at that part of the tale, as if he had been dug sharply in the ribs. But his glare made me ashamed I had said it.

I told him then that I felt no pang about taking Bjarni's sword. Or the large amount of salt, or any of the other supplies I thought necessary. Fuck Bjornshafen. Fuck Gudleif and fuck both his sons.

My father grinned at that.

Taking Bjarni's sword was the worst thing, for a sword then was a thing not to be taken lightly. It was expensive and, more than that, it was the mark of a warrior and a man of substance.

The Greeks in Constantinople – who call themselves

Romans, but speak no Latin – think all Northmen are Danes and that all Danes fight in mail and with swords. The truth is that most of us have only the seax, a kitchen knife the length of your forearm. With it, you can chop a chicken or gut a fish – or kill a man.

You get to be good with it, since mail is too expensive for most. Any good blow will kill you unless you avoid it and only if you must do you block it, so that the edge of your precious seax isn't notched away.

A sword, though, was a magical thing, a rich thing and the mark of a warrior, so not to be trifled with – but I took dead Bjarni's sword out of spite, right off the hook in the hall, while Gudleif grunted and farted and slept. In the morning I was gone early, before he noticed it was missing.

Bjarni would notice but I made my peace with him on my own and prayed to big, bluff Thor to intercede. Then I added a prayer to Odin, made wise by communing with the new-dead, who had hung nine nights on the World Tree for wisdom. And one to Jesus, the White Christ, who hung on a tree like Odin.

'That was deep thinking, right enough,' my father said when I told him this. 'You can never have too much holy help, even if this Christ-following lot are a strange breed, who say they will not fight yet still seem able to field warriors and sharp steel. As for the sword – well, Bjarni won't need it and Gudleif won't mind. Ask Einar for it. He will let you keep it after what you did.'

I stayed silent. How could I tell them what I had done? Pissed myself and run, leaving Freydis to die?

The first sight of those great bear pugs in the snow, maybe two weeks after I had struggled through to her hov, had set Freydis to barring doors and hunkering down. The night it came we had eaten broth and bread by the glimmer of the pitfire embers, listening to the creak of the beams and the rustle of straw from the stalls.

I lay down clutching Bjarni's sword. That, an old ash spear of her dead man's, the wood axe and Freydis's kitchen knives made the only weapons we had. I stared at the glowing embers, trying not to think of the bear, prowling, sniffing, circling.

I knew whose bear it was and, it seemed to me, it had come seeking revenge after all these years.

I woke to soft singing. Freydis sat, cross-legged and naked, the hearthfire glowing on her body, her face hidden by the long, unbound straggles of her streaked hair, one hand holding upright the ash spear. In front of her were . . . objects.

I saw a small animal skull, the teeth blood-red in the light, the eye-sockets blacker than night. There were carved things and a pouch and, over them all, Freydis hummed, a long, almost continuous drone that raised the hair on my arms.

I hung on to the sharkskin hilt of Bjarni's old sword while the dead crowded round, their eyes glittering in the dark holes of their heads, pale faces like mist.

Whether she called them for help, or called the bear, or tried to weave a shield against it, I don't know. All I know is that when the bear struck the wall, the hall boomed like a bell and I jumped up, half-naked, sword in hand.

I shook my head, scattering memories like water drops. A last, brief flash of the curving swipe of paw and her head, spinning, flailing blood to the rafters. Had there been a smile on it? An accusing look?

My father rightly guessed the memories, wrongly assumed I was mourning for the lost Freydis and clapped my shoulder again, giving it a slight squeeze and a half-smile. Then he walked me slowly to the hall across the sun-sparkled snow. The eaves were dripping with melting spires of ice.

Everything seemed the same, but the thralls avoided my eye, keeping their heads down. I saw Caomh down by the shore, standing by a pole with a ball on it – one of his strange White Christ totems, probably. Once a monk, always a monk, he used to say. Just because he had been ripped from his cloister didn't make him less of a holy man for the Christ. I raised a hand in greeting but he never moved, though I knew he saw me.

Gudleif's hall was dim inside, misted with cold light from the smoke hole. The hearthfire crackled, breath coiled in wisps and the figures hunched on benches at the foot of the high seat turned to us as we came in.

I waited until my eyes had accustomed and then saw that someone else sat in Gudleif's high seat, someone with hair to his shoulders, dark as crow wings.

Black-eyed, black-moustached, he wore blue-checked breeks like the Irish and a kirtle of finest blue silk, hemmed in red. One hand leaned on the fat-pommelled hilt of a sheathed sword, point at his feet. It was a fine sword, with a three-lobed heavy silver end to the hilt and lots of workings round the cross guard.

The other hand clasped a furred cloak around his throat. Gudleif's furred cloak, I noticed. And Gudleif's high seat – but not his ship prows. I saw them stacked to one side and the ones that flanked the high seat now were the proud heads of an antlered beast with flaring nostrils.

Hard men, my father's oarmates, who thought highly of him because he was their shipmaster and could read waves like other men did runes. Sixty of them had come to Bjornshafen because he had wished it, even though he did not lead this *varjazi*, this oathsworn band and their slim snakeship, the *Fjord Elk*.

Einar the Black led them, who now sat on Gudleif's high seat as if it were his own.

At his feet sat others, one of them Gunnar Raudi, hands on his knees, cloaked and very still, his faded red tangles fastened back from his face by a leather thong. He looked at me and said nothing, his eyes grey-blue and glassed as a summer sea.

The others I did not know, though I half recognised Geir, the great sack of purple-veined nose that gave him his nickname wobbling in his face as he told the tale of finding me half-frozen and slathered in blood, the headless woman nearby. Steinthor, who had been with him, nodded his shaggy head in agreement.

They were cheerful about it now but, at the time, had been afraid when they found the great white bear dead, a spear in its brain and Bjarni's sword rammed in its heart. As Steinthor happily admitted, to the grunts and chuckles of the others, he had shat himself.

There were two other strangers, one of them the biggest man I had ever seen: fat-bearded, fat-bellied, fat-voiced – fat everything. He wore a blue coat of heavy wool and the biggest seaboots I had ever seen, into which were tucked the baggiest breeks, striped blue and silver, that I had ever seen. There were ells of silk in those breeks.

He had a fur hat with a silver end, which chimed like a bell when he accidentally brushed it against the blade of the huge Dane axe that he held, rapping the haft on the hard-packed hall floor now and then and going 'hoom' deep in his throat when Geir managed a better-than-usual kenning in his story.

The other was languid and slim, leaning back against one of the roof poles, stroking his snake moustaches, which were all the fashion then. He looked at me as Gudleif looked at a new horse, weighing it up, seeing how it moved.

But no Gudleif, just this crow-dark stranger in his chair.

'I am Einar the Black. Welcome, Orm Ruriksson.'

He said it as if the hall belonged to him, as if the high seat was his.

'I have to say,' he went on, leaning forward slightly and turning the sword slowly on its rounded point as he did so, 'that things turned out more interesting and profitable than when Rurik came to me with this request to sail here. I had

13

other plans . . . but when your shipmaster speaks, a wise man listens.'

Beside me, my father inclined his head slightly and grinned. Einar grinned in return and leaned back.

'Where is Gudleif?' I asked. There was silence. Einar looked at my father. I saw it and turned to look at him, too.

My father shrugged awkwardly. 'The tale I heard was that he had sent you into the mountain snows to die. And there was the matter of the bear, which had not been settled—'

'Gudleif's dead, boy,' Einar interrupted. 'His head is on a spear on the strand, so that his sons will see it when they finally arrive and know that bloodprice has been taken.'

'For what?' growled the large man, turning his axe so that the blade flashed in the dim light. 'It was done when we thought Rurik's boy was killed.'

'For the bear, Skapti Halftroll,' said Einar quietly. 'That was an expensive bear.'

'Was it Gudleif who killed it, then?' asked the slim one, stroking his moustaches slowly and yawning. 'I am thinking I have just been listening to Geir Bagnose recount the saga of Orm Ruriksson, the White-bear Slayer.'

'Was he then to weigh the cost when it came at him in the dark?' growled my father. 'I can see you count it up, Ketil Crow – but by the time you got your boots off to use your toes, it would have been your head split from your body, for sure.'

Ketil Crow chuckled and acknowledged the point with the wave of one hand. 'Aye, just so. I cannot count, that is true enough. But I know how many beans make five, just the same.'

'Of course,' said Einar, smoothly ignoring all this, 'there is the woman, Freydis, who was killed. No thrall, that one. Freeborn and there's a price to be paid for that, since her death came because Gudleif let the bear go in the first place. Anyway, the bear was mine and worth a lot.'

My father said nothing about whose bear it was. I said nothing at all, since I had just realised that the pole with the ball Caomh had been standing near was a spear with Gudleif's head on it.

Einar shifted again and drew the cloak tighter around him, his breath smoking in the cold hall as he declared, 'In the end, you can argue in circles about whose fault it was – from Rurik bringing the bear here, to Gudleif letting it escape. And then there is why he sent the boy late into the mountain snow to that lonely hall. Perhaps he and the bear were in this together.'

It was half in jest, but Skapti and Ketil both warded off the evil with some swift signs and grasped the iron Thor's hammers hung round their necks. I realised, even then, that Einar knew his men well.

I said nothing, rushed with a fluttering of memories, like bats spilling from a hole in the ground.

After the bear had slammed into the wall, there was silence, though I swear I heard it huffing through the snow, paws crunching. Freydis droned. The two milk cows bellowed their fear and the bear answered, drove the animals mad and chilled me so much I found myself sitting on the floor, the lantern at my feet, my breath caught, my mouth glued with dryness.

'So Gunnar Rognaldsson, will you tell all this freely to Gudleif's sons when they come? Or, perhaps, you would like to come with us? We need good men.'

I shook back to the Now of it, but it took me a moment to realise that Einar was speaking to Gunnar Raudi. I had never heard his real name – he was always just Red Gunnar to us.

And in a dangerous position, I realised. Gudleif's man and a vicious and deadly fighter, he had been left alive so far because he had been the one to send word to my father about me.

Yet it was clear he and Einar knew each other – and that

Einar didn't trust Gunnar and Gunnar knew it. I saw that Einar would not want Gunnar left to advise Gudleif's sons. Without him they would think twice about revenge.

Gunnar shrugged and scrubbed his grey-streaked head, as if considering – but the truth was that he had no choice. 'I had thought to berth here for good at my age,' he growled ruefully, 'but the Norns weave and we can only wear what they make. I will come with you, Einar. Coldward and stormward, eh?'

They grinned at each other, but it was the smile of wolves circling.

'And you, Bear Slayer?' Einar said, turning to me. 'Will you join your father on the *Fjord Elk*? I strongly advise you to do so.'

He didn't have to say more. Gudleif's sons would revenge themselves on me if I stayed, for sure, and there was nothing for me here.

I nodded. He nodded. My father beamed. Skapti called for ale.

And so it was done. I joined the Oathsworn – but there was more to taking the blood-oath than a nod and a wink, though I only learned that later.

I ate in Gudleif's hall for the last time that night. The partition hangings were ripped down (with some contempt, it seemed to me) to make room for all the Oathsworn to come in. It is the mark of a raiding jarl to have a whole hall and those who partitioned it were admitting they'd given up needing the men for raids and therefore the room for them. The Oathsworn held to the old ways and hated a hall with hangings.

We ate round the pitfire, me huddled and listening to the thunder of the wind on the beams. The fire flattened and flared as stray blasts hissed down the smoke hole and through the hall, while these growlers who had taken over Bjornshafen, just like that, fished mutton from the pot, blowing on their fingers and talking about such strange things and places as I'd never heard of before.

They drank, too, great amounts of ale, the foam spilling down their beards while they joked and made riddles. Steinthor, it was clear, fancied himself as a skald and made verses on the bear-slaying, while the others thumped benches or threw insults, depending on how good his kennings were.

And they raised horns to me, Orm the Bear Slayer, with my father, new-found and grinning with pride as if he had won a fine horse, leading the praise-toasts. But I saw that Gunnar Raudi was hunched and quiet on his ale bench, watching.

That night, as the men fell to talking quiet and lazy as smoke drifting from the hearthfire, I fell asleep and dreamed of the white bear and how it had circled the walls and then fallen silent.

I turned to say to Freydis that her walls were well built; I was sure that we had weathered it, that the bear was gone. I was smiling when the roof caved in. The turf roof. Two massive paws swiped and the earth and snow tumbled in and then, with a crash like Thor's thrown hammer, the bear followed: an avalanche of white; a great rumbling roar of triumph.

Numbed, I pissed myself then and there. The bear landed in a heap, shook itself like a dog, scattering earth and snow and clods, and then got on all fours.

It was a cliff of fur, a rank, wet-smelling shriek of a thing that swung a snake neck with a horror of a head this way and that, one eye red in the firelight, the other an old, black socket. On that same side, the lips had been straked off, leaving the yellow tusk teeth exposed in a grim grin. The drool of its hunger spilled, thick and viscous.

It saw us; smelled the ponies, didn't know which to go for first. That was when I ran for it and so decided the skein of all our lives.

17

The white bear whirled at my movement – the speed of it, and it so huge! It saw me at the door, scrabbling for the bar. I heard it – felt it – roar with the fetid breath of a dragon; I frantically tore the bar off and dragged the door open.

I heard it crash, half-turned to look over my shoulder as I scrambled out. It had risen on hind legs and lumbered forward. Too tall for the roof, its great head had smacked a joist – cracked it – and tumbled it down into the fire.

I swear I saw it glare its one eye at me as it shrieked; I also saw Freydis calmly stand, pick up the old spear and ram it at the beast's ravening mouth. Not good enough. Not nearly a good enough spell, after all. The spear smashed teeth on the already ruined side, snapped off and left the head and part of the haft inside.

The bear lashed out, one casual swipe that sent Freydis flying backwards in a spray of blood and bone. I saw her head part company from her body.

I ran stumbling through the snow. I ran like a nithing thrall. If there had been a baby in my way I would have tossed it over one shoulder, hoping to tempt the beast into a snack and giving me more time to get away . . .

I woke in Gudleif's hall, to a sour-milk smear of a morning and the sick shame of remembering, but everyone was too busy to notice, for we were leaving Bjornshafen.

Leaving my only home and never returning, I realised. Leaving with a shipload of complete strangers, hard men for the sailing and raiding and, worse yet, a father I hardly knew. A father who had, at the very least, watched his brother's head part company from the rest of him and not even shrugged over it.

I could not breathe for the terror of it. Bjornshafen was where I had learned what every child learns: the wind, the wave and war. I had run the meadows and the hayfields, stolen gulls' eggs from the black cliffs, sailed the little faering and crewed the hafskip with Bjarni and Gunnar Raudi and others.

I had even gone down to Skiringssal once, the year Bluetooth buried his father Old Gorm and became King of the Danes.

I knew the place, from the skerry offshore where the surf creamed on black rocks, to the screaming laughter of the terns. I fell asleep at night rocked in the creaking beams as the wind shuddered the turf of the roof, and felt warm and safe as the fire danced the shadows of the looms like huge spiders' webs.

Here Caomh had taught me to read Latin because no one knew runes well enough – when I could be pinned down to follow his hen-scratching in the sand. Here was where I had learned of horses, since Gudleif made his name breeding fighting stallions.

And all that was changed in an eyeblink.

Einar took some barrels of meat and meal and ale, as part of the 'bloodprice' for the bear, then left instructions to bury Freydis and drag the bear corpse in and flay the pelt from it. Gudleif's sons could keep that and the skull and teeth, all valuable trade items, worth more than the barrels taken.

Whether it was worth their father was another matter, I thought, gathering what little I had: a purse, an eating knife, an iron cloak brooch, my clothes and a linen cloak. And Bjarni's sword. I had forgotten to ask about it, it had never been mentioned, so I just kept it.

The sea was grey slate, capped white. Picking through the knots of dulse and rippled, snow-scattered sand, the Oathsworn humped their sea-chests down to the *Fjord Elk*, plunging into the icy sea with whoops, boots round their necks. White clouds in a clear blue sky and a sun like a brass orb; even the weather tried to hold me to the place.

Behind me, Helga scraped sheepskins to soften them, watching, for life went on, it seemed, even though Gudleif was dead. Caomh, too, watched, waiting by Gudleif's head – until we were safely over the horizon, I was thinking, and he could give it a White Christ burial.

19

I said as much to Gunnar Raudi as he passed me by and he grunted, 'Gudleif won't thank him for it. Gudleif belonged to Odin, pate to heel, all his life.'

He turned back to me then, bowed under the weight of his own sea-chest and looked at me from under his red brows. 'Watch Einar, boy. He believes you are touched by the gods. This white bear, he thinks, was sent by Odin.'

It was something that I had thought myself and said so.

Gunnar chuckled. 'Not for you, boy. For Einar. He believes it was all done to bring him here, bring him to you, that you have something to do with his saga.' He hefted the chest more comfortably on his shoulder. 'Learn, but don't trust him. Or any of them.'

'Not even my father? Or you?' I answered, half-mocking.

He looked at me with his summer-sea eyes. 'You can always trust your father, boy.'

And he splashed on to the *Fjord Elk*, hailing those on board to help haul his sea-chest up, his hair flying, streaked grey-white and red like bracken in snow. As I stood under the great straked serpent side of the ship, it loomed, large as my life and just as glowering. I felt . . . everything.

Excited and afraid, cold and burning feverishly. Was this what it meant to be a man, this . . . uncertainty?

'Move yerself, boy – or be left with the gulls.'

I caught my father's face scowling over the side, then it was gone and Geir Bagnose leaned over, chuckling, to help me up with my rough pack, lashed with my only spare belt. 'Welcome to the *Fjord Elk*,' he laughed.

TWO

The voyages of the Northmen are legendary, I know. Even the sailors of the Great City, Constantinople, with their many-banked ships and engines that throw Greek Fire, stand in awe of them. Hardly surprising, since those Greeks never lose sight of land and those impressively huge vessels they have will go keel over mast in anything rougher than a mild chop.

We, on the other hand, travel the whale road, where the sea is black or glass-green and can rear over you like a fighting stallion, all roar and threat and creaming mane, to come crashing down like a cliff. No bird flies here. Land is a memory.

That's what we boast of, at least. The truth is always different, like a Greek Christ ikon veiled on feast days. But if anyone boasts of spitting in Thor's eye, standing in the prow, roaring defiance at the waves and laughing the while, you will know him for the liar he is.

A long journey is always being wet to the skin and the wind bites harder as a result and your clothes are heavy as mail and chafe you until you have sores where the cloth rubs on wrist and neck.

It's huddled in the dark, bundled in a wet cloak, feeling

21

the sodden squash every time you turn. It's cold, wet mutton if you are lucky, salt stockfish if you are not and, on truly long voyages, drinking water that has to be strained through your linen cloak to get rid of the worst of the floating things and no food at all.

There wasn't even a storm of any serious intent on this, my first true faring; just a mild pitch of wave and a good wind, so that the company had time to erect deck covers of spare sail, like small tents, to give some shelter, mainly to the animals.

Einar huddled under his own awning, aft. The oars were stacked inboard and the only one with serious work was my father.

And my task? A sheep was mine. I had to care for it, keep it warm, stop it panicking. At night I slept, my fingers entwined in the rough, wet wool while the mirr washed us. In the morning, I woke with spray and rain washing down the deck. If I moved, I squelched.

The first week we never saw land at all, heading south and west from Norway. My sad ewe bawled with hunger.

Then we hit the narrow stretch of water which had Wessex on one side and Valland, the Northmen lands of the Franks on the other. We made landfall a few times – but never on the Wessex side. Not since Alfred's day.

Even then we kept to the solitary inlets and lit fires only when we were sure there was no one for miles. Nowhere was safe for a boatload of armed men from the Norway viks.

We sailed north then, up past Man, where there was much argument for putting in at Thingvollur and getting properly dry and fed. But Einar argued against it, saying that people would ask too many questions and someone would talk and the news would get to Strathclyde before we did.

Grumbling, the men hauled the *Elk* further north, into the wind and the white-tressed sea.

Three more days passed, during which no one spoke much

more than grunts and even the sheep had no strength left to bleat. For the most part, we huddled in solitary misery, enduring.

I dreamed of Freydis often, and always the same vision: her receiving me on the morning I arrived. She wore a blue linen dress with embroidery round the throat and hem, her brooches had strange animal heads and between them was a string of amber beads. She made no movement save for the rhythmic stroking of the growling cat.

'From the pack, I take it you have come from Gudleif,' she said to me. 'Since he would only miss this journey if he were sick or injured, I presume that to be the case. Who are you?'

'Orm,' I replied. 'Ruriksson. Gudleif fosters me.'

'Which is it?'

'Sorry?'

'Sick or injured.'

'He has sent for his sons.'

'Ah.' She was silent for a moment. Then: 'So were you his favourite?'

My laugh was bitter enough for her to realise. 'I doubt that, mistress. Why else would he send me through the snow to the hall of a—' I stopped before the words were out, but she caught that, too, and chuckled.

'A what? Witch? Old crone?'

'I meant nothing by it, mistress. But I was sent away and I think he hoped I would die.'

'I doubt that,' she said crisply, rising so that the cat sprang off her lap and then arched in a great, shivering bow of ecstasy before stalking off. 'Call me Freydis, not mistress,' she went on, smoothing her front. 'And ponder this, young man. Ask yourself why in . . . how old are you?'

I told her and she smiled gently. 'In fifteen years, you and I have never met, though we are but a day apart and Gudleif came every year. Ask that, Orm Ruriksson. Take your time. The snow will not melt in a hurry.'

23

'He sent me to die in the snow,' I said bitterly and she shrugged.

'But you did not. Perhaps your wyrd is different.'

Then the hall changed, to the one I had sat in under her bloodsoaked sealskin cloak, with the roof caved in. Yet still she sat on her bench, the cat somehow back on her lap.

'I am sorry,' I said and she nodded her head off her shoulders, so that it tumbled into her lap, sending the cat leaping up with a yowl . . .

I woke to the cold and wet, wondering if she was fetch-haunting me. Wondering, too, what had happened to the cat.

Then Pinleg yelled out from the prow, where he was coiling walrus-hide ropes. When he had our attention, he pointed and we all squinted into the pearl-light of the winter sky.

'There,' shouted Illugi Godi, pointing with his staff. A solitary gull wheeled, staggered in the wind, dipped, swooped and then was gone.

My father was already busy, with his tally stick and his peculiar devices. I never mastered them, even after he had explained them to me.

I knew that he had two stones, like grinding wheels, free-mounted. One pointed at the north star and the other was fixed to point at the sun. That way, my father knew the latitude, by seeing the angle of the sun stone. He could calculate longitude by using that and what he called his own time, marked on his tally stick.

I never understood any of it – but at the end of four days I knew why Einar valued Rurik the shipmaster, because we found the land at the point where we were supposed to find it, then my father, leaning over the side, watching the water, announced that a suitable inlet lay no more than a mile away, one where we could get ashore and sort ourselves out.

He read water like a hunter reads tracks. He could see changes in colour where, to anyone else, it was just featureless water.

The mood had changed and everyone was suddenly alert and busy. The sail came down, a great sodden mass of wool which had to be sweatily flaked into a squelching mass and stowed on the spar.

The oars came out, that watch of rowers took their sea-chest benches and Valgard Skafhogg, the shipwright, took a shield and beat time on it with a pine-tarred rope's end until the rowers had the rhythm and away we went.

Pinleg swayed past me, smiling broadly and clapping a round helmet on his head. He had a boarding axe in one hand and a wild light in his eye. It was hard for me to realise that Pinleg was older than me by ten years, since he was scrawny and no bigger than I was.

I wondered how such a runt – his leg was permanently crippled, from birth I learned, so that he walked with a sailor's roll even on dry land – had ended up in the Oathsworn. I learned, soon enough, and was glad I had never asked him.

'I'd leave the sheep, Bear Killer,' he chuckled. 'Grab your weapons and get ready.'

'Are we fighting?' I asked, suddenly alarmed. It occurred to me that I had no idea where we were, or who the enemy would be. 'Where are we?'

Pinleg just grinned his mad grin. Nearby, Ulf-Agar, small, dark as a black dwarf and with an expression as sullen, said, 'Who cares? Just get ready, Bear Killer. Pretend they are lots of bears. That will help.'

I glanced at him, knowing he was taunting me and not knowing why.

Ulf-Agar hefted his two weapons – he scorned a shield – and curled a lip. 'Stay behind Pinleg if you are worried. Killing men is different from bears, I will grant you. Not everyone is cut out for it.'

I knew I had been insulted; I felt my face flame. I realised, with a sick lurch, that Ulf-Agar was probably deadly with his axe and seax, but a slight is a slight . . .

A hand clasped my shoulder, gentle but firm. Big-bellied Illugi Godi, with his neat beard and quiet voice, spoke softly: 'Well said, Ulf-Agar. And not everyone can kill a white bear in a stand-up fight. Perhaps, when you do, you will share your joy with Rurik's son?'

Ulf-Agar offered him a twisted smile and said nothing, suddenly interested in the notching on his seax. Then: 'I have a spear, Bear Killer,' he remarked, with an edge-sharp smile. 'Since you drove your own up into the head of that beast, you may want to borrow it.'

I turned away without replying. Ulf-Agar wanted the tale to be a lie, for it was a task Baldur would have been hard put to manage, let alone a scrawny man/boy. And the night-mare of it hag-rode me to a shivering, soaked waking most nights, which I am sure Ulf-Agar had not been slow to notice.

The nightmare was always one of those where you are running from some horror and yet you cannot get your legs working fast enough – which is what happened when I spilled out of that doorway, leaving Freydis to her wyrd. I was sobbing and panting and struggling in the snow. I fell, got up and fell again.

My knee hit something, hard enough to make me gasp. The wood sled. The bear lumbered forward, spraying snow like a ship under full sail. I had Bjarni's sword still, was surprised to find it locked in my hand.

I picked up the sled awkwardly, stumbled a few steps and half fell, half hurled myself on it. It slid a few feet, then stopped. I kicked furiously and it moved. I heard the bear grunting and puffing through the snow close behind me.

I kicked again and the sled slithered forward, picked up a little speed, then a little more. I felt the hissing wind of a swiped paw, a fine mist of blood on my ears and neck from its ruined mouth as it roared . . . then I was away, hurtling down the hill, the bear galloping clumsily after, bawling rage and frustration.

There was a confusion of snow spray and darkness, a howl from behind me, then the sled tilted, bucked and I flew off, spilling over and over in the snow. I came up spitting and dazed. Something dark, a huge boulder, hurtled past me, still spraying snow and blood, rolling down the hill towards the trees. There was a splintering crash and a single grunt.

And silence.

Shaking woke me and I stared up at Illugi, ashamed that I had fallen asleep at all when everything else was bustle and purpose.

'We are in Strathclyde,' he said. 'We have a task inland. Einar will explain it all later, but best get ready for now.'

'Strathclyde,' muttered Pinleg, shoving past us. 'No easy raiding here.'

The landing was almost a disappointment for me. With my sword in one hand and a borrowed shield in the other – Illugi Godi's, with Odin's raven on it – I waited in the belly of the *Fjord Elk* as it snaked smoothly into the bow of land.

Shingle beach stretched to a fringe of trees and, beyond, rose to red-brackened hills, studded with trees, warped as old crones. There were rocks, too, which I took for sheep for a moment and was glad I had not called out my foolishness.

Since nothing moved, everyone relaxed. Except for Valgard Skafhogg, who bellowed at my father as the keel ground on shingle stones, calling him a ship-wrecking son of Loki's arse. My father bellowed right back that if Valgard was any good as a shipwright, then a few stones wouldn't sink us and, from what he had heard, Valgard couldn't trim his beard. Which was a good joke on his nickname, Skafhogg, which means Trimmer.

But it was almost good-natured as we splashed ashore, to a smell of bracken and grass that almost made me weep.

It was bitter cold and you could taste the snow. The sail was dragged out, unfurled and draped over a frame – not as a shelter, since it was sodden; we only wanted it to dry out a little. Then we'd put it back, for when we returned to this place, we'd be in a hurry to get away from it.

Lookouts were posted and fires were lit for us to dry clothes and, above all, get warm. I staked out the sheep, as I had before, on a long line for her to crop what she could of the frozen grass and brown-edged fern and bracken.

She had little time to enjoy it and I was almost sorry when she was up-ended, gralloched and spitted. Brought all that way in damp misery, simply to be the hero-meal before the Oathsworn went into fight: I identified strongly with that wether.

I wondered about the fires, since the wood was wet and smoked and you could see it for miles, but Einar didn't seem bothered. Now that we were so close, he had tallied that warmth and a full belly was worth the chance of discovery.

My father, now free of any duties, since he had done his part, crossed to where I sat shivering by the fire and trying not to wear my drying cloak until the rest of me had lost some water.

'You need some spare clothing. Maybe we'll get some soon.'

I glanced sourly at him. 'A seer now, are you? If so, tell us where we are raiding.'

He shrugged. 'Someplace inland.' He stroked his stubbled chin thoughtfully and added, 'Strathclyde's not a place to raid these days, never mind inland. Still, Brondolf is paying good silver for it, so we do.'

'Brondolf?' I asked, helping him as he started to erect a shelter from our cloaks, making a frame of withies.

'Brondolf Lambisson, richest of the Birka merchants. He hires the Oathsworn of Einar the Black this year. And last, come to think of it.'

'To do what?'

My father tied cloak corners together, blowing on his fingers to warm them. The sky was sliding into dour night and it would soon be colder yet. The fires already looked flower-bright comforts in the growing dark.

28

'He leads the other merchants of Birka. The town was a great trading centre, but it is failing. The silver is drying up and the harbour silting. Brondolf seems to think he has found an answer. He and his tame Christ godi, Martin from Hammaburg. They keep sending us out to get the strangest things.' He broke off at a thought and chuckled, uneasy as all Northmen were with the concept. 'Who knows what he is doing? Perhaps he is working some spell or other.'

I knew of Birka only from old Arnbjorn, the trader who came to Bjornshafen twice a year with cloth for Halldis and good hoes and axes for Gudleif. Birka, tucked up in an island far east into the Baltic off the coast of Sweden. Birka, where all the trade routes met.

'Is that where you have been all these years, then: searching out dead men's eyes and toadspit?' I demanded.

He made a warding sign. 'Shut that up for a start, boy. Less mention of . . . such things . . . is always safer. And, no, I wasn't always doing that. For a time I thought to have a white bear safely tucked away, the price of a small farm.'

'Is that what you told my mother? Or did she die waiting for your return?'

He seemed to droop a little, then looked at me from under his hair – it was thinning, I noticed – one eye closed. 'Go fetch some bracken for bedding. We can dry it at the fires beforehand.' Then he sighed. 'Your mother died giving you birth, boy. A fine woman, Gudrid, but too narrow in the hip. At the time I had a farm, not far from Gudleif as it happens. I had twenty head of sheep and a few cows. I was doing well enough.'

He stopped, staring at nothing. 'After she died, there didn't seem much point in it. So I sold it to a man from the next valley, who wanted it for his son and his wife. Most of the money went to Gudleif, when I made him fostri. Some he was to keep and the rest was for you when you came of age.'

Surprised by all this, I could only gape. I had known she died . . . but the knowledge that I had killed my mother was vicious. I felt clubbed by Thor's own hammer. Her and Freydis. They'd do better to call me Woman Killer.

He mistook my look, which was the mark of us, father and son. Neither knew the other and constantly misread the signs.

'Yes, that was the reason Gudleif's head went,' he said. 'I thought him my friend – my brother – but Loki whispered in his ear and he used the money on his own sons. I think he hoped I would die and that would be an end of it.' He paused and shook his head sadly. 'He had reason to think that, I suppose. I was never a good husband, or a good father. Always trying to live the old way – but too much is changing. Even the gods are under siege. But when he fell ill and sent for his own sons, thinking he was dying, Gunnar Raudi sent for me and Gudleif knew it was all up with him.'

'So he did try to kill me in the snow,' I said. 'I was never sure.'

Rurik shrugged and scratched. 'Nor he, I think. If Gudleif had wanted you dead, there were easier ways, though Gunnar Raudi wouldn't have gone with it. A sound blade is Gunnar and you can trust him.'

He broke off, looked sideways at me and scrubbed his head in a gesture I was coming to know well, one that revealed his uncertainty. Then he chuckled. 'Perhaps, after all, Gudleif sent you to Freydis to have her make you a man.' His look was sly and he laughed aloud when my face flamed.

Yes, Freydis had done that, popped me on her the way Gudleif used to put me on his horses when I could barely walk. He made you wrap your hands in the mane and hang on until you learned to ride or fell off. If you fell off, he would pop you on again.

When I thought of it, Freydis was much the same. Blurry with the mead I had brought, greasy-chinned with lamb, she had caught me by the arm and dragged me close, stroking my hair and answered the riddle she had set me and I had failed to understand.

'I can manage everything, have done since my Thorgrim, curse his bad luck, fell down the mountain,' she said dreamily. 'The year after that, Gudleif arrived at my door. I can cart dung and spread it on the hayfields, herd cows, herd horses, milk, make bread, sew, weave . . . everything. But Gudleif provided the thing that was missing.'

I couldn't move, could scarcely breathe, though I was hard as a bar of sword-iron and too dry-mouthed to speak.

'Now he cannot and he sends you,' she went on and rolled me on her.

'Come. I will teach you what you were sent here to learn.'

'Good was Freydis,' my father said, himself bleared with fond memories. 'Gudleif swore she was a witch and had made him return every year and stay until he could hardly crawl on the back of a horse to ride off the mountain. If Halldis knew, she kept quiet over it. She was rich as good earth, was Freydis . . . but lonely. All she wanted was a good man.'

I looked at him and he grinned. 'Aye, me too. And Gunnar, probably. In fact, if there was a man who hadn't ploughed that field, then he lived in the next valley but one and was too lame to travel.'

I said nothing. I wanted to tell him of Freydis and her spell and how she had killed the bear with a spear while I ran . . . A vision, again, of that head, lazily turning, spraying fat drops of blood in an arc. Had she smiled?

When I eventually crawled to the side of it, the bear was already dead, the haft of the spear driven clear up and out the top of its skull by the impact with a tree. It had hit the slope and over-run its own feet. It was still a huge cliff of snow, frightening even when still. I saw, numbly, that the hair under its chin was soft and nearly pure white. One sprawled paw, big as my head, was shaking gently.

31

I sat down, trembling. Freydis's spell had worked. Perhaps the price had been her own death. Perhaps she knew. I blubbered and there was no one reason for it. For her. For the knowledge of my own fear. For my father and Gudleif and the whole mess.

Eventually, I was shaking too much to cry. I was half-naked in the cold and had to get back to the hall. The hall and Freydis. I didn't want to go back there at all, where her fetch might be, waiting accusingly. But I would freeze here.

The bear shifted and I scrambled away. A final kick? I had seen chickens and sheep do that with their throats cut through. I didn't trust this bear. I remembered Freydis and my fear, took a deep breath, crossed to it and drove Bjarni's sword into where I thought the heart would be, deep inside the mass of that white cliff.

It was a good sword and I was strong, made stronger yet through fear. It went in so smoothly I practically fell forward on the rank, wet fur; there was no great gout of blood, just a slow welling of fat drops. The sword was in nearly to the cross guard and I couldn't get it out.

Eventually, shivering uncontrollably, I gave up and slogged back up the slope, through the door and into the ruin of the hall, wrapped myself in her cloak for the warmth and waited, sinking into the cold, where Bagnose and Steinthor found me.

It was a bad enough memory to have rattling round your thought-cage. Now, to add to all that, there was a new horror: a vision of me, like a small bear, clawing another Freydis from the inside out, charging out from between her legs in a glory of gore and challenge. I couldn't see the face of the woman, my mother, though.

I shook my head, near to weeping, and knew it was for me more than anyone and wanted to back away from that, ashamed.

My father gripped my forearm wordlessly. Probably he

thought I was mourning Freydis, or my mother. Truth to tell, I was not even sure which myself.

More alone than ever, I picked my way through the camp, where men chaffered and yacked and busied themselves, out into the trees to get bracken, aware of his eyes following me, aware that he was as much a stranger as all the others.

I wondered if he had taken his brother's head, or if Einar had. What must it feel like, to have to kill your brother? Even just to watch him die?

Yet they were still men, these Oathsworn. Grim as whetstone, cold as a storm sea, but men for all that.

Most had wives and families – in Gotland, or further east – and went back to them now and then. Pinleg had a woman and two little ones whom he sent money back to by traders he could trust. Skapti Halftroll had more than one woman in more than one place, but he spent all his money on finery. Ketil Crow was outlawed from somewhere in Norway and had no one but the Oathsworn.

There were others, though, who were men apart. Sigtrygg was one, for he called himself Valknut and wore that rune symbol on his shield, three triangles known as the Knot of the Fallen. It meant he had bound his soul to Odin, would die at the god's command and even the swaggerers walked soft around him.

Einar himself was a mystery, though most people had the idea he was an outlaw, too. Pinleg joked that our jarl, dark and brooding under his sullen, crow-wing hair, had been thrown out of Iceland for being too cheerful. He was the only one who dared joke about Einar.

Later, when bellies were full and the conversation had died, men took to cleaning their weapons, taking great care with the blades to gently grind out all the dark spots they could. Einar stood next to the biggest of the fires and the men gathered silently round him in a half-circle, facing the black sea as it sighed on the shingle. Behind, a wet mist crept stealthily down the mountain.

'Tomorrow, we head inland from here,' Einar said, his dark eyes moving from one to the other. 'Pinleg, you will stay here with nine others and guard the ship and our belongings.'

Pinleg grunted his annoyance at that, but he knew why . . . in a long, fast march, he wasn't the best choice.

He also knew, I learned later, that he would get his share of the spoils, since no one kept anything for himself. In theory. Actually, everyone stole a little: silver dropped down breeks into boot-tops, or stowed in bags under his balls or armpits. Those caught, though, suffered whatever punishment the Oathsworn decided, which certainly started by losing all their booty and almost always included pain along the way.

'We seek what will be easy to find: the Christ temple of St Otmund,' Einar told us. 'It will be the only substantial stone building for miles, with outbuildings of wood, so look for that. We raid it and get out, fast. This is a well-defended kingdom and the days of good raiding here are long gone, so take only what you can carry – no slaves, no livestock, nothing heavy.

'The only thing we must get is a . . . a . . . reliquary.' He stumbled over the foreign word, then looked at the puzzled faces. 'It looks like a chest, well made, well carved and decorated. That we must get.'

'What's in it?' asked Ketil Crow lazily.

Einar shrugged. 'Bones, if everything I hear about such items is true.'

'Bones? Whose bones?' asked Illugi Godi curiously.

'St Otmund, almost certainly,' answered Einar. 'That's what these Christ-followers do with saints. Stick their bones in a chest and worship them.'

'Fuck,' offered Valknut disgustedly. 'More spell stuff. What are they cooking up in Birka?' He made a warding sign and just about everyone followed.

34

'Good question,' growled Skapti. 'What does Birka want with this pile of bones?'

Einar shrugged and looked darkly at them all. 'All you need to know is that they are outfitting us for next year. Every man will get enough for a new set of clothes, top to toe, and the *Fjord Elk* will be fitted with new gear, too. And we get to keep what we take from raids other than what was asked for.'

Everyone fell silent, nodding at that. Skapti hoomed in his throat and growled, 'Just show me where they are, these saints.'

Those who knew better chuckled and Valknut told him: 'Saints are dead followers of Christ. Their chief priests vote the best dead people to be gods in their Valholl.'

'Votes, Sig? Like in a Thing?' scoffed Skapti. 'No fighting for it?'

'They don't believe in fighting,' Valknut said loftily. 'They believe in dying and when they do they are called martyrs. And the ones they think are better martyrs than others become saints.'

People who knew nodded, those who were learning this shook their heads in sceptical disbelief. Skapti hoomed disgust. 'Well, if that's the way of it, then we shall make lots of martyrs tomorrow, with little risk.'

Einar held up one hand, his hair like black water breaking round the stone of his face. 'Don't be fooled. What the Christ-followers say is one thing, yet this kingdom supposedly follows the White Christ and for people who don't believe in fighting, they can make a shieldwall that will turn your bowels to piss if we are unlucky enough to meet one. Move fast, stay quiet and we'll get in and out faster than Pinleg on a woman.'

Laughter and nudgings of Pinleg, who grinned and said, 'I have heard tales of treasure, Einar. Dragon hoards, no less. I would not like to think I am pissing about in the rain chasing some child's firepit story when I could be getting in and out of a woman.'

There was a sudden silence and I wondered why Pinleg had voiced that where others, clearly, had kept their teeth together. Later, of course, I found out why Pinleg could say what he chose.

Einar swept his black eyes over them once more. 'There is such a thing being spoken of . . .' He held up a hand as Pinleg cleared his throat to spit. 'Rest your oar a moment,' he said and Pinleg swallowed. Einar stroked his moustaches, looking round before he spoke.

'This Martin, the monk, is a deep-thinker, who can dive into the world's sea of learning and fish out choice morsels. Lambisson thinks highly of him and keeps him close – and Brondolf is no cash-scatterer, as we know.'

Grim chuckles greeted this and Einar scrubbed his chin. 'I have . . . uncovered some things that make me believe there is more to these Birka matters than is carved on the surface. There's a snake-knot tangle to it, though, so when I know more, you will know more.'

Pinleg grunted and that seemed to be assent. The others milled and muttered to each other.

Einar held up both hands and there was silence. 'Now, we are Oathsworn and have two here – Gunnar Rognaldsson, known as Raudi, and Orm Ruriksson, known as the Bear Killer. You know our oath . . . is there anyone who will stand the challenge?'

Challenge? What challenge? I turned to my father, but he nudged me silent and winked.

Slowly, a man stood, uncomfortably it seemed to me. A second stood with him and my father let out his breath with relief.

Einar nodded at them. 'Gauk, I know you have waited for this moment since your foot went bad on you and you lost the toes last year.'

Gauk stepped into the firelight, his face made more gaunt with the shadows playing on it, and nodded. 'Aye. Without those toes, my balance is gone. Sometimes, unless I am careful, I fall over like a child. One day I will do it in a fight.'

Everyone nodded sympathetically. If he stumbled in a shieldwall, everyone was put at risk.

'So you will step aside, with no fight and no shame?' asked Einar.

'I will,' said Gauk.

'For whom?'

'Gunnar Raudi.'

And that was that. Gauk would be free to leave here the next day with whatever he could carry away and Gunnar Raudi would take his place. My mouth was dry. I realised that the way into a full crew of the Oathsworn was to challenge and kill someone already in it, then take the binding oath. Unless, of course, that someone volunteered to go quietly.

Gauk and Gunnar were already clasping forearms and Gunnar was (as polite custom demanded, I learned) offering to buy what Gauk couldn't carry away on his back. Sweating and chilled, I glanced at the other man as Einar turned to him.

'Thorkel? Are you going with no fight and no shame?'

'I am, for Orm Ruriksson.'

There was murmuring at that. Thorkel was a seasoned fighter, a good axeman and I was, as Ulf-Agar yelped out, only a stripling.

'A stripling who killed a white bear,' my father snarled back at him. 'I don't recall any tales of your doings, Ulf-Agar.'

The little man's dark face went darker still and I knew then what Ulf-Agar's curse was – that of legend. He wanted one to live after him; he was jealous of those who had what he sought and could not steal.

He was welcome to it, I said to myself, since it was a lie and shame made me hide it from everyone's sight, though it sickened me.

Einar stroked his chin, pondering. 'It's hard to give up a good man for an untried one. That's why we fight. How do we know what we get if we don't see newcomers fight?'

Thorkel shrugged. 'No matter what he is like, he will fight better than me, for I do not want to fight at all. Not against the Christ-followers, for my woman in Gotland is one and I promised her – swore an Odin-oath – that I would not raid their holy places. So best if I leave, for if that is the way Birka's thoughts are going, I cannot go with them.'

Einar scowled at that. 'You swore an oath to us all, Thorkel. Is that to be overturned by a promise to a woman? Is your oath to us less than that to a woman?'

'You have never met my wife, Einar,' said Pinleg gloomily, his wiry body swathed in a huge cloak. 'Breaking an oath to her is not done lightly.'

Everyone who knew Pinleg's woman laughed knowingly. Before Einar could answer, Illugi Godi rapped his staff on a stone and there was silence.

'It is not a promise to his wife,' he said sternly. 'It was an oath to Odin. However stupid that may have been, it is still an oath to Odin.'

'Our oath is made to Odin,' Einar argued and Illugi frowned.

'Our oath is made to each other, in the sight of Odin. Thorkel's own Odin-oath may be truer, but I am thinking he must live with the consequence of swearing too many oaths. Anyway, he does not break his oath to the rest of us if one stands in his place.'

There was nodding agreement to that and Einar shrugged and turned to me. 'Well, you take the place of a good man, Orm Ruriksson. Make sure it was worth the trade.'

I stepped forward as bid and clasped Thorkel's forearm. He nodded at me, then moved off.

And that was it. I was now part of the Oathsworn of Einar the Black.

Later, I saw Thorkel and my father head to head in conversation and something niggled at me and worried and gnawed until I had to voice it.

'You arranged it,' I accused and, to my astonishment, my father grinned and nodded, putting a finger to his lips.

'Aye. Thorkel wanted to go, has done for a time. He has an Irish woman in Dyfflin, which is just across the water from here, but made no Odin-oaths over her. By Loki's arse, what sane man would do that, eh?'

'Why does he want to leave?'

My father frowned at that and self-consciously scrubbed his chin. 'Tales of Atil's treasure,' he answered gruffly. 'Thorkel believes it foolishness, thinks Einar's thought-cage is warped.'

'Why didn't he say that, then?' I answered, with all the stupidity of youth.

My father batted my shoulder – none too gently, I thought – and answered, 'You don't say such things to the likes of Einar, unless you have a head start and fast feet, or are prepared to fight. No, Thorkel wanted out when he got here and didn't want to fight for it and didn't want to lose all his stuff.

'This way, he gets to leave safely with a bag of hacksilver – and you get a good sea-chest, a spare set of clothes and a decent shield.'

'I have nothing—' I began and he clasped my forearm, his eyes gleaming in the darkness.

'I did little enough for long enough,' he said. 'I need take big strides to catch up and I will not make old bones on a farm now, I am thinking. So I will spend my shares how I choose.' He paused then and added, 'Keep your lips fastened round Einar. He is a dangerous man when his brows come together.'

So, in the star-glimmered dark before dawn, I found myself assembled with the others, sword in hand, clutching Thorkel's shield with its swirling design of rune snakes, shivering and sick to the pit of my stomach.

We helped shove the *Fjord Elk* back off the shingle before the tide went out and stranded it there for hours. My father, of course, was staying behind since he was shipmaster and Pinleg would need him if they came under attack. So was Valgard, in case the ship was damaged. The eight others who stayed were hard enough men, but were all those who, for one reason or another, were not the fastest on their feet.

I was surprised that Skapti was going with the main body – not that I was going to say aloud that he was too fat to move fast – and more surprised than that to see him wearing a mail hauberk. A few others had mail, too, but had left off the padding of spare tunics usually worn beneath it.

Later, of course, I learned that no clever man expecting a fight and having good mail will willingly give it up and, since the easiest way of carrying it is to wear it, that's what they did.

The two who were leaving said their farewells, hefted their bundles and packs and struck off in the opposite direction from the one we would take. By the time we reached the Christ temple, they would be far enough away not to be considered part of the act. If they moved fast, of course.

Ulf-Agar had unrolled his mail from the fleece it was kept in, the sheep-grease fending off the rust. I thought to try to mend the rift between us and stepped forward to offer a helping hand as he hefted the ring-heavy mail by the shoulders.

Instead, he slapped my hand away and scowled. This was too much and I felt my hackles rise. Then Illugi Godi stepped between us and ushered me away, talking the while as if nothing had happened.

'Good sword you have there, Orm Ruriksson. Here's a tip, though: run it through the fleece of one of those fresh-killed sheep a few times. It's been splashed on by the sea and that rots metal faster than anything I know. Really, you need a sheath for it, but not a soft leather one, since that rots the metal fast, too. Better one made from wood, with a sheep-skin lining. That way you can use the sheath as a good club if you have to . . .'

Out of earshot, he clasped my shoulder in friendly fashion and glanced back to where Ulf-Agar's tousled head was emerging from his mail, his arms flailing. 'You meant well, but I fear you've made things worse. It's a thing among mail-wearers that if you can't put it on or take it off unaided you shouldn't have the stuff. So you just insulted him.'

'I didn't know,' I said, my heart sinking.

'I think he knows that,' answered Illugi Godi, 'but it won't help. Some evil gnaws him, and until he beats it to a pulp you and he will always be glaring. Unless you can fight him, I'd steer away wherever possible.'

My father came up as Illugi strode away and, at his questioning look, I told him what had happened. He stroked his chin and shook his head. 'Illugi is a good man, so you can take his advice. Mostly. Like us all, he has his reasons for being in the Oathsworn.'

'What are his?' I demanded and he shut one eye and squinted at me quizzically.

'You want to know a lot. He thinks Asgard is under siege from this White Christ and our gods are asleep.'

'And you? What are your reasons?'

He scowled. 'You want to know too much.' Then he forced a smile and produced a round leather helmet. 'One of Steinthor's spares. He picked it up last year, but can't wear it himself.'

It looked fine to me – a little too big, no fastening strap and a nice metal nasal. 'Why can't he wear it?'

My father tapped the metal nose protector. 'He's a bowman. Blocks your sighting, does a nasal. Bowmen all wear helmets without them. And no mail – even half-sleeves snag the string. That's why they stay well out on the edges of a fight and pick people off.' He spat. 'No one likes bowmen – unless they are *your* bowmen.'

We clasped hands, forearm to forearm.

'Stay safe, boy,' he said and turned back to the ship.

Einar, helmeted and mailed and wearing two swords in his belt, shield slung over one shoulder, looked at the assembled men. He handed a spear with a furled cloth on it to skinny Valknut. 'Move steady and quiet. Stay together – anyone who stops for a piss or a pull on the way risks being left on his own and we won't be going back to find them. We hit fast and hard, collect what we came for and get out. Don't try and carry off anything that weighs more than you. You'll either fall behind or have to leave it in the end.'

He glanced around one more time and nodded, then took the head of our pack and led us at a steady, fast walk up through the trees, into the night-shrouded land, towards the first silvered smear of dawn.

It was a good pace, uphill. No one spoke and there was silence until the pace began to tell in louder, ragged breathing. That and the shink-shink of slung shields on mail, the swish of the bracken underfoot and the odd clink and creak of equipment was all that marked the passage of nearly fifty fully armed men.

After an hour, Einar stopped us. The sky was milk-white, shading to grey towards us. Somewhere behind that, a winter sun fought to claw over the thin, black edge of the world. Trees were outlined in skeletal black – and there was something else.

It was a dark bulk with a tower and the faint, reddish glow of a light. Everyone saw it; there was a general, hushed business of tightening straps, unshipping shields, hefting weapons.

Einar had us take to one knee, then sent Geir and Steinthor off into the night. Briefly silhouetted against the dawn sky for us, they would be invisible to any watcher from the tower. I rubbed dry lips, hearing my breathing magnified by the helmet's cheekpieces into a rasp. That looked like a powerful strong building – and, as the light grew, you could see other, smaller buildings huddled round it.

Geir and Steinthor slid back. We all listened.

'The light is on the gate in a wooden wall that stretches all round it,' reported Geir, rubbing his dripping bag of a nose. 'The gate is the only way in unless you want to go over seven feet of timbered fence. It was built for defence, was this place.'

He paused, for effect as it turned out, since Steinthor grinned and added, 'But the bloody gate is wide and welcoming open. It's been a long time since anyone attacked them. They have forgotten.'

'A big stone temple and six outbuildings,' Geir added, 'all wattle and withy. A stable, for sure. Perhaps a smithy – I can smell the banked fire and tinsmith metal. There's a good covered bread-oven. The others could be anything.'

Einar rubbed his nose and squinted. Then he shrugged. 'One way in, so that simplifies the planning.'

He rose up and we followed. At a fast pace, we followed Geir and Steinthor, almost running through the bracken and, as we neared the gated wall, where the first rose-light of the rising sun touched the moss-gentled points of the timbered fence, we broke into a silent run, piling through the gate under the light set to welcome weary travellers.

Resistance was slight, almost none. By accident, Ketil Crow stumbled over the watchman, a slumbering man in brown robes, huddled in a little hut beside the gate. Ketil had turned aside and gone into it looking for loot, but couldn't see anything in the dark.

Until the querulous voice revealed the watchman, he thought there was no one else in the building, which was so small and cramped he couldn't get room to swing a slashing sword properly. Ketil Crow was flailing around, while the unseen watchman screamed and then the sword stuck in a beam and, cursing, Ketil Crow couldn't get it out.

By this time, half the company had heard the commotion and, seeing his predicament, were howling with laughter. The watchman, crashing into Ketil and knocking him off his feet, stumbled out of the building, mad with fear and near flying in his panic.

That was when Valknut stepped forward and threw his hand axe, which smacked into the left side of the man's forehead with a sound like dung thrown against a wall. The force flung him sideways and he fell on his back, gurgling like some strange, long-nosed beast, the blood welling out of the mess of his face in a growing pool.

Ketil Crow hurtled out of the building, dark with anger, and the jeers stopped as he swung this way and that. But, as the men congratulated Valknut on his throw – it was generally agreed to be a fine one, since it wasn't a balanced throwing axe – there were chuckles and sniggers in the darkness at Ketil's expense.

Wordlessly, Valknut put one foot on the dead man's bloody chest and, with a flick of his wrist, removed his axe. It came away with a small sucking sound and Valknut, with a brief, blank look at Ketil Crow, wiped the blood and brains on the dead man's brown robe and strode off, axe in one hand, spear with furled banner in the other.

Ketil Crow caught me looking and I blinked at his expression, then wisely found the stone temple with the tower more of interest and trotted towards it.

It was, it seemed, one large hall, with an impressive flagged floor. The tower held no archers, nothing more than a bell. There were two brown-robed figures sprawled, spewing blood on the flagstones. Half a dozen others were penned at the far end of this hall by the rest of the Oathsworn and Einar was head to head with Illugi Godi.

It was a strange place and I gawped. It had benches and a sacrificial altar, which was where most of the people were. Behind the altar, above their heads, was a window, filled with pieces of coloured glass in the shape of a man wearing, it seemed, a glowing hat. The walls, too, were painted with strange scenes.

The dawn light that spilled from that window was like Bifrost, the rainbow bridge, and it stained the altar. I did not know it then, but such a window was as rare as teeth on a hen – I did not see another until the Great City, Constantinople.

But it was nothing next to what was below it, stuck on the wall. Two thick beams, one vertical, one horizontal, held the wooden figure of a man, hanging there by his hands. No, not hanging, I saw. Nailed, through his hands and his feet. He had some strange crown, which stuck spikes in his forehead, and what seemed to be another gaping wound in one side. It was a fine carving.

'Is that their god, then?' I asked Illugi Godi, much to Einar's annoyance.

'The son of their god,' answered the priest. 'The Romans stuck him on those poles, but the Christ-followers say he didn't die.'

That was impressive. I had thought any god who allowed himself to be nailed to a bit of wood wasn't up to much – ours were clever or strong fighting men, after all – but if he had survived all that and come out smiling, this Christ was to be reckoned with.

'Finished?' demanded Einar pointedly. Then he turned to Illugi Godi. 'So where? You are the expert here, priest.'

Illugi Godi squatted, fumbled in his pouch and came up with his rune bones. I saw the brown figures flailing one

45

hand back and forward on their chests, which seemed to be their way of warding off the evil eye. I laughed. Illugi wasn't evil.

He cast; the bones tinkled. He took some fine white sand from his pouch and blew it off the palm of his hand towards the altar, then stood and smiled.

'There,' he said and pointed at the altar. As a hiding place, it wasn't hard to work out – it was almost the only thing in the hov of this hall. And, I saw, the sand he had blown hadn't settled neatly where the altar touched the flagstoned floor. It had sunk into the cracks, which meant it was hollow beneath. He was clever, was Illugi Godi.

Einar and Valknut circled it, but there was nothing: no handle, no mark of any kind. Puzzled, they were scratching their heads when Gunnar Raudi, wiser in the ways of hiding valuables, stepped up, leaned his shoulder into it and gave it a shove.

With a grinding sound, the altar slid back several feet, revealing a set of stone steps. A torch uncovered a small chamber and the contents were soon up and on the flag-stones.

There was a thin silver plate, two metal cups – gold, Illugi said – and a couple of hollow silver columns, which Gunnar Raudi said were sticks for holding fat tallow candles. Strange to relate now, but I had never seen the like and was so marvel-ling at them I nearly missed the next wonders.

Geir came up from the chamber with two chests. The first was clearly the one Einar wanted, a fat, ornate effort about the size of a man's head. The other was flatter; Geir held it up and turned it round. It was studded with coloured glass and had a huge clasp on it, which Geir snapped off easily, bit and announced admiringly: 'Silver.'

Then, to my astonishment, the chest fell open in two halves and loads of leaves riffled. Geir turned it over and over while I stared, my mouth dropped open like a droop-lipped horse.

'It's full of leaves,' I said, wondering. 'With colours on them – and little animals and birds.'

'It's a book,' said Illugi Godi patiently as Geir chuckled. 'The Christ monks make them. It has their holy writings. Like runes.'

Not much, I thought scornfully. Runes were worked on stone, or wood, or metal; otherwise, how would they last? Geir ripped one of the leaves out to show me how this book thing worked and I heard a brown-robed man, one with silver hair, moan.

Steinthor, more practical, grunted with annoyance over something else. 'No women, then?'

'Christ priests don't go with women,' advised Illugi Godi and Steinthor shot him a hard glance.

'Bollocks. I have tupped women before in these Christ places.'

'There are women Christ priests,' Illugi said patiently. 'But they don't go with men.'

'Just as well,' grunted Einar, cuffing Steinthor on the shoulder. 'No time to plough any fresh furrows here and no one is dragging any shrieking women with us. Anyway, why are you here? Didn't I tell you to make sure all these brown-robes were rounded up?'

As if in answer, the air was split with a massive ringing boom, followed by another. There was a moment of stunned panic, then Einar roared, 'The bell. The fucking bell . . .'

Gunnar Raudi was first, spilling into the little chamber at the far end beneath the tower.

The defiant man in a brown robe lasted long enough for a second pull on the rope before Gunnar's blow sprayed his teeth and blood and brains against the opposite wall. The bell, as if his ghost still tugged the rope, continued to boom a couple more times before swinging to silence.

In the main hov of the hall, the men were licking their lips, weapons up, uncertain and on edge. Steinthor, aware that he had put everyone at risk, shrugged apology, ducked hastily under Einar's scowl and scurried off to scout.

Black-raging, Einar swept up the fat chest, indicated to a couple of men to pick up the rest, then turned to Ketil Crow and Ulf-Agar, jerking his chin at the huddled brown-robes. 'Kill them, then join us at the gate. We'll have to move fast now.'

I left, half looking back – Valknut pushed me impatiently through the door as the screams began.

Outside, the Oathsworn gathered silently together. No buildings had been torched, the ringing bell had interrupted that and someone said we should do it now, but Einar pointed out how long it would take to get a fire lit. 'They'll be coming after us,' he growled. 'Now we head for the *Fjord Elk* – and fast.'

With Geir and Steinthor running ahead, he led us off at a fast pace, almost on the edge of a trot. It was full daylight now, but overcast, smirring with rain. I noticed that the birds were mad with song.

We were halfway to the ship, perhaps a little more, labouring up a slope of red bracken, when they caught us up.

Skapti, huffing in the rear, suddenly yelled out and pointed behind us. We all stopped and turned; dark against the browns and withered greens, the horsemen came on, urging their mounts through the tangling bracken and gorse.

'Top of the hill, form a line, three deep,' roared Einar. 'Move.'

The Oathsworn may have been stumbling and out of breath, but they knew their business. I was the only one who didn't.

They slid into three ranks, the mailed men in front, the spearmen second and everyone else in the third. Einar saw me as he strode along the front. 'Guard Valknut, young Orm. Sig, let them see whom they face.'

Valknut slid the thongs from the furled cloth on his spear.

A banner spilled out, white with a black bird on it. I realised, with a sudden start, that it was the Raven Banner. I was about to fight under the Raven Banner, as in a saga tale.

Valknut hefted his axe in his free right hand and grunted at me, 'On my left, Bear Slayer. You are the shield I don't have.'

I nodded. Geir and Steinthor were on the same side, the left flank of the line. On the other, Skapti took station, where there was room to swing his long Dane axe.

Einar chuckled, wiping the drips from the edge of his helmet. 'Not horse, these. Fyrdmen on ponies. You won't have to face mailed horse today, just the fat levy of some local noble.'

I watched the horsemen dismount; saw that most of them were in leather and had shields, spears and axes. Just like us.

One of them, mailed and shouting, bullied them into three ranks, again like us. There were a lot of them, perhaps twenty or so more than we were and they overlapped us. I heard the swish of Skapti's axe, testing range.

The rain was invisible and soaking. We dripped, waiting in the bracken and heather.

Einar shook rain from his eyes and grunted, peering at the men below us. They were in no hurry to come at us and, suddenly, Einar strode over to Skapti. They had a brief, grunting conversation, then Skapti simply dropped his axe and hauled out the heavier of the two swords he wore, the one he called Shieldbreaker. Einar fell in behind us.

Skapti strode to the front, swinging his shield on to his arm. 'We can't wait. That's what they want and they will be bringing up more men, I am thinking, before they take on the Raven Banner.'

There was a general mutter of agreement and Skapti nodded. 'Boar snout. We have to break their shieldwall here, scatter them.'

He strode several paces to the front and everyone seemed

to slide into position like a cunning toy. Shields overlapped, they crowded into a wedge, shoulders hunched into the shields, pushing. In front, Skapti pushed back, as if trying to hold them, his feet skidding on the bracken, a delicate balance between strength and footwork.

Balked, the men shoved; the power of the wedge grew as it moved downhill, with Skapti as a brake. With nowhere to go, I fell in at the rear, still with Valknut.

About twenty paces from the line of the fyrdmen and their overlapped shields, Skapti roared something and the men behind increased their effort. Skapti took two, three steps, raised his shield, lifted his legs off the ground and was shot forward, a huge battering ram at the point of the boar snout.

The fyrdmen's shieldwall smashed apart; men were flung sideways. The Oathsworn were in among them then, the fight a grunting, flailing, slipping, sliding mess of whirling steel and blood and flying bone.

On the fringes, some of the fyrdmen dashed forward; two arrows spanged off their shields and they stopped, seeing Geir and Steinthor nocking fresh ones. They huddled behind their big round shields and backed off, all save two, who came on, heading for the Raven Banner and Valknut.

And me.

Valknut backed off a pace, hefted the axe and then hurled it. It cannoned off one man's shield, spinning through the air into the bodies behind.

With a triumphant roar, he came stumbling at Valknut, who stuck the Raven Banner pole firmly in the ground, whipped out a long seax and, ducking under the swing and the man's shield, kippered him open with a swipe along the belly. He was still running when his stomach opened and all the blue-white coils fell out like rope, tripping him.

The other one came at me. I was petrified . . . but I weathered his first rush; I felt his sword whack on my shield, bounce off the metal rim and just miss my nose.

He hacked a backstroke and, before I knew it, I had done what Gudleif and Gunnar Raudi had taken pains to teach me . . . I slammed the blunt point of my sword at the bottom of his shield, the force of the blow tilting it forward and exposing the whole shoulder and side of his neck.

Then I carved a stroke downward before he could recover. The blade going in felt no different to chopping wood, since it smashed into the shoulder and collar bone, half carving his arm from the socket.

He gave a shriek and fell away, dropping his sword, clutching at the wound as if to fasten the gaping sides together. I stood there, scarcely believing what I had done, my mouth gawping like a dead cod.

'Finish him,' growled Valknut and I looked at him, then back to the wounded man. No, not man. Boy. He fell, lay on his back, chest heaving, no longer even groaning. The blood flowed thickly out of him; by the time I was peering at him, the rain was pooling in the hollows of his unseeing eyes. No older than me . . .

I felt a smack on the back and whirled, sword up.

Steinthor held up a placating hand, chuckling. 'Easy, Bear Killer. That was well done, as neat as any I have seen – but don't gawp at it or you'll end up lying beside him.'

But the fight was over. The fyrdmen – those not groaning or lying like little sacks on the sodden ground – were running, not even waiting to take their horses. The leader was down, carved up under the combined efforts of Einar and Skapti. Panting men knelt or stood, gasping, legs apart, heads down. One or two, I saw, were retching.

Steinthor expertly patted the corpse beside me, gave a grunt of satisfaction and came up with two small slivers of hack-silver and an amulet in the shape of a cross. He tossed the amulet to me and stuffed the silver down his boot. 'Keepsake,' he chuckled and moved on to the next.

Einar was cleaning his sword. Skapti Halftroll was

51

moving among the bodies, making sure the fyrdmen were all dead.

Illugi fed something from a flask to one of our own, who lay shivering in the rain, hands clutching his stomach. Blood leaked between his fingers.

'Tally?' demanded Einar.

Skapti thumbed one side of his nose and snotted. 'Eight of them dead, more who will feel how bad their wounds are when the fear that keeps them running wears off.'

'Us?'

'A few wounds. Harald One-eye's serious; someone carved half his foot off, so we'll have to carry him. And Haarlaug has a belly wound,' answered Illugi.

'Bad?' asked Einar. Illugi paused, moved to the groaning man, knelt, sniffed and then came back to Einar.

'Soup wound, I think, though it will take an hour to be sure. We'll have to carry him and that will kill him, for sure.'

Einar stroked his wet chin and then shrugged. He drew out his short seax and moved to Haarlaug. Around him the other men collected themselves, stripping what they could find from the dead. The soft, silent, smirring rain dripped.

'Haarlaug,' said Einar. 'You have a belly wound. Illugi Godi fed you some of his soup and he can smell it even so soon after.'

He let the words hang there. The man grunted, as if hit afresh. His face, already pale, went to milk and he licked dry lips. Then he nodded. He knew what it meant to smell Illugi Godi's soup from your opened belly.

'Make sure Thurid, my wife, gets what's mine,' he said. 'And tell her I died well.'

Einar nodded. Someone thrust a seax at him and he took it, then wrapped Haarlaug's hand tight round the hilt.

'Give my regards to all those who have gone before,' he said. 'Say to them, "Not yet, but soon," from me.'

Those nearest muttered their own prayers and nodded at

Haarlaug, commending him to Valholl. Now that the moment was on him, though, his eyes rolled in panic and his mouth started working.

Einar was swift, lest Haarlaug lose hold and let his fear ruin his dignity. The short seax flashed across the white throat, leaving a red line and he thrashed and kicked for a few minutes, eyes bulging and Einar holding him, one hand on his mouth, the blood soaking his sleeve.

Then he stopped and Einar placed one hand over his face, closing Haarlaug's wild eyes, leaving it there for a moment, kneeling. Illugi Godi chanted softly, almost under his breath. The blood pooled under Haarlaug's lolled head.

Then Einar rose up. 'Strip him quickly, then we go. Ottar, Vig, get the mail and weapons off that leader and whatever valuables he has – there's a torc round his neck that looks like silver. Finn Horsehead, fetch one of those horses and load Harald on to it. Move.'

In seconds, it seemed, before I had even plodded back to the top of the hill, Haarlaug was a pale, sad shape in the red hillside, laid neatly on his back, hands clasped on the deer-horn hilt of the knife on his chest, the only thing they left. The rest struggled wearily up the hill, clutching a shirt, breeks, boots – even his woollen socks. Ottar and Vig panted to the top, one draped with a mail shirt, the other clutching a sword and an extra shield. Ottar looked back, hawked and spat. 'No way to leave one of our own,' he said. 'He should have been decently howed up.'

I saw the other huddled, still shapes. I couldn't even tell, now, which was the one I had killed.

'Move,' growled Einar and, as he passed, slapped me lightly on the shoulder. 'Good fight, boy. You'll do.'

And that was it. Twenty minutes later we were panting and gasping down through the trees and out on to the wet-black shingle, stumbling up to where the *Fjord Elk* swung.

I remember that I was more afraid trying to board her than

I was in the fight, since she was so far out we had to wade to our chests and, if it hadn't been for them throwing out the boarding plank, none of us would have got on board at all.

As it was, between rain and sea, I landed on the deck, miserable, wet, chafed, shivering and more tired than I had ever been in my life. I couldn't believe that anyone had any strength left, but the same ones who had just fought dumped their weapons, slithered out of mail, took oars and worked the *Elk* out into the wind, where the sail was hauled up and we were off.

And all the time, I saw the boy's eyes, the rain filling them like tears, felt Einar's hand slap my shoulder and heard him say, again and again: 'Good fight, boy. You'll do.'

THREE

We wintered at Skirringsaal, on the southern tip of Norway, because it was too late in the year to get back to Birka, which was further east along the Baltic and frozen in now. Skirringsaal was handy and had all that the Oathsworn needed: drink, food and women, though it was only a summer trade fair, a *bjorkey*, which fell quiet in winter.

Einar grumbled; he'd much rather have foisted himself on some minor jarl who, faced with sixty warriors sailing into his fjord, would have been all hospitality and smiles for the winter. Instead, he was forced to dole out hacksilver and have the men split up throughout the town, paying for roof and ale with locals, who were used to foreign travellers.

Einar himself, thanks to the foresight of the local merchants, got himself a hov in a small boatshed and was able to sit in a makeshift high seat, his prows on either side, and lord it like a jarl, with more than a few of the Oathsworn with him. All of the others dropped in daily to take advantage of the free ale and whatever was in the pot.

Almost everyone bought a slave girl at once – to the relief of those traders who thought themselves stuck with them all winter – and the hov was thus fairly crowded, with nothing to do but repairs to gear, or dice, or play endless games of hnefatafl and get into fights about who won.

That and drink and fucking seemed to make up winter, as far as the Oathsworn were concerned.

Because my father was the valued shipmaster, he and I were in Einar's hov, which was less well built than a turfed hall like Bjornshafen. With so many of us, space by the central hearthfire was at a premium and privacy was a joke. At any one time, one of the band was humping away at a girl and, after a while, it didn't even excite attention, never mind the senses.

Once, I saw the Trimmer, busy with a game, drop one of the 'tafl counters. It rolled practically under the arse of one of the weary slave girls, which was bouncing on the filthy rush floor under Skapti's grunting slams. Without even looking, Trimmer shoved her buttocks to one side, retrieved the counter and went back to the game.

Once over the reluctance at doing all this in front of others, humping slave girls was what I did whenever possible.

Several times I was dragged off one so that she could help prepare the food and, once, was slapped by Skapti when I shouted in anger. His casual blow knocked me into three or four more men, scattering whatever they were doing and, as I lay with my eyes whirling, Einar had to come in and lay about them as if they were a pack of snarling dogs.

He, of course, had his own section, hurdled off at the back. Here, he and Illugi, my father and Valgard Skafhogg would sit and scheme. Sometimes Skapti and Ketil Crow would join in.

In the end, because everyone agreed I would fuck myself to an early grave, I was reluctantly dragged, most days, away from the women. No one but Ulf-Agar minded that a beard-less boy was at the high seat of things.

As the year ground through the skeins of snow, interest in everything waned. Simply getting through to the thaw became the focus of everyone's intent; endless, freezing rain and snow, the grey-yellow ice that formed everywhere, the coughs, rheumy eyes, loose bowels, all became a test of endurance.

Except for Einar, who tried to ignore his own phlegm and fluxes, scheming on regardless, like a man pushing a plough through a stony field.

The riddle of the saint's box had eluded him, it seemed. No one knew for sure, since he never let anyone look at the contents. Instead, he dragged in every trader who was trapped, like him, and had intense conversations with them behind the hurdle.

Then, one day, as the ice dripped from the eaves and men actually started to stagger out of the stinking hov – and it would have reeked to any Greek, used to baths and oiled massages, even before the winter – Illugi, Valgard, my father and Einar were huddled in his little private chamber, as usual.

And me. Youth had made me healthier than the rest and I was still almost permanently aroused. Since everyone else had more or less lost interest in the girls, I could pick and choose and had my eye on one, a dark beauty, almost as dark as the bluemen from the far south who were so prized in Ireland.

I was craning for a look at her as Einar was speaking, which was why I missed most of it and only came in at the end, to hear him say: '. . . before that little shit Martin gets his hands on it. But no one reads Latin here, not even those who think this place is called Kaupang.'

There were dutiful chuckles at that. Foreigners called Skirringsaal *kaupang* because they'd once asked what it was called and someone – probably deliberately – had told them 'a market'. So they had continued to call the town that, thinking that was its name.

Einar sighed and shook his head. 'I hate relying on that Latin-reading Christ priest. It would be nice to know what it is he seeks in this.' He slapped the ornate chest.

'Latin is a pain in the arse,' I said, yawning. 'If they have three words where one good one would do, they use them.'

There was silence and it took me a while to realise everyone was staring at me. Einar's eyes were black, ferocious. 'How do you know that, boy?'

Conscious of his tone, I considered cautiously, then answered: 'Caomh taught me to read it, back in Bjornshafen—'

I never got the rest of it out. There was an explosion of roars; everyone was talking at once. Einar was trying to hit me, scrambling to get up and out of his furs, Illugi trying to restrain him and my father and Valgard arguing with each other, all at once.

Eventually, when it fell silent again, I raised my head. Einar was glowering at me and breathing as if he'd run up a hill. Illugi was watching him, holding his staff across his knees and between me and him. My father and the Trimmer sat staring at me, one astonished, the other stone-faced.

'Can you read this?' Einar demanded, thrusting a few rustling leaves at me, similar to the ones I'd seen torn from that book-chest in Otmund's temple.

'I've never read from this before,' I told him. 'Caomh drew the letters in the sand, or in the dirt.'

It was clearer than that, of course. Easy.

'"The people here were lost to God's mercy,"' I read, squinting at the faded, brown letters. '"They wallowed in their idol worship, until God Himself brought His word to them, though His humble servant, bound in duty to . . ."' I stopped, scanning the lines ahead. 'It goes on and on – do you want to hear all this?'

Einar leaned forward, dangerous-eyed, his voice frosted. 'Read it all,' he snarled.

So I did. Otmund, it seemed, was full of the joy of coming to the lost people of the Karelians and returning them to the fold like so many strayed sheep. He listed, in considerable detail, his unstinting efforts to do that.

His greatest triumph came, it seemed, when he managed to gain some followers among those skin-wearing trolls.

In the end, as the chief declared for the White Christ, the last believers in the old ways stole their god's stone, on which lay the secrets of the tomb, and spirited it away south and across the sea, into the lands of the Krivichi at Kiev and to a chief named Muzum.

'Read that again,' demanded Einar. Sighing, seeing my chance with the dark girl recede by the minute, I worked my way back, took a breath and laboriously read the passage again. My head hurt with the effort.

'Secrets of the tomb?' Einar asked Illugi, when I had finished. Illugi Godi shrugged.

'Might be Atil's treasure,' he grunted. 'Might be a poor kenning on the nature of gods. And Muzum? I know the Krivichi tribes – we passed through their lands going down to Kiev, some time back. There's no chief called Muzum.'

'They always do that, the Latin writers,' I offered moodily. 'That's what I mean about them. They seem determined to write something and make it as long-winded and hard to understand as possible. Usually, if you take the "um" off the end you have a better chance of working out what they really mean with names.'

'Hmm,' mused Illugi. 'Muz? Might be *muzhi*, but that just means Great Chief. Every ferret-face with two horses and a dog calls himself a great chief along the river banks around Kiev.'

'Then we'll just have to find one with a bloody great stone from a god,' Einar grunted, then looked at me and rubbed his chin. 'Next time, tell me what you can and can't do. I wasted valuable time talking to traders – at least half a dozen over the course of this Loki-cursed winter. Now they will be carrying the news of it far and wide.'

'I didn't know that you needed anything read,' I snapped back, annoyance at missing out on the dark one combining with the unfairness of it to make me daring. 'If you had actually unpicked your lips on this, I'd have known.'

Einar considered for a moment – a long year under that obsidian stare – then chuckled. 'Faults on both sides, then. The main thing is I now have someone who can read stuff before Martin the Christ priest does.'

'I can read it if it is kept simple,' I warned him, wishing now I had spent more time with Caomh and his dirt-scratchings. But who knew then that such a thing would be of more use to me than the best way to get gull eggs from a high cliff?

Einar nodded, considering.

'What now?' my father asked. 'Down to Kiev and the Black Sea again?'

'Eventually,' Einar said, 'but we call in at Birka and fulfil our hire. That way we get paid and I find out if Martin and Lambisson say true, since they will not know that I have all the saint's chest has to offer. Orm, not a word to anyone else that you can read the Latin. Mind that.'

I nodded and he grinned and clapped my shoulder. 'Truly, Rurik, you birthed a rare one and I am glad now that you bribed Thorkel to let him take his place.'

My father chuckled and I gawped and everyone laughed at the pair of us.

'Now go and fuck that Serkland woman before your head swivels off its stalk. Not that she'll thank you much – she has the coughs and fever all of those women get coming from the warm lands and I am thinking she will not last the winter.'

Still chuckling we moved into the main hov and, as we broke apart, my father caught my sleeve.

'I did not know that he knew about Thorkel,' he said quietly. 'I forgot that Einar is a deep thinker and a cunning man. We'd both do well to remember that.'

60

Funnily enough, I remembered those words, even as my loins took over the thinking for me. Partly, I think, because Einar was right and the Serkland woman was already too sick to be a good bedmate, but mainly because of what Illugi had said about Atil's treasure.

'You sew your lips on that one, young Orm,' my father said when I mentioned it, looking right and left to make sure no one could hear us. 'That's something we are not supposed to know about.'

'We don't, I am thinking,' I answered.

He rubbed his head and acknowledged that with a rueful grin.

'But this is the same Atil as the tales?' I persisted. 'Volsungs? All of that?'

'All of that,' agreed my father and then shrugged and scowled when he saw my look. 'Learned men believe it,' he argued. 'Lambisson's tame Christ priest, we found out, seems to be seeking it to solve Birka's silver problems.'

I said nothing, but the thoughts whirled and sparked like embers in the wind. If even a tenth of what was said about the treasure hoard of Attila the Hun was true, then it was a mountain of silver you could mine for years.

Sigurd's treasure, culled from a dragon hoard and cursed, if I remembered the saga tale of it, then handed to the Huns by the Volsungs before they fell out.

'Just so,' Illugi Godi said, when I came to him with questions – though his eyes narrowed at the mention of it. 'You should put your tongue between your teeth over this matter, young Ruriksson,' he added.

'No secret here, it seems to me,' I replied and he hummed and shrugged.

'Well, so it would appear. No simple saga tale, either,' he went on. 'The Volsungs are lost to us, vanished like smoke, taking Sigurd Fafnirs-bane and Brynnhild and all the rest, so that the former is now a dragon-slaying hero and the latter is one of Odin's Valkyrie. Remembered for that only and not that once they were people, like you or me.'

I sat, hunched, hands wrapped round my knees as I had once done in Bjornshafen, listening to Caomh tell stories of his Christ saints. For a moment, listening to the steady, firm voice of Illugi, I was back in the red-gleam twilight of Gudleif's hall, full-bellied and warm and safe.

'Atil, too, was once real, a powerful jarl-king of those tribes who live in the Grass Sea, far to the east. The Volsungs thought him great enough to be allies against the Old Romans, so they sent him a wife: Gudrun, who was once Sigurd's woman. With her came a marvellous sword as a dowry.'

'Sigurd's sword?' I asked and he shook his head.

'No. They gave him a sword forged by the same smith who made Sigurd's own. They called it the Scourge of God and while Atil had it, he could never lose a battle.'

'Which made it hard for the Volsungs when they found Atil was a false friend,' I offered and Illugi scowled.

'Who is telling this?'

He was, of course and he hummed, mollified, when I said it.

'Just so. The Volsungs knew they could not win; they were beaten time and again by Atil until they came upon another way. They sent him a new wife, Ildico, in peace. To tempt him to take her, she came with a great treasure of silver – Sigurd's dragon hoard.'

'Cursed,' I pointed out and he nodded.

'On her wedding night, this brave Ildico slew Atil as he slept and waited for the morning beside him, knowing she could not escape.'

We were both silent, brooding on this cunning plot, cold and coiled as a snake, and the sacrifice it had entailed: the Volsungs losing their wealth and Ildico her life, for she was chained to Atil's death throne alive when he was howed up in a great mound of all the silver of the world, including the

62

Volsungs' gift. A mound long hidden, with all those who knew of it killed.

Such revenge we in the north knew well, yet even so, the warp and weft of this sucked the breath from you.

The rest of the winter dragged into spring without much event. Many of us got sick, me included, with streaming eyes and nose and coughing. Eventually, we all recovered – save for the Serkland woman, as Einar had predicted. She caught a fever, which went quickly, Illugi Godi said, through all the stages: tertian, quartan, daily and, finally, hectic.

At that point, with her breath rasping in her chest, she simply gave up, turned her head to the wall and died. Einar gave her body to the Christ priests in the town, but they refused to perform suitable rites over her, since they said she was 'infidel'.

So Illugi Godi commended her to the true gods of the North and then tipped the body into the sea, from a rocky spit a little way out of town, as an offering to Ran, Aegir's sister-wife, to ensure good sea journeys.

That was because the good merchant council of the town wouldn't have a thrall howed up in their own yards – though they took Harald, whose cut foot had festered all through the winter, then turned black to the groin and stank, at which point he died.

Ulf-Agar, myself and a new Oathsworn, a fair-haired, bearded man called Hring, brought into the Oathsworn to replace Haarlaug, carried the Serkland woman out. I remember Hring because neither he nor I joined in Ulf-Agar's cursing about having to carry a thrall to be buried. That and the fact that, because of the lice, he was the first of many to have his head shaved. Perhaps that, the mark of a thrall forced on him by circumstance, made him more aware of her.

As for me, I thought myself the only one who cared, though we had all humped her at one time or another and never had a name for her other than Dark One. But, almost with the splash of her in the black, cold water, I had forgotten; I stopped wondering what she had been in her own hot lands. By the time I was back in the hov, I was already looking for the huskiest of the girls still on her feet and trying to get her off them.

Not long after that all the girls were gone, sold off almost overnight. The winter was done and the *Fjord Elk* was bound for the whale road again.

No one remembers Birka now. Sigtuna, a little way to the north, now sits in its high seat, though people still speak of Gotland as being the queen of the trade places of the Baltic. But Gotland was no more than a seasonal trade fair beside Birka when it flourished.

At the time, I thought Birka was a marvel. Skirringsaal was big, even winter-empty, but Birka, when I first saw it, seemed to me an impossible place. How could so many live so close together? Now, of course, I know better – Birka was a place of rough-hewn logs that could be placed in a few streets of Miklagard, the Great City of the Romans, and not be noticed.

We came beating up to it in driving rain and a wind that wanted to tear the clothes from us. It thrummed the ropes and heaved out the soaking sail.

Because it was so wet, my father shrugged at the idea of hauling it in and the *Fjord Elk* ran with it, cutting like a blade through the black water, throwing up ice-white spray, snaking down the great heave of the sea so that you could feel it flex, like the muscled beast it was named after, rutting in some red autumn wood.

It was here that we lost Kalf to the waves. My father, when Pinleg bellowed out that the great fortress rock of Birka, the Borg, was in sight, knew that the sail and spar had to come down on to the rests and be lashed. If not, we would slice past it and on into the Helgo and the tangle of islands where the ice still gripped and calved off into dirty, blue-white bergs that would smash the speeding *Elk* to splinters.

So we all sprang to the walrus-hide ropes and began to pull, while the *Elk* groaned and bent and the water hissed and creamed away underneath her.

The sail fought us – and one corner of it tore loose, flapping, deceptive. Kalf leaned out to grab it. A mistake. It was wet; he missed; it slapped him like a forge hammer in the face and I just caught the sight of him out of the side of one eye, flying arse over tit, up and out and into the black water with scarcely a splash.

And he was gone, just like that.

Those who had seen it and weren't hanging on to rope sprang to the side, but there was no sign. Even if he had surfaced, there was no hope; we were flying before the wind like a horse with the bit clenched. By the time we had got the sail stowed and the oars out and turned to row back, he'd have stiffened with the cold and sunk.

I saw my father mouth at Einar, the wind ripping the words away into the wet sail. Einar simply shook his head and pointed onward. Illugi Godi made a sign against the evil eye and Valgard roared incoherently at us, then moved in, banging shoulders and urging us to pull down the sail.

We smothered the great, wet, squelching mass of sail on to the spar and lashed the spar to the rests, panting and sweating with the effort. The rowing crew took their sea-chest benches and, slowly, the *Fjord Elk*, like a reined-in, snorting horse, stilled and was turned towards the great wet-black rock that marked Birka.

On it, I saw, was a fortress, a rampart of earth and stone that loomed over the settlement and, at a certain point, Einar had us take down the antlered prows, to show we came in peace and were not about to offend the gods of the land with our arrival.

We rowed on, practically level with the great rock, until

the sound of a horn brayed out faintly on the water and Rurik, sharply, ordered oars to rest. We waited, the *Elk* rolling in the swell, water slapping spray over the side.

'What are we doing?' I demanded of Steinthor. 'Going fishing?'

He chuckled and slapped my shoulder, causing a fine spray of water from the soaked cloth. 'We wait for the tide,' he answered. 'The way into the harbours is dangerous with rocks and only Birka men know where they are. The only safe way in is to wait until the rocks show at low tide – or leave when the water runs really high, like in a storm, and trust to the gods.'

'Harbours?' I ventured.

'They have three,' he said, almost proudly. 'The one to the west they actually made; the other two are natural.'

'Four harbours,' my father interrupted. 'The fourth is the *salvik*, the Trade Place, further to the east. That's for small ships and those with shallow draught, like us. We can berth there without having all those fat-bellied *knarrer* in our way, or paying fees for it.'

Steinthor grunted. 'It is a harbour if you count dragging the ship up the shingle on rollers a harbour. And it's a long walk to the town.'

The swell grew and the *Fjord Elk* moved with it, slow and ponderous, like some half-frozen water insect. We slid into the *salvik* and, with the others, I leaped out, paired myself with Hring on an oar and, using it and the others as rollers, the *Fjord Elk* was ground up over the shingle and the cracking ice pools.

Valgard fretted and tried to inspect the keel, ducking under the oars as we took them from behind and dropped them in front. One cracked and splintered under the stress; Einar cursed, nodding to Valgard to add that to his tally stick of essential refurbishment.

There were other ships, none as big as the *Elk*, but many

of them, it seemed to me, freshly arrived with the melting ice. But Geir and Steinthor grunted and shook their heads.

'Fewer than last time and there were few then,' muttered the former, rubbing his wobbling nose.

Steinthor shrugged. 'All the more ale for us then.'

Down on the strand, under the flapping tent of a patched sail, a trader had spread out a series of tattered furs, on which were bolts of dyed cloth, wool and linen. Next to him, another had set up a simple trestle bench, with amber beads, bronze cloak ringpins, ornaments of jet and silver, eating knives in decorated sheaths and amulets, particularly Thor's hammer made to look like a cross, so the wearer got the best of both Other Worlds.

They looked hungrily at the men swaggering off the ship; a few Oathsworn wandered over, but wandered back swiftly enough, glum. Pinleg, rolling even more because he hadn't got his landlegs yet, scowled and shook his head as he came swaying up. 'Not buying, selling,' he growled. 'Piss-poor prices for anything we want to get rid of. That means we'll have to hang on to it until we get to Ladoga.'

Illugi Godi came up, carrying a live hare by the ears. It hung from his hands, trembling and quiet. He moved to a large, flat rock, which had clearly been used before, and set the hare flat, stroking it gently. It gathered itself into a huddle and shook.

He cut the throat expertly, holding it up so that it kicked and squealed and the blood poured over its front and flew everywhere with its flying, desperate attempts to leap in the air.

Illugi gave it to the sea god, Aegir, in the name of Kalf, who had died in the black water without a sword in his hand, in the hope that the Aesir would consider that a worthy enough death, and to Harald One-eye and Haarlaug. Men stopped, added their own prayers, then moved on, humping sea-chests on their shoulders.

67

It came to me then that the Oathsworn had done one journey, from south Norway, round between Wessex and the lands of the Norse in France, north to Man and Strathclyde, then back and on eastwards to Birka. A journey without trouble and a soft raid, according to the salt-stained men of the Oathsworn. And yet three men had died.

Illugi gutted the hare while it kicked feebly, examined the entrails and nodded sagely. He left the red ruin of it aside, started a small fire from shavings, fed it to life and caught me watching. 'Get me dry wood, Orm Ruriksson.'

I did – with difficulty on that wet beach – and he built the fire up, then laid the remains of the hare on it. The smell of singed fur and burning flesh drifted blackly down to the traders, some of whom crossed themselves hurriedly.

When it was done, Illugi Godi left it on the rock, picked up his own meagre belongings and both of us stumbled up the shingle to the coarse grass and on towards the dark huddle of Birka. On the Traders' Green, which sat opposite the tall, timbered stockade and the great double doors of the North Gate, was a sprawl of wattle-and-daub huts.

Two substantial buildings squatted there, too, made of age-blackened timbers caulked with clay. One was for the garrison that manned the Borg, the great fortress which towered over to our left, and the other was for those like us, visiting groups of armed men who had to be offered hospitality, without the good burghers of Birka having to invite them into their protected homes.

At the gates, two bored guards with round leather caps, shields and spears made sure no one entered the town with anything larger than an eating knife and, since no sensible man would simply leave his weapons with them and hope to get them back later, there was much cursing from those unused to the custom as they traipsed back to dwellings to secure them with people they knew.

Illugi Godi, busy pointing things out to me as we trudged

towards the Guest Hall, stopped suddenly at the sight of one of the Oathsworn, walking up from the beach in a daze, as if frozen.

Puzzled at first, I suddenly saw his face as Illugi Godi took him by the shoulder and turned him to face us. Eyvind, his name was, a thin-faced, fey-eyed man from Hadaland in Norway. My father said he was touched, though he never said by what.

Something had touched him, for sure, and it made the hairs on my arms stand up; he was pale as a dead man, his dark hair making him look even more so and, above his beard, his eyes looked like the dark pits of a skull.

'What happened to you?' demanded Illugi as I looked around warily. The wind hissed, cold and fierce, the night came on with a rush and a last, despairing gasp of thin twilight and figures moved, almost shadows. At the gate and up at the fortress, lamps were lit, little glowing yellow eyes that made the dark more dark still. Nothing was out of the ordinary.

Illugi asked again and the man blinked, as if water had been thrown in his face.

'Raven,' he said eventually, in a voice half wondering, half something else. Dull. Resigned. 'I saw a raven.'

'A crow, perhaps,' Illugi offered. 'Or a trick of the twilight.'

Eyvind shook his head, then looked at Illugi as if seeing him clearly for the first time. He grabbed Illugi by the arms; his beard trembled. 'A raven. On the beach, a rock with the remains of a hare sacrifice on it.'

I heard Illugi's swift intake of breath – and so did Eyvind. He was wild-eyed with fear.

'What was in your head?' demanded Illugi Godi. Eyvind shook his own, muttering. I caught the words 'raven' and 'doom' as they were whipped away by the wind. I shivered, for the sight of one of the All-Father's birds on a sacrifice offering was a sure sign that you would die.

Illugi seized the man in return and shook him. 'What was in your head?' he demanded in a fierce hiss.

Eyvind looked at him, his eyebrows closed into one, and he shook his head again, bewildered. 'Head? What do you mean . . . ?'

'Were you remembering, or just thinking?'

'Thinking,' he answered.

Illugi grunted. 'What thought?'

Eyvind screwed up his face, then it smoothed and he looked at Illugi. 'I was looking at the town and thinking how easily it would burn.'

Illugi patted him on the shoulder, then indicated the pile of dropped gear. 'Get to the Guest Hall and don't worry. It was Odin's pet right enough – but not with a message for you. For me, Eyvind. For me.'

The eagerness in him was almost obscene to watch. 'Really? You say true?'

Illugi Godi nodded and the man scrabbled to collect his things, then stumbled off towards the butter-glow of the Hall.

Illugi leaned on his staff a moment, looking round. I was annoyed; Eyvind thought he had seen one of Odin's ravens, herald of death, and had then gone off, not the least bothered that the doom of it was claimed by another. I said as much and Illugi shrugged.

'Who knows? It could have been Thought . . . That raven is as deep and cunning as Loki,' he replied. Then he looked at me, his fringe of grizzled, red-gold beard catching the lamp glow. 'On the other hand, it might have been Memory – Birka has burned before.'

'You think it a warning, then? Since it came to your sacrifice for the dead?' I asked, shivering slightly.

'On yet the other hand,' Illugi Godi said wryly. 'Eyvind is Loki-touched. He loves fire, is mad for fire. Twice before people have stopped him lighting one on the *Fjord Elk*. Oh, he always had good reason – hot food for us all, dry boots and socks – but he was also the one who wanted to torch all the buildings at St Otmund's chapel, after we knew the fyrd were roused.'

I remembered – so it had been him who had called for it.

'So he was mistaken?' I asked as Illugi hefted his belongings and, with no other word, led me to the Guest Hall.

I wanted to ask him what would happen when Eyvind told the others, but should have realised what Illugi already knew: that Eyvind would say nothing. He would now, as the fear and relief fell away, realise what a nithing he had become at that moment and would certainly tell no one how his bowels had turned to water.

The Guest Hall was spacious, clean and well equipped, with a good hearth pitfire and a lot of boxbeds – not enough for us all, so it was a chance to see who was who in the Oathsworn.

Of course, I ended up on the floor near the draughty door, but that was no surprise. My father got a good boxbed, as did Einar and Skapti and others I had expected. To my surprise, Pinleg got one, too and, after a moment of raised hackles and growling, Gunnar Raudi forced Steinthor out of his. Chuckling, Ulf-Agar watched the archer slouch off, scowling.

'Watch your back, flame-head,' he advised. 'You may be picking arrowheads out of it.'

'Watch your mouth, short-arse,' Gunnar growled back, 'or you will be picking my boot out of it.'

At which all those who heard it laughed, including Steinthor. Ulf-Agar bristled, thought better of it and subsided sullenly, for he had also heard of Gunnar Raudi.

I was surprised how many of these hard men had heard of Gunnar and the respect they held for him. I had always thought of Gunnar as someone who lived for free at Bjornshafen and never questioned the why of it.

Now, it seemed to me, Gunnar was known as a hard man

himself, but was clearly not at ease with it. I wondered, then, why he didn't just leave, for it was also clear that he and Einar were wary as big-ruffed wolves round each other.

I had expected Birka to be much the same as Skirringsaal, but it was different. We had women, sent by the merchants who ran the town, but these were no bought thralls, to be up-ended and tupped without thought. They were respectable wives and mothers, in embroidered aprons, with proper linen head-coverings and a beltful of keys and scissors and ear-cleaners. They had their own thralls – some of them pretty enough – but not for the likes of us to grab at.

They had no fear and sharp tongues and the cold-eyed men of the Oathsworn meekly submitted to having hair and beards trimmed and fingernails cut, as if they were children.

So we had meals and minded our manners, after a fashion – Illugi Godi had to cuff a few heads into shamefaced apologies now and then and so respected was he that he could.

I wondered about Illugi. He was a godi, a priest, of course, but most priests were jarls, too. But in the Oathsworn, Einar clearly ruled. It was bewildering for me, this new life – and for others, too, forced to go into the town to get drunk at one of the ale houses set up for foreign travellers and try out the whores there, though they grumbled at having to spend silver on humping that they could never get back.

But even if someone could be persuaded to part with a girl, taking her back to the Guest Hall was a waste of time, since the disapproving eyes of the goodwives, who came and went as they chose, tended to have a shrinking effect. Things, it was generally agreed, were not changing for the better.

There was news, too, brought by traders in coloured cloth tunics and trousers, some dressed like Skapti, who told of those lost in the cataracts of the Rus rivers that year. Like old Boslof, sucked under Holmfors, Island-force, which was an indignity to a man who had survived the insatiable, boulder-strewn torrents of the Drinker, the Courser, the notorious Wave-force and all the rest of the deadly rapids that marked the route to Konugard – Kiev, the Slavs called it. The last seven were so vicious that the Christ-worshippers called them the Deadly Sins after some tale in their holy sagas.

I also heard about Arnlaug, dead of the squits, despite offering up a good ram to the tree on Oak Island, which the Christ-men were calling St Gregor's Island, the first haven after the last of those seven rapids. Having shat himself with fear going down all of them, it seems this Arnlaug couldn't stop and wasted away, so that he was a husk when they came to burn him.

Burn him they did. They had turned to the old ways in the east, ever since the Kura raid some twenty years before, when two hundred ships, they say, entered that river south of Baku and put the town of Berda to the flame and the blade, all the Mahomet-worshippers there.

In turn, the raiders were attacked by Mussulmen – and the same sort of squits that took Arnlaug – and had to retreat, whereupon those Aesir-cursed heathens had dug up the respectably buried and stripped them of the fine weapons and armour left in their boat-graves.

Now the traders burned their dead instead, as hot as they could make it, so that armour melted. As well, they broke the swords into three pieces, to be reforged across the rainbow bridge, but not in this life.

That, as one silver-bearded, garrulous old veteran of the rivers and rapids pointed out, was in Igor's time, who was seventy-five and his wife, the famous Olga, sixty when they gave the Rus their prince, Sviatoslav, whose wars on the Bulgars and Khazars now strangled the silver life out of Birka.

And everyone nodded and marvelled at the wyrd of it and shook their heads over the future.

They shook their heads, too, over the new trade agreements with Miklagard, the Navel of the World, which meant they could not purchase more than fifty gold pieces' worth of silk and had to have a stamp to prove it.

Nor could groups of more than fifty men, all unarmed, enter that city of New Rome, which they called Constantinople. Ridiculous, everyone agreed – even, admittedly, if fifty gold pieces' worth of silk made a fair number of trousers.

Except, noted Finn Horsehead, if they were for Skapti Halftroll. He'd be lucky to get a pair and a spare out of that much material. And everyone laughed, even the merchants, who grudgingly admitted they were given free equipment and a month's provisions for their return to Kiev, which they now had to do, by law of the Emperor, every autumn. Miklagard's finest did not want roistering Norsemen over-wintering in their nice city.

More to the point, as several men fresh from Denmark's trade port of Hedeby revealed, King Hakon was dead and gone and Harald Bluetooth was now indisputable ruler of both Norway and Denmark after a great battle at the island of Stord in the Hardangerfjord. There Hakon lost both his life and his throne to those who were once both his bitterest enemies and his closest kinsmen.

And Illugi Godi rapped his staff appreciatively on the hearthstones at the news that Hakon had been carried to Saeheim in North Hordaland and howed up there with Odin rites, so that the king who had followed Christ until his moment of death was now revered by the old gods, joining his eight brothers, the sons of Harald Fairhair, in Valholl.

Now the five sons of Eirik Bloodaxe and their mother, Gunnhild, fairly to be called Mother of Kings, were returned to Norway and the armies were broken up. Most, being farmers and good, steady men, had sensibly gone home. A few – too many for some – were now prowling, looking for fresh work or easy looting.

I listened and watched and learned at the feet of these, the

74

wondrous far-travelled, watching their faces in the flickering red firelight. I saw who was for the White Christ and who was not, who was trading and who watched for a chance to raid.

Especially, I watched Einar listen and stroke his moustache and, when he paused, knew that bit of news was more important. Then he would resume stroking and I could see him turning it over in his head.

The tidings of new armed men was what clearly concerned him: competition in a world already crowded with it. The garrison of Birka was made up of rootless men looking for somewhere to put their boots, a wife, a hall, a hearthfire. Einar could see the value of a good sword-arm drop by the day.

'If he does not call me soon,' I heard him confide to Ketil Crow, 'I will have to get his attention.'

I knew at once the 'he' Einar spoke of: Brondolf Lambisson, the leader of the Birka merchants. Einar had sent the saint's box up to the Borg with Bagnose and Illugi the day after we'd arrived. They gave it personally to Martin the monk and had back assurances that Brondolf Lambisson would speak to them soon – and then, nothing.

I never found out what Einar had in mind to attract attention, because the next night one of the leather-clad garrison slouched into the Guest Hall and told Einar he was expected in the Borg.

So Einar called Illugi and, surprisingly, me, to go with him. As I collected my cloak, he took me by the arm and said, almost in my ear, his breath strong with herring, 'Not a word that you can read, let alone the Latin.'

For me, it was exhilarating to be out in the town, under the fitful stars and scudding clouds, following the flash and sway of the lantern as the garrison man led the way down the slippery planked walkways, me dodging rain barrels and trying to keep my feet.

75

I was delighted, amazed and repelled all at once – so much so that Illugi had to cuff my head once and mutter, 'If you swivel that neck any more, boy, your head will fall off. Watch your feet, or you will end in the muck.'

He paused as a drunk staggered up, tried to avoid the group of us, slipped and crashed off the walkway into the stinking mire on one side. 'Like him,' he added, scowling and vainly trying to wipe splashes off his tunic.

Behind us, the drunk spluttered and gurgled and got up blowing, then splashed back on to the planks and squelched unsteadily off.

I have seen the other towns since. Hedeby was bigger, Kiev was better and Miklagard, the Great City, could swallow them both and not notice. But Birka, in the first flush of unfolding spring, was like some wild and garish flower.

Every house had a light and noise from it: laughs, shouts, singing. All the treacherous walkways had people – so *many* people, in streets that stank of cooking and spilled ale and shite. They say, at that time, a thousand people lived in Birka. I had never seen a hundred people in one place at one time.

I scarcely realised we were climbing until the pulsing crowd of humanity slackened, then disappeared, and we emerged from the shadowed eaves of quieter houses almost under the stockade and main gates of the Borg.

Inside, unadorned and massive, the dark masonry of the fortress loomed, sparked with golden glow here and there. A small, iron-ringed door and a flight of steps took us into a flagged courtyard, on the other side of which some more steps spiralled wearily to yet another door.

Through this I stumbled, following the others, drunk on the sheer sensation of it all, spilling into a great golden glow of light from torches on sconces, which made the guide's feeble lantern look as if it had gone out.

The place was hung with rich tapestries crusted with gold threads and embroidered with scenes that, in the flickering light, looked as if they were coming alive. I didn't understand any of them – save a hunting scene – but several had those people with round hats of gold, so I thought they must be to do with the White Christ.

The very floor, of polished wood, seemed to gleam and I felt my boots on it were an affront.

A new figure appeared, nodded to the guide and smiled affably at Einar, quizzically at me and, lastly, offered a fixed politeness to Illugi Godi.

He wore a brown robe tied with a clean, pale rope and soft, slippers. His face was sharp, smooth, clean-shaven, his eyes black and his brown hair cut the same length all round. The torchlight bounced off his bald scalp – no, not bald, I realised suddenly. Shaved and, by the fuzz on it, in need of renewing.

'Martin monk,' acknowledged Einar with a nod. 'Brondolf has news, then?'

'Our master has something to impart, yes,' answered Martin smoothly, then turned to Illugi Godi. 'Still a heathen, I see, Master Illugi? I had hoped Our Lord would see fit to deliver another miracle as we approach Easter.'

'Another miracle?' responded Illugi. 'Has there been one recently, then?'

'Indeed,' answered Martin, almost joyously. 'My own bishop, Poppo, has convinced Harald Bluetooth of the power of God and Christ, who died for our sins. He wore a red-hot iron glove to prove it. So it is that Bluetooth is now to be gathered into the flock of God and given His mercy.'

'Where is Brondolf?' Einar demanded.

'On his way,' replied Martin easily. 'He has asked that I offer you his hospitality – please come to the fire. And who is this?'

Einar jerked a thumb at me and shrugged. 'Orm, son of my shipmaster, Rurik. He has never been anywhere, or seen anything, so I thought to bring him, for the learning in it.'

'Indeed,' mused Martin. 'I see you have seen the Light and been gathered into God's grace.'

Puzzled, I saw him glance at the cross on my chest and was appalled that he should think me a Christ-follower. 'I had it from a man I killed,' I blurted without thinking. Einar chuckled. Martin, unsure whether I had just been witty or stupid, led the way to a table with benches and we sat.

It was here, for the first time, that I found food could be remarkably different. Women came, soft-slippered so that they scarcely made more than a whispering sound, and served up fillets of fish stuffed with anchovies and capers, shellfish which we hooked out with silver picks, cutlets of lamb, bloody-rare, ripe with wild garlic and melting in my mouth, all washed down with wine, which I had never tasted until now.

Food. Until Birka, all food was mud-coloured – brown, or yellow or red – and tasted of fish, even the meat, since we fed livestock on fish leavings. I could hardly breathe for the sight and smell of that table.

And all the while Martin chattered about the storms and the news of Stord and how unfortunate it was that Hakon could not be gathered into the bosom of Christ as was proper, but no doubt God would overlook the heathen propensities of his followers and gather him anyway.

Which prompted a sharp response from Illugi Godi and then they were off into argument, leaving Einar and me behind. I listened with half an ear as Illugi tried to explain that the Vanir were not the same as the Aesir, were older gods and some, like Ull, were not much worshipped.

Einar. I caught him looking at me as I looked at him, and saw that his expensive silver cup was scarcely touched. Then I saw myself as he saw me, cheeks bulging with lamb, gravy on my chin, wild with the sheer, unbelievable sensuality of the whole affair.

I swallowed, sobered. Einar grinned and I followed his gaze to the arguing pair.

Illugi was in heated debate about the tale of Bishop Poppo and the wearing of the red-hot glove and Martin was smiling and answering him blandly.

Suddenly, as if a veil was whipped away, I saw, as I knew Einar did – had done since we arrived – that Martin was stalling. The wine, the food – even the argument – were all a feint, as when a man looks for an opening under a shield.

'Where, then,' Einar demanded, 'is Brondolf?'

If he had hurled the silver cup to the polished wood of the floor he couldn't have created more of a silence. Martin looked round, blinked and sighed.

'I had hoped he would be here to tell you himself, but it seems that he has been caught up in events,' the monk said in his gentle, accented voice. 'Things are happening in the wider world – Bluetooth, for one – which have to be dealt with.'

'What was in the saint's box?' asked Einar quietly.

Martin shrugged. He paused, then answered, 'Bones. Some writings, but not what I had hoped.' He rose and crossed to a small chest, opened it and took out a cloth bag, which chinked softly. 'Brondolf is disappointed in me, I fear,' he went on with a wry, deprecating smile, which twisted his face into a gargoyle mask for a moment. 'He is now looking for more . . . practical . . . ways of restoring Birka's fortunes, since my poor efforts have failed.'

'And what were these poor efforts?' asked Einar, leaning forward so that the black pillars of his hair framed his face, making it even more pale than usual, his eyes deep-sunk pools. I was reminded of Eyvind, who had seen Thought, Odin's raven.

Martin spread his arms dismissively and smiled. 'I thought I had found a great ikon of Christ, one which would have made a church in Birka a pilgrimage for Christians everywhere. It seems I was wrong.'

'What was this ikon?' asked Illugi. Einar's dark-pool eyes

79

never left Martin's face and made it hard for the priest to broaden the smile. I knew, at that moment, he was lying and the vision of a great mountain of silver, Atil's hoard, made my heart lurch. It could be real after all.

Martin spread his thin-fingered hands – stained with what seemed to be burn marks – and shrugged. 'It scarcely matters, Illugi,' he said smoothly. 'You know how many there are. Like so many others, this turned out to be a fake. If you took all the knuckle-bones of St Otmund and assembled them you would find a miracle. He had four hands, at least.'

Smiling, he stepped forward and placed the cloth bag in front of Einar with a soft, chiming chink. 'Brondolf thanks you for your efforts. You are free to go where you please.'

The air grew still and no one moved. It was as if we were all frozen and the longer the moment went on, the more painful the attempt to move became.

Then Einar, with a swiftness that startled us up like swallows, scooped up the bag and stood. In a second, there was nothing but movement, as if that had released us from some spell. Einar strode off without a word. Illugi Godi, I saw, sensed that something had happened but wasn't sure what. Politeness stayed him long enough to thank Martin and offer all the usual platitudes and get them in return.

For my part, I saw the monk's eyes flick, just once, to the door. On the back of it, on a hook, hung a hooded cloak.

Einar waited for us in the courtyard, where a fresh, clean, cold wind drove out the cobwebs, streamed out our hair, hissed over the flagstones and rattled the little gate as we were quietly ushered out and handed a lantern. No guide back to the Guest Hall, then.

'You might have had more regard for hospitality,' chided Illugi Godi and Einar, only half listening, grunted a reply.

'He paid in silver, in a town where silver is scarce as hen's teeth. He wanted no argument and he wanted no bartering for goods on tally sticks. He wants us gone, does Brondolf

Lambisson – but had to leave it to the monk, such a delicate thing. So what could have been more pressing to him that he could not come himself?' He turned to me suddenly. 'What did you see?' he asked.

I knew at once what he meant, felt strange, as if perched on a cliff like some fledgling gull, waiting for a suitable wind, working to that moment of hurling off and trusting to new wings.

'He was lying,' I said, sure of it as I was of my own palm. 'Brondolf is somewhere else, as you say. Since he is so important, it must be someone more important than him. Since, I am thinking, there is no one more important than him in this place, then it must be a foreigner and a chief at least . . .

'And the monk was waiting for us to go, for he has business abroad.'

I told him of the cloak on the back of the door. Illugi's eyes widened and Einar halted, so that we all nearly ran into him. He turned to me, a grim smile on that pale face. I wished he wouldn't do that, since it was worse than no smile at all.

'Most men think in a straight line,' he said, barely audible over the town's noise and the wind. 'They see only their own actions, like a single thread in the Norns' loom, knotted only when they thrust their life on others. They see through one set of eyes, hear through one set of ears, all their life.' He stared at me. 'To look at things through someone else's eyes is a rare thing, which cannot be learned. To those with the gift, it is not hard, nor complicated. But, to survive and be more than any others, it is essential. You have that gift, I am thinking.'

I was stunned and swelled with it. In that moment, I almost loved the great, glorious being that was Einar the Black, yet, even then, the very gift he praised me for slipped a memory, the blade-bright thought: this man had snicked off the head of Gudleif, for almost no reason other than he could.

We tramped back to the North Gate and were almost out

when a figure loomed from the dark, with others behind. I saw Gunnar Raudi, Ketil Crow, Bagnose, Pinleg and others, wild-eyed, wild-haired – and sober.

Gunnar Raudi's grim face, grimmer still in the play of lamplight loomed up to Einar and said, 'Ulf-Agar is missing. Steinthor says men took him.'

FOUR

'They were armed,' Steinthor growled. 'Armed and in the town, Einar.' He held out his forearm, showing a rough strip of bloodstained cloth, the ends whipping in the wind. Around him, Einar, I, Illugi and others gathered, stone-grim.

'Who were they?' demanded Einar.

Steinthor shrugged. His eye was closing to a fat-puffed slit. 'Six, maybe seven,' he said. 'We left the ale house at the harbour and they came after us. Danes, it seemed to Ulf-Agar and me, and looking for trouble, for we had offended no one.'

'Let's get there,' snarled Skapti Halftroll. 'Weapons or no weapons, I'll grind them.'

There were savage chuckles at that and a few began to push past Einar on the wooden walkway, but he thrust out an arm and stopped them. 'Wait. Let's find out more. Steinthor, why did they take Ulf-Agar? And where did they take him?'

Steinthor touched his eye speculatively, squinting at Einar. 'That's the strange of it. They came for us and we thought it was just a fight. I wasn't up for it much, having been light on my drink, but Ulf pitched right in. Then I saw the weapons come out – long blades they were and too long to be hidden under a cloak and brought in. Someone turned a blind eye to that.'

'Now you can do that,' called someone from the back and there were more chuckles. Steinthor spat and touched the eye again.

'If it had been the edge of that blade, I would be a dead-eye, for sure. But it was the upswing that smacked me. Knocked me to the ground, right off the walkway and into the mud and shit. When I surfaced, they were hauling Ulf away and he was not making a move, hanging between two of them. He might be dead.'

That silenced everyone.

'What did you do then?' asked Einar. 'Stand there and drip?'

'No, I did not,' retorted Steinthor hotly. 'I followed them, thinking they would kick the shit out of Ulf-Agar and leave him. I thought they had picked on him for some reason I did not know – he can be an annoying little turd, as anyone will tell you.'

'Indeed so,' Einar agreed, nodding into the chorus of harsh chuckles. 'But they didn't, or else we would be binding his bruises.'

'No,' agreed Steinthor. 'They hauled him to one of the warehouses at the main harbour. There were a lot of men there and two boats, high-prowed and gilded and bigger than the *Elk,* that were not there yesterday.'

This set everyone muttering. Illugi Godi looked at Einar and Skapti hoomed a bit, then said: 'Two *drakkar*? What *varjazi* has two boats that size?'

'None,' muttered Einar, stroking his moustache. 'Nor could a *varjazi* persuade the merchants of Birka to ignore their laws on weapons. Only a real power could do that.'

'Such as one who now rules two lands?' Illugi Godi said mildly, the wind whipping his hair into his face.

'Bluetooth,' Einar said and the name leaped from head to

head, swirling away on the wind, setting fire to mutters and darkly exchanged looks. He looked at me. 'You had it right enough. Someone more important than Brondolf Lambisson and a foreigner.'

Bluetooth, new King of the Danes and Norwegians. Somehow, he had heard of the Oathsworn of Einar's *Elk* and their quest for some treasure. It seemed to me – and, I knew, to Einar – that he had heard more of it than we had, to seize one of us and put him to the question. It did mean, I was thinking, that you had to take Atil's treasure hoard seriously, for surely no one would go to these lengths over some muttered foolishness about a saga tale? Surely he had not come after us over that?

There were chuckles when I hoiked this up, wide-eyed and wild-haired in the Birka wind.

Einar, though, frowned, for it had been revealed then that just about everyone knew the supposed secret of Atil's treasure. And, of course, Einar was going to the same lengths over the foolishness of a saga tale and he did not like to hear that voiced.

'Perhaps so,' he growled. 'I would like to know who has been sent by the King of Norway and the Danes. And what this someone wants with Ulf-Agar.'

'We must get him back,' said Illugi and there were mutters of approval at that.

Einar nodded. 'We swore an oath to each other,' he said. 'It is Ulf-Agar's bad luck that he knows nothing that would help Bluetooth in this matter, so we will do it quickly, before they kill him by accident.'

'And,' muttered Illugi, 'you don't know just what Ulf-Agar knows. Fox-eared, that one.'

'He is, right enough,' murmured Einar, then, louder: 'Orm, go with Steinthor, who will point out the warehouse. Watch it carefully. After that, Steinthor should go to the Guest Hall and have his wounds tended.

'Geir Bagnose, you will go to the fortress, to the gate there. A man will come out, cloaked, perhaps hooded. He has a face like a weasel and will be scurrying, I am thinking, like a rat out of a hole. I want to know where he goes without him knowing he is followed.'

Then he turned and led everyone else back to the Guest Hall.

Suddenly, there was just me and Steinthor on the dark street of greasy timbers, in a town now quiet save for a distant shout or two and a barking dog. The buildings were shadowed mounds, angular howes through which the wind whipped.

Shivering, I followed Steinthor as he limped between the houses, first this way, then that. Then he stopped and pointed. I saw a building slightly apart from the others and beyond it the black sea slapping an oak jetty. A lantern swung wildly, dancing weak yellow light over a door in the building. Two figures moved, stamping and dragging cloaks round them against the wind.

With a brief clap on my shoulder, Steinthor was away into the night, the fire and the ale. Bitterly, I watched him go, pulled my cloak tighter around me, up over my head and hunkered down in the lee of a fence, feeling the sodden ground soak into my boots.

The building the fence enclosed was a wattle hut with a patch of garden, now muddied. Inside, I heard chickens murmur to each other and two voices talking, though it was too faint for me to hear the words. I only knew that one was low and one was higher. It made me feel all the worse out here, with the rain spitting in my face and the wind swooping and swirling. On the black water, prows danced.

The voices tailed off. Someone snored and, far away, a dog yelped furiously.

Then I heard the first shriek from the warehouse and stiffened. I looked around, but there was no one. If Einar and the others didn't come soon . . .

Another shriek, half whipped away by the wind. I clenched my teeth. Still no sign of anyone.

On the third scream, I could stand it no longer. I moved down towards the warehouse, edging always into the shadows, which took me away from the door and the wild lantern and the guards, round to one flat end of the building, then round again to where the curved back wall stood on a strip of ground, falling away to the shingle and the spray-lashed water.

There were bulky shapes here; I scrambled over discarded barrels of rotting wood, old sodden wool that had once been a sail, frayed rigging, worm-rotted spars. I was sure I was blundering around like the clapper in a bell; every time I made a sound I froze in one spot and waited. But nothing happened.

Another shriek, louder this time.

I found a door, slightly recessed, and had to quietly clear old cordage from in front of it, so I knew it wasn't used.

It was rotted and knot-holed, which let me peer through. I saw faint light, as if from a lantern, but nothing moved. I pressed on the door . . . nothing. I pressed again, harder – and it gave with a soft sigh of rotting splinters and insect husks.

I had an eating knife, the length of my finger, and it felt ridiculous clutching it in one sweaty hand while the blood thundered in my ears and I waited for the rush of feet and the flash of three feet of edged steel.

Nothing – but the next shriek nearly made me piss myself, so loud it seemed. It tailed off abruptly and I swore under my breath. Only bloody-minded stupidity was making me do this, I reasoned. I didn't even like Ulf-Agar.

But I knew the real reason, of course. I had sworn the oath and, if it had been me, I'd rather know there was the hope of someone coming for me, than that I was doomed.

It was so dark I had an arm out in front of me, the knife held in the fist of the other, taking one slow, rolling step after another. I had the impression of beams, of a wooden floor, caught a spit of rain on my face and, looking up, glimpsed stars through the ruined roof, then clouds scudded across and they were gone.

There was rubbish everywhere: a series of traps for the unwary. I took two steps and almost went on my arse when my foot skidded off what felt like the shaft of an oar. I gave up, crouched down, started to slither across the floor, waiting all the time for whoever was in the darkness to erupt at me.

As the sweat ran in my eyes I swore that I could see them, waiting just ahead, so that my breath stopped in my throat.

I sent a nest of mice rustling off, exploded a ball of cockroaches, which ran all over my arm, almost to my face and, despite myself, I gasped aloud and slapped them off. Then I relaxed; if the room was filled with armed men, they were deaf or dead.

I crept towards the lurking shape, moving so that the faint glimmer of light silhouetted it and not me. Then I realised what it was and almost shouted out with the joy of relief. A prow. A gods-cursed, arse-wipe of an old prow.

I was wiping my face and trying not to weep with relief of the moment, when it suddenly struck me that the light seemed to be coming from the floor. I found a knot-hole in a door – there was a cellar.

The square of wood came up smoothly, revealing a set of wooden steps and, compared to what I had been in a moment ago, a lot of light. I lay down, craned my head as far as I could and spotted there was only one way: a passage, with a lantern stuck up on a niche on one wall about halfway down.

I crept down on to a stone floor and the reek of old hides and spoiled food. I started along the corridor and had almost reached the lantern on the wall when something flickered, a gleam and no more. I stopped, crouched, looked again. It was gone. I moved my head – light bounced off metal. I peered at it: a small bell, one of several strung on two or three strands of black horsehair, stretched across the passageway at ankle height.

I hunkered back and blew out gently, considering, searching, thinking. If I had set such a warning, so easily stepped over if found . . . I saw the second one, at neck height to a man. Half-hunkered and awkward with caution, I slid between the two and on down the passage to where it ended in a blank wall and two doors, left and right.

I considered. The door left was closed, the one right slightly opened. I listened to the closed one, watching the open one. Snores from the closed one. No noise at all from the other, but there was light there – and heat.

I pushed it and it scraped open on the dirt floor, along a groove worn there with use. It was dimly lit and a sharp smell of smoke and sweat and blood hovered. There was a fire, like a forge fire of charcoal in a metal brazier. Wooden-handled implements stuck out of it. Silhouetted against it was the figure of a man, naked to the waist and muscled, the sweat-grease gleaming in the red light of coals.

Beyond, blood-red in the light, hung between two beams by his thumbs, his toes barely touching the ground, was a naked Ulf-Agar, head swinging, face hidden by his tangled hair. Dark patches marred the white of him and something black ran down his chest in a slow, viscous trickle.

I took two steps and the figure heard and turned, lazily, expecting someone else. I gave him the little knife, searching for his throat but missing by a long way and having Odin's luck. It went in his left eye up to the hilt; it must have killed him instantly.

He went backwards, his mouth the ragged shape of a scream that never came, dragging the knife out of my hands, crashing down on the brazier and rolling off in a spill of sizzling coals at the feet of Ulf-Agar. His head came up slowly as I put my foot on the dead man's forehead and hauled the little knife out, then sawed at the thongs that held Ulf's thumbs.

'You . . . ?'

'Can you walk?'

He fell into my arms then, almost to his knees, recovered and shoved himself upright. There were wet, red burn weals all over him and his speech was mushed where they had burst his lips and splintered his teeth. The hilt of a sword, I thought as I steadied him.

Then the door was shoved further in and someone stepped in. 'Hauk? Starkad says—'

He saw us then and I made to run at him with the little knife, but Ulf-Agar gave a growl, a low, terrible sound that froze me to the spot. He moved swiftly, but unsteadily, snatched something from the brazier and slashed the man across the face.

With a howl, the man fell, blood all over the hands he clasped to his face. Snarling, bloody froth all over his chin, Ulf rammed the white-hot iron down, through between the man's knuckles, leaning on the thing with all his might while the man writhed and screamed, pinned like a worm on a hook.

The reek and sizzle of it snapped me to life. I crashed heavily into Ulf, knocking him sideways. 'Let's go,' I hissed. 'Follow me.'

I got out of the door as the one opposite opened, inwards. I booted it as hard as I could and it flew back, sending whoever was behind it sprawling, then I dashed on. Behind me, Ulf-Agar lumbered like some strange dark dwarf.

I heard the bells tinkle as I went through them – fuck it, everyone knew of our presence now, so alarm bells scarcely mattered. I hit the wooden steps, flung myself up and into the dark warehouse, darker still after even the little light we had had. I was lost in it, couldn't work out which way was which, whirled in a complete circle, then realised I was alone.

Below, at the foot of the stairs, Ulf-Agar felled someone with a meaty smack, then howled at the men in the passage beyond. I could see only the sweat-gleam of him and the whirling red bar of the hot iron.

'Fuck! Get *up* here. Others will come . . .'

He heard me, backed up the stair, leaped through and slammed the door on them, standing on it. I heard them rush the stairs, the clatter as they thumped on the door. Ulf rose an inch or two; he was too slight to keep them down.

I saw light, caught him by one wrist. 'This way . . .'

I was at the front door, the one with the swinging lantern – that was the glimmering light I had seen. I hit it, smashing hard, my shoulder hunched into it. The door held and I bounced back into Ulf and the pair of us went over. Behind, I heard the trapdoor bang up and light spilled out, silhouetting the men who stumbled up the steps.

'Odin's . . . hairy . . . arse,' Ulf gasped, getting to his feet. 'It's barred on the inside, you oaf. Lift it . . .'

He had no time for anything else. The men from the cellar were on him and metal clanged as he parried and leaped. Two of them, armed with wicked long seaxes and gleaming, frenzied eyes. In the half-dark, stumbling over debris, with no sound other than Ulf's curses and everyone's ragged breathing, they closed in.

I heaved up the bar in a trembling frenzy now; the door flew open, figures suddenly loomed up and a voice – such a familiar voice, a voice that filled me with a sickening leap of such relief I almost lost control of my bladder.

'Stand aside, Orm!'

And big Skapti, clutching a fat wooden club, hurtled through the door, just as a meaty smack sounded behind me and Ulf howled. Then I was shouldered out of the way, slammed sideways out of the warehouse, where I caught my heel and fell. I lay, looking up at the rushing figures, saw Valknut, his face briefly lit in a snarling mask, Ketil Crow,

91

almost throwing himself into the warehouse, Gunnar Raudi and his red flag of beard.

Then Einar stood, looking down at me, his hair streaming like night in the rising gale. His grin was sharp, wolfish. From inside the warehouse came the thwack and crack of wood breaking bone and laying open skulls.

'I told you to watch, young Orm.'

My tongue stuck to the roof of my mouth; I meant to tell him of the shrieks in the night, managed only the word: 'Scream,' and he nodded, as if I had told him the whole tale.

Valknut and Skapti appeared, a limp Ulf hanging between them, his feet dragging as they hustled him out of the building. After him, thrown out bodily, came a stranger, followed by Ketil Crow and the others.

'Is he dead?' Einar asked Skapti, who shook his head, his beard rippling in the wind.

'Beaten, burned, a bad cut on one shoulder, but alive.'

Einar jerked his head in the direction of the Guest Hall, then turned to where the stranger was climbing to his knees, his head hanging, gasping like a winded pony. Bloody drool hung in strands from his mouth.

Einar bent, grabbed the man by his hair and hauled the head up. 'Who is your jarl? Whose *drakkar* are these?'

The man's eyes rolled and there was a great dark mark all along one side of his face. His voice, mushed from his smashed mouth, was hard though. 'Fuck oor murrer.' He tried to spit, but only succeeded in slicking his own chin.

'Starkad,' I said, suddenly remembering the name shouted by one of them – the one, I also remembered, with a sickening lurch, who wouldn't be shouting anything any more, from a mouth rammed full of white-hot metal.

Einar's head came up with a snap, like a hound on a scent. He looked at me, then the man at his feet, drew out a long seax from under his cloak and jerked the man's head back.

'Time to go, Einar,' Pinleg warned, looking down at the harbour, where shouts and lights split the darkness.

'Starkad Ragnarsson?' Einar demanded of the man, ignoring Pinleg. The seax came to his nose and the man saw what would happen, blinked, swallowed snot and blood and then nodded. Einar flicked the seax up anyway, gave a sharp curse and flung the man's head away, so that he sprawled, panting and writhing like a whipped dog, the blood spurting from his split nose. Ketil Crow kicked him viciously as he passed.

They moved swiftly, in a tight group – or as tight as they could along the wooden walkways – Ketil Crow bringing up the rear, turning now and then like a huge elk at bay. We caught up with Valknut and Skapti, a moaning, half-conscious Ulf between them.

As we neared the gate out of the town, there was a flurry of discarded clubs, blades stuffed inside tunics and Ulf-Agar was swathed in Skapti's heavy blue-wool cloak, to hide his state. Like a party of drunks we spilled out of the gate, past the two bored, cold, envious guards and on to the Guest Hall.

Inside were only Oathsworn – all the women had been told to leave – and all of them were armed. Illugi had Ulf-Agar set down near the fire and bent to look at him, peeling off Skapti's cloak. Skapti took it back, staring at the ominous stains with distaste, before bundling it up and moving to stow it in his sea-chest.

Einar put mailed guards on the door, then sat by the fire, elbow on one knee, stroking his moustaches. The Oathsworn spoke in low, quick tones, sharing the tale of the battle; now and then a sharp bark of laughter rang out.

There was a great thumping at the doors and everyone fell silent, half crouching in the red twilight like a pack of feral dogs, eyes narrowed. Steel gleamed. The thumping came again and a faint voice.

'It's Bagnose,' said one of the mailed guards. Einar indicated to open the Hall door and Geir stumbled in, growling.

'Fuck you, what took you so long? Thor's farting up a gale out there and you keep me . . .' Geir fell silent, seeing the red-lit faces of armed men all staring at him, seeing that something had happened.

Einar didn't explain, simply summoned him. 'You followed the little monk?'

'I did,' said Bagnose, looking round for ale. Steinthor, naked from the waist and strapped with ragged bindings, handed him one and Bagnose grinned and swallowed. Einar waited patiently.

'He went to the Trade Harbour and a timber hov there. No, not a hov . . . a Christ temple of a sort. Half-built. He met someone there.' He paused, grinning, and took another swallow, then saw Einar's eyes growing dangerous. 'Vigfus. Old Skartsmadr Mikill himself.'

Vigfus. Vigfus. The name was spread in mutters around the Hall until someone – Hring, I thought – asked the question I wanted to ask. Who the fuck was Vigfus?

Einar ignored it. 'Has he a ship?'

'A solid, fat *knarr* in the Trade Harbour. And maybe twenty or thirty men – good fighting men, too, fresh from Bluetooth's wars, though these ones are from the losing side, I am thinking.'

Einar stroked his moustache for a moment, then looked up at Illugi. 'Illugi Godi and Skapti and Ketil Crow: we will talk this out.'

'We should get out of this hall,' growled a voice from the back. 'We are trapped here.'

'What do you think will happen?' Einar shot back.

'Bluetooth's man, this Starkad, will come. If we don't come out, he will burn us until we do,' answered one called Kvasir, nicknamed Spittle.

Einar laughed, though there was no cheer in it. 'Bluetooth, last I heard, was King of the Danes and Norway. Birka belongs to the King of the Swedes. He might be offended if Bluetooth's war hounds ran around killing and burning people in this main trade town.'

'No king cares about Birka. Birka is its own master,' Finn Horsehead pointed out. 'Lambisson is master here, in the name of the King of the Swedes. If the king still is Olof, that is. Eirik was fighting him for it, last I heard, and since Eirik is also known as Victorious, there's a clue as to which one to put your money on.'

There was laughter at that.

'Lambisson it is who has allowed Bluetooth's men into Birka with full steel in their hands,' answered Valknut. 'Which gives you a clue as to whom to put your wager on for treachery. He is a practical man for money.'

There was more grim laughter at that. Einar scanned the faces, seeing the half-fearful, half-savage looks and the eyes gleaming in the red firelight. 'Stand out in the wind if you want,' he shrugged. 'But Illugi, Skapti, Ketil Crow and myself will talk this out. Quietly, over some ale, in this warm hall.'

There were mutters about holding a proper Thing over something so important and fresh arguments began. Someone – I was sure it was Eyvind – said loudly, 'Burn.'

Geir Bagnose blew froth off his fresh horn of ale and began to skald, loudly and with feeling. I winced as I realised he was making poetry out of the rescue of Ulf-Agar and, though I knew why he did it, wished he didn't. But men stopped arguing to listen.

My father slid in beside me and clapped me on the shoulder. 'You did well.'

'I shat myself several times,' I answered truthfully. 'I should have waited . . . but he was screaming fit to shave the hairs off your arms.'

'Aye,' my father agreed, 'he was bad handled at that—' He broke off as men raised voices in appreciation of a particularly good kenning about 'grim eye of the wyrm', it being a clever play on my name. 'Just as well Ulf is out of his head,' he added. 'He'll hate this.'

'He played his part,' I argued. 'He was defending my back in the end, armed only with a hot forge-iron.'

'Let's hope Bagnose puts it in, then,' my father chuckled, then raised his voice as Geir stopped to take another pull at his drinking horn.

'Well done, Bagnose. Now that the Hakon's skald, the Plagiarist, is silenced by the death of his king in Norway, there's service there for a good court verse-maker.'

Geir raised his horn in acknowledgement, wiped his lips, then stuck the tip of the horn in the earth floor to keep it upright while he continued extemporising verses.

'Just thank the gods he isn't Skallagrimsson,' my father added and I hastily made a sign against the evil eye. Egil was a famous poet, but a man with blood behind his eyes and a great elk head with beetling brows that, it was assuredly reported, you could hit with Thor's hammer and not dent. He was also as mad a killer as a wounded boar and not a man whose ale-elbow you wanted to nudge.

Which reminded me of our predicament – and questions I had. 'Who is Starkad? And this Vigfus? And—?'

'One foot first, then another,' my father answered, leaning closer and dropping his voice. He ticked them off on his blunt, splintered-nail fingers. 'Starkad Ragnarsson is one of Bluetooth's best, a man loved by women and feared by men, as they say. He is possibly the only man Einar fears, so we should fear him, too. He has the reputation of a good boar dog – once he has sunk his teeth in, you will never get his jaws out save by slaying.'

I mulled that one over moodily, while my father raised another finger.

'Vigfus – no one has ever called him anything else. Apart from Skartsmadr Mikill, Quite the Dandy, which he hates. It seems he always dresses in the dark, as they say, for he has a worse way with clothing than Skapti Halftroll and the Oathsworn have had dealings with him before . . . certainly we know his like. He always manages to have some band of followers, all hard men, not to be trusted.'

'Like Einar?' I offered wryly and my father frowned and shook his head.

'No, lad. Einar believes in oaths; he will hold to them. Vigfus is as treacherous as a snake with a foot on its tail.' He sighed and scrubbed his chin. 'There are too many players in this game,' he added gloomily.

'What game?' I retorted. 'We don't know what we are playing.'

'No, I don't understand it,' agreed my father, then shot a sideways, almost sly look at me. 'Einar thinks you are a deep thinker,' he went on, rubbing his beard. 'What do you make of it all?'

I considered it. This King Bluetooth had heard there was something, enough for him to find two ships and armed men, for he had also heard the Oathsworn were involved and knew them as grim men in a fight.

He must have learned that before the Oathsworn came for me in the Vik – that already seemed an age, another life. I looked back on it and saw this boy stuffing gull eggs in the hemmed loop of his tunic and, though I knew it was me, he was already a stranger. In so short a time I had become a man and a killer of men.

'Aye, just so,' agreed my father. 'We were with the Danes of Hedeby, then headed for the Vik, since it was on the way to Strathclyde. But no one was loose-mouthed in Hedeby – and after that we came for you, word having reached me.'

'Can you be sure of that? I remember Pinleg spoke of Atil's treasure on the beach at Strathclyde – how many more knew in Hedeby?'

He made a mouth like a cat's arse and scrubbed one hand through his thinning hair, which was answer enough. 'And Vigfus?' he asked.

I shrugged. 'Why should Lambisson have just the

Oathsworn sailing for him? But there must be a good haul at the end of it, to be worth the outlay on more than one band, for men and ships are not cheap.

'It is possible that he is making sure no one group knows everything about what he seeks – even if it really is Atil's treasure – only a little part of it. And he won't be happy that Starkad is here. He will not want the likes of Bluetooth setting his hands on whatever it is he seeks.

'But I am thinking this Vigfus is not Lambisson's man. He is Martin's man and the Christ priest takes such pains to meet him in secret that there is the stink of treachery in it.'

'Just so,' said Einar's voice behind me and, turning, I saw him, black as a scowl in the firelight. Behind him, Skapti and Ketil Crow were moving among the men, talking in urgent, quiet voices, clapping shoulders. Bagnose's epic – thank the gods – had been brought to a halt.

Einar hunkered down beside the pair of us. 'You have the right of it again, young Orm,' he said. 'Now we know the players of this game, we must find out what the game is.'

'And the rules,' I offered.

He looked at me, cold-eyed. 'There are no rules.'

'None?' I asked, far too boldly. 'What of the oath we swear – is that not a rule?'

'It is an oath,' he replied with a thin smile, 'which is different. You are young and will learn the difference. I was young once and walked by myself. I counted myself rich when I found a comrade I could trust. And I could only trust one who would swear an oath.' He turned to my father then. 'Rurik, take the Trimmer and the men Ketil Crow is picking. Make the *Elk* ready for sea.'

'In this gale? I'd be hauling her higher up the shingle . . .'

'On the dawn tide, we must be gone from here.'

'To where?'

Einar looked at him for a moment, then grinned. 'The whale road.'

My father ran his age-veined hand over his face, saw Einar's face, blank as stone, nodded and got up. He wanted to speak of hidden rocks, but saw it was pointless. Einar wanted away, in any direction – and fast.

I realised men were moving, swiftly and efficiently to pack, moving sea-chests and gear. Some were stripping off their mail, which I thought strange.

'Here's the way of it,' Einar said to me quietly. 'Men will make the *Elk* ready, others will take all our gear to the Tyr Grove, a place of birch trees not far from here. Illugi Godi knows it and will lead them.

'I will need a few, enough to make a good group in the dark. And Orm, the Bear Slayer. We will fetch the little monk and be on our way before anyone knows the better.'

I blinked and swallowed.

Einar clapped me on the shoulder. 'And we will walk through the gates with only our eating knives and friendly smiles, to try and meet with Lambisson and the little monk, for good sound reasons. Of course, once we do, we will make sure the little monk stays.'

I swallowed again. 'And Lambisson?'

Einar shrugged, his mouth in a twisted grin, then rose and moved to give Ketil Crow some urgent, low-voiced instructions.

In a daze, I collected my cloak, realised it was filthy from the warehouse and tried to brush some of the worst off. I thought of using my knife to scrape it, but when I attempted to pull it from the sheath, I found it was stuck fast. When I eventually wrenched it out, I saw it was gummed with dried blood.

I remembered the man's eye, felt the suck as I pulled the knife out. I had not been aware of it at the time, being eager to cut Ulf-Agar free, but the gods never forget and made me remember it now. I knew it was Loki's doing when I felt the sick rising in me.

Bagnose grinned at me, hefting a sea-chest and helping Steinthor with another. He winked as he bustled past. Two others were making a seat out of two spears and a cloak, to fetch Ulf-Agar away.

Some saga hero, me. Sitting trembling in the midst of this preparing host, trying not to throw up all that lamb and wild garlic over my salt-crusted boots.

Einar came over, holding a long seax in a soft leather sheath and a handful of leather bindings. He handed it to me, then undid my tunic belt, hiked it up and undid the strings of my breeks.

I clutched them to me, but he indicated, grinning, for me to drop them. Loud hoots of laughter greeted this. Then he started to show me how to strap the foot-long seax to the inside of one thigh, high up under my balls. Red-faced, I stopped him, fumbling the thing on myself, aware of my prick shrinking under the stares.

'You'll impress the women when you sit,' rumbled Skapti.

'But not when erect,' growled Kvasir Spittle from the crowd and everyone laughed, the high, savage laughter of men about to stare Thor in his red-bearded face.

I hauled my breeks back up and Einar nodded, looked around the company and raised one hand. There was a short, deep-throated 'hoom' and then only the noise of men moving, gear clattering, feet shuffling. In seconds, it seemed, the hov was empty, with not so much as a discarded strap-end to show anyone had been there.

Hring and Skapti came up, carrying the spear and cloak bed I thought made for Ulf-Agar. Eyvind was there, and Ketil Crow, Gunnar Raudi and Einar, who looked at me and said, 'Lie down and be dead, Orm. But give me that amulet from your neck first.'

Bewildered, I lay on the contraption and was bundled up in two cloaks, swathed head to foot, along with four long, naked swords. Einar grinned down and, just before he covered my face, said, 'Remember: be still and dead, Orm Ruriksson. There's more than one way to kill the bear.'

I felt him place something on my chest, then rocked violently as I was lifted. I heard the wind hiss and thump round the houses of Birka, but felt nothing through the swathe of cloaks. I smelled sweat and piss and blood, though, felt the weight of the wool, heard sounds dull almost into stillness and the night transform into a hotter, dryer blackness, clutching me like an eager woman.

I was not happy with it, the lurch and sway and the press of the wool and the feel of trying to suck air through it, thick as gruel. My eyes were blinking sweat; the edge of one blade, I swore, was slicing into my thigh with every stumble they made. I felt my lungs contract and my heart was banging against my ribs like a door in the wind.

We stopped. Someone said something, too indistinct in the wind. Then Einar, gloomy and sombre, announced: 'One of ours is dead . . . a Christ-follower, as you can see. We need your little monk to speak properly over him and do what rites the Christ-men do.'

The answer was gruff, almost offhand and I heard Einar spit. 'It happened no more than an hour ago – in the town you are supposed to guard. Where were you, then, when the men from the *drakkar* had their swords and axes out, running riot in the streets?'

The guard grunted, shamed to silence. Another voice sounded, much closer. 'Stabbed, was he?'

'Stuck through like a pig,' agreed Skapti sorrowfully.

I felt the cloth twitch back and the guard grunted. I lay, muscles frozen, willing my closed eyelids not to quiver. The cloth twitched back and Gunnar's growl came low and fierce: 'Have a care and respect, little man.'

'No offence,' I heard the guard say hastily. 'I remember the boy from earlier. A shame. Pass through – though I think it unlikely you will get much from that monk, who somewhat lacks the proper hospitality all Christ-followers are supposed to have.'

'Our thanks,' Einar replied and the corpse bed lurched on.

'Tell the guard at the door that Sten passed you,' the guard called after and again Einar called his thanks.

Beyond earshot, he turned and hissed anxiously to the others, 'Where's Eyvind?'

No one knew. Muttering curses under his breath, he led us up the steps, to where another guard stood at the hall door. Einar recited the same story, used Sten's name and, suddenly, there was a flash of blinding light as the cloaks were peeled back. I almost lost a finger in their rush to get the swords out in that empty antechamber.

Einar held up one hand. 'Quiet, as you would tickle trout from a stream, or your woman's fancy. We grab the monk, give him a dunt – no more, mind – that will lay him out as dead, then put him in the corpse bed and trust the guards don't see, in the dark, that we are one more walking out than walking in.'

It was a good and daring plan, as everyone agreed afterwards. But, as Gunnar Raudi pointed out, plans are like summer snow on a dyke and rarely last more than a few minutes.

Which is what happened when we sneaked into the room where Einar, Illugi and I had dined. It seemed an age ago, but the dishes were still there.

And so were the soft-slippered servants, clearing them away.

'Fuck—'

It was all anyone had time to say. There were four of them, all O-mouthed and frozen. There were six of us and they were still scrabbling on the polished floor when our nailed boots scarred a way to them and steel flashed in their faces.

Three died in a welter of sprayed blood and muffled shrieks. The fourth found Skapti sitting on him, driving the air from his body, slamming his head casually and rhythmically into the floorboards. I hadn't even moved, found I had stopped breathing and started again with a savage, hoarse intake.

'The monk?' demanded Einar, leaning down to the dazed, battered thrall. His shaved head was bleeding, his eyes rolling. He had shat himself and Skapti, sniffing suspiciously, stopped sitting on him in a hurry, which had the added effect of allowing the man to breathe and talk.

'There . . .'

Gunnar Raudi and Ketil Crow sprang forward. Skapti whacked the flat of his sword on to the thrall's head, which slammed it back into the floorboards. Blood seeped from the thrall's ears, I noticed.

Skapti moved on and probably thought he had been merciful in only knocking the man unconscious. I reckoned, from the rasping breath and leaking blood, that the man would almost certainly die. Even if he didn't, he'd probably be witless, like old Oktar, who had been suspected of releasing the white bear at Bjornshafen.

The following summer he had been kicked in the head by a stallion and blood had come out of his ears. He had survived, with a big dent and no mind enough to keep him from drooling, so Gudleif had had him sacrificed, in the old way, his blood sprinkled on the fields, as a mercy. Another wyrd death to lay at the den of that bear – and, of course, at the feet of my father.

A series of shouts and a scuffle snatched me from these thoughts. Ketil Crow arrived, more or less behind Martin the monk, who smiled smoothly at Einar – much to all our bewilderment. 'Excellent,' he declared. 'How did you plan to get me out?'

'How do you know we planned to get you out and not just lay you out?' scowled Ketil Crow. Einar indicated the corpse bed Hring was dragging in and Martin's smile grew broader still.

'Clever,' he said, then, briskly: 'There is a woman next

door. She will be the one for that bed, well covered. I will, if I may, borrow a cloak and helm – from Orm, who is my size—'

'Wait, wait,' growled Einar, scrubbing his stubbled chin. 'What's all this? What woman?'

Martin was already pulling the cloak from my unyielding shoulders, trying to prise my leather helmet off. I slapped his hands away.

'Lambisson does not esteem me. He will be back soon, having realised that the woman I had brought here is more valuable than anything else he seeks.'

'Valuable?' demanded Einar.

'She knows the way to a great treasure,' Martin responded, tugging, then rounded angrily on me. 'Let it *go*, you idiot boy.'

At which point, angered beyond anything I had experienced in my life, I swung my sword in a half-arc. It was wild – a bad swing entirely, as Skapti said later. It hit the monk high on the head, but with the flat, not the edge. He went down like a sacrificed horse, gone from a twisted-faced little weasel of a man to a heap of rags on the floor.

Einar bent, studied him for a moment, then stroked his beard again and nodded admiringly at me. 'Good stroke. Hring, bring the little rat round. Let's find this woman . . .'

We moved to the door, opened it as cautiously as possible and Ketil Crow moved in, followed by Gunnar Raudi, then me. Einar and Skapti stayed outside.

It was dark, lit only by a horn lantern, guttering low, and fetid, a strange, high smell which I came to recognise later as fear and shit in equal measure. Ketil Crow knew it well, for it put him into a half-crouch, blade held low in his left hand, hackles up. Behind, Gunnar Raudi moved to the left. Naively, I bumbled on, past Ketil and on to the middle of the room, to the only furniture in it: a low bed with a pile of rags.

It was only when the rags moved that I realised it was human . . . or had been once, at least. There was a droning sound, a long muttering, then a sobbing – such a sound as to crack your heart. I backed away, my own hackles up. Perhaps this was the fetch of a woman who had died . . .

Gunnar poked the rags with the blunt tip of his sword and they moved rapidly, scuttling like an animal, reached the end of a length of chain and stopped. A head came up, framed with tangled, greasy hair, face pale as the moon and with two wild, bright orbs staring back at us. The woman – if woman it was – gabbled something which sounded vaguely familiar. Ketil Crow advanced slowly and, from the door, Einar's impatient voice growled for us to get the bloody woman and be done with it.

'It's chained up,' Ketil Crow said.

'It stinks,' added Gunnar. 'And it's chained by the foot.'

'Then cut the fucking thing,' hissed Einar. Behind him came slapping sounds and a low moan as Martin was brought back to life.

'The foot?' I gasped, aghast at such an idea, but knowing either of them was capable of it. Gunnar shot me a scornful scowl.

'The chain, you horse's arse.' And he nodded to Ketil Crow to get on with it, but got only a scowl.

'Use your own blade. I like the edge on mine.'

'By Loki's hairy arse!' roared Skapti, barrelling in and knocking everyone aside, the huge Shieldbreaker sword soaring up. The pile of rags that was a woman saw it, screamed once and flopped. The blade whirled down; the chain shattered at the point where it joined an iron fetter.

Skapti swung round, his eyes boar-like and red. Instinctively, Ketil Crow and Gunnar backed away.

'Now you pair of turds can carry her,' he growled. For a moment, Ketil Crow's eyes narrowed dangerously and I watched him, for I knew if he struck Skapti it would be from behind. No sane man would face an armed Skapti in a confined space.

Instead, he grinned like a wolf on a kill and moved to the woman. I followed Skapti outside, where Martin was sitting up and shaking his head, dripping from the contents of a ewer Hring had thrown on him. Hring, smirking, was trying to force the pewter pot inside his tunic, flattening it into uselessness as he did so.

Einar hauled the monk up on to unsteady legs and clapped him playfully on the shoulder. 'Sore head, eh? Now you be quiet and nice, or I will let the Bear Slayer loose on you again.'

Everyone chuckled – save me and Martin.

'I will want to know more of this, monk,' Einar went on. 'But, for now, we will follow your plan. Orm, give him your cloak and helm, for I don't think Brondolf Lambisson will want him gone from here and may have left instructions to that effect. Lower the woman on to the corpse bed and cover her up. Then we can leave.'

They had completed their task, were hefting the bed and moving from the wreck of the room, when the door opened and Brondolf Lambisson strode in, holding a small chest close to his own.

There had been no warning for him. One minute he was coming into the neat, warm hov of his fortress, slippers on his feet, a nice warm hat on his head; the next he had stepped into a nightmare wreck of a room, reeking of shit and blood, littered with corpses and come face to face with the last six armed men in the world he wanted to meet.

He had time to give a strangled yelp and whirl back out of the door, though, hurling the chest straight at the nearest, which happened to be Skapti and Einar. It hit Skapti on the shoulder, smacked Einar on the forehead and dazed him. With a cry, Skapti dropped his end of the corpse bed, blocking the doorway.

'Ah, Odin's bollocks . . .'

Einar was clutching his head, cursing so hard I made a sign against angering the very gods he maligned. Blood stained his fingers when he removed them.

Skapti started to lumber after the fleeing Lambisson, but Einar grabbed him. 'No. Time to row hard for it,' he said through pain-gritted teeth.

Hring picked up the chest and shook it. It rattled with coin and he beamed at Einar.

'You have a head for business right enough, Einar.'

The answer was a dangerous growl and a shake that sprayed everyone with warm droplets, like a dog climbing out of a stream.

Martin stumbled forward, my hand on the nape of his neck. He tried once to shake me off and I tightened my grip, at which he gave up struggling and trembled, part with anger, but mainly with fear.

'The chest,' he managed and Einar took it from Hring, opened it, shot a look full of questions at the monk.

'On the thong . . .' muttered Martin. Einar started raking about in the chest.

'Time to go, Einar,' warned Skapti. 'Lambisson will raise the whole Borg in another blink.'

Einar fished out a leather loop, dangling from which was a heavy coin, punched with a hole to take the thong. It swung, gleaming in the flickering lights.

'The woman had it round her neck,' Martin said, thick-voiced with the pain in his head.

We all craned to see it, but it was just a medallion to me.

'See it,' Martin urged. 'On one side and the other . . .'

Einar turned it over and over in his fingers, while Skapti hovered by the door. 'Einar . . . in the name of Thor, move your arse.'

'On one side, Sigurd . . .' Martin wheezed. And I saw it, as it turned and flashed. On one side, the head of Sigurd, slayer of Fafnir. On the other, the dragon head. 'Volsung-minted,' he went on. 'From the hoard Sigurd took. There is no other coin like it out in the world.'

Skapti slammed the doorpost with his forehead and roared his anxious frustration at us all.

'All the others, its brothers and sisters,' Martin breathed, 'are buried with Attila the Hun.'

Then we were out into the little room, composing ourselves and stepping as quietly as we could, controlling our ragged breathing with effort, to face the guard on the steps.

'Wouldn't that weasel-faced little fuck help then?' asked the guard sympathetically. Beside me, I felt Martin stiffen and poked him meaningfully.

'No. We will do it with our own rites,' answered Einar and moved on, keeping his head turned as far from the man as possible, so the blood wouldn't show.

We were halfway down the stairs when Einar stopped. A red flower bloomed in the dark, beyond the Borg walls. Shouts followed it. Another flower bloomed. The guard above us peered disbelievingly.

'Fire . . . ?'

'Eyvind,' said Einar bitterly, as if the very name was a curse. Which, of course, it turned out to be.

Just then, the fortress alarm bell clanged out. Lambisson. The guard on the steps whirled, confused. Helpfully, I said, 'Must be a fire in the town. That will be bad in this gale.'

The guard nodded, now unsure of whether to rush to the gate and find out, or stick to his post. Instead he said, 'Get on now. Hurry.' Then he turned into the fortress.

'Move!' hissed Einar, but that was a whip we didn't need. We almost scampered across the main gate, where the guards were staring. Only two now – it seemed Sten had taken the others to help against the fire, which was luck, since he seemed to know my face.

The ones on the gate couldn't give a rat's arse whether we

had found a monk or given our comrade suitable burial, being too busy craning to see what was happening.

They waved us through and we headed off along the walkway, moving towards the town wall. The reek of smoke, shouts, a whirl of sparks and flame showed that Eyvind's handiwork was excellent. I remembered the raven, the doomed voice of Eyvind saying: 'I was looking at the town and thinking how easily it would burn.'

A group of men and women with buckets charged past us, pushing along the walkway. Shouts whirled away with the wind, but some were louder up ahead, where a fresh red flower bloomed.

'There he goes!'

Eyvind stumbled from the cover of darkness, vaulted a fence, fell on the walkway and got up again. He was wild-eyed and seemed to be laughing. He saw us and sprinted. Behind him, a crowd of pursuers made ugly noises.

'Fuck his mother,' hissed Ketil Crow. 'He'll have them all down on us . . .'

There was confusion. All the weapons were hidden with the woman on the corpse bed. Eyvind, half stumbling, laughing with relief, charged up the walkway to us, to safety and his oathsworn oarmates.

Einar stepped forward, whirled, wrenched my breeks to the knee and whipped out the hidden seax, all in one movement that left me frozen in place – which was just as well, since I felt the wind of that edge trail past my naked balls.

Eyvind was trying to speak, gasping for air. Einar stepped forward, for all the world as if to embrace him, and drove the seax up under the ribs and straight to the heart. Eyvind simply collapsed like a bag into Einar's arms and he promptly threw the luckless dead man back towards the pursuing crowd, sprawling him bloodily on the walkway.

He turned to me and said, 'Pull up your breeks, boy. This is no place or time to have a shit.'

Then he swiftly – piously – laid the bloody blade on the chest of the swathed figure on the corpse bed, switched a covering edge over it and signalled us to move on.

Some of the baying pack had seen what had happened, others further behind had not, saw only that their quarry was down and a boy was trying to take a shit in the walkway. There was laughter, confusion.

The crowd milled up to the dead Eyvind like some giant, slavering cat whose prey had suddenly dropped dead before it could be played with. They pawed it with kicks for a while, then started to string up the corpse as we passed.

The owner of the house they wanted to use was arguing furiously about having it hang from his eaves. More sparks whirled on the wind from the last fire Eyvind had started. Not one of them queried how he had died or that we had done it with a weapon we shouldn't have had. It was, I noted numbly, pulling up my breeks, as if we were invisible.

We went through the town gate, out past the garrison, now stumbling into life in response to the clanging bells, the shouts, the fires.

In the confusion, we melded into the darkness beyond. When I looked back, it seemed the whole of Birka was burning.

FIVE

As my father said at the time, we should have hauled the *Elk* higher up the shingle, for this was no time to be out in a boat.

It was bad enough scrambling up the straked sides of it in the dark, with the freezing water sucking and slapping you, but once aboard, the rowers bent to it and took her out to where the black waves were white-tipped with fury in a howling night.

Then we fought the storm and the fear of splintering on Birka's hidden rocks; three men leaned on the steering oar and the rest of us huddled in a sort of dulled stubbornness. I was charged with looking after the woman, who moaned and rolled eyes made even whiter by the night and gabbled incessantly in some tongue that almost approached the familiar.

In the blue-white flashes of lightning which seared through even closed eyes, I could see the pale face of her, like a skull, hair plastered slick to it, eyes sunk in deep, dark pools, mouth opening and closing on her meaningless sounds. I wrapped her and myself as tight as I could in a sodden cloak and her arms went round me.

We leached warmth from each other as the *Elk* staggered

111

forward recklessly into the night and, at one point, I saw Illugi Godi, standing alone at the prow, an axe in either hand, chanting prayers. Then he threw them overboard, an offering to Thor, master of the wind and rain.

Dawn came up like thin milk in a bowl. We were alone under the great, white pearl that is the inside of the ancient frost giant Ymir's skull, which is the vault of the sky. The wind no longer roared at us, but hissed a steady, cold breath, driving us north and east, up the great, grey-black, glassy swells, spilling white spray from their frayed ends – my father had instinctively headed for Aldeigjuborg, which the Slavs call Starya Ladoga.

The *Fjord Elk* slid up them, water foaming aft, staggering now and then as the bow knifed and water swirled down the deck into the nooks and crannies of her.

She was a good boat, the *Elk*. Not a longship in the sense everyone thinks they know: those are the *drakkar*, expensive warships built to carry warriors and not much cargo, with barely four or five paces in the beam. You can't travel far in a longship before all those men need water and food you haven't got and you have to call in somewhere to replenish it.

Nor was the *Elk* the fat-bellied little trading *knarr* that ploughs stubbornly through the blackest seas with tons of cargo in her well.

Which was why Einar did what he did next. Later, I worked out why. Vigfus in his little *knarr* would wait out the storm before heading north in search of the god stone he thought we were after. He had too many men for such a little ship and such overcrowding would be deadly in a storm, for such a ship depended on its trim to stay afloat.

Starkad, also, would wait, since he dare not risk his expensive ships. However, he would then race hard as those dragons can sail, aiming to make it to the same place faster than any of us and before his stores ran so low his men starved and thirsted. He would know where to go, because Lambisson would tell him, having no choices left.

So Einar spoke with Valgard and Rurik, huddled together, with much shaking of heads on their part and much curled lip from him. In the end, they broke apart and Einar announced: 'Shields and oars.'

There was a general shifting around at that. Those who knew what was about to happen seemed as uneasy as those who hadn't a clue. Gunnar Raudi scrambled up to me, forking a lump of bread out of a leather pouch and handing it to me and the woman. In the light of day, she looked no better, seemed no more sensible – but she chewed the bread avidly, which was a good sign, even if her dark eyes were strange and pewter-dull.

I caught Gunnar's sleeve as he turned to go, asked him what was happening.

'We run,' he said and flashed a gapped grin full of half-chewed bread. 'Hold on tight.'

Shields were fetched out, the bosses knocked from their centres and carefully stored in pouches, along with the rivets. The oars were run out, which was a puzzle, since I already knew it was madness to try rowing in that swell. Perhaps they were going to try to turn the ship for some mysterious hidden land my father had found in his seidr way.

Then the bossless shields were slid down on to the oars, which were turned blades flat to the sea. The shields were locked in place on the side and the oars couldn't even be moved. I had never seen or heard of this before; quite a few others were similarly puzzled. But those who knew looked grim about it.

The oars, uniformly fixed in place, stuck out pointlessly, blades flat to the swell, like the ridiculous legs of an insect.

'Up sail!' roared Rurik.

No – a mistake, surely? In this wind and swell? We would run so fast we'd go arse over tip, plunge the bow into the

113

waves and swamp her. I had heard such things – we had no keel for such travel . . .

But the crew sprang to it, the spar lifted off the rests, the great sail, soaked despite the sheep grease and seal oil, flapped, strained, bellied out like some grass-fed mare and the *Elk* leaped like a goosed goodwife.

The ignorant gasped and some yelled out with fear, but the *Elk* shook itself and sped ahead, the oars acting like the deep keel it didn't have.

My father came across to me, squinting up at the sail, then back to the steering oar, where Skapti stood braced with it under his armpit and three others waited close by, in case he had to try to turn.

'Not that he could,' my father chuckled. 'We run hard, fast and true – faster than anything. The *drakkar* will fall over themselves under full sail in this sea and are too big to try this trick – we have near half as much again on them and are rigged so that the inside of every wave adds more speed.'

It was true and men hung on as if about to be swept away. The *Elk* . . . flew. It planed up one side of the swell, surfed down the other, kissing the water with the oars, sweeter and faster than anything, while the wind thrummed the walrus ropes and, if you leaned out, you could see parts of the crusted strakes not normally exposed except during careening.

'Get your arse inboard,' roared Valgard, catching me by the belt and hauling me in with a cuff. I did not care. I was exhilarated, drunk on the sheer beauty of it.

Once, as a boy, I had dared to ride Gudleif's best and fiercest, Austri, named after one of the dwarves who sit at the four corners of the sky. With no saddle or bridle or reins I sprang on him and he had taken off. His mane whipped my face, the wind ripped tears from my eyes, but I felt the surge of him under my thighs and calves, the sheer power and grace as we flew in a thunder over the meadow.

114

Of course, the red weals of that mane had given me away. Gudleif had beaten me for it but, through the snot and tears afterwards, I was still mazed in the feeling. The *Elk* did the same for me that day, too.

Gradually, as they grew used to the wonder of it, men relaxed – until Valgard had them watch the oars, lest one catch the water too hard and shatter.

I lay next to the softly muttering woman, feeling the heat of her, watching the weathervane swoop and soar with the rise and fall of the swell in long circles, listening to the endlessly-repeated sound that went with it, from the creak of the mast stays, the thump as it shifted in its socket, the snake-hiss of the water under the keel, the deep-throat hum of the wind in the ropes, like a struck harp.

Towards midday, I reckoned, a watery-eyed sun came up and everyone cheered; it was the first sun we had seen in a long time. Martin the monk watched Illugi Godi give thanks for it, his face dark as the black water under the keel. Einar watched Martin, stroking his beard.

Gunnar handed out sour milk and gruel and wet-mush bread later, together with a half-cup of water. The woman's dull-eyed muttering only stopped when she ate, but even that was half-hearted. She felt hot and I palmed her forehead, which was clammy.

'How is she?' demanded Illugi, suddenly appearing at my side. I told him and he checked, grunted, moved to Einar and spoke with him. He nodded, looked at the sky, then called Rurik and talked to him. My father rubbed a hand across his wild, thin hair – a sign I now knew spoke of his unease – and moved to the side.

He studied the water for a long time, on both sides of the boat, looked at the sky, squinted at the weak sun, which was losing itself in a milky haze. He said something to Einar, who nodded and hauled Gudleif's already tattered fur tighter round him.

Water dripped from my nose and we ran on towards night, heedless of land, of skerries, of shoals, of anything. We were on the whale road.

As the light thinned, Einar waved me to him and murmured to Ketil Crow, who fetched the monk. With Illugi Godi, we huddled under the little upturned *faering* which stood as the nearest thing to a shelter on the boat and which, of course, Einar claimed as his due.

'Well, we are escaped, monk, and at no small cost. Now tell us why you should not go over the side as a sacrifice to Thor,' he growled at Martin.

I refrained from saying anything, because the taste of it was bitter in my mouth. The cost was Eyvind's and he had paid it in full, betrayed by the man who had made much of oath-swearing. That and the fact that the time to have thrown the monk overboard was at the height of the storm, when Thor and Aegir needed an offering.

Martin, wet and miserable and cold, with a great black bruise down one side of his face, sniffed snot into the back of his throat. Gone was the smooth, urbane scholar who had invited us to dine, but the drowned rat that remained still, he thought, had some teeth.

'You would do well to treat me better, Einar the Black,' the monk answered bitterly. 'I hold the secret of what you want, after all.'

'The god stone holds that secret,' answered Einar coldly. 'Between Illugi, who can ken the runes, and Orm, who reads Latin, I think we can prise out the secret. Give me another reason to keep your feet dry.'

Martin glanced sourly at me and nodded, slowly. 'I wondered how you had known of the stone. I had not thought a boy would have such learning, though.'

He had marked me, that was clear, and the knowledge of it made me shiver. He seemed, to me, far too calm and cool about it all. To Einar, also, I saw.

'Indeed,' said Einar and nodded to Ketil Crow and another burly man, Snorri, who had a god mark on his face almost the same shape and in the same place as the monk's bruise. They grabbed Martin; he shrieked and struggled, but they wound a good rope round his ankles and hauled him up the mast a little way, where he waved wildly and swung.

Einar stood, stretched, yawned and farted. Then he drew out a little knife I had not seen before, too small for a fighting seax and not his eating knife. He grabbed the little monk's left hand and sawed off a finger at the first joint. Blood sprayed; the monk howled and jerked. Einar examined the digit, then tossed it casually over the side.

'This is a magic knife,' he said, bending close to the monk. 'It can tell lie from truth and every time it finds a lie it will remove a finger until all are gone. Then it will start on toes, until all are gone. Then it will start on your prick and your balls . . .'

'Until all are gone,' chorused those in the know, with roars and huge, knee-slapping laughs.

'Just so,' said Einar, without the hint of a smile.

'Let me down, let me down . . .'

He babbled well, did Martin. He wet himself – we knew because it steamed pungently – and prayed for oblivion, but his White Christ didn't hand him that, for it was well known that a man upside down, with the blood in his head, can't faint. He pleaded, offered everything in this world and, by virtue of his knowing his god personally, the next.

And he revealed everything. That Atil's treasure existed. That the god stone didn't matter, but the woman did. Vigfus, it seemed, had been sent to where the god stone originally stood, after Martin had found that the Christ ikon he sought had been taken there to be forged into part of Atil's treasure: a sword, it seemed.

This was part of the gifts given to Atil by the Volsungs when they knew the only way to defeat that almond-eyed

117

snake of a steppe lord was by sacrifice and cunning – a final great gift, of swords and silver and a bride, one of their own, a seidr witch called Ildico. Who killed him on their wedding night.

Martin, seeking clues, had sent Vigfus to find the forge, or any reference to swords or spears. Vigfus, who couldn't find his arse if someone shone a light on it, failed to find anything, had seized the woman who now shivered and raved beside me because the local heathens seemed to hold her in high esteem, in an attempt to force the knowledge from them.

They had attacked Vigfus, killed more than a few of his men, and forced him to flee back to Birka with only the woman.

Martin, however, had seen the amulet she wore for what it was, had then remembered St Otmund and his mission, thought perhaps there might be a clue in his writings about the forge and sent us to Strathclyde. But there had only been reference to a god stone.

'So,' Einar demanded, while the monk's blood dripped fatly on the deck and the snot ran into his eyes, 'why are you now fearful of Lambisson, whose purse you have plundered for all this? If you are on the track of the Great Hoard, surely he would be pleased?'

The monk hesitated for the first time. 'I . . . he . . . we simply disagreed. On a point of principle . . . Let me down. I will be sick.'

'A point of principle?' Einar growled, narrowing his eyes. He reached for the mutilated hand and the monk howled.

'No, no . . . wait, wait . . . the ikon. It was the ikon . . .'

'That's what Bluetooth wants,' I said, suddenly realising. 'This Christ charm. To convert the Danes with. For that bishop who wore the red-hot glove.'

And Martin was sick, spilling it into his nose and his hair, choking on the slime-green of it until Einar, seeing he might well die upside down, nodded to Snorri, who lowered him to the deck. Seawater was thrown over him until, shivering and wretched, he could breathe again.

'Has Orm the right of it?' demanded Einar.

Martin, unable to do anything else, nodded and retched.

'So,' Einar continued, 'Bluetooth knows nothing about Atil's treasure, only that there is a god charm the Christ-followers revere. You did not tell Lambisson of it, but spent his money finding it for yourself . . .' He was stroking his moustaches, thinking, thinking. 'What is this Christ charm everyone wants?' he asked, giving Martin a kick.

The monk spluttered, wiped his nose, coughed out an answer. 'A spear. Once. Thrust. Into the side of our Lord by the Romans.'

'Ah,' mused Einar.

Illugi Godi nodded sagely. 'Touched by the blood of a god, it would be a powerful thing.'

'Forged now into a sword,' someone said. The whole crew, I realised, was spellbound, for the monk's answers had been screamed out for all to hear.

A sword. Made from god-touched metal. It was saga stuff, mother's milk to the likes of us. There were great things in the world: silver hoards, fine horses, beautiful women. But no prize was better than a rune-spelled sword.

'And the woman? What is she to this?'

Martin spat and heaved in breath. He looked like a rat fresh from a cesspit. 'She is of the blood of the smiths who made the sword. She . . . knows where it is.'

No one blinked at that, though some shot anxious glances back towards the woman, for a witch was bad luck on a ship. Bad luck anywhere, I was thinking.

'Does Vigfus know this?' Einar demanded and Martin, rocking back and forward, ruined hand cradled in his good one, shook his head and whimpered.

'He knows of the god stone, though,' Ketil Crow offered. 'He will seek it, not knowing it will do him no good – nor us, for it will bring him in the same direction as we travel now.'

'A runesword,' growled Einar, ignoring him. 'A man with that would be a hero king indeed.' He looked around and grinned. 'A man with that, a mountain of silver and a crew like the Oathsworn need fear no kings.'

They whooped and cheered and pounded on each other, the deck, anything. As it died away and they went back to duties, or to huddle against the mirr, Einar turned, his grin fading as he saw my face, which I foolishly failed to disguise. Its black, scowling ugliness made him recoil a little.

'That's a face to sour milk,' he noted, annoyed. 'When everyone else laughs.'

'Except Eyvind,' I pointed out, 'who is not here.'

Then he knew, as did Illugi Godi who was close enough to hear and put a hand on my arm.

'Eyvind broke oath with us,' Einar growled. 'He put us all in danger with his Loki curse for firing everything.'

'An oath is an oath. The one I swore did not say that foolishness or a curse made it worthless and got you killed.'

Illugi Godi nodded, which Einar caught. His scowl deepened. 'I think you are smarting because you had to lose your breeks in the street,' he said slowly. 'It seems to me that your gift is in need of maturing before it is of use to me. It seems to me that you would be better staying with the woman.'

He stared at me and I knew I had been mortally insulted and was entitled to be angry. But this was Einar and I was so new I squeaked still. I quailed under that glass-black gaze.

'I will call if I need you,' he added and jerked his head in dismissal.

I stumbled away on watery legs and slumped down next to the woman. I heard Einar bark something angrily at Illugi and then there was silence, save for the creak-thump of the mast and stays and the hiss of the keelwater.

My father and Einar then huddled briefly and Martin was

dragged over to join them. It was clear that a course was planned.

The sail came down, the shields and oars came in – you could not heel the boat over on a tack otherwise – then the men bent to it and hauled the *Elk*'s head round on to the new course, where the whole ship was rerigged once more and sprang into its mad gallop.

I did not have to ask my father where we headed, for it was obvious: to the forge where the woman was taken. She was going home.

The rain fell, the woman muttered and rolled her eyes up into her head and the *Elk* sped on, out along the whale road – and nothing was the same again.

Four days later the woman was burning with fever and babbling and Hring was casting hooks on lines behind, baited with coloured strips of cloth in a forlorn attempt to catch fish.

But, as Bagnose observed gloomily, they would have to be flying fish to catch up with the *Fjord Elk*. Meanwhile, the water in the stoppered leather bottles was being filtered through two layers of fine linen to get rid of the floaters.

Then an oar snapped with a high, sharp sound as a blade finally caught sideways on to the waves. The shards flew, the butt end leaped up and the shield slammed back across the thwarts. A man howled as it cracked his forearm.

And Pinleg, in the prow as lookout, called out, 'Land!'

My father turned expectantly to Einar, who glowered and said nothing. So my father gave a short curse, then yelled out, 'Shield oars inboard. Sail down. Move!'

For a moment, I thought Einar would leap to his feet, and braced myself to spring at him. But he only shifted, as if cocking a buttock to fart, then settled again, stroking his beard and staring blackly at the deck.

The speed came off the *Elk* like ice melting under salt. It felt like we were wallowing suddenly.

'To oars.'

Stiff, wet, we climbed up and took position on our sea-chest benches. I hauled with the rest of them; the head of the *Elk* came round, slowly, slowly, and she started to inch her way across the swell, rolling like a drowned pig now, all grace gone.

We slithered into the shelter of a bay, with a low, grey headland where tufts of harsh grass, tawny as wheat, waved softly and patches of green showed through the russets and yellow. Seaweed and lichens crusted the stones studding a beach of coarse, wet sand, meadow-grass was already sprouting shoots beyond that and there was a flush of green shoots on the birch and willow clumps. Two small rivers trickled together to empty into a shallow tidal estuary.

We splashed ashore, dragging the *Elk* a little way up the sand, as far as we could on shaky legs and on that tide. Birds sang and the resin-tang of life was everywhere. When the sun came out, everyone was cheered; Bagnose began more verses and the Oathsworn swung back into the rhythm of things.

But nothing was the same.

Shelters were built, short-term affairs of springy branches roofed with wadmal cloth, the stuff we used to repair tears in the sail.

Some men took off on a hunt, having spotted deer slots, Steinthor and Bagnose among them, quartering ahead like hounds. Hring and two others dug trenches in the sand shallows to catch tidal-trapped fish, while I scuffed along the wide curve of the beach, gathering dulse and mussels until my back ached.

By nightfall, fires were lit and everyone had eaten well. The hunters had come back with some small game and a wild duck, shot in mid-flight by Steinthor, who claimed it was a lucky strike, though others disagreed. Bagnose, on the other hand, had missed and was still grumbling about having lost the arrow.

People began to dry out clothing and I had managed to wrap the woman in something warm, in a dry hut where a fire was lit just for her, since Einar knew her value. He had also paired Martin and me to make sure she lived and if ever anything spoke of his anger with me, that was it.

I was less angry than I thought I would be. Caring for the woman was a lot better than the back-breaking task I would surely have been given: four hours of bailing out the *Elk* for Valgard.

And there was something about the woman. I had stripped her with the monk's help, although he was less than helpful since he insisted on doing it with his eyes averted, which was awkward, to say the least.

In the dim, gloomy light of the horn lantern, guttering because the whale oil in it was thick and old, she was fish-belly white, so that the bruises and welts stood out on her skin.

Illugi Godi, when he arrived with a wooden bucket of cold seawater for compresses, sucked his teeth and glared at Martin when he saw it.

'Vigfus,' sighed the monk mournfully, hugging his ruined hand under one armpit. 'He misused her, I am afraid.'

She lay, feverish, open-eyed and staring, but seeing nothing. I cleaned a lot of the filth from her, saw the flare of cheekbones and the full, ripe lips and realised she was a beauty.

'A princess, perhaps,' Martin agreed, wringing out the cloth. From outside came the mutter and growl and bursts of raucous laughter that marked contented men relaxing. I wanted to be there. My father was there and I saw, with a sharp pang, that I didn't fit with him, or them. That perhaps I never would.

'I'm hungry,' I said. 'I will watch her if you fetch food.'

Martin scrambled to his feet, wincing. I could almost feel the throb of that wounded finger, which he should have had cauterised, lest it fester and the rot spread so that his hand or even arm might need to come off. I told him so and he paled, whether at the idea of losing the limbs or having it seared with a hot iron, I did not know. Both, probably.

The woman stirred on the pallet of soft rushes and cloth, spoke again in that infuriating speech, so near to something I could understand, yet still foolishness. Her eyes opened; she saw me, stared, said nothing.

'How do you feel?' I asked. Nothing.

'I am Orm,' I said slowly and patiently, as to a child. 'Orm,' I added, patting my chest. 'You?' And I indicated her.

Her mouth moved, but nothing came. After all that babble, I thought wryly, now there is no sound at all.

Martin reappeared with two bowls of what smelled like meat stew. There was bread, fire-dried and with most of the mould cut off, and his arms were full of leather cups and a matching bottle.

The woman saw him and thrashed wildly, backing away. I held her, made soothing noises, but her wild eyes were fixed on him and she bucked and kicked until, exhausted, she couldn't move.

'Leave the food and go,' I said, 'otherwise she will be like this and no help to herself. Or Einar.'

He blanched at that name. 'I did nothing to her,' he bleated. But he left my bowl and cup and went.

I fed her small portions of the meat stew, which she sucked greedily, but seemed too weak to make much of. But when I looked, a fair bit of it had gone down her neck.

'Hild,' she said, suddenly, as I wiped gravy as gently as I could from lips whose fullness, I realised, had a lot to do with being swollen and split.

'Hild,' I repeated and grinned, pleased at this progress. She almost smiled, but her lips cracked open and oozed blood and she winced. Then, abruptly, she stiffened.

'Dark,' she said, staring at me, though I realised she couldn't see me at all. 'Dark. Alone. Dark. In the dark . . .'

Her eyes rolled up to the whites and she was gone, back into the babble. But I had understood her, saw now that she spoke some broad dialect of which I could understand one word in four. It was some form of Finn, which I had known because of Sigurd, Gudleif's other fostri, who had come from that land.

A tear squeezed, fat and quivering, from under one eyelid and rolled down her neck. When Illugi Godi came with salves he had made for the bruises and welts, I told him what had happened and he sat back on his heels and considered, pursing his lips. A louse moved in his beard and he plucked it absently and crushed it, still thinking.

'Well, at least Einar will have some more of this puzzle, but whether it solves anything is harder to tell,' he mused. 'At least he may be more pleased with you, boy.'

'Not I with him,' I responded and he nodded sadly.

'Aye, he is in the wrong. Eyvind deserved better and to break an oath is a bad thing. I think he knows it, too.'

'Perhaps the message from Odin's raven was meant for him then,' I offered and Illugi looked at me cautiously.

'You have too many years for one so young,' he muttered tersely and left, leaving the salves behind.

That night I dreamed of a white bear I couldn't seem to avoid, one with black eyes who chased me round a wind-lashed room full of spars and sails and finally landed on my chest, a great weight, bearing down . . .

I woke with something warm and heavy on my body, the hut lit only by the remaining embers of the fire. I tried to sit up but a hand shot out, long and white and strong enough to shove hard on my breastbone and force me back on to the bed.

Her hair was hanging down in mad tangles, her cheek-bones flaring in the red light, her eyes clear and black – black as Einar's own, I noted. There were shadows under them and harsh lines carving the sides of that slapped-red mouth. The strong hand which fastened me to the bed had stark blue veins, proud on the pale skin.

Mesmerised, I watched her sway above me, lean down, stare into my eyes.

'Orm,' she said and I could not move. 'I know what you seek. I know where the forge is. I went there, but was too big to get in, too afraid. The other . . . the Christ priest's hound caught me. But I must go back. Take me back. I have to find a way to the dark . . . to the dark place where she is.'

And she was gone, fallen forward on to me, with no more weight than a husk and for all that it was a thump, it drove no breath out of me – just the opposite. I found myself holding her, caging her as her head lay on my chest, with the Thor hammer/cross biting into her cheek.

And I fell asleep like that, holding her – though, in the morning, she lay asleep in her own pallet and I wondered if I had dreamed it, but she woke and smiled at me and I saw that she was scarce older than I was.

And then she talked.

After I had fetched her gruel and water, I went to Einar and found him cross-legged under an awning, fixing the boss of his shield back on. Men were busy with tasks; I saw Hring, out in the *faering*, trying for fish at the mouth of the estuary.

I sat down opposite Einar and waited, Eventually, he deigned to look up at me, taking some rivet nails from his lips under the black waterfall of his hair.

'The woman is called Hild,' I told him. 'She is a Finn and her village is two days up the coast from here. Her father was called Regin and his father before him and so on back into the dim. Every smith was called Regin and the village name is Koksalmi.'

The black eyes fixed mine. 'How can you talk to her?'

'One of Gudleif's other fostris was a Finn. I learned enough from him.'

Einar stroked his moustaches and looked towards the hut. 'What makes this Finn woman so special?'

'She is revered because she has the blood of the old smiths,' I went on. 'There is no smith there now and has not been for many years. The last one made the sword for Atil, she says, and no one but her knows the way into the forge now. All those with the blood seem to know it, but of this part I am unclear. She, too, I think. It does not seem to be a secret passed on, just something that . . . is.'

'Why is the forge important? Why is she?'

I nodded, having anticipated that. 'The monk found out that this magic Christ spear he sought had been taken there long ago and sent Vigfus to see if it was still hidden there and, if so, get it. When Vigfus failed, he tried to seize Hild, seeing she was so esteemed by the villagers and hoping they would hand it over in return for her life. She fled, to the forge, I am thinking . . .' I stopped, for here her tale had splintered into fragments.

'And?'

I shrugged. 'Something happened there. Something that drove her into the clutch of Vigfus – but something that haunts her dreams still.'

'A fetch?' demanded Einar.

I nodded. The restless spirit of the dead, the fetch, sometimes invaded other bodies, or walked around in their old shape until some strange design of their own had been accomplished. Everyone knew it.

'She says she must get back to the forge. I don't know why, but it seems if she does, she will know where the Atil sword now lies. And the hoard with it.'

Einar stroked his moustaches. He had, I noticed, shaved his cheeks and his hair was washed and nit-combed clean. I felt my own filth more as a result.

'Interesting,' he mused. 'Vigfus is far behind and heading in the wrong direction, towards the god stone that is no use to him. Starkad knows only this village by name and seeks a Christ ikon that no longer exists in the same shape.'

'So, if we can get to this forge and the woman really does then know where the hoard is . . .' I added.

'We can leave them all behind,' finished Einar. He tapped in a rivet and nodded sombrely at me. 'You have done well. Let us forget the unpleasantness between us. You have, as Illugi Godi is pleased to remind me, an old head on young shoulders.' He squinted at me. 'Shoulders which, I am noticing, have filled since last autumn.'

He rose, moved to his sea-chest and rummaged in it, coming out with a long hauberk of mail. It was, I recalled, the one stripped from the dead fyrd leader after the fight at St Otmund's chapel.

I caught it when he threw it at me and, when I slipped it on over my raised arms, the weight made me stagger a little, but it fitted well round the shoulders and was suitably loose round the waist that a cinched belt would take the rest of the weight off.

He nodded. 'Take it. You have earned it.'

I bowed to him, as I had seen others do with Gudleif, and that pleased him. I fastened on my swordbelt and swaggered back to the fires, one hand on the hilt, salt-stained seaboots stumping.

There were good-natured catcalls and jeers and backslaps when the rest of them saw it – and not a few envious stares from older hands, who would have loved such a gift and thought a beardless youth didn't deserve it.

My father was prouder than I was of it and offered advice on its care. 'Roll it in a barrel of fine sand for a day,' he advised and everyone hooted tears at that – fine sand for a day. On this gods-cursed shore.

But all the time I was thinking to myself that I would not

trust Einar, oath or not. And, across the fire, I saw the fierce, yellow-eyed stare of naked hatred that came from Ulf-Agar, for all that he was still weak and bruised.

Life, I thought, bending and wriggling the mail off, to the thigh-slapping roars of laughter at this first attempt, was simpler when I climbed sheer cliffs for gull eggs.

SIX

The way the tales tell it, raiders from the sea always arrive out of the mist. Even our own sagas have followed this in recent times, with high-prowed shapes, black against the sea mist, sprinting for the unsuspecting shore to spew out armed warriors like strewn dragon teeth.

This, I know now, is because the only ones who can write about it at all were usually not there and heard it from those who hadn't sailed anywhere. Monks, the curse of truth.

And the truth is always less than the tale. We arrived at a place called Kjartansfjord out of a mist thick as gruel, gliding on black water and moving so slowly an old man swimming could have overtaken us.

Out in front, in a leaking coracle of withy and sealskin, was Pinleg, a torch in hand and more oil-soaked wrappings at his feet to keep it fed. I was on the oar and a long line ran back to the prow of the *Elk*, so that it looked as if we were towing her.

In fact, we were making sure there was nothing that would splinter her, while not getting lost in the mist ourselves.

In the prow of the *Elk* I could see my father, peering at the water. Beside him, swathed in my long, hooded cloak, was Hild and it was her we had to thank for being able to find this fishing village and fjord at all, which lay at the mouth of an estuary, further east and north than we cared to be, right up in the Karelian lands of the Finn.

Some twenty miles up the river lay her home – and the forge – so she knew the landmarks and that was just as well, for even my father's skill would never have found this place in the fog.

We crept in, like fearful sheep. Those not at the *Elk*'s oars were armed and grim, for no one could be sure what waited for us here.

'Ship,' called Pinleg and waved the torch side to side, a signal for the *Elk* to back water.

'It's a *knarr*,' he added a moment later and looked at me, licking lips that were as dry as my own, despite the slick mist-wet that soaked us. We waited, slipping so slowly through water so flat and still it could have been ice; we made scarcely a ripple on it.

'Not Vigfus,' Pinleg said a moment later, the relief clear in his voice, 'but I don't know whose ship it is. Besides it, there are only fishing boats.'

The *knarr* turned out to belong to Slovarkan, a trader from Aldeigjuborg. A number of the Oathsworn, being Rus from Novgorod and Kiev, had wives and family in that place, which stood at the mouth of the Tanais, and which had featured in my dreams ever since I'd heard someone say of my father that he was 'off down the Tanais'.

In my daydreams, the Tanais was a silvered serpent of a river, gliding through a land of fables, rich with treasure and adventure.

It doesn't exist at all, though, being a single name for the Volkhov, the Syas, the Mologa and all the rivers, portages, rapids and cataracts that lead from Aldeigjuborg in the north to Kiev and, eventually, the Black Sea. Along the Tanais came glass from Serkland, silk from the far Cathay lands, narrow-necked bottles from east of the Caspian, embroidered pouches from the lands of the steppe tribes – and, once, silver from beyond the steppe, from places with names like Tashkent.

But, as Slovarkan bemoaned moodily, when he realised we were less of a threat than he'd first thought, there was no silver. Sviatoslav, the great Prince of the Rus, was thrashing about against the Bulgars and the Khazars and had stopped the flow. Some, Slovarkan added darkly, were saying it was even worse, that the mines of Serkland and Tashkent were played out, which probably meant the end of the world.

We listened politely and sorted out our gear, made shelters on the shingle and, when the sun burned off the mist, went up the beach to the huddle of houses that marked the small village to try to tempt the fled people back.

Small was too big a word for it. Its name – Kjartansfjord – was bigger than it was. It was a fishing port, loud with screaming gulls and whitened with their shit. Its one big feature was a stone-built jetty where the terns dipped and wheeled. The shingle beach was webbed with strung nets.

Einar, I knew, would rather not have stopped here at all, would rather have used the mist to sneak past into the river and on up it without trace. But we needed food and water and ale. We needed time to dry out, repair, replace – but the best we could find in Kjartansfjord was some coarse, hard bread, some new rope, ships' nails and all the fish we could store away once the people realised we hadn't come to rob them.

In the end, they robbed us, which was what always happened when the Oathsworn tried trading.

Slovarkan had a cargo of hoes, axes, saws and spades, practical stuff likely to be in bigger demand than exotic bottles from east of the Caspian – but he also had three dozen bolts of good wool cloth in various colours. Since Einar had a bucket of silver, both parties were delighted to trade and a morning was spent weighing, clipping and sorting hacksilver while the ragged Oathsworn went off with cloth to try to replace the worst of their clothing.

Einar, at first, was all for sailing on upriver the next day, as Slovarkan's *knarr* slipped out on the tide, southbound. He was convinced that either the trader would meet Starkad, or Starkad's *drakkar* would arrive at any moment.

Of course, Valgard and Rurik then pointed out that the *Elk* needed attention and that, if Einar sailed it upriver, he was as good as penned like a sacrificial ram. Better, they said, if the *Elk* hauled off down the coast a way with a minimum crew. Repairs could be done – nails had worked loose, the mast stays were frayed – while the rest went on to the forge.

That day, under wool-cloth shelters – no one wanted to stay in the stinking fish huts of the locals, even if it pissed down – two things happened that made Einar decide to send the *Elk* away.

The first seemed innocent enough. Pinleg was Odin's man – I found out why this day – and very devout, almost as deeply as Valknut. Whenever we made landfall, he would make a cairn of stones and decorate it with raven feathers, much frayed with use, that he kept for the purpose.

There were also Christ-followers – Martin the monk was now to be found sitting with them – and it had never been a problem. But that weasel of a monk knew what he was about and it was this day that made Einar realise what a danger he was and made me wish I had kept my blade edge-on to his tonsured head.

I was sitting, boiling leather strips to soften them and wrapping them round the metal rim of my shield before they hardened. Then I would tap them home with some rivet nails I had managed to get.

I had wanted to do this since the fight at St Otmund's chapel, when the boy's sword had bounced off the rim in a shower of sparks. The wild bounce of it had almost laid my

133

cheek open, so I had decided then to give an enemy edge something to bite on rather than leap off.

Not that it had done that boy any good. I remembered the rain pooling in his open eyes and shivered, at which Hild placed her hand quietly on my shoulder. She was sitting behind me, braiding my hair, which had grown long and was falling in my eyes as I tried to work on the shield.

I felt the touch and tried not to let my face flame. The winks and nudges of the others, the first time she had done something like this – repairing rents in my cloak – had made me wish she'd go away. Since then, I found myself enjoying her company. I was almost happy.

In fact, we exchanged smiles, her lips still chapped and swollen. She liked to be busy – it kept her from thinking too much. But nothing kept her from those moments of . . . absence . . . when her eyes rolled up and she was gone elsewhere. Into the dark.

Valknut said this sort of failing sounded to him like the falling sickness, for someone in the farm next to the one he was born on had it: a girl, he recalled. He said it was a disease that came from some Roman king, the one who was so great all the subsequent Roman kings took his name for their glory.

'She used to fall like a cut tree,' he remembered. 'Then she jerked and thrashed and foamed at the mouth, much like a man I once saw hit with an axe that laid his head open so that the inside fell out. But she was whole. Her family were used to it and all of them carried strips of leather to shove in her mouth, otherwise she would have bitten through her own tongue.'

But I did not think this was the same thing at all – or, if it was, it was a lesser version. Hild did not foam at the mouth or thrash. She just hugged herself and wailed and went away somewhere else.

I was enjoying the feeling of her at my hair as I tapped away at the shield and was aware, on the edge of my vision, that Pinleg was at his little cairn, reciting from memory the forty-eight names of Odin.

And Hring walked up to him, stood for a moment, then said, 'We think you should pull that down, for it is a heathen affront to good Christ-men.'

All those who heard it were so astonished they couldn't speak. I saw that all the Oathsworn's Christ-sworn, about a dozen of them, were standing apart, with Martin the monk lurking at their back. I saw, too, that he and Einar were looking at each other across the shingle, a battle of eyes as harsh as two rutting deer locking horns.

Pinleg stopped his reciting and slowly turned to face Hring, leaning slightly to one side as he favoured his good leg. 'Touch that cairn,' he said quietly, 'and I will take off your head and piss down your neck.'

'You are an arch-pagan,' Hring persisted, but he stumbled over the word, so that all those who heard knew it was not his own, Pinleg included. Einar caught Illugi Godi's eye, jerked his head slightly and Illugi moved to intercept the quarrel before it went too far. But he arrived too late.

'Arch-pagan,' repeated Pinleg and curled his lip. 'You can't even say it, you arse. I hear the words, but the voice belongs to that dung-faced little fuck hiding behind you all.'

Hring flushed at that, for it was true and he was aware that he had delivered his challenge badly. Embarrassment and frustration made him stupid. 'He has two good legs, though,' he said.

There was the briefest of pauses; the world held its breath. It was unspoken, but a rule, that no one made a joke of Pinleg's crippled limb. Even Hring knew he had gone too far. Perhaps, like me, he had reasoned that runty Pinleg was no danger.

When the focus of the quarrel then landed up in his balls, swung with considerable force, driving the air out of him with a savage whoof and the pain into him with a leap of blinding tears, he should have seen sense.

Instead, writhing, his hands clutched between his legs, he screamed out through the snot and tears and pain: 'Holmgang!'

Once out, it couldn't be put back. The news that Pinleg and Hring were to fight spread and even those away on a hunt hurried back.

Illugi Godi, after consulting with a grim-faced Einar, had the proper area paced out and roped off with strips of cloth and as much true ceremony as could be mustered under the circumstances. Then Pinleg and Hring appeared, stripped to the waist, bareheaded and armed with sword and a shield.

The holmgang was simple enough. You fought in an enclosed area with no armour and the same weapons. If you put one foot outside – going on the heel, as it was called – you lost. If your blood was spilled, you lost. If you ran, you lost – and were counted a nithing, with no honour. The only other way out was to win. There's a lot more ceremony and a few more rules, but that's the weft of it and all anyone standing in the square of it needs to know.

Pinleg looked ridiculous, a white body with ribs showing, scrawny as an old chicken. Another of the Oathsworn, who had never seen him fight, actually jeered. Hring was much more powerfully built and stepped up, swinging his sword to loosen his arm.

But I saw Pinleg was muttering to himself, that his head was shaking and I felt the hairs all over my body prickle.

They stepped into the roped area and Illugi Godi began the ritual, cleansing the combat, making sure no bloodprice penalty lasted with the winner from his friends or family.

And all the time Pinleg muttered and his head shook. Little flecks appeared at the corners of his mouth and I believe, around then, Hring began to realise the awful truth and just how much of a mistake this was.

Illugi Godi stepped out of the ring. Hring boldly slapped sword on shield and fell into a crouch. Pinleg stood for a moment, then his whole body spasmed, spittle flew from his mouth as he screamed, the shield went flying to one side and he launched himself across the ring.

I had never seen a berserker. I have heard all the tales since, about them being shapeshifters, turning into bears, or that they got their name from wearing bearskins, or that it was really wolf pelts.

Some say they chew strange herbs, or drink bark brews to get into the state of it, but the truth is that a berserker is a frothing madman with a blade, a man who does not care if he lives or dies as long as he gets to you and kills you. And the only way to kill one is to cut the legs off and hope he can't crawl as fast as you can run.

Pinleg lurched like a troll on wheels, faster than anything I had ever seen, his neck out, his chin jutting. It reminded me, in that fleeting moment, of the snake-headed white bear when it roared at me after falling through the roof.

Hring was taken by surprise, overwhelmed. He had no chance. There was simply the shrieking and then sickening, wet chopping sounds as Pinleg, spraying strings of saliva, hacked Hring into bloody pats of meat and kept on hacking.

'Fuck . . .' said someone.

Kol Fish-hook, one of Hring's Christ-following friends, moved as if to drag Pinleg away, but Einar roared, 'Stay. If you value your life.'

And, realising what they were dealing with, the circle moved cautiously backwards as Pinleg carved and roared.

When he finally ran out of screams, he stood, soaked in blood, his hair sodden with it, his face a mask of clotted red, save for the eyes, which seemed to dull suddenly, like the sea under a cloud. He slumped to his knees, drooled a little, then he fell forward on his face and snored.

Einar stood up as Illugi Godi and Valknut moved to carry Pinleg away. 'You should know that one of the forty-eight names of Odin is Frenzy,' he said, sweeping his black-ice gaze round us all. 'Know also that anyone else who decides what

137

religion will be followed in the Oathsworn will have me to deal with. I will not be as merciful as Pinleg and kill you quickly.' Then looked at Martin and said: 'You made this. You clean it up.'

Stunned at what he had seen, Martin stumbled forward to where the red ruin that had been Hring lay. Einar would not let anyone help him and, when Martin took up an arm to try and pull the bloody thing away, it tore free in his hands and he fell backwards on his arse into a puddle of blood.

Everyone laughed, even the Christ-sworn, then turned away in sorrow and disgust. Hring had found his death and it had not been a good one. Arguments broke out about whether he would make Valholl, given that he had been a Christ-follower when he died. Some of the others were uncomfortable with this, realising only now what following the White Christ really meant.

I watched as Martin, his robes soaked with red, gathered up and hauled off the bits and suddenly realised I knew nothing much about Hring other than that he liked to fish and he had been the only other one to help consign the Serkland woman to the sea when she died at Skirringsaal.

But something had happened here. Hring had broken his oath and I knew it was because Einar had broken his oath with Eyvind.

I think Einar knew it, too, so that when Valknut came up and announced that Ulf-Agar was gone, it was just another turn of Odin's subtle revenge. Or Loki's. Who knew?

'One of the fishermen saw a limping man get on that *knarr* just before it left,' Valknut added.

'He has broken his oath as well,' I said and, for the first time, Einar's black eyes would not meet mine.

The next morning, I stood on the shingle in another spring *mirr* of rain and watched the *Elk* slide out and away from the village. All around, watching with me, were the Oathsworn, all but a dozen – all the Christ-men – who had gone with my father and the Trimmer to safety down the coast.

Watching, too, was Martin, his ruined hand still tucked under one armpit, the puddle at his feet tinged pink from the blood that still seeped from his brown habit. He wore a leather collar now and a leash that attached him to Pinleg like a hound.

When the *Elk* had all but vanished into the rain mist, we turned in ones and twos and started to collect our gear. Hild, who had a spare cloak that had belonged to my father, had more of my essentials, wrapped in a bedroll.

With scarcely a word, falling into the familiar routine, we formed up, with Bagnose and Steinthor questing out in front, and started the long march upriver, to Koksalmi and the forge.

Hild knew the way, but Einar didn't trust her, so she was kept close to his side, with Pinleg and the leashed Martin. He would have leashed Hild, too, but Illugi Godi, knowing I would cause trouble over it, persuaded him, I think, that it would be better to have the woman on his side, not an enemy.

We climbed, for an hour at least, through birch and alder, where the sun slanted. As the trees thinned out, we halted, waiting for Bagnose and Steinthor to come back from scouting ahead. It gave everyone a chance to adjust straps and the weight of pack and shield.

I looked back, rubbing a raw place on my neck, feeling the wind, a good onshore blow hammering from a sea that sparkled. Below, somewhere to the right, the river meandered, reed-lined and narrowing.

Hild hunched on a rock, arms wrapped round her knees. 'Can you walk?' I asked and she looked up. Her eyes rolled, focused, rolled again. Then she nodded. I bent to take her bundle as well as my own and her hand, clawed and fierce, caught my wrist. From under the curtain of her hair I heard her say: 'She is waiting. She will guide me. She told . . .' The voice stopped, the slanted eyes grew slitted with cunning. 'No one is to know,' she hissed.

I liked her – I believe I loved her, in that way first love is. At least I thought I did, because she was the first woman I did not want to upend and fuck. I never thought of doing that casually with her, though I sometimes grew hard thinking of her white body in the dark.

Yet even then I couldn't seem to see it without the weals and the bruises, couldn't see her face gasping in passion without her eyes rolling up, white and dead, and hearing that Other voice, sometimes a hiss, sometimes a rasp.

I now knew that I was afraid of her, of her magic. If it had been me, I would have turned her loose, for all the lure of Attila the Hun's hoard.

Bagnose and Steinthor strode back in, spoke with Einar, then loped off again. The Oathsworn rose, shouldering their burdens, and we set off across a wide, pale plateau carved with rocky gullies and studded with knuckles of green-spotted grey stones. Here and there were stands of birch like white sentinels and mountains rose on either side, faint and purpled in the distance.

Gunnar Raudi fell in step with me, glancing sideways from under the faded red of his tangled curls. 'Faring well, young Orm?'

'Well enough, Gunnar Raudi,' I answered, in between breaths as we stepped out.

He was silent for a while and there was only the creak and clink of gear, the grunts and pants of labour. Eventually he said, 'We have come a long way in a short while.'

'Indeed,' I answered, wondering where all this was leading.

'It seems to me you are marked,' he went on slowly and I looked at him warily.

'Marked? By whom?'

He shrugged. 'Odin perhaps. But marked. And Einar knows it.'

'Einar?' I was lost now.

He caught me by the arm and we halted, men filtering round us, some with muttered curses at our blocking the trail. 'You are Einar's doom, I am thinking,' he said in a low, urgent voice, looking right and left, waiting until we were out of earshot. 'Everything bad happened to him after you came.'

'Me?' I answered, astonished, then thought I saw what he was about. 'You and I boarded the *Elk* at the same time. Why are you not Einar's bane? Why me, Gunnar Raudi?'

'I thought of that,' he replied, perfectly seriously and so honestly I felt ashamed at my suspicions. 'But the white bear was a sign . . . Einar came because of you, took you aboard because of the bear. I do not know which god stole his luck – Odin is my bet, though – but he used you to do it.'

It was nonsense, of course, and I could not shake the feeling he was up to something, so I shook my head and shouldered my gear.

'Einar believes this,' Gunnar Raudi said and now I saw why he had stopped me. Our eyes locked.

'Truly?'

He nodded. Then he clapped me on the shoulder. 'We'd better run, young Orm, or be left behind.'

Towards evening, we hit meadow grass, still yellowed but with new shoots coming through. Then, as the first stars appeared, Bagnose and Steinthor quartered back to Einar's side.

'We saw cattle,' said Bagnose.

'A bull and three milch cows,' added Steinthor.

'And a boy with yellow hair watching them,' finished Bagnose.

'Did he see you?' asked Einar and got a curled lip from the pair of them. He stroked his moustaches and then announced that we would camp in a hollow, fringed with trees, that we had left behind some minutes before. Only one fire was to be lit and that for cooking, in the centre of the dip, where it wouldn't be seen.

Later, after we had eaten, he called me to where he sat, with Gunnar Raudi and Ketil Crow and Skapti and Illugi – all the Oathsworn's faithful hounds.

'Orm,' he said, his face tomb-dark on the other side of the fire, his hair a shroud for it. 'Tell me the truth of it. Is Hild right in the head enough to go to her people and let them know we mean no harm?'

I thought about it, and found myself scrubbing my chin like my father did – found, also, that there was a down there to be scrubbed. I wasn't considering the question – Hild had enough sense for the task – but what it meant.

It meant, I reasoned, that Einar was worried about the villagers, which was sensible. After all, Vigfus's crew had been routed by them and they were, presumably, hard-enough fighters. It meant that he wanted to see if he could persuade the villagers to help. If not, he would stamp them, swift and hard, in the dark.

It's what I would have done.

The problem was, as I told him, that I didn't think Hild would want to do it, that she was following her own saga here and needed to be in that forge. I believed, too, that if we had any hope of reaching the end of this whale road, we needed her to be there.

And the good people of Koksalmi wouldn't stand for that.

'You think they would kill her?' Einar asked. I nodded. Skapti hoomed and then spat in the dying embers of the fire.

'How do you know so much? I know you cared for the woman, but she is out of her head half the time. And you are a boy – Frigg's tits, you have not even been with us a season, are barely big enough to fit in that mail you strut in.'

I bridled, half rising, and big Skapti waved a placating hand. 'Easy, easy – I meant no insult by it. Do not mistake me for a bear, young Orm.'

There were chuckles and I lost my anger in embarrassment and scrubbed my face again. 'She will lead us to the forge if

142

you give her leave and trust her to do it,' I said, with only a slight twinge of fear that I was wrong. 'Perhaps we can stay quiet and sneak in and out, no harm done.'

'I thought the forge was in the village?' growled Ketil Crow.

'No. From what I understand, it is in a small hill nearby. The villagers count the place as a god place, but they fear it, too, and never go there, from what Hild says.'

This was stretching the cloth a great deal. It was what I had garnered from Hild's ravings, which was not quite the same thing as a straight fact.

Einar considered it, then nodded. 'In, out and then we move west and south, to where the *Elk* lies,' he said.

'And on to somewhere,' Skapti rumbled, 'where there is something on the cookfire that isn't fish.'

The next morning was misted, tendrils of it snaking round our ankles, lying in the hollows and under the trees like smoke.

We had been moving for no more than a few minutes when we broached the cap of a hill. Below, the mist roiled down the slope as the morning sun burned it off and the bare hillside led down into the beginnings of a fair-sized forest, where the river sparkled.

Hild stood and pointed, right across the river and the trees, to a great craggy outcrop, almost bare save for stunted stands of fir. 'The forge lies under that,' she said, then turned to the north. 'And the village is an hour that way. I came here sometimes, but she . . .' She broke off, wrapped her arms round herself, moaned slightly.

Ketil Crow, looking dubious, glanced at Einar. Hild swayed and Illugi steadied her. I moved to her side and heard her say, as if fighting for breath: 'The old entrance is closed. Barred. Only from the top. Barred, Orm. You understand? Barred . . .' Her eyes rolled and she fell against me.

'Fuck,' said Skapti. 'Now we'll have to carry her.'

'What was all that growling about?' demanded Einar. I

told him as we moved on, four men sharing the burden of Hild, on another spear-bed.

We moved through the whispering trees, splashed across the fast-running, knee-high stream and on, up to where the ground started to rise and the trees thin. Then there were only withered efforts, like a crone's clawed hands, and Einar called a halt as Geir Bagnose and Steinthor came sliding in.

'We found a track,' said Bagnose.

'And a door.'

It was the faintest of trails, and it led to a hacked-out entrance. Sunk a little way into it was a stout wooden door.

'It was a mine once,' someone noted and when we looked, we could see the faint remains of the old wooden slats which had carried ore carts long ago.

'This door is a good one,' remarked another, whose name I knew to be Bodvar. He had been a woodworker and knew one when he saw it. 'But it has been repaired a few times, here just recently.'

He pointed and we saw the difference in weathering, the thick new cross-planks.

'Vigfus,' muttered Einar and we all saw the remains of axe scores, where his crew had tried to cut through. It was clear someone had come and repaired the damage caused after they'd been chased off. Which meant, of course, that they were not entirely afraid of their mountain forge.

Skapti gripped the edge of a cross-plank and heaved. When nothing happened, he pushed, then stopped, shoved his helmet up and scratched. 'There's a thing,' he said. 'It's barred from the inside. I can feel it.'

'So there is someone in there,' said Ketil Crow and chuckled nastily. 'Perhaps we should knock.'

'That's what Vigfus did,' Valknut said, pulling off his helmet and wiping the sweat from his brow. 'Look where it got him.'

'The thing of it is,' said Bodvar, 'that this door has not

been opened in a long while. Look, there's an old bird's nest in the angle of that hinge.'

He was right. And the more we looked, the older the door was and the longer it had been shut. There was silence and Einar stroked his chin. Finally, he said, 'Bagnose, Steinthor, see if you can find another way in round this rock. The rest of us will go to where Hild said to go – the top.'

'This is a mountain,' protested Steinthor. 'It will take hours to go round the whole circle of it.'

'Then get started,' growled Einar and they left, splitting to right and left. The rest of us hefted our gear and got ready to climb. No one spoke. If challenged, they'd have said they were saving their breath for the task, but their minds were on dwarves and trolls and other things that lived under mountains, guarding the secret of treasure.

I thought most were chewing over the prospect of turning up some of Atil's hoard – and a few droop-lips were just stupid enough to think that it was actually buried here.

But I was wrong. Everyone was too busy wondering who had barred the door inside the mountain.

SEVEN

Long, painful, sweaty. There – to say it takes three words and I wish it had been as easy to get to the top of that gods-cursed forge mountain. But I remember the climb as being tough, mainly because I was wearing mail: the weight of a small boy on my shoulders. That and all the other stuff – two shields, because I felt guilty and offered to share the burden of one of those who had to carry Hild up it on the spear-bed.

At the top, I was too busy ripping off my salt-stained boots and woollen socks to care about a cairn of stones. The cold air on my aching, throbbing feet almost made me moan with pleasure and, after I had inspected the rawest bits, I then took time to look around.

Everyone else was in a similar state. Men wriggled out of mail, stripped off layers of linen and wool, sat with their heads lowered, dripping under the unexpectedly warm spring sun. Skapti's face looked like it would burst.

But Einar, if he was suffering, showed no sign of it. He stood, pensively staring at the cairn and the poles that surrounded them. Every one but four of them bore a skull, leering and weatherbeaten. The four that didn't had recognisable heads, with eyes gone, lips peeled back, strips of skin pecked from cheeks.

146

'Vigfus's men,' said Valknut, who was nearest me, massaging his calf muscles.

I shed my mail like a wriggling snake, then wandered over to have a closer look. The heads were ruins; you couldn't tell if they'd even been men, save for one who had a fringe of beard left.

The cairn was waist height, with fallen stones around it. When I looked more closely, I realised it wasn't a cairn, but a ring of stones round a blackened opening. Peering down revealed only more blackness.

Ketil Crow joined me, as did a few others. And, of course, Bodvar picked up a stone and dropped it in. There was a short pause, then a faint splash.

'A well?' queried Bodvar.

'On a mountain top?' responded Ketil Crow with a curl of his lip.

'I wish you had not done that,' Illugi Godi said, frowning at Bodvar, who merely shrugged.

'If not a well, what?' demanded Skapti, lumbering up.

'A smoke hole,' said Einar absently, then kicked one of the stones at his feet. We all saw that the blackening was an age of soot.

'For the forge,' someone said, enlightened.

'His charcoal is a little damp,' commented Valknut and there were chuckles.

We milled and peered and argued this and that for a while. Einar stood and thought and, apart from the whirr and song of birds, there was only the muttered rant of Hild, that constant background noise we had all become used to.

'Rope,' said Einar. There was some – Valknut had a length; two others had coils of it round their waists. Einar had a fire lit, made a torch, held it over the hole and let it drop. We all watched it fall, turning lazily, trailing sparks. We saw the shaft, where it suddenly widened out, the gleam of water – then the torch hissed and was gone.

147

'Take a sounding on that,' ordered Einar and the ropes were knotted firmly, then a bearded boarding axe tied to one end and lowered. When the rope end was reached, it still hadn't gone slack and that meant some two hundred feet. We hauled it up and found it dry.

'That's a deep hole,' muttered Skapti uneasily and everyone agreed. Deep holes were to be avoided: the lair of dragons or black dwarves.

'Let's find out how deep,' said Einar and had us take off the leather neck straps from our shields and fasten them to the rope. Then we lowered it again. At 250 feet, the rope went slack and, when it was hauled up, the last twenty or so was wet.

'So, now we know,' said Einar. 'Who will be lowered, then?'

There was a shifting from leg to leg and a studious attempt to be looking somewhere else.

'I would go,' offered Skapti and everyone groaned and laughed.

'Just so,' said Einar. 'Someone small and light, then.'

'Send the Christ priest,' shouted someone. 'He's scrawny enough.'

There was laughter and Martin's face went white. But Einar shook his head, tugging on the leash a little. 'The black dwarves will eat him,' he said. More laughter.

'I will do it,' offered Pinleg and there were nods and some appreciative noises at his bravery.

'Can you swim?' added Einar and Pinleg acknowledged his lack with a wry wave.

It took me a while to realise they were silent and all looking at me.

'Can you swim?' asked Einar.

I swallowed, for I swam like a fish, the legacy of some-times falling off those black gull cliffs. I could lie, but Gunnar Raudi knew, so I nodded.

There was a single exhale of relief and a few hands clapped

148

my back, more because the owners weren't going than at my courage.

Skapti knotted the rope into a kind of sling, which made it a seat rather than round my waist, which cut the wind from you. They made a new torch and I climbed on to the crumbling edge of the cairn, while Skapti wrapped two coils round his ample frame and braced himself. Two others, shoulders humped with muscle from rowing, stood to help him.

'Jerk the rope twice to have us stop,' he growled.

'What if I need to come up in a hurry?'

'If the dragon is burning your skinny arse,' he replied, 'we'll hear you scream.'

As the others laughed, Einar lit the torch. Then I kicked out and started down.

At first they went so fast that I clattered off the sides, but I yelled up to them, my voice bouncing crazily in my ears and they slowed the descent. Turning slowly I was lowered, down and down and down into the dark shaft, the torch guttering.

I saw a small, round opening midway down, set into one side of the shaft like a dark lidless eye. I almost called out, but then I was sinking below it and, suddenly, out of the shaft entirely.

There was the impression of airiness, a great expanse of vaulted rock, which the torch only dimly revealed. Water dripped and the air felt damp and cold and smelled musty. When I saw the water gleaming red in the torchlight, I jerked the rope and stopped.

Swinging gently, I lowered the torch a little, peering around. There was nothing but water. I swallowed the dry spear in my throat and realised I had no way of telling them to haul me up save one.

So I yelled. The sound boomed off the wall. I was jerked up like fish bait, shot back up the shaft so quickly I hit the sides and yelped in pain, which only made them haul harder.

I almost shot out into the sunlight, the torch falling back into the darkness.

I was cursing them as they dragged me over the side of the cairn stones and, when they saw I was unharmed, everyone laughed at my fury. I didn't think it was funny; both my elbows and one knee were bloodied.

'You've had worse humping on a dirt floor,' observed Skapti, hauling me up and grinning. Then they all wanted to know what I had seen.

'A shaft, widens out into a chamber full of water,' I revealed.

'That much we found out without lowering you,' Einar grunted.

'There isn't much more,' I bridled. 'Short of going in the water and swimming about in the dark, I couldn't find out more.'

'It might come to that,' Einar growled and I saw he was serious. The thought of being in that black water in the pitch dark shut me up and focused my mind. I remembered the opening, and thought more about it.

'I am thinking that there is something of the heathen sacrifice about this place,' Martin the monk said slowly. 'I can smell it.'

'You . . . have the . . . right . . . of it.'

The voice was weak, but so unexpected that we all whirled and stared. Hild was upright, swaying, her face bloodless.

'The only way in is here,' she said, speaking in a rush, as if trying to get it all out as fast as she could. 'Was once to be my fate . . . All who know go into the dark. There is a way to the door if you can find it. If you do, you can choose – to unbar it, or stay. No one has unbarred the door since the woman of the first smith. She went in for her sin, gave sin and secret to her children.' She paused, sagged. 'My mother is in there. When I had provided a daughter, that was to be my fate.'

We all chewed that over. Martin crossed himself. So that was the 'dark' Hild spoke of, the 'she' who haunted her. Her mother. In the black pit of that forge, probably mouldering at the bottom of that lake. And if she still spoke to her daughter, she was a fetch of rare fierceness.

'They threw them in, all the smith's daughters?' demanded Valknut.

'The heirs of Regin,' muttered Illugi. 'I have heard that name before . . .'

The others, even though they did not know the whole of it, were equally uneasy faced with this. Like them, I was thinking that a village capable of heaving their own down a hole were not ones to walk up to as a stranger.

I was so petrified I couldn't stand – and I wasn't going swimming down there, even if Einar cut my bollocks off with his truth-seeking knife.

'There is an opening, midway down,' I babbled to Einar. 'The edges are smoke-blackened, upwards, but not beneath. I think that is the true smoke hole.'

Einar glared at me. 'Can you get in it?'

I paused, trying to think, then nodded. As I peeled off my tunic, I felt Hild's black eyes on me. She was wrapped like a corpse bundle in my cloak and shivering in the warm sun.

'Bodvar, you and Valknut pick three more and go back to the barred door. When Orm here reaches it, he may need help. Send back for the rest of us to come, too.'

Both men groaned at that. The idea of tramping all the way back down that gods-cursed hill was not appealing. On the other hand, I saw, it was still better to them than going down the shaft. And Einar had spoken of 'when' I reached the door. Not 'if'.

I felt Hild at my side, her hand on my naked arm. I looked into the dark eyes and saw fear. But not for me, I thought as I turned away, stuffing a firestarter and my eating knife in my boot.

At the edge of the loose-stone cairn, Einar caught my arm, his black eyes like nails on my face. He said nothing and, after a moment, let me go.

Then I was down the shaft again, torch in hand. When I got to the round opening, I had them stop and swung for a bit, studying it. Then I hooked myself near it, slid my feet in to the knees.

It would be a tight squeeze and what to do with the torch bothered me, for I couldn't take it lit, but maybe couldn't fit with it unlit and stuffed in my belt. And I didn't want to be in the dark wherever that smoke hole ended.

In the end, I worked it out. I undid my breeks and hauled the ties out of them. As they slid and flapped round my boots, I stubbed the torch into sparks and embers, fastened my breeks cord to one end and made a loop at the other.

In the dark, I looped it round my neck, then slithered further into the smoke hole, let go the rope and was alone. In the dark. In a hole no bigger than a burial chamber.

It went down at a sharp angle, as it had to, but I was offering up extravagant sacrifices to all the gods, Aesir and Vanir and any others I could think of, that it didn't get narrower. My hands were out above my head, palms flat on the rough stone – a natural crag, this, I thought with the part of my mind not screaming in terror at the fact that my nose was so close to it.

Like a tomb. Dark . . . I hit an obstacle and stopped. An obstacle. Solid. I was stuck.

There is no feeling like that. The hardest thing I ever did was not scream and thrash. I felt the weight of it above me, had the sweat of fear and labour stinging my eyes, heard the rasp of my own breath in that hot, cloistered dark.

I lay, hands up behind my head, palms flat, pushing. Nothing. My feet were on something solid. I brought my knees a little way up, hard up against the roof of the shaft until I felt them puncture and bleed to try and shove against the obstruction – and found nothing beneath my feet.

I blinked away sweat and gasped and tried to think. It bent. Of course it did. It turned from an angled shaft to a straight one.

I wriggled, legs lowered, felt them slide down and was just sighing with relief when I realised that if it angled down it was a sheer drop. At which I shot forward, ripping the skin from the palms of my hands, straight down, crashing into something that seemed soft, though the hard edges of it cracked my head and an already battered elbow.

There was a choking dust, too. I couldn't breathe; it was smothering me. I thrashed, then lost the last of my courage and, gibbering and choking, floundered out of what I thought was a bed and tumbled, this time on to something hard.

I saw light then, but it was inside my head, and when I eventually groaned upright and felt the place that hurt, it came away sticky. But I was breathing, though I could taste the swirling dust still.

I hauled myself together, along a ladder, it seemed. The torch was still attached, mercifully, and both knife and firestarter were in my boot. Using the firestarter in the dark was no problem and the first brief spark was so bright in that place that I saw, at once, that I was on an ore-track, the 'ladder' being wooden rails.

The next spark, then the next and the dried mosses caught into faint pinprick embers. I blew, slowly and carefully, nurtured it into a flame, fed that to the torch and, suddenly, I had light.

I was in a square chamber. I had fallen maybe ten feet and what I thought had been a bed was the metal-edged forge, the soft landing being the remains of charcoal ash, now settling slowly. I was black with it.

There were barrels and, next to them, a sagging table with dust-shrouded tools. The ore-tracks I lay on stretched ahead and behind, into darkness both ways, half buried in rubble spill. An old shovel lay discarded on them.

153

I got up, wiping the sweat from my eyes, torch held high. The forge still had the bellows, but when I touched them, they sighed to dust. The anvil, however, was what caught my eye. It was layered with dust and cobwebs, at least as heavy as two Skaptis and rusty. But it had a split in it, deep as the first joint of my finger, across its width.

I spat dust out and moved to the sagging table, passing the barrels and seeing the dark contents spilling from two of them. I bent and sniffed, tasted iron: they were filing and discards. The other had held sand. On the other side of the table was a stone tub which had, presumably, held water for quenching.

The tools seemed to be the sort of thing you would have in a forge: hammers, pincers, mallets, all cobwebbed and rusting. And, on the wall above, something that gleamed.

I moved the torch closer and saw a ledge hewn out of the rock. Above it was a long, single string of runes. I couldn't read them and the thought struck me that it was strange that a Northman could read Latin, but not runes.

In the ledge lay what appeared to be a batten of wood, seemingly oiled and fresh. It had a squarish head, with two bright rivets holding a nub of shining metal, a thumb-length sticking out of the wooden shaft and neatly sheared off. I didn't touch it – after the bellows had fallen apart, I didn't want to touch anything. I was sure the rubble spill had come from the roof; the sheer weight of that place pressed on me.

But it was more than that. There was something about that piece of wood that kept me from touching it, that was strange and Other and I could not work it out.

In the end, though, I picked up a heavy hammer, rusted iron with an iron shaft, too. Having a weapon made me feel better. What good it would do against the fetch of a dead woman was another matter.

I backed away, considering, trying to orientate myself so that, when I chose a route out of that room, I wasn't heading off down into some labyrinth of forgotten and dangerous mineworkings, but towards that barred door.

I was still trying to work it out when the torch guttered and my heart nearly stopped. I looked wildly at it, but it was nowhere near burned down. I held it up; a breeze caressed it and I cursed myself for a ninny and followed where the breeze was coming from.

The door, when I finally saw it, was almost an anti-climax. The bar was stiff and I had to force it up with the hammer until it finally toppled out. Then I shoved, heard shouts, saw a sliver of light and then fingers curling round the exposed edge of the door.

With a wrench and a shower of dust, it racked open, spilling sunlight into the shaft. I shuffled out, my breeks manacling my ankles.

Valknut loomed up, Bodvar and the others behind. They stopped, recoiled, stared. Then Valknut seemed to sag, wrapped his arms round himself and reeled away. Bodvar pointed, his mouth working.

Scared witless, I whirled round in case something was creeping up, but there was nothing. I heard them gasp and wheeze and choke and, with a sudden burst of fury and shame, realised they were helpless with laughter.

It took them ages to recover and my sulking only made it worse. Bodvar actually volunteered to reclimb the hill to get the others because, he said later, he'd have burst from laughing.

Valknut later admitted he'd thought it was a black dwarf stumping out to tell them all to piss off, his hammer at the ready, and had nearly wet himself with terror. The relief when he saw who it was made him laugh all the more.

I saw the funny side. Eventually. The door opens and there is a boy, naked but for his boots, his breeks tangled round his ankles, black with charcoal dust, streaked white with sweat runnels and blood . . . I would have hooted, too.

I was still like that an hour later – though my breeks were up and the sun a lot less warm, so that I was shivering and goose-bumped. I needed water to wash, but there was none spare for that, so I stayed black and gave everyone a fresh laugh.

Einar nodded appreciatively, as if he knew what I had done. Ordinarily I would have swelled with proud delight at this, but there was too much doom about Einar now for me to hold him in such esteem.

More torches were lit and I led them, less four to guard the open door, back to the forge room, Hild staggering at my side. Martin kept darting eagerly ahead, just like the dog Einar had made him, tangling his leash and making his keeper, Skapti, curse.

We crept in and I showed them what I had found: the forge, the bellows, the barrels and the table.

Both Illugi Godi and Martin the monk dropped to their knees, to the astonishment of all – what could have made that pair worship together? They, too, were astonished, not realising what the other had seen.

'The spear,' Martin breathed reverently. 'The spear . . .' He couldn't say anything else, just sat with his hands clasped and prayed.

'That?' queried Ketil Crow. 'There's only a shaft.'

'It is – was – a Roman spear,' Martin said, his voice filled with awe, then he bowed his head and actually sobbed. 'But the pagan devils have removed the long metal point, steeped in the blood of Christ. May God punish them all.'

Ketil Crow, with a scornful look at the weeping monk, stepped forward, making to pluck the spear-shaft from its ledge. Illugi Godi's voice was booming loud when he roared: 'Stay!' He pointed to the rune line. 'A runespell. A new one. A new runespell.'

That stunned us all. Valknut dropped to his knees and bowed his head at the enormity of it.

There were few runespells. Odin himself, who had hung nine days on the World Tree, had only ever learned eighteen, as Illugi now reminded us.

'And had a spear thrust into his side, too,' Pinleg growled pointedly to Martin. 'But at least he got Knowledge out of it.'

'Was it?' interrupted Valknut. 'I thought it was Wisdom.'

'Perhaps the pair of you need to hang on the same tree,' Illugi Godi said wryly. 'That way one of you would have the wisdom or knowledge to shut up.'

'It's all pagan nonsense,' Martin declared.

'Take your prize, then,' Einar offered. 'Surely some pagan nonsense is no danger to you, under the protection of your god? After all, didn't your Bishop Poppo wear a red-hot iron glove and come to no harm?'

Martin licked his lips, looked as if he would try it, then settled back like a sullen dog.

Ketil Crow, shaken at his narrow escape – the runespell might have cursed him, or worse – wiped his dry mouth with the back of one hand. Unless you know what you are doing, you walk warily round a runespell, neither speaking it aloud nor laying a hand on it.

'There's no rust on that spear-shaft,' Valknut noted and I blinked, realising only now what the strange Otherness had been. No rust. Or dust. Or cobwebs. Everything looked as if it had been made the day before.

There was a general backing away. I saw Hild stagger, heard her mutter, moved closer and put one arm round her shoulders. She was cold, but sweating and swaying wildly, like a mast in a high wind.

'So what happened?' demanded Ketil Crow. 'Did they forge a sword out of bits of an old spear? Is that the right of it?'

'Essentially,' muttered Illugi Godi, leaning forward to study the runes and speaking absently, his voice sounding like a man speaking underwater. 'It was written here by someone . . . who

157

knew . . . how to do it well. For the smith to copy on to the sword he was forging.'

Ketil Crow shrugged. 'I can't think that you would get much of a sword out of some old spearhead,' he scoffed and Illugi peered briefly at him.

'Depends on the spearhead. With the blood of a god on it . . .'

He left the rest unsaid, but Ketil Crow had it terrier-gripped and would not let go. 'Not one of our gods.'

'A god is a god,' Illugi remarked. 'Ours are more powerful, obviously . . .'

Martin's snort stopped Illugi, but Ketil Crow wanted no theological debate. He kicked the metal forge moodily, for he had wanted lots more – treasure, swords, all the stuff of sagas. 'I still don't see that a sword made from an old spear is much of a weapon.'

'Perhaps you should look at the anvil,' said Einar laconically, 'where they tested it.'

That great cut across the anvil, where the smith had tested the edge of his blade, made Ketil Crow click his teeth sharply together. Everyone craned to see and Valknut gave a low whistle of appreciation.

'Deep. Through mail, a cut like that. And helmet-steel, maybe more. Solid iron, that anvil.' He turned and nudged Ketil Crow. 'Some spearhead. Some sword.'

Ketil Crow scowled, but it was half-hearted and the old, avaricious glow was back in his eyes.

'What's this?' asked a voice and everyone turned, thrusting torches. The man – a grey-bearded veteran called Ogmund Wryneck because of a head-jerking tic he had – stood looking up another shaft, behind the barrels. The wooden rungs of a ladder led upwards.

'Well spotted, old eye,' Einar said, clapping him on the shoulder. He stepped on the ladder, moved up one rung – and it fell apart with a puff of rotting wood.

'Well, that's that,' he said, then looked at me. 'A strong lad, bracing himself, could work himself up that shaft with a rope if he had a mind.'

'He could,' I answered bitterly. 'When you find one, ask him.'

Illugi Godi, impatiently grabbing the nearest torch, was almost nose to rock now, poring over the runes and muttering, but careful not to touch. But he was not so engrossed that he could not try to grasp more. He turned to me, his eyes wild.

'Yes, yes, you must. There might be another runespell. Think of it! Another spell.'

'Or a sword,' added Ketil Crow enticingly.

'Or some of Atil's treasure,' said Einar. The rest of the faces round me glowed with the greed of it and their eyes burned on me.

Fuck your runes, I wanted to say. Fuck your magic swords. Fuck you, too, godi. You haul your holy arse up the shaft if you feel so strongly about it.

Yet, at the same time, I was taking the offered rope, coiling it round my waist, looping the torch round my neck again and heaving myself into the shaft.

In the end it was an easy climb. The rungs broke into dust, but there were rusted metal sockets for them and they stayed intact for the most part, so it was simple. At the top, I lit the torch and looked around.

There was a collapsed shelf and more barrels, whose splayed staves spilled the contents out. There was a chest which looked interesting, but only because I tried to move it and knew it was heavy and perfect as an anchor for the rope.

I slung it down, told them that the room was too small for everyone and then turned back to the other thing I had spotted. The door.

It was half open, swung limply on sagging hinges and revealed, at first, what seemed to be an old wooden-framed

159

bed and a collection of rags. Then I realised the rags had form; white gleamed. Bone.

As Einar panted up the rope into the room I realised, from the hanks of hair and the remains of jewellery, that this could be Hild's mother. Einar, peering over my shoulder, rubbed his moustaches and nodded when I offered my explanation.

'Interesting,' he said and then pointed out the obvious, which I had overlooked. 'If it is, she could have unbarred the door, got out and returned to her child.'

That made me jerk. Perhaps it wasn't her, after all, but some other luckless relative – a grandmother or older – but why they hadn't walked out was still a mystery. However, as I pointed out to Einar and Illugi, the only two who came up, best not to mention this to Hild.

They nodded, though I wasn't sure they heard. Illugi was too busy hunting for more runes and stirring up only the old dust of dried beans and insect husks. Einar, however, was at the metal chest and working a seax into the rusted lock.

It gave with a dull sound and he lifted the lid. We all peered, half expecting gold, swords, gem-studded crowns. Instead, there were a lot of cloth bundles which, when we unwrapped them, unveiled a series of blackened tin plates, some bound together through holes with the remains of leather thongs.

'Like the book of leaves in St Otmund's temple,' I pointed out and Einar nodded, rummaging furiously and annoyed that there was only this and the metal was only tin.

'Indeed,' said Illugi, his eyes gleaming, 'that's what it is. Hold the torch closer, Orm. Let's see . . . Yes, runes. Excellent . . .' A moment later, he straightened, the disappointment palpable. 'Apart from advice on never allowing two blades to lie across each other and a list of plants to rub into the anvil to give it more strength, there isn't much here on smelting that I haven't heard before.'

'Useless, god-fucked place,' muttered Einar moodily. 'No treasure, no clues.'

'There is the runespell on the wall below,' Illugi said brightly.

'Know what it says?' demanded Einar.

'I think it is something about truth, or being true. And there's an eternity rune in there, which means long-lasting. And, of course, it all depends on how you cut them . . .'

'You have no idea, do you?' Einar challenged and Illugi shrugged, grinned sheepishly and admitted that to be true.

'It seems to be what you'd expect to find on a good sword – a runespell to make a blade true and long-lasting,' he said. 'But the runes are old, different from the ones we know now.'

The shriek made us all jerk, an ear-splitting sound that bounced off the walls, ringing the whole place like a bell.

'What the fuck . . . ?'

Einar was down the rope in a fast slide that must have flayed skin from his palms. I followed, only marginally slower, since I was almost certain I knew who had screamed.

I was right. Hild stood in the centre of a ring of wary warriors, clutching the spear-shaft to her chest. She was still as a carved prow, her eyes wide and staring at nothing, her mouth open and chest heaving, as if she could not breathe.

'The monk made her do it,' Bodvar said. 'We were all thinking it a bad idea when she started to, but that little rat said someone had to and it might as well be her.'

Einar glared at Skapti, who tugged the leash so that Martin jerked. Halftroll shrugged and said, 'He wasn't wrong, Einar. Someone had to risk it.'

Martin, straightening, adjusted his cowl and smiled. 'I was right. I have been right all along. This Hild is linked to the sword made here, a powerful weapon now thanks to the blood of Christ on that holy spearhead they used to forge it.

'The heathens may have perverted the Spear of Destiny,

but the blood stays true. True also is the blood of the smiths – she knows where the sword is and so also where the Great Hoard is.'

'Kill the little fuck now,' growled Ketil Crow.

'He has the right of it,' announced Hild in a strange, gentle, calm voice. 'I am linked by the blood of the smiths who made this sword.'

'How many spears were stuck in this Christ, then?' Finn Horsehead demanded to know. 'For I have heard that the Emperor of the Romans in the Great City has hundreds of Christ ikons, from a little cloth with the god's face on it to a crown made of thorns. And a spear that was thrust in the side of this Jesus as he hung on his tree.'

'False. I have the real spear,' snapped Martin angrily and Einar whacked him on one ear, sending the little monk stumbling.

'You have nothing at all, monk,' Einar said in a voice thick and slow as a moving glacier. 'You have your life only by my leave.'

Hild shook her head, as if scattering water from her. 'I know where the sword of Attila is. I can take you there, far to the east, along the Khazars' river.'

'Where in the name of Odin's arse is that?' demanded Einar.

'I know,' said Pinleg like an eager boy. No one laughed now, not after what they had seen him do. 'It's down the Don,' he announced triumphantly.

'The Don?' repeated Einar.

'That's Khazar territory,' insisted Pinleg. 'If it is the same Khazars who spit little arrows at you and worship the god of the Jewish men.'

'The same,' Hild said and there was silence, loud as a clanging hammer. The shock of it all was still chilling us when one of the door guards came in out of the dark tunnel, blinking into the light.

162

'Rurik says to come quick,' he told Einar, 'for something has happened.'

'Rurik? What is he doing here?'

We charged out, back along the passage and into the daylight, where the weak sun seemed searing and blinding. Blinking, we saw Rurik and Valgard Trimmer and four others. My father, grim-faced, stepped forward and I saw he had a bloody, unbound cut along the length of his forearm, seeping thickly through the rent in his tunic.

'One of Starkad's ships came,' he said, 'with Starkad and Ulf-Agar. There was a fight; eight of us were killed.'

'How did you get the *Elk* away with so few?' demanded Einar.

My father paused, scrubbed his face and the sickening realisation was dawning on us all before he even told us.

'We didn't. We came overland, with Starkad hot on our heels. We left the *Elk* burning to the waterline.'

EIGHT

It was at that moment that most saw how Einar's doom was on him and most blamed it on the fact he had broken his oath. Einar, too, knew it, but he needed the crew still – more than ever at that moment – and I saw him meet his wyrd standing straight and with Loki cunning.

'Well,' he said with a whetstone smile, looking round the stunned, angry faces to men who knew they were stranded on a hostile shore. 'Now we need the Oathsworn.'

And he turned, moving away from the forge mountain as the sun started dying on the edge of the world, heading uphill.

There was a flurry of mutters, argument traded for argument. One or two, either those who had worked it out, or those who would follow Einar into Helheim, shouldered their gear one more time and loped after him, long shadows bobbing. One was my father. Eventually, the others followed, grumbling about everything and especially why they were going uphill yet again.

'Hold, I'll bind that,' I called and my father turned, grinning at the black sight of me.

'You need to wash behind your ears, boy,' he growled and I laughed with him and tore up my last clean underkirtle from my bundle to use on his forearm. It was a long, wicked cut, oozing blood.

'Seax,' he grunted.

'You should have kept out of the way, old man,' I said with a smile. His eyes, when they met mine, were brimming. He had lost the *Elk*. I felt it for him, but could do nothing more than concentrate on my knots and finish the binding.

'What now?' I asked him as he turned away and, to be fair, he knew what I meant at once.

'In the end, everyone will see the same thing,' he said quietly. 'Einar broke oath and the gods are taking his luck. So now every man will be wondering what it will cost him to do the same.'

'Einar broke oath with Eyvind, so I can break oath with Einar,' I replied angrily. 'So can you. So can anyone. The gods can find no fault with that, surely.'

My father patted my arm gently, as if I was still a child. 'You are new to this, boy. Use that gift Einar prizes you for and I am proud of you for.'

Bewildered, I could only stare. The others, grumbling and still arguing, were hefting their stuff and following on up the hill, into the twilight.

My father smiled and said, 'Can you break your oath to Einar, yet keep it with me?'

I saw, with a shock of clarity, what Einar had meant. We had sworn an oath to each other, not just to him, and that would keep us bound, for the more his luck went bad, the more he stood as a monument to what happens when you break the oath.

Yet the worse his luck got, the more we suffered. It went round and round, like the dragon coiled round the World Tree, tail in mouth.

My father nodded, seeing all of that chase across my face. 'An oath,' he said, 'is a powerful thing.'

I brooded on it all the way back to where we camped,

halfway up the forge mountain, where Einar sat alone, arms wrapped round his knees, his face hidden by the crow wings of his hair. There were no fires, little talk and, when it was too dark to check blades and straps, men lay down and, if they had them, wrapped themselves in cloaks and tried to sleep.

I wondered if, like me, they felt the doom of it all: a band, oathbound to an oath-breaker, followed a madwoman on a quest after treasure that was more fable than real. A skald would not dare make it into a saga tale for fear of the laughter.

More than likely, I realised later, they were brooding and miserable because their sea-chests had all gone up in flames, with everything they had left in them.

Skapti and Ketil Crow made sure men kept watch, though I was excused after my labours of earlier. I sat and worried at the problem like a hound with a well-chewed bone, so lost in it that it took me a long while to realise that Hild had come up, silent and stately, hugging the spear-shaft to her like a baby.

She said nothing, just sat down, not quite beside me, not far away. Although I couldn't see him in the darkness, I was aware of Martin, watching, waiting. I was glad he was still leashed to Skapti.

Dawn was another milky-gruel affair, with a creeping ground mist that disturbed everyone, but they generally agreed that Einar, doomed or not, was still a deep thinker for battle. He had taken us above the mist and anyone creeping up would, sooner or later, have to step out on to that bare, cragged skull of a hill and meet us fairly.

Some, of course, were all for getting away, but Ketil Crow, Skapti and the others put them straight: it was far too late for that. Starkad had sent men to follow Rurik and the survivors from the *Elk*. He was coming and there would be a fight.

And all this time Einar said nothing, though he was found already on his feet dressed for battle and wearing a dark blue

166

cloak, fastened with an impressive ringpin of silver, worked with red stones. He spent the morning staring down the hill at the mists, stroking his moustache, while men sorted out their gear and checked and rechecked straps and shields.

Then, like an eerie wind, there came the sound of a lowing horn, distant and mournful.

'That's not clever,' muttered Valknut. 'He'll have those villagers out.'

The horn sounded again, closer. Einar whirled, his cloak billowing, and pointed silently to Ketil Crow, Skapti, Valknut – and me. He looked at us all from eyes deep-sunk as mine shafts, then spoke as if his teeth were nailed to each other. 'Skapti, make sure the monk stays fastened to you. He is what Starkad wants most. Orm, keep the woman with you also. Brondolf Lambisson will have told him much, but he knows little of the woman and nothing of how valuable she is to us. Valknut, break out the banner and guard it.'

He paused, turned to Ketil Crow, whose languid stare never wavered. 'If I fall,' he added, 'you take the Oathsworn back to where the *Elk* was burned. Starkad's ship is there. It is my intent to cut them up badly here. He has one ship, will have left guards and has, I suspect, a hundred men here, perhaps fifteen or twenty guarding his *drakkar*. It may be possible to take it and that is what I intend.'

Again he paused and gave a twisted smile. 'None can escape their wyrd,' he growled, 'but there is no reason why the Norns should have an easy weave of it and I will postpone the final shearing of those three sisters yet.'

We watched him stride off and no one spoke. It was the first time he had come close to admitting his doom and it was unnerving, so that you didn't want to be close to it. We broke apart and went to our tasks.

I was concerned about Hild. I could hardly leash her to me and so would have to stand with her to make sure she didn't take it into her head to run off. That meant I couldn't

167

stand in the shieldwall and, apart from the fact that every blade was needed, it would have been the first shieldwall ever for me. Mailed, I would have been in the front rank, the place of honour – though those in it called themselves the Lost. Except, I thought moodily, I would miss it, guarding this girl.

'You look like a sulky boy,' she said brightly. 'All you need is to scuff the ground with a toe.'

Guiltily, I shot her a look, then chuckled at how right she was. Some front-rank warrior me. She sat, primly adjusting the ruins of my cloak. I saw she wore a pair of men's breeks, too, last seen in Valknut's pack. Saw, too, that she was calm, alert, completely unlike the rolling-eyed maniac of before.

Almost too calm, in fact. As she turned and smiled a lavish smile, my heart turned and my stomach, too, because there was something unnatural about it.

'When the time comes,' she said, 'we will run that way.' And she pointed left, to where the ground dipped into brush.

I had no time to query it, for the horn-blast was on us. Bagnose and Steinthor flitted out to the wings of the forming line and the shieldwall went up with a deep roar and slam as shields locked. The banner unfurled with a snap and, craning, I saw figures filtering out of the mist, forming into a line. A banner flew there, too, and the shock of seeing another Raven Banner was like cold water. When all was said and done, we were fighting our own.

A figure came forward from them, hands raised to show they were empty. He wore a splendid gilded helmet and a flaming red cloak over his long mail hauberk. When he got closer, he peeled the helmet off, to reveal a shock of tawny hair and beard and bright, ice-blue eyes above a wide smile. Starkad.

'Einar,' he called. 'Your ship is ash; your men are too few. All you need do is hand over the monk and what you found in this place and you can go where you will.'

Einar nodded, as if considering the offer. 'What you say is true enough. Yet you talk, which means you are not sure of winning, even with all your men. No doubt you have been told of the Oathsworn and you are right to be afraid. Is Brondolf Lambisson with you? Let him tell you of encountering the Oathsworn, as he did in his own hov. Better still, he could show you his keks and the shit on them.'

There was grim laughter at this and a flurry from the ranks behind Starkad, which broke to let Brondolf Lambisson through. Dressed in mail and with a fine helmet and shield, his red-faced anger was plain, but his words didn't carry far enough for the Oathsworn to hear, so they jeered at him, clashing sword and shield until he gave up.

'It seems you are determined to visit your own doom on those around you,' Starkad countered, which was cunning and would have flustered a lesser man. But Einar had courage and wit enough, even with the crows practically pecking out his eyeballs.

'Ah . . . you have been speaking with Ulf-Agar, I am thinking,' he said, craning as if to see round Starkad. 'Is that nithing here?'

Reluctantly, a figure stepped out, mailed and well armed, but limping slightly. He said nothing, but glared and pointed at Einar with his sword.

Einar shook his head sorrowfully.

> 'Cattle die and kinsmen die,
> Yourself will soon die,
> Only fair fame never fades . . .'

His voice rang out the old lines and even I saw Ulf-Agar jerk with shame and anger. Einar, in a voice of ice, added, 'Fair fame has eluded you, Ulf-Agar, for all you sought it. Fame – yes. Men will remember you as an oath-breaker and

169

that you do not stand straight and tall next to the likes of Orm, the White-bear Slayer.'

And it was my turn to jerk with shame, when the Oathsworn cheered and banged their swords on their shields, yelling my name.

Starkad recovered well, though, and his pleasant smile never slipped. 'Well, it seems a fight is certain on this bare hill,' he called out, loud enough for all to hear. 'But why waste good lives? Let's you and I end it, Einar the Black. If I win, your men are free to go or join with me. If you win, likewise.'

Einar shrugged, knowing he could not refuse it with honour. 'When,' he said, stressing the word, 'I win, your men will just go. I want no part of Bluetooth's hounds. Except for Ulf. I want him.'

'Agreed,' said Starkad and I saw Ulf-Agar's face pale and his mouth move, but he had no say in it, being a nithing even in the eyes of those at his back.

So Starkad came up, though the lines held their places. He shed his cloak, hauled out a beautifully hilted sword, settled his fresh, clean shield, which was decorated with a swirling design, and then tapped the edge twice, lightly, with his sword.

Einar, having dropped his cloak, hauled out his own weapon and unslung a pocked and scored shield. The pair of them circled in a wary half-crouch.

There was a flurry, a tanging of metal and they parted. Einar whirlwinded steel, hacking lumps off that fine, new shield; Starkad backed up, dropped, swung at Einar's legs and he only just leaped back in time.

It went like that until both men were breathing heavily and it was clear that Starkad was stronger and better. His shield was almost wrecked though and I still had hopes – until, in a move all later agreed was as fine a trick as they'd seen, Starkad hooked the fat pommel of his sword inside Einar's shield, wrenched it sideways and cut downwards, in one smooth movement.

Einar was no fool and leaped back, but the blade slashed the shield loops and he had to throw the ruin away. Blood sprayed from his slashed hand as he did so. Starkad's grin was wolf-yellow.

He closed; Einar backed off, backed off further, then suddenly hurled forward, catching inside Starkad's sword with his own and forcing it wide, launched himself on to Starkad's shield. His helmeted head tipped back, came forward like a siege ram and would have splattered Starkad's nose if it hadn't been for the iron guard.

Stunned, Starkad fell backwards. I remembered falling on the hard edge of the forge with the side of my head and knew how Starkad was feeling. Bright lights and sickness: he was doomed.

But he rolled and Einar's cut sliced his leg open from knee to boot top, so that he roared with the pain of it. Lashing with his legs, he tangled Einar, who fell. They flailed wildly at each other and missed.

It was then that the ranks of his men split apart, shouting.

At first we thought they had treacherously decided to run at us. Then we saw the figures, the hurled javelins. They wore no helmets, had no armour, but they had fistfuls of throwing spears and long knives and there were lots of them, spilling out from the thinning mist, right into the back of Starkad's men. The villagers from Koksalmi had woken up.

Einar and Starkad broke apart, panting, staring at each other. Starkad, cursing, limped sideways, away from him, pointing his sword. The blood squeezed out of his boot toes when he moved.

'Later,' he gasped.

Einar saw what was happening, got to his feet, swirled up his cloak and issued swift orders. The Oathsworn started to melt backwards, away from the fight, leaving Starkad to deal

171

with it and taking this chance. It occurred to me, as I took Hild by the arm, that Einar was right – he still had some gods on his side and the Norns' wyrd wasn't so easily woven for him after all.

'This way,' Hild said, almost cheerfully, and I remembered, chilled, her earlier quiet statement.

She was right, too – the villagers had sent men to the flank. They spilled out to my left and she led us to the right, into the brush. I stopped, though, as Skapti lumbered up, dragging Martin on his leash.

Two villagers hurled javelins at the big man. I saw him hit. I couldn't believe it, but he was hit. The javelin went into the back of his neck and came out of his mouth and he stopped and fumbled, then tried to feel round to grab it and haul it out, but couldn't. Black blood gushed out and he looked at me with a stare of pure astonishment and crashed down like the end of the world.

I wanted to dash to him, but Hild held me back and pulled and pulled. I saw Martin jerk the end of the leash from Skapti's twitching hand. Our eyes met, a single locked, mutual glare, and then he scuttled off.

I left, numbed, stumbling after Hild down the slope. Skapti. Gone.

We came out on to the flat in a scrabble of scree and panic, panting and gasping. Hild stumbled too far and slipped over the bank of the river into the water with a sharp scream and a splash.

Frantic, I hurled myself at the edge, saw her floundering in the shallows and more concerned with hanging on to that gods-cursed spear-shaft than getting out. I grabbed her hair and yanked, angry and afraid, and hauled her out.

'You were always the one for humping,' said a voice, vicious as a bite.

Ulf-Agar stepped from the bushes. He had lost his helmet and his shield, but was still mailed and had a long and wicked sword. 'Now it seems you have to drag a corpse out and fuck that,' he added. He moved towards me, dragging his leg where it had been sword cut in the warehouse fight in Birka.

I remembered him, sweat gleaming in the musty twilight, swinging that cooling red branding iron – the one that had left the wet, slow-healing weals all over his body – as Starkad's men closed in.

I remembered him guarding my back as I foolishly bounced off the door I could have opened easily if I had thought more about it. I heard him yelling at me to do it, blood spraying from his smashed mouth. Of all the injuries, that was the worst, especially for the likes of him – teeth were more precious than silver for, without them, you sucked gruel where real men chewed meat and bread. And that, too, was my fault, in Ulf's head.

That same mouth was twisted on a face triumphant with hate and I knew he could not be brought to the same memories of then, that reminding him of how I had freed him would simply fuel the fire that ate him. I cursed the gift Einar prized so much: by stepping back in my head I could see that Ulf wanted to be me and could not. So he would destroy me instead.

Yet the hate made him stupid and blind. If he had been sensible he would have said nothing, simply struck. Having said something, he would have stayed beyond sword reach, knowing his limp slowed him. He would also have realised that I had learned something from the first time he had reckoned me no more than an untrained idiot boy who had, unaccountably, come into all Ulf-Agar's luck in a Loki trick.

But he did have a brain after all. And when I whirled and drew my sword and swung it in a scything arc, all in one swift, practised movement, I released it from the cage of his head.

The edge took a chunk out of the right side of his skull, clean as taking a slice out of a boiled egg. He never even had time for a look of astonishment. And what came out of his opened head was a strange spray of grey pasty stuff, tinged with watery blood and yellow gleet.

I left him still alive, it seemed, for his mouth was working and his limbs were twitching and I could have sworn he saw me drag the bedraggled Hild away, leaving him to the hunting packs of villagers. Even in death, I thought viciously, he'll be shunned. His head's too damaged even to warrant being stuck on a pole round that shrine. Truly, when the gods set their faces against you, you are fucked.

I came across Pinleg, loping quietly ahead. I balked at joining him, not knowing his mood, but he was calm, even cheerful. I told him of Ulf-Agar and he spat.

'Good. And you got the woman. Einar will be pleased. I know where he plans to gather, so let's move.'

We scuttled swiftly along, then stopped to get our bearings. I wiped the sweat from my face and looked at Pinleg. 'I saw Skapti hit.'

'I know,' he growled, almost annoyed. 'Silly big arse.'

'He's dead,' I urged. 'For sure.'

'Of course,' said Pinleg, lumbering off. 'No one could have lived with a sharp stick poking out of his gob.'

'But he's dead,' I wailed and he stopped, whirled and grabbed my tunic. I froze, waiting for the spittle and the steel. Instead, he stared at me nose to nose, his breath rank with fish.

'I know,' he said softly, then let me go and patted my arm. 'I know.'

We met Valknut and Ketil Crow and Einar. The Oathsworn drifted up in ones and threes, panting, sweated, wearing or carrying all they had – everything else had been left behind. There were too many missing – but I spotted, with a leap of the heart that surprised me, my father trotting up, grey-faced and with fresh blood soaking through the sleeve of his tunic.

I went to him and he nodded and grinned at seeing me,

but shook his head when I moved to check the blood-soaked bindings.

'I leak like a sprung tub,' he admitted cheerfully, 'but I am not sunk yet, boy.'

Like the others, he met the news of Skapti's death and the monk's loss with cold silence, but Ulf-Agar's death brought a satisfied grunt.

'Well, boy,' my father said admiringly. 'You are surprising even me, who watched you grow for the first five years of your life and saw what a wolf-pup you were then.'

This was new and I wanted to know more, but the others were growling their own appreciations and a few hands thumped my back. I half expected to hear that familiar, deep 'hoom' from somewhere, but it was gone for ever.

'Now we run, hard,' Einar said, once we had splashed across the river and into the trees. 'We beat what's left of Starkad's men back to their own ship and take it. That's the only way off this gods-cursed shore.'

It was bitter, that journey, for the land seemed to want to scream out its beauty and the new life of spring while we grimmed our way through it, bleak with the loss of Skapti and the others, on towards an uncertain fate.

We went through belts of woodland, great oaks and ash burgeoning with fresh bud, and across swathes of fresh green, studded with small blue and pale yellow flowers. Thorn trees drooped with early blossom and every breath of wind scattered sprays of white, while the birds blasted their throats out.

And, black as a lowered brow, the Oathsworn moved swiftly, a pack of dark wolves that had no joy in any of it.

So fast did we move that we were brought to the little sheltered bay by my father and his uncanny knack just as the sky velveted to dark and the first stars frosted.

Einar halted the grey-faced, panting pack of us – the last

few miles had seen more frequent halts, mainly because Hild was exhausted. But I had seen Pinleg grateful for it, while my father and Ogmund Wryneck and a few others sank down with relief, with hardly the strength to suck up their drool.

Bagnose and Steinthor went wearily out at Einar's command, while the rest of us hunched up in a hollow, hearing the wind hiss over the tufted grass that led to the beach and out to the sea. I tasted the salt of it on my lips. Strange how we had longed for the feel and smell of land when afloat and now longed for the touch of ship and spray now that we were ashore.

No one spoke much, save for Einar, muttering with Ketil Crow and Illugi and my father. I couldn't hear much of it, but I guessed some: my father would be there to tell Einar whether a ship could be worked out of the bay, whether wind and tide were favourable and, if not, when they would be.

Ketil Crow would have counted heads and knew how many of the Oathsworn were left – I reasoned about forty, no more, for we had left some on that forge mountain and whether dead or scattered didn't matter. They were gone from us, like Skapti.

After a while, as a moon slid up, scudded with cloud, Bagnose came back and had words with Einar, who then called us all round him in that shadowed hollow.

'Steinthor is watching Starkad's *drakkar*. It seems all his men are ashore, with a nice fire and ale. They have posted two sentries only.' He grinned, yellow-fanged in the dark. 'That's the best of it. The rest is that there are about sixty of them and they are well armed. But they are out of mail and have no thought of danger. So we form up and move, now. Move fast and hard, break them and go for the *drakkar*. If we can scatter them and board, we can get away, for the wind and tide are right for it.'

And, of course, I was given Hild as my task. I was becoming

176

tired of it, to be truthful, for she unnerved me now with her quiet, knowing looks and calm, black-eyed smiles.

So the Oathsworn scrambled wearily out of the hollow, formed into a loose line and loped off in a rough boar snout. I was in the middle, with Valknut and the Raven Banner unfurled and moving steadily beside me.

We came up over the tufted grass and on towards where Steinthor hid and I saw the red flower of the fire and the great expanse of blackness that was the sea behind it. There was a faint lantern swinging there, almost certainly on the prow of the boat, which swung on the end of a stout rope and an iron anchor in the shallows.

When Steinthor saw us, Einar waved for him to form up. He paused, stretched the bow and, as we came up, an arrow whirred into what seemed darkness to me. Moments later, though, I almost stumbled over the corpse of one of the sentries. Half-turned, I saw Pinleg stop, head bowed. He spotted my worried look and waved. 'Go on, Rurik's son. I will catch you up and race you to the beach.'

And he grinned, so I did as he said. It was the last he ever spoke to me.

When I joined the others, they were pausing, for no longer than a single breath, a mere shortening of stride, to let the line form. Then, at the moment the men by the fire all saw us, looming out of the darkness like a frowned eyebrow, Einar yelled, 'Boar snout.' He hurled himself at the apex of the rough triangle, but he was no Skapti and it came in far too fast and loose.

There was no firm shieldwall to hit, though. We ploughed, roaring, through men who were already scattering in all directions, jogged past the fire, hacking sideways at anything that came too close and, when we hit the water, splintered apart and kept going for the ship. I saw Gunnar Raudi grab a man and heave him up, then leap, miss and splash back down into the water.

I was knee-deep and thrashing through it, blinded by spray, hauling Hild along, trying to keep both of us upright while that damned spear-shaft she would not let go of took both her hands and left me to support us both. Men sprang for the sides and the anchor rope, swarmed up . . . we were going to do it.

I gained the side and hauled up and over, then reached down for Hild, while others were wildly dragging themselves, panting and dripping, over the side of the massive ship. My father was screaming at men to get to the oars, for others to get the sail-spar hauled up off the rests.

And I saw the men on the shore forming, swiftly, expertly. They had no armour, only some had helmets, but all had a shield and a sword or an axe or a spear. They were veterans, were Starkad's men and not about to be shamed by the loss of their ship without a fight for it.

The shieldwall formed with a slap and a roar and then they were jogging forward and I knew, with a sick lurch that made me so frantic I almost tore Hild's arm out of her socket getting her aboard, that they would be on us before we gained enough distance.

Then, suddenly, something broke from the shadowed shallows to our right. There was a blood-chilling shriek, a burst of spray and a blur of movement. Like a troll on wheels.

Pinleg came in a shambling run of screaming, whirling death. They didn't know who it was, but they knew what it was and the shieldwall almost fractured there and then. When Pinleg hurled on it, slashing, biting, screeching, it did, like a still pool hit by a stone.

'Haul away, fuck your mothers!' roared my father and the oarsmen, panting, soaked, white with fatigue and riven with panicked frenzy, dug and pulled, dug and pulled.

The sail clattered up, the wind filled it and the great serpent *drakkar* slid away into the night, away from where the ends of the shieldwall closed, from where swords rose and fell and the bundle of men, like a pack of snarling dogs, stumbled this way and that over the beach, through the fire, hacking and slashing.

One or two tried to break off and run at us, but Bagnose and Steinthor fired at them and, though their strings were soaked and the arrows went wild or short, it made Starkad's men think about it.

We slid into the dark, further and further, faster and faster, until only the red flower was left to mark the place.

That and the shrieking of Pinleg, so that we never heard him die. It was generally agreed that if we didn't hear it, it probably never happened and that he is fighting still, on that beach.

The rowers gave up quickly, exhausted. They barely had the strength left to haul the oars inboard and stow them; one or two even fell down where they were and slept. Certainly everyone collapsed into some sort of deathlike sleep, even Einar.

But Ketil Crow and Illugi and Valgard stayed awake in shifts, manning the steering oar of the huge *drakkar* and plotting a rough course by the stars until my father was more himself and could turn his talent to it.

And I saw it all, dull-eyed and slumped in some strange almost-sleep, hearing the shrieking of Pinleg, seeing the astonished look on Skapti's face, made strange by the great, bloody point sticking straight out of his mouth.

By dawn, we were alone on a gently heaving swell, hissing over it steadily, the grey light brightening into a cold, crisp, clear day. One by one the Oathsworn grunted stiffly into this new day, as if astonished they were there at all.

And then we saw what we had got.

It was perfect, from the graceful swan-necked, lavishly carved bow and stern, down the grey-painted strakes of the hull, up to the huge belly of the sail, sewn in strips of three

179

colours – red, white and green – so that the ship looked like some bright banner, sluicing along the swells, hissing through their breaking tops like a blade.

There was carving everywhere, even cut in fluted chevrons on the oarblades, which added to their bite and recovery, I was told. Panels, carved and painted, shielded the steersman from the weather and the steering oar was carved in whorls, to aid the grip. And the weathervane was gold – gilded, Rurik corrected, but no one listened. It was gold, could only be gold, in this marvellous ship.

There was more: all the crew had left their sea-chests on board. There were clothes and jewellery and money and armour and weapons. There were rings and eating knives and cloaks with fur collars, for this was Bluetooth's *dreng* – his chosen men – and nothing was too good for them.

There was another huge bolt of cloth, too small for a sail, but in the same striped colours, which my father revealed was for use as a tent when anchored.

There were barrels of stockfish, salted mutton and water. There was even a specially built firepit in the centre of the tiny cargo space, with solid firebricks and a slatted iron grill, so that you could have hot meals and never need to stop or slow down.

The only things missing were the proper carved prowheads, which were probably still back on the shore, removed as was custom.

'First chance we get, lads,' Einar promised as the booty was divided up, 'we will have new elk heads made. For no matter what this ship was, it is the *Fjord Elk* now.'

They all cheered and, after everything had been found and argued over – even though there was three times as much as any one of the remaining Oathsworn could have used – Illugi Godi supervised the boiling up of mutton on the marvellous firepit and everyone ate a hot meal and agreed it the best they had ever tasted on this most marvellous of ships, which carried some 140 and could be sailed by three.

'Though the gods put fire in your arses if we hit a flat calm and you have to row her,' Valgard growled when he heard this. Which thought made everyone quieter, for it was a heavy beast of a boat to be rowing crew-light.

'Don't worry, there will be others joining the Oathsworn soon enough,' Einar told them and again they cheered. And he had, it must be said, brought them from the wolf's jaws to a rich prize, so that, like me, they almost forgot that his doom had brought it on them and that men had died.

But even so, the four remaining Christ-followers now reverted to Thor's hammer and were shamefaced that they had ever considered the White Christ, for it was clear to all that some gods still favoured Einar and the Norns were having to unravel some of what they were trying to weave for him.

Still, there were many, like me, who sat pensively, wondering just what we had won from Koksalmi. A useless old spear and a madwoman raving about a treasure hoard only she could find for us. And this marvellous ship and its riches.

We had lost much to weigh against that: Martin the monk had escaped, while Skapti and Pinleg and more besides were dead.

Worse than that, I was thinking, there is only so long you can fend off your wyrd when it is laid on you.

NINE

We stood with heads bowed on the headland, where the wind hissed in from the sea, bringing the smell of salt and wrack and watched as the sweating men Illugi had hired shifted the man-sized stone into position, heaving on ropes to pull it upright.

It shunked softly into the pit dug for it, where lay spearheads and rings and hacksilver, all given by the Oathsworn as an offering to Pinleg and Skapti and the others we had left behind.

Illugi, who had overseen the purchase and sacrifice of three fine rams – one for Pinleg, one for Skapti, one for all the rest – turned to where I stood, with Hild, Gunnar Raudi and a few others. And Pinleg's woman, Olga, a big, blonde Slav with fat arms and the faint hint of a moustache.

She was not beautiful – standing beside the pale, fey Hild she looked as solid as a heifer and as handsome – but she had a strong face and her chin was set, even if her eyes were damp. Her hands, with their chafed-red knuckles, gathered the heads of two tawny-haired children into the warm comfort of her apron. A boy and a girl, they were clearly bewildered by all this and their mother's obvious grief.

'What would you have on it?' Illugi Godi asked as the mason stood by, head cocked attentively.

'His name,' she said, tilting her chin defiantly. 'Knut Vigdisson. And those of his children, Ingrid and Thorfinn.'

Knut Vigdisson. It came as a shock to realise Pinleg had had a name, like any other man. And named after his mother, too. A good Norse name, like those of his children, though his wife was a Slav here in Aldeigjuborg, that great cauldron of peoples.

Knut Vigdisson. Pinleg was a stranger to me with that name. Still, he had one – Skapti didn't even have that, only the one the Oathsworn had given him. Halftroll.

Illugi Godi nodded and then asked, politely: 'May we add something on our own behalf?'

That was for form. If it was agreed, the Oathsworn would pay for the stone, which would stand on this spot and shout Pinleg's and Skapti's fame in the ribbon of runes waiting to be cut, and commemorate the others lost with them.

We had agreed it earlier with the carver. Their names and Pinleg's children's names would be added to the simple testament that they were the Oathsworn of Einar the Black, who raised this stone in their honour and then, simply: '*KrikiaR – iaursaliR – islat – Serklat*'. Greece, Jerusalem, Iceland, Serkland.

Others wanted something like 'They gave the eagles food' or something even more dramatic and never mind the expense, but Illugi held to what had been agreed earlier at a meeting of everyone, Einar included. I had not realised, until then, how far-fared the original Oathsworn band had been, or how long they had been on the whale road.

Hild said, as we turned away from the windswept headland: 'You lost friends over this matter. I am sorry for it.'

Surprised – she had not volunteered so much speech since the forge mountain, weeks before – I blinked and tried to think of some polite reply, but failed. So I said what I thought, which Illugi Godi always said was best. Experience, even then, with so few years on me, had taught the opposite.

'I was wondering if Skapti had anyone to mourn for him besides the few of us,' I said. 'If he had a name other than Halftroll, I never heard it uttered.'

She nodded, hugging – as always – the ruined Roman spear-shaft to her. 'It is hard to lose friends,' she agreed, sadly.

I took a slight breath, formed up and charged. 'You would know. You have lost your mother and all your friends. You can never return to the village you came from. Not that you would wish to, I suppose, considering what they had planned.'

There was a pause and I wondered if I had gone too far, too soon, but she nodded, blank-faced. We walked on down towards the road that led back to the smoke-stained wooden sprawl of the town.

Behind, I could hear Gunnar Raudi and the others raucously toasting the stone, the carver, the helpers and the dead as was only right. Ahead, Olga walked, solid and ponderous, beside the tall, spare figure of Illugi, nodding as he spoke. On either side, the tawny-haired boy and girl, un-affected by the death of a father they had barely known, scampered and laughed in the spring sun like new lambs.

'At my first bleed,' Hild said suddenly, 'my mother told me a secret that her mother told her. Then she gave me to the tanner's wife. Not long afterwards, she offered herself to the forge mountain, as my grandmother had done, for it was expected.

'They were not bad people in Koksalmi, but they believed in the power of the smiths. The village had been chosen, long before, to be the place where something great would happen, to ensure that the Old Gods survived for ever.'

'The Vanir, you mean?'

'Older still.' She fell silent and I saw her knuckles whiten on the spear-shaft, so I tried to comfort her.

184

'Still, you are safe now. You have faced the curse of the forge and are better for it.'

'Better?'

Confused, I waved a wild hand. 'When first we met you were . . . sick. Now you seem well again. Calmer. I am glad of it.'

We walked on in silence for a moment, then she turned and laid one hand on my arm. 'Do you like me, Orm?'

Flustered, I felt my face flame. I started to stammer and saw the strangest thing in her eyes. Sadness. I stopped, unable to say anything.

She leaned closer to me. I felt the butterfly wing of a kiss on my cheek and then she pulled back. 'You have been kind. But keep clear. Do not try to . . . love me. Or you will die.'

Her gaze was as sharp as the spear that had once graced the Roman shaft she held fiercely in both hands and, for a moment, I wondered if she would try to stick me with the nub end that was left. Then she whirled and dashed along the road in a flail of skirts. As she passed Illugi Godi and Olga, they looked back at me, both united in the surety that I had offended her in some way.

Not long after, as we came to the sea gate of the town, Olga gathered the purse Illugi gave her – Pinleg's share – and her children and went off. Illugi Godi came to me and jerked his head at where the faint roars drifted; Bagnose was composing verses in a good skald saga for the dead of the forge mountain. 'Should you not be there?'

'I was tasked with looking after Hild,' I replied moodily.

He smiled. 'It seems our captive princess does not wish to be looked after,' he replied. 'What did you do?'

'Nothing,' I answered sharply, then sighed. 'I don't understand women. Well, not this one, anyway. She seems to like me – then looked as if she'd stick me with that spear.'

'She is a strange one,' agreed Illugi, 'even allowing for the wyrd of her life so far.'

185

'Strange, too,' I mused, 'the way she babbled like a child when first we met. I could understand one word in five, if that – and only because it was like the Finn tongue, but different. She has a secret told to her by her mother and, it seems, told mother to daughter back into the mists. But she has no daughter herself and was so badly handled by Vigfus that it has addled her. She is more to be feared than ever, I am thinking.'

'Yes,' mused Illugi. 'And the way she clutches the spear-shaft, like a child with a doll.'

We passed into the town proper, on to the wooden walk-ways between herds of huddled houses.

'Martin the monk told me he found the girl through the writings of that Otmund,' he went on, 'the one who was made a saint and whose church we raided. He wrote about the villagers and their beliefs and managed to convert some of them.'

In which case he was a braver man than I, for I would not have argued with any of the people of Koksalmi. Not without an army at my back.

Illugi chuckled, but it seemed bitter. 'Brave or stupid,' he said thoughtfully. 'Those unconverted ran him and his followers off. I believe then that those who had stuck to the old gods took this god stone away, for they knew others like Otmund would come and seduce more villagers to their lies. The White Christ is winning.'

I looked sharply at him and saw his worried face. Then it cleared and he smiled.

'But Martin believed that the girl would lead him to the Great Hoard somehow, being linked to the sword the smiths made for Attila. The stone, he reasoned, was not necessary.'

'Martin is a rat,' I spat, 'and I wouldn't trust him to tell me a dog's hind leg was crooked. Anyway, Atil's hoard is a tale for children.'

'No,' answered Illugi. 'That part is true enough. When Atil

was dead, never having been beaten in battle – because, it was said, of his fabulous sword – his men carried him into the steppe and howed him up in a burial mound made from all the silver taken from those he had conquered. They say it was so tall, snow formed on the top.'

There was silence while we both tried to wrap our heads round that monstrous idea of riches, but it was too much and made my head hurt. It all made my head hurt and I said so.

'True,' Illugi agreed, 'That Christ priest, Martin, seems to be able to swallow it all down, though, but you are right about him being untrustworthy. He thought to cross Lambisson with a false trail using the god stone. Perhaps he wants the treasure for himself.'

I shook my head. Treasure of that sort did not interest Martin, that much I knew. The Spear of Destiny, as he called it: that was what Martin wanted. With that he would become a high priest in his religion, and convert even more to the Christ cause.

Illugi frowned when I spilled this out, but he nodded. 'Aye, you have the right of it, I am thinking. He will be back after that shaft, so we must keep a close watch on it.'

'On Hild,' I spat, bitterly, 'for she will not relinquish it without a struggle. It is some sort of talisman to her now.'

'Perhaps so,' Illugi mused, then frowned. 'It is possible there is some Christ magic in it, a subtle, seidr sort of magic that will turn her to the Christ side. Still, a risk we must take if we are to keep her content, for she will not lead us to the hoard if she thinks we are being false with her.'

This sucked my breath away, said so matter-of-factly. Lead us to the hoard? She could no more lead us to a hoard of silver than I could kiss my own arse and I said so.

Illugi's eyebrows went up. 'Martin seemed certain of it,' he answered.

'Martin, we agreed, was a Loki-cunning, crook-tongued,

sleekit-as-a-fox horse turd who could not be trusted to tell you a raven was black,' I roared back at him, hardly able to countenance that he believed this.

'He believed his Christ charm, the spear, was in the forge and he was right about that,' Illugi answered mildly. 'Have you noticed anything about that, young Orm?'

The wind having been sucked out from my sails, I floundered. 'Noticed what?'

'The spear-shaft that Hild will not relinquish. The wood is blackened; the rivets are rusted.'

'It is old – if Martin is to be believed,' I replied pointedly and he looked steadily at me.

'Older than anything we have seen,' he answered. 'Yet, in the forge, on its ledge, under the runes . . .'

I felt a shock that prickled my body. He was right. I recalled it then, gleaming polished wood, the little nub end and rivets like new. I shook my head, as to drive the memory away. 'A sea journey. The salt . . .'

'Perhaps – but so quickly?' Illugi mused. 'And what kept it gleaming new all those years on that ledge?'

'I . . . don't know,' I confessed. 'What?'

He shook his head, stroked his beard. 'I don't know either. The runes maybe – that was a powerful spell. Perhaps it ages because the blood of this Christ of theirs, who hung on the cross-tree and was stabbed with it, if you believe such a thing, has been removed with the metal shaft they used to forge the sword. Perhaps both.

'But it ages, Orm, it changes – and there is more. Like a . . . talisman . . . it helps Hild find her way to where the sword lies.'

I can see the enlightened curl their lip at this. Pagan stuff for skalds, for saga tales. The priests of the White Christ have banished this darkness from our minds, they claim proudly. Yet now we have the Devil and his minions. We no longer have Odin, who hung on the sacred tree with a spear wound.

188

Instead, we have Christ, who hung on a cross with a spear wound.

On the beaches at Bjornshafen, I had conjured up trolls and dragons for me and my small warriors to fight with wooden swords. We knew they were all around us, unseen, waiting for the unwary, and just hoped they were far away from the affairs of men at that moment.

And runes were magical, everyone knew. I had heard of runed helmets that brought an enemy to their knees and mail that could not be pierced – though I had never come across any. But I was young and better men said it was so.

Yet, here was this, the world of Other, of gods and frost giants, black dwarves and trolls and magic runes, clutched to the bosom of a young girl under the spring sun of a strange, exotic town. Perhaps, after all, she had the way to a hoard of silver . . .

We had gasped our way north and east, sliding into the River Neva and then into the mouth of the Volkhov, heaving and panting at the oars, far too few to row this new *Elk* unless we had the flow of the tide and no wind in our face.

Cursing, with the breeze at our back – and unable to hoist sail, since that would have sped us too fast to stop in a river of shallows and currents we did not know – we laboriously brought the new *Elk* to final rest in the harbour of Aldeigjuborg.

So weary were we, in fact, that we did not notice the glances at first. In a harbour crowded with *hafskips* and *knarrer*, the great, beautiful *drakkar* stood out like a gold ring in the gutter and the whole harbour had stopped to look at us.

I raised my head to swallow welcome water and was captured by the sheer strangeness of it all. Birka had been a port of foreigners, I had thought, but this place, this Ladoga as the Slavs call it, was a different world entirely.

There were throngs of people here, all of them bright and dazzling in some way. Slovenes, Vods, Ests, Balts, Krivichi, big Svears with loud voices and sober clothes, even bigger Dregovichi and Poljanes from Kiev, wearing dazzling colours and fat trousers like Skapti, carrying long curved swords with no crosspieces on their carved wooden hilts.

There were shaved heads, ones with thick braids over one or both ears, or one at the back, or combinations of all of them. There were flat, clean-shaven faces, ones with moustaches which trailed off the end of the chin in wisps, full beards, braided beards, wild hair, carefully manicured locks, ones braided with beads and silver rings.

And there were goods: honey in pots, seal and deer hides, the furs of beaver and fox and great barrels of fine grinding stones, feather pillows and salt in sacks. There was even a sledge, big as a cart, waiting on the jetty to be taken somewhere.

And everyone stopped what they were doing to look at the magnificent jarl ship, crewed by a third of what it should be, by hard men with too much new finery and too many weapons to have come by it all honestly.

Einar stroked his stubble thoughtfully and announced: 'We sleep on board tonight.'

Which was only sensible, though everyone grumbled. They had survived death, rowed until the calluses split and wanted dry land, hot food, ale and women. But Einar had only to point out the sea-chests and what they would lose if the ship was raided in the dark and they unpacked the fancy awning tent and slung it up.

That night, Einar allowed half to go and get drunk, on pain they drank through their nose, as the saying goes – answered no questions and gave no drunken boasts. The next night, it was the turn of the other half and so it went on.

We never moved from that traders' fair awning of a tent;

we grew to like sleeping aboard and going about our business in shifts. When we had paid our harbouring dues to the town official and his well-armed bodyguard and showed no aggression and, more to the point, started spending, the town relaxed.

Hild and I went ashore once, me following her like a faithful retainer, armed – there were no restrictions here, though that was changing – with sword. As the days progressed, I wore finer and finer clothing.

I bought new boots, new breeks – blue, striped with silver wire and fat, like Skapti had worn – a fine dark-blue tunic, a green cloak with a rich, red-enamelled pin, a new wooden sheath lined in greased sheepskin for Bjarni's old sword.

I swaggered in Hild's wake, knowing that everyone who saw me knew I was off the *Fjord Elk*, aware of them nudging each other and saying, 'Go and look at her, she is the finest ship afloat and her crew are warriors all, even the young one there.'

And Hild bought clothing, too, to replace the tattered remnants of her own, so that, next day, we wandered the merchants' booths with her in a new dress and sparkling apron, hair unbound. I bought her a braided silver fillet for her brow, which she accepted and wore without protest, but without seeming enjoyment either.

But she looked just like a fine princess, with a fine prince by her side. We ate meat on wooden skewers and drank honey mead and I enjoyed that day. I remembered it afterwards, when all was darker. Even she seemed to enjoy it, though it was hard to tell – and she never took more than one hand off that spear-shaft, not once.

It ended, I remember, with the first of the recruits climbing the shoreplank to the deck of the *Elk*, where Einar waited. Gunnar Raudi and Ketil Crow and others had been out spreading the word everywhere that the fine ship and its hard crew were looking for good men not afraid to swear a *varjazi* oath to each other and live with the consequences of that.

When we got back to the ship, we had to push through a throng of them, all out for a piece of the luck that had gained Einar's crew riches and a fine ship. I wanted to shout out the truth to them, but thought better of it.

'Six skills I know,' I heard one say. 'I play 'tafl and scarcely make a mistake reading runes now. I can row and ski and shoot and use both spear and sword.'

And they were all variations of that. Those who passed Einar's scrutiny – I never knew what he saw, one way or the other – were tallied up by Illugi and told of the oath they would swear, in a ceremony to be arranged when we had all the men we needed.

When Einar was unsure, he would turn to Ketil Crow and raise an eyebrow and that man would wave a languid hand and ask something like: 'You are coming to a hall for the first time, walking up to it uninvited as a guest, but certain of hospitality nonetheless. What are you looking for?'

Those who answered that they were making sure where the doors were, in case they had to get out in a hurry, were hired. Those who stammered, or looked lost, or grinned and said 'the women' were sent away.

On the day of the stone-raising we had tallied up the last of them – the most Oathsworn that had been, according to Valknut. One hundred and twenty of us, almost the full complement of a *drakkar*, and Einar had thought carefully about what came next.

He had bought two fighting stallions, would match them as was the custom, then sacrifice the winner to Odin. On that altar of ground the Oathsworn – all of us – would swear the oath that bound us together once more. Even Einar.

It had been Illugi Godi's idea and, judging by the way luck had been running, Einar was probably right to think there was a chance it would work. He was still working his way to Atil's hidden hoard, sending Illugi to try to flush out any references to it, like ducks from a marsh, while giving nothing away himself.

I did not put my thought – that there was no stone raised to Eyvind anywhere – to either him or Illugi. But the wyrd was working on Einar and, on that very day, it caught up with us all.

A few days after the stone-raising, the Oathsworn gathered on the Thingvallir, a patch of grass-tufted ground just outside the walled stockade of Aldeigjuborg.

It stretched along the river southwards and had a large flat altar-like stone embedded in it, near which the town had erected a wooden totem statue to Perun. Since, with his hammer and his big, brave bearded face, he was so like Thor as to be his brother, this satisfied Norse and Slav alike. Even though the Great Prince of Kiev, Sviatoslav, wasn't a Christ-follower like his mother, Olga – who was sainted for it later – he was tolerant enough. After all, he was half Khazar and they, I had been told, had chosen to follow the faith of the wandering Moses-men, which seemed beyond kenning; not only were they the very ones the Christ-men hated for having, they swore, killed their Christ, but the original Jewishmen were in Serkland, many miles away, and everyone else around was a Mussulman. Perhaps that was why Sviatoslav fought them, though some said it had more to do with them dominating the eastern trade routes.

Others, round the fires of a night, said that the Khazars were descendants of the Huns and had been sky-worshippers until not so long since. They had changed religion, these men assured us, because their chiefs, whom they called khans, were elected as being favoured of the gods. If they failed just once, it meant the gods no longer favoured them, so they were killed; naturally they thought it a good idea to change this religion. And they had chosen the god of the Jews because they had Christ-men on one side and Mussulmen on the other and thought it deep-minded cunning not to annoy their neighbours.

193

There were a few dark glances shot at Einar over this and a couple of muttered comments about how the original Khazar religion seemed smarter. If Einar heard it, he made no sign.

But the whole thing was puzzling, that you could put on gods like a cloak on a cold morning. The more I discovered about the gods of the world, the more of a mystery they seemed to be and, for all my long years, I have still not fathomed it.

Once or twice a year, then, the scraggy black cattle and big-fleeced sheep were scattered off this Thingvallir and it was used to settle lawsuits and discuss, in public, town matters.

In reality, the town was run like Birka, by a group of the richest merchants, all elected by each other. Now and then it pleased them to make it appear that everyone had a say.

The status of Aldeigjuborg was awkward. Originally, the Svears had founded it as a trade centre and it was still supposed to be a part of what would become Sweden during my lifetime, when Olaf, the Lap King, united the Svears and Geats.

Since there was no Sweden and no strong ruler of the Svears – at that time, no one even knew who it was, only that there was a fight for it – the town went its own way and the Norse ran it.

But it was full of foreigners – Slavs and Khazar merchants, mainly – and Sviatoslav and his bold sons were stamping their mark, carving out a Rus kingdom from Kiev, in all directions. They controlled Novgorod, which we called Holmgard and, in all but name, held Aldeigjuborg as well and preferred to call it Starya Ladoga.

Einar had made it known that the Oathsworn would be having a ceremony on the Thingvallir, to coincide with the festival of the Dawn Goddess, Ostara, the one the Saxons call Eostre and the Christ-men were calling Easter. Hundreds turned up to help broach the barrels of mead and ale and wolf their way through acres of spit-roasted meats.

Of course, a few grumbled about the fact that there was no Year King to sacrifice, only a good horse, but they were old and remembered the old ways. No one seriously thought these days about burying a Year King in the field and eating bread made from that grain to share the miracle of rebirth.

Nor were the Greek priests, brought from Constantinople by Sviatoslav's mother, a barrier, since they celebrated the festival, too, it appeared. Illugi Godi, of course, was enraged by this.

'See them,' he railed, as the gorgeously accoutred priests paraded down the muddy walkways, swinging censers and droning. 'It's not enough that they should declare the true gods are nothing short of paltry bandits, but they have the nerve to steal our worship for their own.' He paused and hawked loudly, then spat. The nearest priest turned, beard quivering, and saw Illugi, recognised the staff and scowled.

'Turds,' Illugi growled. 'Easter, they call this, as if we can't see they have stolen it.'

'Maybe they already had a festival of their own,' offered my father, scrubbing his head as he did when he was unsure.

'Ha! And a god who hung on a tree and was stabbed with a spear?' Illugi argued, thumping his staff on the walkway.

My father looked at me, shrugged and gave up. I grinned. It was, after all, a celebration of my Name Day. Neither of us could actually remember the exact day, my father being drunk at the time, as he admitted, so I had always celebrated changing age at the festival of Ostara.

And, in this one, I was now sixteen years old and a man.

Not that that mattered to Einar – later, as the mead and meat was being enjoyed, I was standing guard to Hild, watching and sober. Valknut, well drunk, was trying his hand with the flamestick belonging to some fire-dancers. The spear-length, burning at either end, was tricky at the best of times but the lean fire-dancer spun it round his body expertly.

Valknut, in contrast, had twice set his hair on fire trying it and Gunnar Raudi, the second time, was gasping with too much laughter to help him put it out. In the end, he threw the contents of his ale horn over Valknut, who went around for a long time with a strange, lopsided hair-style and the trailing smell of his charred locks.

Moodily, I managed to persuade Hild to see the fighting stallions. They were good, well-chosen beasts – a black and a grey – and, though I'd had no hand in picking them, I was impressed by their quality.

Betting was fierce and loud and, as I watched, a group of half-a-dozen men approached me, led by Valgard and my father.

'Orm, lad, the very man we need,' roared the Trimmer. 'You know fighting horses, your father tells us. Who will win this?'

'We will share our winnings with you, Bear Slayer,' said one of the men with them and that made me blink. He was one of the new ones, a man older than me with a faint white scar marring the red wind-beaten face up beside one eye. I had never spoken to him and, if I had, would have treated him as one would an older head. But here he was, deferring to me, calling me 'Bear Slayer' in a way that let me know he had heard the tale – probably Bagnose's verses – and was impressed by it.

Yet, even as I felt the heady rush of that, I remembered Ulf-Agar, the man who had wanted the taste of this more than life itself; I saw his twisted mouth and his yellow eyes.

My father – as usual – mistook my pause for reluctance and clapped one shoulder. 'Orm, for me, lad.'

'Not the grey,' I said. 'It will not be strong enough.'

My father closed one speculative eye, then whirled on the others and raised his hands in triumph. 'My son has spoken on the day he becomes a man. Now let us make money out of it.'

196

And they went, a few throwing me a backward glance. I saw admiration and envy there in equal measure.

The horse-fight was almost ready to start; people were drifting in from all over the open area – a few of them wet, where they had been trying to walk logs on the river, because no boat big enough could be sailed up it so they could walk the oars.

I placed my own bets with a few of the locals and watched the brave and drunk dart at the fighting stallions with sticks, trying to goad their favourites to anger by sticking them up the arse or in the balls. The horses were tethered on long lines, but well apart from each other and were already all bared teeth and flying hooves, so it was a dangerous business. I saw one man, slowed by drink, hirple away holding his ribs, already purpling into a huge, horseshoe bruise and almost certainly broken.

It was then that I saw Gunnar Raudi, moving urgently through the crowd towards me, almost running and looking back over his shoulder. 'Orm, move,' he yelled as he came up. 'Back to the *Elk* . . . Hurry.'

'What . . . why?' I said, bewildered. He shoved me and I staggered. Then he looked back, grunted and dragged out a seax from under his cloak.

'Too late.'

Four men hurtled out of the crowd, which parted rapidly, since they were armed with long knives and one had an axe as well.

I blinked and stood in front of Hild. Einar had told everyone to come with only eating knives, since drunken quarrels were best settled with feet and fists. But, as Hild's guard, I was mailed and armed with a sword, since Einar took no chances with his key to a fortune. I had cursed it at the time as being hot, uncomfortable and unnecessary, but I hauled my blade out and offered thanks to Thor for it now.

The men paused at that. I swept up the hem of my cloak

197

and looped it round my shield-arm, partly to keep it out of the way, partly as a padded block for a cut. Gunnar Raudi and I waited; the crowd yelled and someone shouted.

The men realised they were surrounded by enemies and that, if they were to get this done, they had to be quick. They were good and fast, no thugs. They came swooping in, three on me, with one to keep Gunnar busy.

I took a cut on the padded cloak that sliced it. Another cut me under that arm, on the ribs, the blow sending me staggering and spraying rings from the mail. I slashed and one fell back with a shriek, sword flying, fingers clutching at a bloody shoulder. My backstroke carved the lower jaw off the axeman, but I was wide open and would have taken a hard cut to my sword-arm that the mail maybe would not have absorbed.

Except that Gunnar Raudi nutted his man on the forehead, springing blood from them both and sending the man reeling. He lashed sideways a second later, the blunted point of his seax catching the man who would have cut my arm. It didn't even break his flesh, but the blow drove the wind from him with a wheezing grunt.

That gave me time to smash the pommel in his face, spraying his teeth and blood. Someone yelled: 'Bear Slayer. Bear Slayer,' and blades flashed, showing how many had ignored Einar's orders.

The men fled, dragging each other away through the crowd, some of whom were not even aware of what had happened. Gunnar, shaking his head to get the blood out of his eyes, winced and clearly wished he hadn't done that. He sank on one knee.

'Is it bad?' I asked and he grinned up at me, blood trickles running either side of his nose.

'I've had worse,' he said, climbing back to his feet as others swept around us, demanding to know what had happened.

'I don't know,' I answered, truthfully enough, too

concerned with the rent in my good new cloak – and worse, the sprung rings in my mail. My side, too, felt like I had been kicked by the screaming horses. 'Ask Gunnar. He had just come to warn me when they burst out after Hild.'

Einar and Ketil Crow came up, with Illugi Godi loping behind, in time to hear Gunnar growl, 'They weren't after Hild. They were after Orm.'

'Me? Why?'

'Good question,' said Einar, looking at Gunnar, who was mopping the blood from the split in his face and accepting, with a grateful grin, a horn of mead. He drank, then passed it to me and wiped his lips with one bloodied hand.

'I saw Martin the monk,' he said. 'He was pointing you out to those ones.'

'Me or Hild,' I argued, but he shook his head.

'You.'

'Martin the monk? Are you sure?' demanded Ketil Crow. Around us, the crowd had gone back to preparing for the horse-fight, save for those of the Oathsworn – the ones who knew of Martin, I saw – who were alert, hands near their hidden weapons.

When Gunnar nodded, Ketil Crow and Einar exchanged glances and fell silent.

Illugi Godi examined Gunnar's head and grunted, 'You'll live. Orm, can you wriggle out of that mail? I want to see that wound.'

It was harder than it looked and no one offered to help, of course. It slithered like a snakeskin to the ground eventually and I straightened up, holding my breath and feeling as bloodless as I looked. Both Illugi and Hild, I saw, were peering closely at my ribs as my tunic was hauled up.

'If Martin is here,' I said to Einar, 'then how did he manage it, save with Starkad?'

'Starkad is dead,' Ketil Crow growled. 'I heard it on good authority from the crewman on a *knarr*, who came upon the other *drakkar*. He died of wound fevers, from a cut on his leg.'

I looked at Einar, who said nothing.

'The other *drakkar* took his body back, wrapped in wadmal and salt, for Bluetooth to see,' Ketil Crow went on.

'How long have you known this?' I asked.

'Not long,' Einar replied absently. 'If it is true.'

Ketil Crow's thin-lipped silence was better than words. He clearly believed it. Wanted to believe it. If Starkad was dead and the other *drakkar* gone back to Denmark, then we were one enemy less. A big enemy, too.

'If so, where did Martin come from?' demanded Illugi Godi.

'Vigfus?' I ventured and Einar's brief, lowered-brow gaze told me he had considered that. There was something more there, too, but I could not quite grasp it.

'Well,' he said, eventually, forcing a smile, 'there is a horse-fight to be enjoyed and an oath-swearing after. If you are not fit to stay, Bear Slayer, I will hand Hild to two others and you can return to the ship.'

'I will go with him,' said Hild quickly. Einar looked from her to me and had the grace to keep his thoughts from his face. He bowed acknowledgement, but I said I was fine to stay.

'Stay sober and don't take part in the wrestling,' Illugi Godi said with a smile. 'Later, I will bind it with salves. Best to leave the mail off.'

When he had gone into the crowd, I pointedly looked at the mail, then at Gunnar. He grinned his understanding, picked it up and helped me into it.

Hild frowned, clutching her spear-shaft talisman. 'Illugi just said not to do that.'

'Illugi is not the one armed men are after,' I pointed out.

Gunnar bent to me, under the pretence of adjusting the hang of the mail on my shoulders. 'Thing is,' he whispered, 'I recognised one of those men. Herjolf, the one they called

Hare-foot, from the next valley to Bjornshafen. Remember him?'

I did, vaguely, a lanky man who came over with sheep to sell now and then, memorable only because of the long-boned feet that gave him his nickname.

'The further you go,' I mused, 'the more people you meet that you know.'

Gunnar hawked and spat. 'I don't believe in such wyrd,' he growled, while a bemused Hild looked on, one to the other. 'He was here after you. I am thinking that, if we find out where the other men are from, you could probably spit from one of their hovs to the other and all from the Vik.'

'What are you saying?' I demanded.

'Gudleif's sons are here,' he replied and wandered off to get his horn refilled.

That crashed on me like an anvil and left me stunned. I shook my head with disbelief. Half a year ago – less – I had no enemies at all and now they were lining up to swing a sword at me.

Gudleif's sons. How had Martin got in with them? At the fishing village, perhaps. He could have reached that and met a ship with Gudleif's vengeful sons on board. Or perhaps he was with the surviving *drakkar* and Starkad's body when they met another ship with Gudleif's sons.

No matter. The wyrd of it was that Bjorn and Steinkel, no older than me and whom I had never seen, were out for bloodprice for the slaying of their father. And not just from me, I remembered.

'Who is Gudleif?' asked Hild.

'A fetch who won't lie peacefully,' I answered and her head came up sharply at that, the knuckles whitening on her talisman spear-shaft.

I made my way through the milling, cheering crowds as the horses fought, seeking out my father. I found him as the grey foundered, reeling backwards on his hind legs, the black's teeth in his neck. Screaming, the black bore him to the ground and pounded him to a red ruin as the crowd roared.

'Orm, Orm, you were right and we have won a fortune,' my father roared, beaming and red-faced. 'How did you know, eh?'

'No matter,' I began, but he had the others round him, wanted to bask in the reflected glory of his clever son and insisted.

'White socks,' I said, speaking quickly. 'The grey had white socks on the rear hocks. The hair grows white round old wounds or bad bone . . . His hocks gave out, because they were weak. A fighting horse that can't stand on his hind legs won't last long.'

My father beamed; the others nodded, impressed. I caught his arm and dragged him aside. He came, realising now that something was up.

'There was a fight,' I said and his eyes widened, examining me, seeing the missing rings on my mail shirt.

'I am unhurt. Gunnar Raudi cut his head giving one an Oathsworn kiss.'

'Shits! How many? Where are they? Einar must know . . . He won't want anything to mar this day.'

'Too late,' I said. Then I told him of my and Gunnar's suspicions.

He sagged a little, the joy of the day withered away. 'Odin's balls,' he said, shaking his head wearily. 'Vigfus, Starkad, now my nephews . . . I am getting too old for all this, Orm.'

'And me,' I replied with feeling, which made him laugh a little. He straightened and nodded.

'Right. You have the right of it. Fuck Gudleif and fuck his sons, too. If Einar has his way today, none of them will be able to touch us.'

That made me blink a bit and my father laid one finger along his nose and winked.

At which point, a hush fell on the crowd as Illugi Godi

stepped up, rapped his staff and began the words of conse-
cration.

It went well. The winning horse, streaming sweat and
exhausted, was expertly dispatched, the blood from its cut
throat drenching the altar stone, the head removed and stuck
on a pole alongside, while the carcass was hauled off to be
butchered and eaten. The heart would be left on the altar
and Illugi would watch to see what bird came to it first.

Then, one by one, the Oathsworn, new and old, stepped
forward and recited their oath of blood and steel and promise,
in the eye of Odin.

When it was my turn, it seemed to me that, on the other
side of the altar, where the smoke from the cookfires shrouded
the river, Skapti and Pinleg and other faces stood and watched
silently, pale figures with glittering eyes, envious of the living.

In front of them all, like an accusing finger, was Eyvind.

Einar was last to swear and his voice was strong and clear.
Just as he had finished, at the moment when Illugi would
close the ceremony with a prayer to Odin, there was a stir
and heads turned to look at a party of horsemen, riding on
to the Thingvallir.

There were six of them, led by a seventh. They were all
mounted on splendid, powerful horses, bigger than our little
fighting ponies. They were all mailed and helmeted, with
shields slung on their backs, long spears balanced in stirrup
cups and curved swords in their belts.

You could not see any of their faces because they had veils
of mail drawn across them and the leader wore a splendid
helmet with a full-face gilded mask on it, a bland sculpture
of a beautiful youth. A huge horsetail hung from the point
of it and blew silver-grey in the wind.

Amazed, everyone watched as they cantered up and swung
into a line. The man with the masked helmet leaped off, light
on his feet for someone in mail and leather. Only his legs,
with baggy red silk trousers tucked into knee-high leather

boots, had no armour and the mail hauberk hung low, so that they were protected when he rode.

He wore two curved sabres in his belt – the mark of a chieftain, so I had been told – and a magnificent, fur-collared cloak of midnight blue fastened with a silver clasp that was probably worth a couple of farms back in the Vik.

When he unclipped the face-plate and pulled off his helmet, it was a disappointment, for there was no gilded youth, only a boy with pimples. But there were a few intakes of breath and the name leaped from head to head like a drumbeat.

Yaropolk.

The Prince, son of Sviatoslav, was young, round-faced and wisp-bearded. Round his neck was a ring of fat, egg-sized glowing lumps of amber, the tears of the sun. His whole head was shaved, save for a hank of black hair, braided and bound with silver bands, hanging over one ear. I learned later that his father was similarly shaved and that, half-Norse though they were, this was their Khazar clan mark. He stepped forward, tossing the helmet up and back to be expertly caught by one of his men. For all that he was barely as old as me, he played the part of a prince well.

Einar went down on one knee, which didn't surprise me. In his place, I'd have gone down on my face.

'Welcome, great lord,' Einar said smoothly and Yaropolk nodded, smiling. Einar waved and Ketil Crow came across, moving faster than I had ever seen him, with a huge silver-banded drinking horn, bought specially for the purpose, I realised later. Yaropolk drank, for all the world like a man who had just dropped in for a chat, then handed it back to Einar, who also drank.

When he had finished, Einar raised the horn and announced that, with this, he was pledging his oath and his life and his band of followers to the *druzhina* of Prince Yaropolk.

Who graciously accepted it in a voice somewhat spoiled by it breaking here and there. Then Illugi Godi recited his prayer to Odin, but kept it short, since Yaropolk was a follower of the Christ like his grandmother – though his own father stuck with the old gods. A great statue of Perun still stood in Novgorod, but a church was being built nearby, it was said. I saw both myself later and realised that old Perun's time was limited when the bird-shit was left on his stern face. Later, of course, the Perun totem in Kiev, gilded moustaches and all, went into the river at Vladimir's orders.

But this was a stunning moment for all of us, save those in the know. It meant the Oathsworn were now personal retainers of one of the most powerful leaders in the realm and anyone attacking us, attacked him.

In one clever 'tafl move, Einar had forestalled all his enemies and, in the feasting and drinking that followed, it was generally agreed – even by those who should know better – that Einar's luck was holding.

It was left to Hild to sober us all up as we gathered round the dying embers of the fire, somnolent with food and beer and mulling on the events. Nearby, a couple were humping with noisy enthusiasm and I was, at one and the same time, annoyed by the presence of Hild, which kept me from doing the same, and acutely aware of her and the fact that other women had lost their savour because of her.

She, if she heard anything at all, or thought anything on the matter, gave no sign. She sat, blank-faced as a benign little statue – and then she spoke. 'I have heard,' she said, 'that the *druzhina* of the Princes of Kiev are powerful forces.'

And everyone nodded and agreed that this was so.

'Horsemen, for all the nobles of Kiev are horsemen,' she went on. 'They fight with the bow and the spear and the sword, from horseback, on the open steppe. The Khazars they war against fight the same way.'

And everyone agreed that this was so.

'So . . . why does he need Norsemen, who fight on foot?'

We all looked at each other, for it was a very good question. Around then, some of us began to wonder.

As the couple reached a gasping end, Hild stood, calmly smoothed her dress, cradled the spear-shaft and drifted into the twilight and back to the ship. And I, of course, climbed wearily and painfully to my feet and followed, hearing the chuckles, aware that 'Bear Slayer' was giving way to 'Hild's Hound'.

The next night, resting by the cookfires, we did not have to worry the bone she had dropped on us. It was announced that the army of Kiev was gathering in that place, to march all the way south, almost to the Black Sea, down the Don river to the Khazars' city there. Sviatoslav would lay siege to it and finally remove this block to the eastern trade routes. And you can't, as Einar airily pointed out, take a walled city with horsemen.

'So you will get us all killed before we can reach the hoard,' grumbled Valknut, but Hild shook her head, her eyes fixed on Einar, who tried to avoid hers. She was quiet, coiled like a snake.

'The city is Sarkel,' she said. 'It lies on the Don. The place we seek is nearby.'

'So you say,' I offered moodily, half to myself, and was surprised at the growls that supported this.

'Orm has the right of it,' Finn Horsehead grunted, jerking his shaggy chin towards Hild. 'It seems to me that we put much of our trust in this woman, who does not inspire me, for one.'

'Nor me,' agreed Kvasir Spittle. 'If she knows so much of it, have her make a chart we can follow.'

Einar looked from one to the other, then back to me and his eyes tightened at the edges as others muttered assent to all this. I swallowed a dry spear in my throat under that gaze.

Einar shrugged and turned to Hild. 'Well, then – will you draw this chart?'

'No.' It was a handslap on a wet stone, a flat refusal that made us all blink.

Finn regarded her with one eye closed. Then he looked at Einar. 'You have a magic knife that would change her mind.'

'Would you trust a chart made that way?'

More growls and mutters, as they realised that she could lead them anywhere.

Kvasir scrubbed his head vigorously. 'I just don't like the idea of trailing after a . . . a . . .' He stopped, stumbling on the rocks of it.

'A witch,' Hild answered for him, her gaze as black as Einar's. She laughed, a low, throaty sound that raised hackles on everyone. She was trembling.

'You will, I am thinking, have to trust me on this, lads,' Einar said easily, laying one hand gently on Hild's shoulder, so that she stiffened and was still. 'Have you ever seen a chart that made sense anyway? Eh, Rurik? Who uses a chart?'

My father stirred uneasily and said nothing. He looked at me, a gaze as heavy and dark as a slab of slate.

'With or without a chart,' Einar said softly, 'the road still leads to Sarkel. If, at the end of it all, young Orm is unhappy, then he can come to me and say so.'

No one spoke. Einar turned away, propelling Hild in front of him. The talk and arguing only started to grow when they had vanished from sight, Ketil Crow and Valknut trailing after like dogs.

'That was . . . ill-advised,' my father growled, sliding up to me and shooting hard looks at Finn and Kvasir. They avoided his gaze and shuffled their feet.

'I said nothing but what was on my mind,' I protested and my father grunted with annoyance.

'Best if you rein that in from now on, Orm,' he said, his gaze flinty. 'For if you anger him, neither I nor Illugi – nor these here,' he added scornfully, glaring at Finn and Kvasir, 'will be able to prevent what happens next.'

There was a soft chuckle in the twilight and we all whirled nervously to face it.

Gunnar Raudi swaggered into the firelight, picking his teeth with a bone needle and looked us all over, grinning and shaking his head. 'You look like boys caught pulling off behind the privy,' he mocked, then spat on the fire and spoke into the sizzle. 'Einar's doom is on him. One day you will all have to face your fear of him.'

'And you are not afraid of Einar?' snarled my father, a little more savagely than I thought necessary.

Gunnar shrugged. 'Wyrd is wyrd. It is not mine, I am thinking, to go down under the edge of Einar's fame. I will consider fear when I see the edge of his blade.'

'When you go down under the edge of Einar's blade,' countered my father bitterly.

Gunnar Raudi's teeth were bloody with firelight when he grinned.

TEN

The fur market of Novgorod dripped under a fine mirr of rain that had been falling since dawn and, no matter how hard they tried, the pelt-sellers couldn't keep their wares dry under awnings and ended up dragging waterproofed wool over them, destroying any attempt at display.

The richer traders, those with solid edifices, huddled under the eaves, hardly bothering to rouse themselves since custom was so slight.

'This is a dangerous business,' my father growled, dragging his cloak further up over his head. Einar thumbed snot off his nose and said nothing.

'You are just wet,' I told him and Valknut chuckled. But the truth was that I thought he was probably right. The rain had soaked my perfectly good cloak and the mud had splashed up my fine fat breeks even on the walkway.

The hollow-socket stare of dead animals followed me from under every sheltered eave and from every trestle: long-snouted wolves, fox, highly prized sable, scabby rabbit and mottled hare. There were deer hides and antler-bone for the carvers and, slung from a hook in the middle of one room, a huge bear pelt with the head still on. The stink of hides from the tanners and leather-workers slunk to my nose now and then, brought by the wind and scarcely dampened by the rain.

I tried to be cheerful and failed and I knew the reason. I no longer had Hild to consider. Illugi Godi was with her all the time now, whether by Einar's order or her demand I could not be sure. But she ignored me as completely as she could and I should have been happy with that, but wasn't.

Everyone else knew why, of course – or thought they did. They nudged each other and grinned at my new, permanent scowl and at every pointed Hild slight.

I touched the seax strapped in the small of my back, under the cloak, and felt the rain trickle down my neck. For days we had been hunting for Martin, or Bjorn, or Steinkel. You wouldn't think it so hard in a town, but I discovered that a town is worse than a forest. You can hide everywhere and anywhere.

But Einar wanted him and I knew why. Martin knew of the Great Hoard and that we had Hild, who knew how to get to it. The gods knew how he had collided with Gudleif's sons, but what none of us wanted was to have him flapping his lip to the likes of Vigfus, or anyone else, in pursuit of his own dreams.

I took on this task with enthusiasm. We were stuck in Novgorod until the spate ended; the rivers were too fast-running to travel until at least May, perhaps June. Down at Kiev, eighteen days at least by boat, the river rose around fifteen feet and spread from about half a mile wide to five or even six miles wide.

Eventually, we heard that someone had seen a monk that might be ours and we listened to that one, because they said this monk wasn't of the Roman church, but Western. Since most of the monks and Christ priests in Novgorod were Greeks from Miklagard, we thought this monk likely to be the right one.

And so here we were, looking for Skudi the Finn in the

Shelonskaya district, across the bridge from the Podol, the riverside quarter. Skudi was a man who had promised, for a price, to deliver this monk up to us. So Einar, me, my father and Valknut went to him, trying hard to look like Gotland traders.

Einar, of course, smelled trap, but decided that more men might be too easily spotted and scare off the prize. In the rain of the market, though, I wished we had brought those men and more. I kept seeing thugs in every lumbering, bearded shape, every untrusting face smeared with fat to keep it dry.

Valknut found the Finn, who did not seem to warrant a shop at all, since he huddled on a bench in a cloak with a rat-chewed fur collar, sparse hair splayed on his skull and a calculating look in his watery blue eyes.

'This is Skudi,' Valknut said and the man nodded, hearing his name. I didn't speak so much Finn, so tried East Norse, while my father offered up West and Valknut, to my surprise, added Greek.

In that complex maze of tongues, we managed to haggle out a suitable price and, at the same time, warn the Finn that Einar would slit him from balls to chin if he proved false. Einar fished out a purse from under his armpit and sorted out full silver coins from the collection of sliced and whole and slivers in the bag. The Finn looked at them, shook his head and went off on a long rant in three languages.

'Tell him that's all he is getting,' Einar warned, narrowing his eyes. But that wasn't the problem and I sighed. This was getting complicated.

'He won't take *srebreniks*,' I said. 'Says there's not enough silver in them.'

The *srebrenik* was a new Rus coin, minted in Kiev from the same design as the favoured Serkland *dirham*, but the silver flow was now a trickle and the Rus ones had less in them than the Arab coins.

211

'His own lord mints them,' growled Einar, 'and that's what he pays us in.'

'Doesn't matter to him. He wants old Rus *kunas*, or Serkland *dirham*. Or *milaresia* from Byzantium if you have any.'

'Fuck him,' answered Valknut and his slit-eyed gesture with a thumb across the throat was eloquent in any language.

But Skudi was a trader and I had to admire him; he was used to hard haggling and never even broke into a sweat. Instead, he pointed to the silver torc round Einar's neck, given by Yaropolk as befits a lord to his commanders.

'That's worth more,' spat Einar. 'He's a cunning little swine, I will give him that.'

I made swift calculations and shook my head. 'No, it isn't. It's a Rus *grivna* of silver, worth twenty five. The *kuna* is the same as a *dirham* here. He is losing slightly, but he can sell the torc for more since it is pure silver.'

Einar blinked. He had another couple of such rings, as befits a jarl, so could afford to miss this one. My father scrubbed his head furiously and Valknut just glared. Then Einar shrugged, bent the torc off his neck and tossed it to the Finn, who bit it with black teeth and nodded, grinning.

'How you keep track of all this *kunas* and *dirham* and srebrooniks . . .' muttered my father. 'My head hurts with it.'

'*Srebreniks*,' I corrected and marvelled at them. I had already learned a valuable lesson: the Oathsworn and all the other bands like them were good at getting loot, bad at keeping it. A good trader would have the purse from under their armpit without having to beat them into the ground first, providing he could keep in his head the worth of all the different coins swirling around trade centres such as Kiev and Novgorod.

'Just make sure he doesn't play us false. I liked that neck ring,' growled Einar moodily.

The little Finn made the silver circle vanish inside his shirt, then swept his ratty cloak over his head and scuttled out into the rain, us following, looking right and left and expecting trouble.

We left the furrier quarter and the tanner stink behind, splashed and slithered down the walkways until, suddenly, Einar stopped and said, 'That's Oleg's hov.'

We all stopped and Valknut caught the Finn before he could go any further. Oleg, third of the sons of Sviatoslav. Vladimir and our own new lord, Yaropolk, were the other two, though Vladimir was born of a thrall. All of them circled each other like wary young dogs, kept from each other's throats only by their father, the mighty Prince of the Rus.

The wooden structure was impressive, but strange, with wooden pillars holding up a portion of the eaves, under which two fully armed guards looked at us with barely disguised amusement and caution.

The Finn gabbled furiously and, between us, we managed to work out that the monk was part of Oleg's retinue and lived and worked in a place round the back.

Einar stroked his dripping moustaches and then hissed to Valknut to take a casual stroll round. 'Try to see him but not be seen,' he growled. 'There's nothing we can do here and now, but we will come back when there is less chance of being seen.'

We moved, hauling the reluctant Finn with us, to the shelter of another building, away from the eyes of the guards, and waited, trying to look innocent. We all smelled like wet dogs.

Valknut was back swiftly, shaking himself free of rain. 'It's him, right enough. Two young boys with him, about your age, Orm. He is scribbling away in the dry, with a brazier of hot coals, the turd.'

'Those boys will be Gudleif's sons,' I said and my father

213

agreed. Einar released the Finn, who vanished into the mirr without a backward glance.

'We will come back at night,' Einar said levelly. 'And put this monk to the question.'

I didn't bother reminding him that the monk was protected, as part of Oleg's retinue, as we were in Yaropolk's. He knew that already, but what was making him chew his nails was whether Martin had told Oleg anything of our business.

So we were back under the same building hours later, when the rain had stopped, in the pitch black of a moon-shrouded night. There was a lantern spreading butter-yellow where the guards had been, but they were gone and the great timber doors closed. I knew that the hov was where Oleg sat during the day, dispensing justice, interviewing, all the things such princes do.

We slid round the side of the building and spotted the glow of another light, spilling from an unshuttered window. Valknut nodded at Einar and we all moved to the place, a mean timber outbuilding to the splendid hov.

Einar wasted no time; he hoofed in the door with a crash and rushed in, seax out.

Martin yelled and fell off a high stool; the youth with him – only one, I saw – went white with fear and scrabbled for the sword he had laid too far away. Valknut swept it up by the baldric and dangled it tantalisingly in front of him, grinning.

'Martin,' said Einar, as if greeting a long-lost friend. The monk rose from the floor, using the time to recover his composure. He smoothed his brown robe – new, I saw – and lifted the stool up. Then he smiled.

'Einar. And young Orm. Yes, lots of old familiar faces here.'

The boy's head came up and a flush brought colour to those chalk-white cheeks at the sound of my name. My father spotted it, too. 'Which one of my nephews are you, then?' he demanded.

The boy licked dry lips. 'Steinkel.'

'Where's your brother? Bjorn, isn't it?' I asked and he shrugged. Valknut, at a look from Einar, slid back into the darkness to make sure we weren't being ambushed.

Martin climbed back on to his stool and recommenced his work, grinding stuff in a bowl. He caught me looking and smiled. 'Oak galls in vinegar, thickened with gum from Serkland and some salts of iron,' he said. '*Encaustum*, from the Latin *caustere*, to bite. But you know that, young Orm, for you can read Latin. But you cannot write in any language.'

Now I knew the reason for the yellow-black scorch marks on his fingertips – which was one of the few familiar signs about him now. He had both grown and withered since I had seen him last. He had a beard now and his bald patch – a tonsure, I had learned – was freshly shaven. Yet he was thinner and something had chiselled away at his face, sinking his eyes deeper, while they blazed with a strange, yellow fervour.

He waved at the litter on the table in front of him, while Steinkel trembled and everyone else waited to hear what Valknut found outside. So we listened to Martin.

'These are what will make you and your kind fade to nothing and the word of God triumph,' he went on, grinding slowly and smiling at Einar.

'What is my kind?' Einar countered and Martin's mouth went thin.

'Doomed,' he said.

The silence was something you could taste.

'These are rolls, for tribute and taxes,' Martin went on, to the chink-chink of his grinding. 'These poor heathens used to make marks on tally sticks and even strips of birch bark. But you can't run a kingdom like that. Oleg values me, for I can tell him who owes what and when. In time, his sons and his sons' sons will know. The mixture bites into the vellum and leaves a mark. As my words will bite into the future and leave a mark.'

'Aye, you are a clever man, right enough,' Einar answered, unfazed. 'Once before you showed me your cleverness.' And he drew out his little knife and nonchalantly trimmed a thread from the weave on one cuff.

Martin winced at the memory and I saw him pause in his grinding to touch the scabbed stump of his finger. Then he recovered his smile. 'If you had not come to me, I would have come to you, Einar,' he said easily.

'Just so,' Einar replied. 'It was lucky for us both then that you showed these bold lads and their friends where to find me and mine. Such polite messengers.'

Martin shrugged. 'These boys came to me because I am a priest and they are baptised Christians. When they told me who they were, I knew whom they sought. That was God's work.'

'Just so,' my father said. 'Your god must be pleased at the helping hand you gave him to point these young lads and their killers in our direction. Some guidance from a Christ priest. Are you not supposed to tell them not to kill?'

'You killed my father . . .' Steinkel declared sullenly.

'I did indeed, nephew,' my father said and I looked at him, shocked. I had always thought it had been Einar. 'He killed my bear,' my father went on. 'And he tried to kill Orm here—'

'Enough,' Einar interrupted and glared darkly at Martin. 'Why would you have come to me?'

Martin put down the pestle carefully as Valknut came back in, looked at Einar and shook his head.

Martin said, 'Take the boy outside.'

Steinkel's head whipped from one to the other, bemused, angry. When Valknut grabbed an arm, he pulled back. 'What are you up to, monk?' he yelled, his voice high and shrill. Valknut wrenched him into an embrace, whirled him round and took the collar of his tunic at the back of the neck, twisting it tight so that it choked him. He hauled the boy up so that his toes danced furiously for a grip on the floor, then the pair of them staggered through the door and into the night.

Einar cocked his head expectantly at Martin, who sighed and put off sharpening his writing quill. 'I have told Oleg nothing,' he declared. 'In return for this continued silence, I want the return of my Holy Lance.'

'Your what?' demanded my father.

'Hild's spear-shaft,' I told him, 'which she won't like to give up.'

My father looked from one to the other. 'Why does he . . . What use is that? It has no point.'

If he meant it as a joke, no one laughed. I looked at Martin and knew. 'He has promised Oleg,' I said. 'In return, Oleg has promised . . . what? A Christ church in Kiev, or here in Holmgard?'

Martin's smile was blade-sharp and twisted. 'Kiev. And when he succeeds his father, he will make me bishop there, with the blessing of the Pope. This country seeks a new and Christian religion.'

'And it won't be the Greek one from the Great City,' I finished for him. He inclined his head generously in my direction.

'There are two more of Sviatoslav's sons,' my father growled, 'who may not fall in with this great scheme.'

Martin shrugged. I saw he was confident of switching allegiances to whichever brother triumphed – if he had a great Christ charm to promise.

Einar was silent for a moment. Martin and he exchanged sword-cut glances across the room, each knowing what the other was thinking. What was to stop Einar killing Martin now and thus shutting his mouth?

The fact that he was Oleg's man and that would mean trouble. Steinkel would know who had done it, so he would have to die. His brother would suspect, so they would have to find and kill him, too . . . there was too much blood, even for Einar.

'How do I know you will keep your word, monk?' demanded Einar flatly.

'You will surely kill me if I don't,' he replied easily, 'and I will swear it on the Christ cross, an oath if you will. You like oaths, Einar.'

There was a moment of deadly stillness. I saw visions of blood everywhere and then Einar shook his head and I breathed again.

'Swear on your Christ-god if you will,' he said quietly. 'Swear also to Odin.'

Martin hesitated, then nodded. A pagan oath was easily broken in Martin's mind, but one to his own god might hold. Of course, Einar would try to kill him anyway, as quietly and secretly as possible and everyone saw that – including Martin. It would be a harder task to find him after all this, I was thinking.

As we drifted into the night, I was less easy about taking the spear-shaft away from Hild and said as much. No one had a thought on it as we made our way back to the *Elk*.

In the end, it was surprisingly easy. She held on tight to it, white-knuckled, until Ketil Crow – none too gently, it seemed to me – prised her loose from it. I expected rants, rages, even those rolling-eyed fits.

Instead, she sank down on the deck with a weary sigh, slumped like a sack.

Ketil Crow and Illugi Godi went off into the night to deliver it and witness Martin's oath. As they left, with my warning to watch out for my cousins, doubly mad now, I would wager, she looked blackly at Einar. 'There is a price to pay for this,' she said and the blank chill of it made me shiver. Even Einar, sunk in morose contemplation of the subject, was jerked back by the simple vehemence of it.

'Can you still find the howe of Attila?' he demanded,

alarmed, and she nodded, her eyes startling pits of pitch in the yellow lantern light.

'Nothing will now keep me from that burial place,' she declared. 'But I will need something from you.'

We moved to Kiev not long afterwards, in a mad, shouting, frantic chaos of boats and men, leaving Valgard and a dozen Oathsworn with the *Elk*.

Novgorod was as far as foreign ships went. All the traders were forced to the Rus boats: the *strugi* and the larger *nasady*, which were expensive, but could withstand Baltic storms and the grind of dragging them over portages. It was as sound a way as any of making sure the Prince of Kiev controlled the river trade.

But the traders stayed in the crowded anchorage this time, fuming and cursing, because every boat had been taken by Sviatoslav to move men and gear swiftly down to Kiev the Golden. From there, we'd move across to the Don and down it to face the Khazars.

I remember the journey as one of the laziest I have ever had. The only lazier one was the sail down the Don afterwards.

As part of Yaropolk's *druzhina* we had nothing to do. Local rivermen poled the boats and all we did was clean our gear, admire each other in our new cloaks – the colour of old blood and the mark of our *druzhina* status – and speculate on whether the women in Kiev would be better than those in Novgorod.

They were. Everything about Kiev was better and it roared with life, swollen by people from everywhere. Entire tribes had arrived: Merians, Polianians, Severians, Derevlians, Radimichians, Dulebians, and Tivercians and names even seasoned traders had barely heard of.

They came with horses and dogs and women and children, bringing an incredible babble and swirling life to the place,

219

and we strode through them all, brighter threads in this rich tapestry, a head taller than all of them, rich in dress and ornament and swagger.

The city heaved with life and colour, from the cherries drying on the rooftops of the *khaty*, their timber and clay houses, to the pears and quinces that glistened in the sun on bowing branches.

Down the Zalozny road came caravans from Serkland with spice, gems, satins, Damascus steel and fine horses. Up the Kursk road still came a vital trickle of silver, which the Volga Bulgars traded from mines even further east. From Novgorod, though, which should have been sending wool, linens, tinted glass, herring, beer, salt and even fine bone needles, came nothing but us, gawping and spitting and roaring.

Kiev was starting to swelter in the heat of a summer sun and Illugi Godi grew increasingly morose, even as the Oathsworn hurled themselves delightedly into the whirling welter of it, hunting out drink and women.

'Enjoy it while you can, boy,' he declared, leaning on his staff as I leaped down on to the jetty, joining a dozen others heading into the teeming streets. 'There will be disease and worse if we stay here for long.'

I waved to him, but I didn't care. The spectre of Hild was like a silent, accusing finger these days. She spent most of her time huddled close to Einar, sharing the gods knew what – not love, certainly.

And then there was my father. I had tried to bring up the subject of Gudleif, of the first five years of my life, of my mother, but he had dismissed it all with a wave, as something of no consequence. Yet it was his brother and I wanted to know . . . even today I don't know what I wanted to know. That it bothered him. That I could help. That we were blood kin right enough.

Instead, it was as if we had shifted three or four oars down from each other. If it kept up this way, we would be on different boats, he and I.

I wanted drink and women that day in Kiev.

I got them, too. Even now, I can remember little of it and even that is probably what I was told by others. There was a party of Greeks, engineers sent by the Miklagard Emperor. They had been in Kiev for months cutting timber and building huge siege engines in jointed sections for easy transport and they knew the best places to go.

There were women and I remember humping on a table and was told I had taken a wager I could hump the fattest, ugliest one in the place and won, despite Ketil Crow being convinced I could never get aroused enough with the one chosen. But, as Valknut pointed out, the difference between a reasty crone and Thor's golden-haired wife, Sif, is about eight horns of mead.

I had that and more. I had never drunk so much and remembered only being hauled up out of a pool of my own mead vomit, my hair sticky with it. There was water that left me dripping, but I couldn't feel it. I couldn't feel my lips, or my legs. Then memory left me.

Later, I learned that I had been carried back to our Rus riverboat almost in triumph – dropped a few times by the unsteady bearers – and flung on my own fur-lined sleep-bag.

What I do remember – I still jerk awake sometimes in the night remembering – is being kicked and the sound of screams. I saw figures and flames and someone yelled – in my ear, almost, so that my head burst in bright colours of pain: 'Arm yourself, you fuck, we're boarded.'

That staggered me half-upright. I found my sword and fumbled for my shield in the half-light of dawn, bleary-eyed, trying to work out where I was. Keep them next to you, we had been told. Always next to you . . .

I was on the deck of the Rus boat, which was shadowed with figures who screamed and slashed. Booted

221

feet thundered; blades clashed; shields thumped. I saw Ketil Crow hurl himself like a growling terrier into a pack of men, slashing wildly, then retreat before they recovered enough to hit him back. His mail gleamed redly in the wild torchlight.

I lurched towards him, the half-formed idea of standing on his shieldless side in my head. As I got to him, three men moved forward, half-crouched, wary, but determined. I didn't know any of them, but I knew the threat of a bloody great Dane axe when I saw one.

The blow came and slammed into my shield with a sound like a falling tree and I staggered under it. Ketil Crow, grunting and panting, was struggling with the other two, being awkward for them because he was left-handed – but the man with the big two-handed axe was mine alone.

Another blow staggered me backwards, then he swiftly reversed and aimed a whack with the butt on my sword-arm, but my own wild flailings bounced it up and it hit the edge of the shield, then the side of my head.

The flare of light and pain was a whole world; nothing else existed. I couldn't see and I heard only a vague screaming. Something monstrous smashed against my shield-arm – then the world hoiked itself back into the Now, where it was me howling, the Dane axe was whirling round again and I was on one knee.

He was good, the axeman. He gave up trying to splinter the shield and thumped the axehead against it, trying to knock it down, then swiftly reversed to try to butt me in the face. Staggering, the drunk fumes burned away in a fire of fear, I managed to fend that off and get to my feet.

As I did, he hooked the blade behind the shield, wrenching it forward to try to break the straps. The butt end stabbed out once more when this, too, failed. It caught me slightly on the chest and even that made me grunt with pain.

He backed off a little, then came in again, snarling and

222

scything the axe low, trying to cut the feet from me. I scampered backwards, collided with someone and battered behind me with the shield, not caring who it was.

He saw an opening, roared the axe back in a half-arc, mouth open in a tow-coloured beard, hair a mass of wild straggles. It slammed into someone to his right and caught. He raged and tore it free and it came whistling round with a flap of cloth attached from someone's cloak – but I avoided it, then struck my first blow, which just missed his forearm.

He leaped back and we paused, heaving for breath. Around us was madness and struggle, but the arc of the Dane axe had cleared a circle round the pair of us, as if by some spell.

'Not bad, Bear Slayer,' he taunted. 'For a boy.'

I sucked air in past the raging brand in my throat. I knew I was dead, that he was better than me. I realised, too, that he knew who I was; he had sought me out. My fame would be the death of me.

He hefted the axe, twirled it deftly in both hands like the fire-dancers do with their flaming poles. It was meant to fix my gaze, like a rabbit to a stoat, but I had seen Skapti do this trick and watched his feet instead. He took a step, closing for the flurry of blows he knew would end it.

I braced myself, a whimper tearing from between clenched teeth. A horn blew. He paused. It blew again. He grinned, yellow teeth in that yellow beard, and pointed the axe at me with one hand.

'Not now, but soon, Bear Slayer.'

Then he lumbered heavily to the side of the Rus boat and hurled himself over. I heard him crash to the jetty even as I was on my knees being sick.

The tally was eight wounded: none dead and none so serious they couldn't grumble over it. They had lost one dead, sunk in the river in full mail, and had carried off their wounded.

And one captured. Who turned out to be one of us.

I recognised him: Hogni, who had spoken up proudly to Einar about his skills. 'I can row and ski and shoot and use both spear and sword,' I'd heard him say.

Now he was lashed upside down from the raised mast spar, where he twisted slowly, blood running down his face and off his dangling hair to the deck, while men, still panting and binding wounds, snarled at him, even those who had been his oarmates. Especially those who had been his oarmates.

Einar paced, his mail making soft shinking sounds. He was a controlled, deadly calm, like the black sea on a rising wind. Hild was gone and that had been the purpose of the raid, which Hogni, on his watch, had allowed. One of the raiders had been careless, I heard people tell each other, and the alarm was raised, which was Odin luck for us.

'I don't need to know who did this,' Einar growled at the man swinging in front of him. 'I know who did this – and Vigfus will pay for it.' He leaned forward, his little knife out. 'I need to know where he is, though, and you will help me.'

There was a flick of his wrist and a scream from Hogni as his finger joint whicked off into the darkness.

'This is a magic knife,' Einar began and I lurched off, away from what was to follow, my guts churning and my head full of Thor hammers. And in the midst of all that, the flare-bright fear of that Dane axe.

I was as doomed as Einar. The bear had been a lie. The first man I had killed had been more inept than me, the second was a lucky strike with a small knife. Then there was Ulf-Agar who had almost killed himself with foolishness. I had never fought a serious fight and knew now that I would die if I did, because I simply wasn't that good at it. Worse, the Bear Slayer was a prize death for anyone to boast of; they would be springing out of holes in the ground after me.

I was retching on nothing when my father came and hunkered down beside me, grunting with the weight and awkwardness of mail. He handed me a leather cup and I drank, then blinked with surprise.

'Watered wine,' he said. 'Best cure for what ails you. If it doesn't work, use less water.'

I drank more, paused to retch it up, drank more.

He nodded appreciatively and scrubbed his stubble. 'I saw you with the axeman – you did well.' I looked sourly at him and he shrugged. 'Well, you are alive, anyway. He looked like he knew the work.'

'He would have killed me.'

My father punched my shoulder and scowled. 'None of that. You're not a whining boy any more. You should take a look at yourself first chance you get. A young Baldur, no less, vulnerable only to mistletoe.'

I drained the cup and never felt less like Baldur.

My father tossed the empty cup in one hand, then started to lever himself up, grunting with the effort. 'Come on. Einar wants us. Hogni has been singing on his perch.'

'Mail,' I said, suddenly realising. 'That's mail . . . that's my hauberk.'

My father grimaced and wriggled in it. 'Bit tight round the shoulders, but not much. Another season of rowing, youngling, and you'll find this too small.'

'Why,' I asked pointedly, 'are you wearing it?'

My father's eyes widened at the implied challenge. 'Einar had all those not out on a drunk armed and mailed. He is as nervous as a cat with its arse on fire. With good reason, as it turned out.'

I remembered now. Ketil Crow in mail, Einar, too, and a dozen others. My father mistook my silence and dropped the cup, then bent over at the waist and, hands over his head, shook himself like a furious, wet dog until the iron-ringed shirt slithered off at my feet.

'I am done with it,' he growled and stalked away. I wanted to call him back, but it was too late and something was nagging me. But my head thundered and wouldn't let me think straight.

Hogni wasn't thinking at all; the last thing to have gone through his head was Wryneck's axe. When I came up to the silent band collected round Einar, Hogni was being wrapped in his own cloak and weighted with a couple of stones.

They lowered him over the side with scarcely a splash, the ripples rolling golden in the rising sun, and I was pleased to see that there were a few green-grey faces in the hard-eyed huddle.

Those whose heads had been clearer to start with – all in mail, I saw – were grim and angry. Not only had a prize been stolen from them – even if some of them did not quite know why she was a prize – but it had been done by a pack they considered dogs rather than wolves.

Worse yet, one of their own had been an enemy and that made neighbour uneasy about neighbour, oath or no.

'Let her go, I say,' muttered Wryneck, scratching the fleas out of his grey beard. This made a few heads turn, for old Wryneck, along with Ketil Crow, Skapti and Pinleg, had been one of the originals of Einar's band.

'She holds the secret of treasure, old eye,' Valknut said, in a tone that reminded me of old Helga talking to the wit-ruined Otkar.

'Watch your mouth round me, you rune-hagged fuck,' Wryneck replied, amiably enough but with steel in it. 'I know what she is said to hold. I have not seen any of it yet save for a single coin with a hole through it and I am thinking she is too much trouble for such a poor price. We should let her lead Quite the Dandy around by the nose for a time, while we go and raid something with money in it.'

It was something when a wise head such as Wryneck started in with thoughts such as these. There were some chuckles at his bluntness, but muted ones, for Einar was close. If he heard, he made no sign.

226

Instead, calm and seemingly unconcerned, he thumbed his nose, stroked his moustaches and said, 'Ketil Crow will pick a dozen men. Take only weapons you can hide under cloaks or inside tunics. Those chosen have five minutes to get ready, for we have little time to spare.'

The newer men, oathsworn only weeks before, were the most eager to go, to prove to the others that no more of them were false. Ketil Crow, of course, wanted some trust-worthy heads with them and, of course, I was chosen.

It was my wyrd.

ELEVEN

The sunlight was painful, even filtered through the dust that matted hair and clothes, dulling all colours to a faded memory.

The sight of the milling crowd of hawkers and their haggling customers, draymen hefting great leather wineskins or rolling barrels, butchers with carcasses slung over their shoulders and hucksters with trays of sweetmeats, covered against the dust and flies, hazed and danced before my eyes, bringing bile to my throat.

On one side, under an awning, I tried to keep my eyes open against the painful glare that seemed to make my head throb worse than ever, sneezing in the dust. It was hot and heavy with stinks from the dye-makers nearby; the smell of stale piss made me gag.

A little way up, Bagnose was turned towards me, trying to catch my eye from under a ludicrous straw hat, which he fondly believed would hide his face from any one of Vigfus's band who might actually recognise him. How he hoped to avoid it was anyone's guess, I was thinking bitterly, when he had a face like a baby's rashed arse and a nose that wobbled and could light his way in the dark. Even people who had never seen him before would notice him.

The crowd thinned a little as we made our way, weaving in and out of the disorderly street traffic, to where the rutted way turned sharply into the dye-makers' district. Then I saw Bagnose take off his hat, scrub his sweat-soaked, straggled hair and put it on again. I knew it was a signal, but couldn't remember what about – then I saw the two men.

They stood in the doorway of a tannery, heedless of the reek. Beside them was the man we had followed, a tall, rawboned man with white hair and the fiercest red face and exposed arms I had ever seen. Steinthor knew him as White Gunnbjorn and he was a Norwegian with a reputation as a hard fighter.

Behind me, four more Oathsworn tried to look innocent and busy at the same time and were failing so badly I wondered if we would get much closer. I slid a hand up the back of my tunic and loosened the seax, feeling the sweat-damp there and wishing it had been raining as an excuse to wear a cloak and hide a proper blade beneath it.

Bagnose nodded to me, then walked forward with unhurried steps. He stopped, turned and looked incredibly interested in the whole hog's head a butcher was lugging through the crowd, dripping blood and trailing flies.

Another man had joined White Gunnbjorn, not tall, but so thin he seemed taller. He had a sharp face and stringy hair round the sides of his head only, while his beard was long and combed and forked, the ends fastened with ribbons the same colour as his leg-bindings, which were purple. That and a loose, red silk tunic, fat breeks the colour of cornflowers and a belt made of silver lappets made him easy to place, even though I had never seen him.

Vigfus, called Skartsmadr Mikill – Quite the Dandy.

Gunnar Raudi wandered up, as if he had just encountered me in the street, his eyes hard above the cheery grin, his face sheened with sweat and his frosted red curls tucked under a round wool hat that must be broiling his head.

'Vigfus,' he said and I nodded. He glanced back, to where Einar was well hidden from any eyes that might know him, and inclined his chin. Presumably he got an answer for he took a deep breath, adjusted his belt and walked unhurriedly up the street towards the four men on the wooden steps of the tannery.

I followed, slightly behind him, and knew the others were following me. I saw Bagnose turn, too, moving up behind the sweating butcher and his grisly load, using it as cover to get closer.

There was a blur of movement, blasting into the pain in my head, into the glare that had slitted my eyes. Stunned, I could only watch as a spear arced out of an alley to our left, whicking across the street towards Gunnar Raudi. They had left a cunning watcher and we had all missed him.

The gods know how Gunnar saw it – even he did not know much beyond a flicker at the edge of his vision. He dropped a shoulder, spun in a half-crouch and the spear missed him, the shaft scoring across his shoulder, plunging on into the dimness of a booth, where a screech announced its arrival.

The street was in uproar. Gunnar crashed into two men carrying a bale of cloth; I stood and gawped, until something smacked ringing lights and exploding pain in my head.

'Move, you rat fart!' roared Bagnose, surging forward.

I stumbled, collided with a screaming woman, fell to one knee and raised my head, blinking dust and confusion. I saw Gunnar Raudi vanish down the alley after the spear-thrower, roaring his anger and fear in that direction.

Bagnose had skidded to a halt, since White Gunnbjorn and the two others were whipping out lengths of sharp steel and coming in his direction, slowed only by the skittering, yelling crowd getting in their way.

And Vigfus was bolting into the tanners' building.

I sprang up then and I will never know why – stung by Bagnose's slap, or even my own fear, perhaps. I ran, swerving round White Gunnbjorn, hearing Einar and the others roaring their way up the street behind me, blades out.

For a moment, the transition from dazzling light to the dim twilight of the tannery blinded me and I skidded to a halt, blinking. Then I caught the brief gleam of silver from Vigfus's belt as he skittered up a set of wooden stairs. I was after him, knife out, taking the stairs three at a time.

He bolted down a narrow work hall and shot round a corner into a room bright with daylight from opened shutters. I followed, cursing the worn-smooth soles of my leather boots on the wooden floors. I slid as if on bone skates, straight into a table, scattering shocked tallymen and their sticks and birch-bark notes.

Amid the shouts and the clatter and the pain of a bruised shin, I saw Vigfus reach the end of the room and thought I had him. There was no way out.

Save the open-shuttered window, which he took with a long-legged leap.

Cursing, I scrambled to my feet, fisted a red-faced, shrieking tallyman in the chest out of the way and sprang to the same window.

Beyond was the slanted short roof of the eaves, looking out over the sprawling yard of the tannery and its huddle of buildings. Between was crammed with vats, wooden frames, strung lines and milling, near-naked, sweating men hooking stinking hides on to long poles or feeding fires under boiling vats. The heat and acrid stink sucked the air away, as if I was breathing through wet linen.

Vigfus was skittering along the wooden shingles. He fell over a rope slung up for washing and rugs, rolled and, for one glorious moment, I thought he was over the edge and done for.

But he stopped himself, sprang up to all fours and looked back at me, for that moment like some strange spider. I thought he was set to come at me, so I slid to a halt and

231

brought the blade up. He twisted his mouth into a scornful grin, sprang upright and raced along the short roof, stopped, looked both ways, then leaped outwards, his arms at full stretch, seax in his teeth.

I gawped. He had to be lying in the tannery yard, hopefully head first in a vat of piss. I ran to the spot – but there was nothing. Then I saw the rope, slung slantwise between buildings, backed up, took a deep breath and did a truly foolish thing, brought on by youth and the sudden grim obsession not to let the fart get away.

I stuck the seax in my teeth and dived out at the slender arc of rope.

I hit it, grasped, swung – as he must have done – and crashed towards a square opening, the shutters half closed.

I splattered the flimsy framework to shreds, felt splinters rip into my arm and plunged into the room beyond in a welter of flying wood, reed flooring and straw from a bed pallet that exploded under me.

I fell and rolled and came up tearing the seax from my mouth and slashing wildly, but the room was empty and all I managed to do was cut my tongue and the side of my mouth.

I saw the doorway, blocked by a simple curtain. I ripped it apart and found myself in another open hallway, filled with shrouded door openings. Stairs led down into the gloom and the smell of pine and tanners' piss was heavy. I felt blood and sweat trickle and spat more on to the floor. The side of my mouth stung with the sharpest pain of them all. I was panting and soaked and desperate at the thought I had lost him.

I ran to the first room and frantically tore aside the hangings on the door openings: boxes, bales, dead rats, live rats. The next one was a room with another square opening blazing with light on the splintered debris of fresh wood; the one after that was a room with a straw bed and nothing . . .

A room with a smashed opening and shards of wood littering the floor. Where he had come in. And gone out again.

I sprang to the window, stuck the seax in my tunic and snaked out of it. I hauled myself upwards this time, on to the sloping wooden shingles, baking in the heat and so dry they cracked like ice. I slithered, cursing, on the ones that came loose.

I saw him then, his red tunic torn and fluttering, one purple leg-binding trailing and the fancy ribbons on one fork of his beard ripped loose. He glared wildly at me and scuttled down the tiles and over the far side.

Odin's arse, would he never stop running? I skated after him, saw the short drystone wall he had dropped on to – astride it, I noted savagely – and was clambering up on, limping painfully and clutching his cods.

People were yelling at us from the tannery yard and on the other side of the wall was the street. I dropped heavily on to the wall, managed not to slam it into my groin, swayed alarmingly for a moment, then caught my balance as Vigfus walked along the uneven, crumbling, narrow wall-top, hands out for balance.

Then I saw Einar and Gunnar Raudi and others, spilling into the tannery yard – but the wall was too high for them to reach him.

He saw them at the same time as I did, reasoned at the same time as they did and avoided the weapons they were preparing to hurl at him by leaping down the other side of the wall, with a curse, to the street below.

'Go round, go round!' I shrieked and they all turned and headed the long way round the buildings, elbowing people out of the way.

They'd never make it in time before he vanished, so I leaped after him, trying to cushion my fall by landing in a trestle of stacked fruits. I came up scattering more people and sticky with juices. Angry shouts followed me as I got up, limping. It had been a bad landing anyway and I was flagging now.

Vigfus wasn't in much better shape, but he was starting into a run when I hurled forward in a flying dive and caught the last, trailing edge of his fancy purple bindings.

He gave a sharp yelp as he went over, clattering in to the dusty ruts full on his face. He scrambled away, kicking at me, his face a mask of fury and bloody mud.

Then I saw, with a sick horror, the bone-white head of Gunnbjorn, trotting through the yelling, milling people, hurling them aside to get to his jarl. Vigfus scrambled up and White Gunnbjorn grinned and made for me, a blade in his hand. His eyes, I saw were strange, colourless – even his lashes were white.

'Leave him,' Vigfus gasped. 'Help me – get out of here. Einar is coming.'

Gunnbjorn snarled at me, then hooked a shoulder under his master's armpit and hauled him up. They were four steps further on when, nearly sobbing with the sheer anger and frustration of watching them get away, I hurled the seax.

It whirled through the gap between us and smacked Gunnbjorn in the back. There was a crack and he shrieked and collapsed in a heap, knocking Vigfus over in front of him.

Gunnbjorn was flailing, trying to reach his back, gasping for help. Vigfus, cursing, saw his state, scrambled up and hopped off, vanishing into the milling throng. I tried to follow, but the pain in my ankle made me shriek as loud as Gunnbjorn, so I fell and Einar and the rest found me, sprawled in the street, pounding it with my fists, face streaked with blood and snot and sweat.

Gunnar Raudi rolled me over, had two men haul me up. Einar hunkered down by Gunnbjorn, who was moaning and still trying to reach his back.

'Take it out,' I heard him groan. 'I can't feel my legs. Take it out.'

There was nothing to take out. The seax was no throwing knife; the haft had hit him on the spine and broken something vital.

Einar rolled him over surprisingly gently and spoke quickly, for we didn't have much time left before someone hefty and armed came to find out what the trouble was.

'Gunnbjorn,' he said, 'you are done for.'

'It would seem so,' the man answered painfully, through clenched teeth. His face was as white as the bone hair plastered limply to his skull, even through the patina of dust. His eyebrows and lashes were white; his eyes were not colourless, I saw, but a faint shade of violet.

'I can let you die as a man,' said Einar, 'with a good blade in your hand and a bench in Valholl.'

You could see the nod in Gunnbjorn's eyes, even if his neck could no longer make it.

'Or I can leave you here,' he said, 'in this street, where you will probably live long enough to be carried to a bed and cared for a little, until you die a nithing.' He paused and shrugged. 'Perhaps you may even live. I have seen such. A man I saw once in Miklagard had a marvellous seat with an awning and was carried about by thralls after having his legs crushed under a ship he was careening.'

Having made the point, he leaned closer, dangling Gunnbjorn's own knife by the blade, haft tantalising inches from the man's palm. 'Tell me where Vigfus is going with the girl,' he said.

Gunnbjorn moaned.

'He left you to die here,' Einar pointed out.

Gunnbjorn's voice was scarcely above a whisper now. 'I have a mother, Hrefna Ulfsdottir. In Solmundsteading in the Vestfold . . .'

'I will send word that you died well. And the purse under your left armpit.'

He closed his eyes then, already seeing the ravens. 'The

Sea Storm. The howe of the Sea Storm, looking for Atil's hoard. The girl knows. To the north-west, one, maybe two days, she says.'

Einar dropped the knife-haft into Gunnbjorn's palm at the same moment he slit his throat. Then we left, while the blood pooled into a scarlet mud-puddle beneath his head and the street emptied, for no one wanted to answer questions about a dead man.

It was like being on the sea in a swell. We crossed the seared steppe under a sun like a fist, kicking up puffs of black soil as we moved over the rolling yellow grass, heading for the next green line on the horizon.

Eventually, the line would thicken, grow larger, haze out of the heat into stands of pine and alder and birch. The slow, undulating steppe was studded with them, each huddled like a herd of living creatures round a gulley, where water trickled sluggishly to the Dnepr. Under the trees was heady with resin, thick with needles and mulch, and an even more oppressive heat. But it offered shelter from what we feared most: Pecheneg horsemen.

It was, as Valknut never seemed too tired to point out, a truly bad idea, heading out on to the steppe on foot, with no more than two days' hard flatbread, rank cheese and some of the dried meat strips the Rus horsemen used.

They stuck it under their saddles and cloths, where the horse sweat softened it and juiced it up – mare sweat tasted better, they swore – but we had no such luxury and, at the third forest of the day, I stopped trying to chew it and swore it would be better kept to repair my boot soles with.

'Give it here,' shouted one of the band, a pox-faced half-Slav called Skarti. 'I'll stick it down my breeks for you. Same idea, different sweat.'

They laughed, this dripping, evil-smelling bunch. They panted like dogs and filled leather bottles with river water, softened bread and meat in the stream before trying to eat it, gasped on their needle couches with the weight of the heat – and joked.

Einar had to turn eager men down when he told them of his plan and that he needed sixty good men from the company to get Hild back. He had sent word to Sviatoslav and his three sons that men of Prince Vladimir's *druzhina* had broken oath and run into the steppe, taking with them a slave from Einar, and that he had gone to bring all of them back. That, he hoped, would excuse his own absence.

Einar's assured calm had gone, replaced by a morose nervous energy, where he stroked his moustaches feverishly and gave every sign that his luck had deserted him.

Then the chosen sixty had struck off north and west, following the signs Bagnose and Steinthor, those two tracker hounds, were leaving as they followed the spoor of Vigfus and his crew to the mysterious howe of the Sea Storm.

And I had gone with them, despite Einar and Illugi and everyone else's misgivings over my strapped-up ankle and the limp I'd had before we'd even started.

But I was determined and Einar didn't put up too much resistance to it. I caught Gunnar Raudi's eye as we started out across the steppe and remembered his words to me, his warnings. Einar, I thought, would be pleased to have me founder on the plains outside Kiev, where he could find a good, sensible excuse to leave me for dead.

The prospect was another good argument for staying behind, but I was more afraid of looking afraid than anything else. That fair-fame trap was closing like steel teeth – I was the Bear Slayer, after all, the young Baldur. I had to go to the howe of the Sea Storm.

'What the hell *is* the Sea Storm?' Einar had demanded of Illugi Godi, after sending men flying on errands everywhere and gathering gear for the pursuit. He added, in a muttered afterthought. 'What is she doing?'

'It is no secret in these parts. Dengizik, the Sea Storm, was a Hun lord,' Illugi corrected. 'They know his name round here. They say he was Atil's son.'

Einar's head came up and he and Illugi looked at each other, exchanging the gods knew what in their glances.

'Perhaps there is a clue there to Atil's hoard,' I offered. 'Maybe that is Atil's hoard and she is leading them to it.'

Einar swung his glare at me, pure black ice, and I felt the weight of it. I should have stopped then, but somehow could not, as children do when they start in on horse-goading for the first time. A savagery comes on them then that those who know watch for, dragging the offenders away and cuffing them round the head.

'I think not,' Illugi offered pensively. 'This Hun tomb is one everyone knows and almost certainly has been raided already. Atil's hoard, it is well known, is hidden.'

'Just so,' I said, testing the ankle now that I had slung all my gear on. 'So well hidden that a madwoman knows how to find it.'

Einar stayed silent, busying himself with his own gear, but Illugi frowned at me as a signal to stop, but I was dancing on the fire-mountain edge now, fearless and capering.

'Hard to say who is more touched,' I went on, not looking at anyone. 'Her with her rolling eyes and shakes and sure wisdom that she knows where these riches are hid, or all of us for following blindly after.' Then I gazed straight at Einar and said, 'Maybe she is your doom. Sent by Odin, who does not like oath-breakers . . .'

I got no further, for his hand was on my throat and his black eyes so close to mine I could feel the lashes on my cheeks. I could not breathe, dare not move.

'You have not been with us long, Rurik's son, but already I am regretting being so indulgent for your father's sake.'

His grip tightened and I felt my eyes bulge like a frog's.

'Einar,' said Illugi warningly and even through the roaring

in my ears I heard the anxious sound in his voice. The steel fingers closed a little harder.

'An exchange of views?' enquired a new voice, barely heard through the thunder in my head. 'Or are you offering a kiss of peace, as the Christ-men do when they promise friendship?'

The fingers relaxed a little and Einar's voice was booming, even though he spoke in the softest of growls: 'This is no matter for you, Gunnar Raudi.'

I tried to look for him, but Einar's eyes were locked on mine still, great tunnels, like the entrances to dwarven caves.

'I shall not speak on it, then,' said Gunnar easily. 'I have another who will do that.'

The soft sucking sound of a blade from a sheath was echoed by Illugi's indrawn breath. 'Hold this,' he declared, deep and stern and I knew, without seeing, that he had his staff up. 'Gunnar, put peace-strings back on that. Einar, let the boy go. There is nothing but doom in this for all.'

The release, when it came, was sudden enough to make me fall to the ground, coughing, my throat thundering with pain and every breath in it a rasp with thorns. When I could finally look up and take Illugi's offered wrist, I found my legs shook.

Gunnar Raudi, his snow-in-bracken hair tied back with a leather thong, stood easily, casually, one hand on the hilt of his sword. Einar, his lips like a scar, stood opposite him, the black cloak of hair framing a face pale as a winter moon.

Illugi stepped forward between them, as if to sever some unseen rope that seemed to be leaning them towards one another.

'This Hun lord,' he went on, as if nothing had interrupted the conversation, 'was the Great City's enemy, so it is believed. He fought them in his time and was slain for it by a general called Anagestes. He was brought back to the steppe lands to be howed up.'

The tension, like a sail emptied of wind, flapped once and was gone. Einar grunted, stuffed gear into a leather bag and looped it over one shoulder. His shield went over the other. No one was taking mail, despite the threats: the heat was too great for that.

'Well, one thing is certain,' Einar said, offering a grin free of any mirth. 'Our Hild is leading him a little dance out on to the steppe.'

Our Hild. Like she was his sister. I watched him combing his hair to try to rid it of the worst of the nits, then tie it back with a leather thong against the heat. My own crawled with lice, but I would not shave it, as others did, since that was the mark of a thrall and I could not bring myself to go so far, sensible or not.

Einar shouldered past Gunnar Raudi and I swear I saw the hair on them rise, like the hackles on wolves, as they brushed against each other. My throat ached and I knew that there would be the mark of five livid bruises on it.

Our Hild. She was no more 'our Hild' than I could fart gold, but Einar clearly thought she was one of the Oathsworn, whether she had sworn or no. He did not, for an eyeblink, imagine that Hild could be playing him false and Vigfus was on the correct track, which was my thought on the matter at the time. Wrong, of course.

Illugi Godi looked once at Gunnar Raudi, then at me and shook his head. 'You are fools, the one for his loose gob, the other for getting into a pissing contest with the likes of Einar.'

'If you don't want to get your toes wet,' answered Gunnar Raudi with a chuckle, levering himself off the doorpost, 'then keep your shoes away from my pisser.'

Illugi raised a defiant chin and his staff, the mark of his rank, but Gunnar merely grinned at him and swaggered off.

'Asgard seems a little deaf to you these days, Odin priest,' he threw back over his shoulder as he went – and I saw Illugi flinch, his head drooping for the first time that day.

240

There was no hint of any of that now as Einar took a knee, sweat-gleamed and grinning, to face the lolling-tongued dog-men he had led into the Grass Sea.

'We must be close,' he called out, glancing at the sun as it started to die, slow and glorious on the edge of the world. 'Tomorrow we'll be on them and get our Hild back.'

The men growled appreciative responses, muted and weary in the heat.

Einar climbed slowly to his feet and hefted his shield and gear to more comfortable spots. 'For now,' he grinned, 'we move.'

'Our Hild,' I muttered morosely as I got up and Illugi, passing, heard it and cocked his head quizzically.

'Our Hild,' I repeated. 'She has suffered nothing but hard knocks from us. He even took away the one thing she had, that bloody spear-shaft. And yet he imagines she is "our Hild".'

'She suffered worse under Vigfus and Lambisson,' Illugi reminded me sternly, leaning on his staff, 'from which we rescued her.'

I grudgingly admitted that and he eyed me carefully as I limped forward.

'Make no mistake with Einar, though,' he went on, for my ears only. 'He calls her "our Hild" because that is what she is. Not Vigfus's, or Lambisson's, or the property of Martin the thrice-cursed monk. Ours, Orm. As the *Elk* is ours. As the silver hoard is ours. I would watch my sullen face and loud tongue round Einar these days. You have become . . . unlucky . . . for him. Next time he may rip the throat out of you.'

I looked straight back at him and saw the harsh lines etched in his face, lines of worry and strain, and Gunnar Raudi's words came back to me. I saw the gods were crushing our priest with their apathy these days and he could find no way to speak to them that would get them to listen.

'I know it,' I replied and slapped my leg. 'Let's hope my limp gets no worse and he has, with all sadness, to leave me behind, eh?'

'He would do it,' Illugi said.

'I have always known that, I am thinking,' I said flatly. 'The difference here, today, is that now so would you, Illugi Godi. A good offering to appease whatever gods Einar has annoyed, eh, godi? Better than a fighting horse, you think?'

I left him, savage with the triumph of the moment, turning away and limping after the others, out of the twilight forest and on to the baking steppe. Later, I was ashamed of myself for having said it, for Illugi had been patient and good with me. But too much had happened by then.

We reached another huddle of trees as the darkness grew and the stars came out. We had no fires and the night was cold, so that those who had decided not to burden themselves with cloaks found themselves shivering, doubly cold after the baking heat of the day. We shared, then, huddled in twos and threes, silvered by a great wheel of stars and moonlight in a perfect, clear night.

In the washed silver of early dawn we were up and assembled, coughing, farting, sniffing, chewing. Men shivered, took a final piss and sorted out their gear, knowing Bagnose had come in during the night with news.

The tomb was found and Vigfus with it, led by the nose to it, it seemed to me, following on after Hild. Steinthor was watching the entrance even now.

Einar listened and nodded and clapped Bagnose on the shoulder, then looked over the wolf-eager faces round him, their breath steaming in the dawn chill, and nodded, smiling. 'This is the edge of a big stretch of forest,' he said. 'It is cut up by lots of gulleys and some of them are quite steep and choked with brush, so watch your feet. Our enemy is no more than an hour's walk away, at what seems to be a set of stairs leading to an entrance high in the side of a

242

ravine. With luck, we will trap them all inside and smoke them out.'

He looked at me and his smile widened, so that the feral-sharp teeth at the side of his mouth were exposed, yellow and gleaming. 'Like a bear hunt, eh, Orm?'

The others chuckled. Einar had them bound to the enterprise with the promise of an easy victory and the luck of the Bear Slayer at their command. You had to admire him.

Bagnose hadn't been wrong about the gulleys and the brush. I had been congratulating myself on keeping up, despite the ankle, but this last section ended at the entrance to a sheer-sided gulley, with a river splashing down the middle of it. When Bagnose silently signalled a halt, I sank down gratefully, feeling the pain, as if someone was shoving a hot brand straight through my ankle-bones.

I wanted to look at it, but dared not take the boot off, or remove the bindings, for I knew it would swell like a dead sheep's belly and that would be that. Instead, I stood in the stream and felt the cool water soak into my boot and wash round the throb of my foot.

A bird whirred and insects hummed as we followed the stream, straight towards what appeared to be a vertical wall of exposed rock. The stream curved round and disappeared and I heard the distant splash of water from a fall. The heat was crippling and there was no air at all, for all we were near water, just a strange stillness. Even the plagues of insects had vanished.

Steinthor and Bagnose appeared as we came up, so nonchalant that we all relaxed, for they swaggered out openly, as if there was no danger.

'They went in about two hours ago,' Steinthor said, wiping his streaming face with a cuff. 'They camped at the foot of those steps last night and spent most of the morning cutting what tall trees they could find to make a bridge at the top. Then they went up.'

We all saw the steps, rough-cut in a half-spiral up one side of the gulley. I started for it and something smacked wetly on my bare forearm. I rubbed it absently, then noticed it was water, but gritty.

I looked up at a strange, brass-coloured sky and wished my father with us, for he knew weather better than anyone and this was nothing I had seen before. I have experienced it twice since, trading down the Black Sea and again in Serkland.

Einar left a dozen men at his back and led the rest of us up the steps. At the top, with room for only one or two, we found it was an outcrop, round which the stream bent. Below, spilling from the far wall, was where the stream began, in a waterfall, whose spray was wonderfully cooling.

Spanning the gap between the outcrop and a wide ledge was a rickety bridge of warped timbers, the wood Vigfus and his men had been cutting. On the ledge beyond lay a scatter of bones around what appeared to be three or four sapling stumps, emerging out of the rock.

Steinthor grinned at our confusion, for he had crept up this far and worked it out. 'Grave robbers from before,' he said, pointing. 'Look – those were spears, weighted to shoot upwards when that area was stepped on. Right up the crease.'

'Traps,' Einar said and the word was passed down the line on the stairs, from head to head like a leaping spark. 'And traps,' he added loudly, to take the sting out of it, 'mean treasure.'

He strode out on to the timber walkway, took three swift steps and was on the ledge, moving cautiously to where the spear-stumps remained. Ketil Crow followed and the next man, the ever-jesting Skarti, paused nervously, eyeing the chasm under the rickety timbers and the unknown dangers of the ledge beyond. The sweat trickled down between the old pox lumps of his face.

We all waited patiently. Since Vigfus's men had all made

244

it, it seemed to me there was little danger left, but there was also no harm in letting someone else go first. When Skarti reached safety, turning with a grin of relief, we all cheered him.

On the ledge, which was broader and wider than it looked from the level of the stream, about another dozen of us congregated; the rest remained on the steps. A wind breathed and sighed up the gulley, rustling the tinder-dry brush, bringing a welcome coolness.

There was an entrance, blocked once by masonry, which now lay in thick chunks. Illugi Godi picked one up, turning it in his hands. It had symbols on it, or the remains of them. There were more symbols, age-worn, on either side and, with surprise, I saw they were truncated Latin – I knew the words *Dis Manibus*, recognised *ala* and started to work out the others

'That big turd with the Dane axe,' Steinthor said, indicating the masonry chunks. 'He can use the blunt end, too.'

I remembered the yellow beard, the grin, the axe, and shivered.

'They call him Boleslav,' Steinthor went on. 'Saxon, I think. Tough, though. Carved his way through this . . . stuff.'

'Roman,' Illugi Godi said. 'I have heard of this. They make a gruel and plaster it on like daub, but it sets hard as stone.'

'What are the markings?' demanded Einar and winced as a sudden flurry of wind blew dust at us.

Illugi shrugged. 'Warning? Curse? A request to knock? I can hardly even try to work out what is in pieces.'

'Latin,' I offered, running my fingers over the sigils. 'They say this is the tomb of Spurius Dengicus, khan of the Kutriguri. Carried here to be buried under the eye of Rome by his brother, Rome's friend, Ernak.'

'Spurius Dengicus? That's Roman, not Hun,' said Eyjolf, whom everyone called Finnbogi, since he was from those lands.

245

Illugi, who knew a few things himself, answered: 'They gave him a proper name for his tomb, doing honour as befits his status. But no respectable Roman family would want their name associated with a steppe lord, so the Roman chiefs found a family that had died out, only the name remaining.

'So it is that all adopted Romans are called Spurius,' he finished.

And so it was. Nowadays, of course, anyone who is considered a shifty lot, not quite what he claims to be, is called Spurius in the Great City.

'Anything else we should know?' demanded Einar, with a pointed look at Illugi. 'Anything that will actually help us, that is?'

I frowned and traced the worn letters. 'There's something about not disturbing his rest,' I offered.

With perfect timing, there came a distant wail from inside the dark opening, a wolf of a sound that set everyone's hackles up. Men backed away; even the ones on the step heard it.

'Odin's arse,' snarled Bagnose suddenly, 'what is happening to the sky?'

Most of it seemed to have gone, eaten by a towering wall of darkness. Even as we looked at it, yellow lightning flickered and the wind rushed at us, like the fetid breath of a dragon, lashing us with a stinging rain filled with grit.

'Thor's goats' arses, more like,' shouted Steinthor above the sudden roar of wind. Men yelled and huddled. Those on the lower steps started to go down, those higher up pushed those behind.

'There's no shelter there!' bellowed Einar above the sudden howling swirl of the wind. 'Up here, into the rock.'

They staggered up and Gunnar Raudi, with Ketil Crow, bent to hold the timber frame, frantic – as were we all – that it would topple, or be swept away and leave us stranded up here. Thunder cracked; the yellow heavens roiled and Illugi

Godi stood upright, staff in one hand, both arms upraised.

'All-Father hear us!'

'Move your fucking fat arses!' screamed Ketil Crow as men stumbled up the steps and across the ledge and into the dark opening like a line of frenzied ants.

'All-Father, hear us. Send your winged ones to bind the wounds of the sky. Ask Thor why he rides his goat chariot over us. Lift us from this field of battle . . .'

A man, caught off-balance by the wind, shrieked his way into the chasm, disappearing beneath the waterfall.

'All-Father . . .'

'Save it, godi, no one is listening to you,' snarled Einar and spat into the dust and mud-brown sluice of rain. 'Run, if you value your life.'

And I ran, limping, heedless of the pain, into the dark opening of the tomb.

Inside, someone had sparked up a torch, but the band huddled as close together as possible in the half-light of a stone passage, shivering, wet, cold in the sudden chill of stone. There was a taste of old dust and bones in my mouth.

'Well done for the torch,' Einar panted, coming up with Ketil Crow and Gunnar Raudi, the latter hauling the rickety timber bridge after him. We paused, all sweat and gleaming eyes in the dark, as another of those low, mournful moans drifted up from the light at the other end of the passage.

Light from a torch none of us had lit.

The storm grumbled. Einar pushed his way through the packed mass of us in the narrow passage and peered to where the yellow glow was.

'Well,' he said. 'Such a light in a dark place always means there is gold there, as anyone knows.' He turned, his grin startling in the dark. 'At least it means someone is home. Perhaps they will offer us hospitality on a stormy night. Ale and meat and women.'

The laughs were forced, though, and he moved on, stepping boldly while we cringed and waited for the springing spear or worse.

Nothing happened. We followed, cautiously, out of the passage into a wider area, part natural cavern, part construct. An arch, made from Illugi Godi's liquid Roman stone, led through to where the torch burned brightest and I thought to point it out to the priest – then saw his face, anguished, dead-eyed. He had called his gods and heard nothing but anger.

Shields up – those who hadn't lost them in the panic outside – and blades ready, we crept forward.

Beyond the arch, we all stopped. There was an even wider area, flagged with great squares of stone. The middle squares were bisected lengthways by small ridges, only just raised above the surface, and where one large square of stone should have been was an opening, from which came a faint torch glow.

More light, guttering in the wind hissing from outside, spilled from the red torch held by Hild, who was hunkered next to the opening, head cocked like a curious bird.

As we came in, there was that echoing groan from below and she turned and looked at us, a beautiful, beatific smile set in a face milk-pale, below eyes as black and dead as a corpse. Everyone saw it and came to a sudden halt.

'Hild . . . ?' I asked. She turned those eyes on me, without losing the smile, then looked down into the darkness, holding the torch high.

'Walk only on the raised ledge,' she said in a harsh voice. 'Beyond is a door, barred now. It leads down and round to where Dengizik sits with his warriors. Do not step off these ridged ledges or, like Boleslav, you will pay the price for violating Dengizik's last fortress and lie prostrate at his feet.'

There was another whimper, which I now realised was Boleslav in agony. Hild rose then, in a fluid, fast movement like nothing she had ever done before and thrust the torch

248

at where Einar stood, pale under his crow-wings of hair, which stirred in the heat from the flames.

'I led them down, then left while they gawped, slipped back and barred the door on them. Only Boleslav was left here and I let him come to me, as he did once before. Only this time I kept my legs closed and my feet in the right place, while he did not.'

Her laugh was cracked. Dry-mouthed, sweating, we all peered down the great square hole into the room beyond. Torches flared and there were crowds of men, I saw.

'There are hundreds of them,' muttered Bersi, wiping his mouth with the back of one hand.

'Those are Dengizik's soldiers,' Hild said harshly. 'Vigfus is among them now, trying to work out how to get back here. He has seen Boleslav fall.'

'So he's trapped?' demanded a voice: Wryneck, I recognised. 'Good. Leave him there. When the storm blows out, we can leave this gods-cursed place.'

'What of the treasure? And he might manage to climb back up through that hole,' demanded someone else.

Bersi snorted and spat. 'Let's come back in a few weeks,' he said, 'and see who is left and who has been eaten.'

'No!' Hild's voice was the flat of a sword struck on stone. She quivered as with a fever, but there was no white to the eyes she glared at Einar and her pointed finger was like a blade. 'Kill Vigfus. We agreed. Kill Vigfus and all his men. Then we go to Atil's howe.'

Einar nodded. No one spoke. He stepped on to the narrow ledge, no wider than the palm of his hand, and, lightly, gracefully, took three quick steps and was across.

Swallowing, I took the torch from Hild, staring at her. She stared back and I had to look away from those eyes, like beads of jet. Behind them lurked . . . something else, something even darker.

Ketil Crow was equally graceful; Wryneck, after a quick

wipe of his dry mouth, shuffled waveringly across and then I followed, seeing figures below me and the sudden spark of tinder. One by one we crossed.

Einar nodded. 'We finish Vigfus here, lads. There is no escape for him now.'

We agreed. The words gnawed me, kicked in the thought that had eluded me since the fight on the Rus boat. It crashed on me like a sluice of cold water.

She had planned it with Einar. She had spotted Hogni as one of Vigfus's men and had told Einar and then given him her price for leading him to Attila's silver, for giving up her precious talisman, the spear-shaft.

Vigfus. Who had beaten and raped her and now faced her vengeance.

She had plotted with Hogni, pretending to want away from Einar and all with Einar's knowing. He had tried to trap them on the Rus boat – that's why he had all the men armed and mailed, for he knew there would be a raid. But when Vigfus wasn't part of it, he let them take her, thinking then to trap Vigfus in the town.

That had also failed, which wasn't part of the plan . . . but he had trusted that he knew Hild well enough, that she was leading Vigfus to where he could be finally trapped and slain. All he had to do was follow, to this place.

He had sweated a bit and lost sleep over it – but she had kept her part in the bargain.

I sank down then, drained of all feeling. There was cleverness in it and ruthlessness and that was no fault. But there was also a coldness and something sick and black as rot.

Once, when I was hunting wild honey late in the season and thought I'd found a comb in a tree hollow, I had boldly thrust my hand in, for speed can foil bees made sluggish with cold. I had plunged into stickiness and triumphantly seized a handful and pulled it out – only to find the slick remains of dead bees and old comb, a stinking mess that made me gag.

I knew where this malignant rot came from, too. Einar, I thought, had made a bad bargain, no matter what he believed Hild would do for him now. Whatever Hild was before she was something else now, something . . . Other . . . and something that had a plan all of its own.

She wanted, I was thinking, to get to Atil's howe. Had to. Needed us to help her do it – and what then?

Einar's eyes were too full of silver to see clearly and, worse, he was dragging us all along, I saw with cold despair, in the shackles of our own oath honour.

He and Valknut forced out the huge stone beam that barred the equally heavy stone doors. No one wanted to ask how a slip of a girl like Hild had managed to shut and bar the door on her own.

We started down the stairs, reached a landing which led to the left, then continued to where Vigfus's torches lit the room beyond. Two steps further down, we stopped, amazed, afraid.

The room was lined with men, armoured in cobwebs and rotting leather and rusting metal lappets. They sat, cross-legged, spears upright and butted into round holes in the floor. A few elaborately helmeted heads had toppled, some skeletal hands had slipped from the spears, but Dengizik's faithful sat on, in the same position they had once taken up on the day the tomb was sealed.

The enormity of that stunned me into sitting down on the lowest stair. They had marched in, sat down, butted their spears and died. Poison? Perhaps, though I would not have been surprised to learn that Dengizik's faithful guard had simply stayed sitting until they died of starvation and thirst.

They sat in neat lines flanking a flagged approach running from the stair to where Dengizik sat, equally armoured, on a stone throne, a great cross on one side . . . no, not a cross. Cross-shaped, but from the arm of the T hung hair. Horsetails:

251

the standard of a Hun chieftain, I learned later. A great, ornate helmet was set on the top of it and I realised this was because the withered thing on the throne had no head.

I got to know those standards well, for the Khazars, who would not have been out of place at Attila's side, had them, too, as well as the strange disc-standards that marked them as Jewishmen – but I never again came across a howed-up steppe lord with no head.

Nor were the lines quite as neat now as they must have been for centuries. The tilting stones above opened on both sides and Boleslav had slipped down one on the left, straight on to the grounded spears of the long-dead.

His weight had snapped the old wood; he had crashed into the dusty corpses beyond and rolled out on to the flagged approach. Now he lay at Dengizik's enthroned feet, pierced through chest and belly, finished off with a merciful throat-cut.

All that strength and skill, I marvelled, remembering him spinning the giant Dane axe, laid low by a slip of a girl. And I shivered at what he had done to her to deserve that impaled death. I knew well enough and half the shiver was for me.

Do not love me, she had said.

Vigfus stepped forward, splendid in gilded mail and a marvellous helmet that had been new for his great-grandfather, which covered the whole face save for the mouth and eyes and had gilded eyebrows and two huge raven feathers.

Behind and on either side were his men, desperate-grim and hefting their axes and swords and spears. There was only one sure way out of that room and that was to go through us and there were not nearly enough of them for that.

Someone flitted past me, back up the stairs and I almost followed, thinking we were well out of it – then I saw it was Bagnose, heading back to the opening, which lay above the room, nocking an arrow as he went. Steinthor, I presumed, was already there.

'I suppose,' Vigfus said, scowling, 'there is no bargaining here.'

'None,' replied Einar with a twisted smile.

'One to one to settle this, winner lets the others go?'

Einar shook his head, chuckling. 'What – and let all this planning go to waste? How does it feel, Quite the Dandy, ladies' man, to have been so trapped by my lady?'

Vigfus narrowed his eyes at the full import of what had been said. His men looked anxiously from one to the other.

'If she is your lady,' Vigfus snarled, 'I wish you well of her. You pair are suited. Personally, I found her a poor, cold, dry hump – but she seemed to want more, so I let my lads have a go. Most preferred to find a goat.'

Some of his men chuckled. Most, realising that that poor, cold, dry hump was what had led them to this wyrd, were less amused.

'Enough talk,' said Einar coldly and snaked forward. An arrow hissed from the opening above and one of Vigfus's men screeched and plucked at the shaft through both sides of his neck. Men closed, steel crashed, shields whumped under blows.

I was cautious, I ganged up with old Wryneck on one man and, between us, we cut him down in a flurry of blows, me hacking deep scores in his arms and one calf, Wryneck battering lumps off his head and swearing.

Another hurtled out of the darkness at us and I twisted to face him. Pain sprang from my ankle and I grunted and stopped. Wryneck clashed with his man and I barely managed to deflect a blow meant for him.

An axe whirred out of nowhere and clattered off Gunnar Raudi's shield. My opponent, black-bearded, screaming, cut a vicious diagonal slash, which I sprang back from. His momentum carried the blow into one of the dead warriors, who exploded in a great eruption of dust and dead insects and toppled sideways. An arrow from above then smacked

Black Beard between the shoulder blades, propelling him straight at me, so that he fell on his face and slid to my feet.

His shield smashed into my injured ankle and I went down, sick with the pain of it, dropping sword and shield to clutch the thing, howling. Wryneck, too busy with his own man, never spared me a glance.

Through the sparkling lights of pain in front of my eyes, I saw Einar cut his man down with a swift series of feints and strikes and vicious shield punches. He turned then, to where Gunnar Raudi was trading blows with Vigfus, who scorned a shield and had a boarding axe in one hand and a long seax in the other.

They cut and leaped and spun, elbowing Dengizik's dead men aside with curses. The chamber filled with the dust of old death, the fear-stink and blood of new.

Vigfus was good, too, and I remembered him spidering across rooftops, swinging in and out of shuttered openings, leaping to grab a rope in mid-air. Fast and limber, for all that he had no sense of dress at all.

Twice Gunnar Raudi had almost lost his sword to the boarding axe, Vigfus swirling it round to trap the sword in the curve of its beard, flicking his wrist to lock it, then trying to wrench it out of Gunnar's grasp.

But Vigfus's magnificent helmet was a hindrance and you could see why sensible warriors had given that type up for one with a simple nasal: you couldn't see anything out of the corner of your eye and, in a whirling fight like this, that was suicide.

Gunnar circled. Einar came up behind him and I thought he was moving to Gunnar's sword side, to make it two on one. As he did, Gunnar Raudi stiffened, half turned – and Vigfus's axe hurled round and took him between neck and shoulder, cleaving deep in a splinter of rings and bone and blood.

My scream was lost in the echoing shrieks and yells of the battle. Einar flung himself over Gunnar's body at Vigfus, roaring his challenge, spittle flying. I half stumbled to where Gunnar lay, blood pooling thickly on the dusty floor.

He was gone, already white, barely able to speak. His lips moved in the frosted berry beard, now bright with new, vicious red spilling from his mouth. If he had something to say other than with those frantic eyes, I never heard it. When they glazed over, I closed them.

Vigfus, fingers curling on the wire-wrapped handle of his axe, crabbed sideways, elbowing aside another fighting pair, one of whom aimed a brief, speculative cut at Vigfus as he did so.

In that helmet, he almost missed it, was left off balance and clattered into another of the Oathsworn, who then stumbled into another of those dead warriors, impaling himself on an age-blackened spear.

I have been asked by bright-eyed youngsters who have never fought for their lives with shield and steel what it's like. I never tell them that it is four or five minutes of mad fear and luck, of slashing cuts and savagery, of shit and blood and shrieking.

The sagas tell it better and the one about the battle between Einar and Vigfus would, no doubt, have been memorable for its superior, clever kennings and nobility. Reality was different and vicious.

Einar, snarling, his sword dripping blood, slashed at Vigfus in a flurry of steel and Vigfus danced sideways, raised himself on his toes and swung the axe downwards in a vicious arc, screaming as he did so.

It took Einar's shield just below the rim, a solid pine on pine wheel of wood, and split it lengthwise. With a swift shrug, Einar was out of the straps, both hands on the hilt of his sword and Vigfus, still holding the buried axe, was jerked sideways by the dead weight of the dropped shield.

Too late, he released his grip. Einar's two-handed blow spanged off one side of that helmet, took Vigfus on the top

255

of the left shoulder with the splintering crack of bone and sheared down through mail, bone, flesh and sinew until it popped out of his armpit with a sucking sound and a spray of ruined iron rings.

Vigfus roared, spun away from his falling arm and clapped his remaining hand over the great rush of blood from the stump. The second blow crushed mail rings into his ribs. The third slashed a steak out of his thigh. He went down, bellowing as Einar hacked shreds off him until there was no more noise.

The others of his crew tried to give up, but Hild would not have that. Screeching, hair flying like a Valkyrie, she demanded they all die.

Two of the Dandy's men threw down their weapons and Einar cut them down where they stood with a few swift strokes. After that, the others fought on with the desperate ferocity of the cornered, but it was short and they were all chopped to bloody ruin by packs of Oathsworn.

Then there was silence, save for the pant and gasp of ravaged lungs. Someone was puking, hard and noisy, and the impaled man was growling and yelling as others tried to lever his arm off the spear-point. The iron stink of blood was everywhere; the floor of the tomb was slushed with viscous red mud.

And I sat there in a widening slick of Gunnar Raudi's blood, his head in my lap, watching the other sluggish pool form slowly from the stab wound in his back.

TWELVE

Eight men were dead; twenty-four more had wounds, some of them deep. In the stunned twilight of battle, Ketil Crow and Illugi took me under the armpits and hauled me up and away from Gunnar Raudi.

I let them, numbed by what I thought I knew, never taking my eyes off Einar. Had he stabbed Gunnar Raudi in the back, hard enough to wound, to distract him? In that half-light and confusion I turned it over and over and still it vanished like smoke.

In the end, I knew, with a deep, sick feeling, that he had, but there was nothing I could do. He was, I thought with a flush of fear, as fetch-haunted as Hild. And had broken his oath yet again in that mad moment.

Then I kept hearing Gunnar Raudi's warnings and knew, with a nauseating certainty, that I would be next.

None of it would bring Gunnar Raudi back. Illugi and I, working without a word between us while the others bound up wounds and sorted out their gear, cleaned Gunnar Raudi as best we could and laid him out on his back, hands folded on his sword. I had to tear strips off his underkirtle to bind his shoulder back to his body, rather than have that terrible gape, so like a lipless mouth.

Einar came across after we had done this, stared down at the body and where we hunkered near it. 'A good man,' he said. 'He died a good death.'

I could not speak. Blood leaked into my mouth from biting the inside of my lip to keep from screaming at him: You killed Gunnar Raudi. You killed him. Like you killed Eyvind.

Einar ordered him laid at the feet of the throne, where the mouldering, fur-rotted remains of Dengizik sat, skeletal hands on the stone arms, the fur rim of his rusting helmet festering on his neck.

Everyone wanted out of that place, especially when Hild drifted like silent smoke down the stairs, to stand over the carved remains of Vigfus and smile her beautiful, fey smile.

'Dengizik has no head,' Einar noted, his voice cracked with dryness.

'The Romans took it and put it on a pole,' Hild answered, her voice seeming sucked out of her in a hiss. 'His faithless young brother Ernak, who would not stand with him against the Great City, had permission to take the body, on condition the Romans sealed the tomb, lest his fetch return. Five hundred years and more it has sat here. My mother told me this.'

There were looks flying one to another, from eyes round and white with fear. Tongues snaked over dry lips as the dust settled, mote by mote and almost sibilant. No one liked talk of a fetch in such a place.

'Is there anything we need from here?' Einar demanded of her, his voice crow-harsh in the blood-reeked twilight.

'Not for me,' she answered, soft as the rustle of a shroud. 'But this is Atil's son and those swords were made by the same smith who forged Atil's blade from the end of the Christ spear. My distant kinsman, Regin the Volsung.'

Two swords lay across the cobwebbed, dusty brocade of Dengizik's robed lap, but no one even wanted to go near them, never mind claim them as spoil.

We left that place, treasureless and afraid, not even having looted Vigfus's men. By the time we had got back across the timber bridge – knocking it spinning into the waterfalled chasm after everyone was safely across – and down the steps, the storm had ended. The sun was out, the sky a clear-washed cloudless blue, and the ground steamed in the heat. But every leaf had a muddy wash, rapidly drying to dust in the heat.

At the stream, we refilled leather skins and bottles, soaked our heads, and considered how best to go on. There were seven of us with wounds likely to slow everyone down and I was one of them, but we were paired with others who helped us back up the brush-covered ravines and on to the steppe.

Thereafter, it was simply a long world of pain, step by fire-laced step, hour after hour, back to Kiev.

That ankle has never been right since; it aches in cold weather and, now and then, simply gives out and throws me over like a sack of grain, always when I am trying to impress with my gravitas and dignity. Each time it flicks pain at me, I remember Gunnar Raudi.

Others suffered much more. By the second day, the man whose forearm had been speared was running a high fever and his arm had swollen like a balloon. By the time we reached the outskirts of Kiev he was being carried in a cloak held at all four corners by his oarmates, drenched in sweat and moaning piteously, while the arm had turned black to the armpit.

Illugi tried what he knew, a potion made from bark of aspen, quickbeam, willow and wych-elm: fifteen barks in all made up this one. It failed, so he tried a poultice made from the ashes of burned hair and everyone con-tributed some, even Bersi, whose waist-length flame-red hair had never, ever been cut and who believed it bad luck to do so.

It was certainly bad luck for Illugi's patient, who died thrashing in his sleep that night in Kiev, having made it to safety. I watched him being wrapped for burial and knew only that his name was Hedin and that he had once kept bees in Uppsala.

On the open steppe we had spotted distant horsemen, beyond arrow range and moving with us like a pack of questing wolves. But they did not come near and everyone agreed it was probably because we had come out of the tomb. Perhaps, it was argued, they thought we were fetch warriors and did not dare to contest us.

I thought it was because of Hild, the only one unconcerned by them. She walked with bold, long strides in her red half-boots, swishing the skirt of her long, blue, red–embroidered dress and only slightly soiled overmantle, a Rus *zanaviska*, her dark hair spilling free.

She was the perfect picture of a Norse maiden – until she turned to look at you and you saw that almost all her eyes were almost entirely black, all dark pupil, with only a thin corona of white. Regin's kinswoman and, if you knew of him, you could see the resemblance.

'Is that the same Regin from the tales, then?' demanded Bersi during one rest halt, when we all hunkered and panted, wiping sweat out of our eyes. 'Sigurd's oarmate?'

'So she seems to say,' Skarti growled, glancing uneasily at where Hild sat, neat in her dress and staring at the horizon.

'Not an oarmate,' growled Bagnose, putting one finger to his nose and snotting to the side.

'Eh?'

'Not an oarmate,' repeated Bagnose. 'Regin had Sigurd as fostri. He was brother to Fafnir, who became a dreaded wyrm through gold-greed and a curse. Regin was a skilled smith, though, who made Sigurd a marvellous sword. Sigurd killed Fafnir the wyrm and ate his heart, which gave him wisdom to see Regin planned his murder, so he killed Regin, too.'

260

'That's a lot of killing, it seems to me,' Steinthor said, 'even for a saga tale.'

'Over a hoard, too,' noted Bersi and we all fell silent, brooding on that, until it was time to move off.

'It's all just tales for fucking children,' growled Wryneck. 'Why we bother with this is the only mystery in it.'

Two other men died in Kiev, of the same sort of thing, their wounds swelling and turning black. A Greek doctor, whom Illugi summoned in desperation, shook his head and said the men must have had something get in the wound, a miasmic rot that festered their injuries.

We never told him where we had been, but knowing looks were exchanged. Dengizik's reach was long, it seemed, and everyone agreed that it had been deep thinking not to have taken his swords, even if they had been Regin's work.

We wrapped and buried our dead in Kiev and I listened to Illugi's soft, long chants on the wyrd of men, one usually sung by mothers mourning children.

Deep into the night before the army left for Sarkel it went on, for Gunnar Raudi, for all the others who had died and, I was thinking, hunched up with my chin on my knees, for Illugi himself and his lost gods:

'Hunger will devour one, storm dismast another,
One will be spear-slain, one hacked down in battle;
One will drop, wingless, from the high tree,
One will swing from the tall gallows,
The sword edge will shear the life of one,
At the mead-bench, some angry sot,
Soaked with wine, his words too hasty,
Will cut one down and make his wyrd.'

A thousand barrels of ale, fifty thousand sheep, the same in bushels of barley, the same yet again in bushels of millet and wheat. Sixty thousand horses, ropes, awnings, tents, hoes, mattocks . . . I heard all this when accounts of the siege were being studiously written up by scholars in the Great City, years later.

I remember one old beard, pen poised, blinking at me as we sat with olives and bread and wine on my pleasant balcony in the Foreign Quarter, enjoying the breeze across the Horn from Galata.

'How many cheesemakers?' he asked and frowned when I laughed.

I told him a number, but I doubt if there were any. I never saw a decent cheese in all the time we floated with Sviatoslav's army down the Don, or sat under those rune-tiled walls at Sarkel, sweating and fevered and scheming and trying not to die before we got rich.

If we had needed cheese, though, Sviatoslav would have provided it. For a man who famously made war on the run, as they say – no wagons, no means of cooking, just strips of leathery meat sweat-soaked under a saddle – he had changed his methods for the attack on Sarkel.

I saw him once, while sweating to load arrows and barrels of salt mutton – no pork, for half of his army wouldn't eat it, for one reason or another – on the boats, already packed with timbers and Greek siege engineers. There was a great commotion along the river bank, men cheering and breaking off what they were doing to run and line the route a caval-cade was taking.

It was Sviatoslav, cantering along in a cloud of dust at the head of his *druzhina*, mailed men with horsehair-plumed helmets and bright blue fur-trimmed cloaks, mounted on magnificent horses. In this heat, they would be baking ovens, but the forest of their lances never wavered.

He was visiting each of his sons and it was Yaropolk's turn, but we were too late to turn out smartly for it. To Einar's annoyance, the Oathsworn greeted the moment like gawping yokels, stripped to the waist, streaked and sweating

262

and loading gear like slaves – mainly because we didn't trust the slaves to do it properly.

I don't know what I had expected, but the ruler of the Rus, of Kiev and Novgorod, who controlled from the Baltic to the edge of the territory ruled by the Romans of Miklagard, was a burly little man with a nub of nose and a yellow beard.

He wore white tunic and trousers, like all the Rus under their armour, but his were dazzlingly clean. His head was shaved save for that silver-banded braid over one ear. There was the sparkle of a huge gold ring in the other.

'Not much to look at, is he?' grunted Bersi, pausing in his lifting. He wiped his brow, his great mane of red hair plastered to the middle of his back with sweat.

'You can tell him that when he shoves a stake up your arse and leaves you hanging there,' countered Wryneck, swigging watered ale from a skin. He wiped his snow-white beard and tossed the ale skin to me.

'Is that what they do here? For what?' demanded Bersi incredulously.

'For some, it is saying the Great Lord of Kiev is not much to look at,' a voice broke in and we turned to see one of the magnificent cavalrymen, helmet held in the crook of his arm, his bald head glistening.

He was smiling, as was the boy with him, a lad of about six or thereabouts, so the panic that had gripped us fled. I squinted up at him while others moved quietly, examining the boy's horse and gear, the beautifully crafted mail of the man, the great metal fishscales of his lamellar coat.

We marvelled and questioned. Three years it took to train a cavalryman in the *druzhina* of a Rus chieftain, we learned. Six for his horse.

The horseman spoke good Norse – East, of course, but most understood him. We admired his two sabres, his lance, the mace that dangled from one wrist, the cased bow.

263

'Are the Khazars the same?' I asked and he smiled down at me.

'Not so brave or good-looking,' he replied. 'But they are the same; all cavalrymen are. You need to be mad to be one and your horse doubly so. It takes the same time to train them – half the army has Khazar blood in them anyway. We always end up fighting our relations in these affairs.'

We chuckled and said it was the same in the north. I tossed him the skin and he drank and gave it back, wiping excess off his moustaches.

Suddenly, Yaropolk was there, with Einar at his stirrup, both scowling.

'Father is leaving, brother,' the pimpled Yaropolk said pointedly to the boy, then flushed and inclined his head graciously to the man. 'Uncle,' he said and we now realised, with a shock, that the boy was young Prince Vladimir and the man Dobrynya, his uncle on his mother's side. The uncle now raised his helmet, slipped it back over his head and then raised one hand in salute.

'Prince Vladimir,' acknowledged Einar and the boy paused as Yaropolk rode off.

'I like your men, Einar the Black,' he said in a sweet, unbroken voice. 'If you survive Biela Viezha, we shall speak again.'

And he was gone, leaving us in a cloud of dust. Einar stroked his moustaches thoughtfully.

'What was all that about?' demanded Bersi. 'Was that really a Rus prince?'

'Kingship was what it was all about,' grunted Einar. 'When you are born to a thrall woman, you need more of it to survive.' Then he bent to a barrel and heaved. 'Back to work, you useless farts.'

As we fell into the rhythm of passing barrel and sack, someone said plaintively, 'What the fuck is Biela Viezha?'

The White Castle, the Slav name for the Khazar fortress

at Sarkel, was what it was. The great, white-limestone fortress on a dun-coloured rise in a bend of the Don, almost at the Black Sea was what it was. The greatest insult to the Rus was what it was, for they had to pay ten per cent on every trade flotilla that went up or down from the Black Sea and politely beg for permission to do so.

All the way down the Don, floating gently, poled by yelling, sweating Chud rivermen, we had taunted the accompanying horsemen, who rode and walked their mounts along the north bank of the Don, as sweaty as we were cool.

They were the heavy horse; the lighter ones, the bowmen who rode fat-headed, short-legged, hairy dogs of ponies, were further out, wheeling like flocks of starlings on the far steppe, keeping the Khazar scouts at bay.

If there was any fighting, we never heard of it; we spent most of the time dicing, lazing about, trading fighting tips and hurling apple cores and rye-bread crusts at the luckless, sweating cavalrymen, who took it all in good part, it seemed to me.

But when we saw the White Castle, we knew why they didn't mind. It was dazzling, blinding white and the walls were huge and solid, with four towers and two gates and a bloody great ditch. I had been told that the Khazars had cities of tents and flimsy structures, easily destroyed and just as easily rebuilt. Even their palaces were just mud brick and they lived in them only during the winter.

Not Sarkel. It will come as no surprise to anyone to learn that the Great City had a hand in building it, ever-helpful to balance the power in the area. Sarkel was built with solid pillars and Roman know-how – and now they had sent their cleverest men and their biggest engines to knock it down, which is statecraft to these Romans.

As our boat was manhandled into the shore, one of the horsemen broke away and trotted over to us, peeling off his helmet to reveal a beaming, sweating face with a huge curl of moustache. 'Welcome, sword-brothers,' he chuckled and swept his hand towards the huge edifice squatting on the plain. 'I hope you enjoyed the rest and the apples. Now it is time to play your part.'

We looked at each other, then to those yellow-white walls on which we had to hurl ourselves and no one was smiling when he trotted off, his bellowing laugh drifting back to us, echoed by his companions.

He had to wait to see us suffer, though. The first days were spent tumbling out everything that had been brought, while horsemen raced off everywhere and dust hazed the world. At night, the cookfires were a field of flickering red blossom.

In two weeks, Sarkel had been cut off and the engineers were doing things with the timbers they'd brought. Spearmen – not the *druzhina* like us, but the great mass of unarmoured levy, sucked in from every tribe for hundreds of miles – stacked their weapons and dug level pits and raised platforms.

We all watched, fascinated, the first time three of these great efforts lobbed sheep-sized boulders across the steppe at the walls to get the range. They hit with a booming crash and a great puff of dust – but nothing happened; nothing collapsed. Disappointed, we went back to the sweaty, stinking job of scraping and boiling cowhides for glue to help fix the assault towers we would use.

That night, hunkered round our own collection of cookfires, we chewed flatbread, sucked down a good meat-gruel, endured the insects and traded our thoughts back and forth.

'There's no place left to shit,' Bersi complained.

'Sit here,' offered my father.

'Shit,' Bersi clarified. 'No place to shit. I'm fed up with stepping in it, everywhere you go.'

It was true enough. I'd heard the army was anything from sixty thousand to a million men and either could be true, though such a number was impossible to get inside your head.

All I knew was that there were a lot of them and even

more animals and women and children. Even for people like us, who'd grown up with shit, things were getting out of hand.

Illugi Godi said there would be trouble over it. People would start to get sick. Einar said that, tomorrow, he would have a place marked out and a pit dug. Everyone would shit there and nowhere else.

'Don't try it drunk,' advised Wryneck, who claimed to have had done this sort of thing before, 'or you'll fall in and stink for a week. If you even get out again, that is.'

But it was Ketil Crow who said what we all wanted to say. 'When are we leaving this?' he growled at Einar. 'Before we get slaughtered on those walls, or die of shit-sickness here, I am hoping to hear you say.'

Einar stroked his moustaches. 'We need to plan it well.'

'Plan what?' demanded Valknut, who was burned dark as a Fir Gorm, the black-men thralls from the very south of the world, so that only his eyes and teeth were seen clearly in the twilight. 'We know where to go – what else is there?'

'Of course,' said that quiet voice from the dark behind Einar. 'That's all you really need, after all.'

She was like a cold wind through an open door. Everyone fell silent under the weight of her renewed presence, but Ketil Crow just half glanced at her, irritated, then spat in the fire. 'Do we know where to go?' he demanded. 'I am wondering why I am following some hag-ridden Finn woman.'

'You think I do not know the way?' Hild challenged, squatting so that her knees came up almost round her ears, the dress pooled in her lap. Her feet, I saw, were neat and bare.

No one spoke, or looked at her long, but Ketil Crow looked from her to where Einar sat, his back to Hild, staring at the fire from under the wings of his hair and saying nothing.

'The others may be afraid of you,' Ketil Crow growled, 'but I am not. If you prove false in this I will rip you from cunt to jawline.'

Hild did not flinch, though a few of us did. Instead, she smiled that fey smile. 'It is good you are not afraid, Ketil Crow,' she said in a voice like the whisper of bat's wings. 'You will need that courage, I am thinking.'

Einar stirred then, half turning to where Hild crouched like some black spider. He shook his head and stroked his moustaches again. 'There's more than just finding it,' he said.

'So you say,' growled Wryneck, 'but I am with Ketil Crow in this matter. It seems to me that a witless girl is about to lead us into the sea of grass. I never trusted women and that has always stood me in good stead.'

'You won't become old and rich,' declared Hild suddenly, in a growl so unlike her own voice that everyone froze. The wind hissed, flattening the fire. Wryneck hawked and spat, deliberately loudly, a sneer of sound.

'You bicker like women,' Illugi declared scornfully. 'What has Einar to say on this?'

It seemed to me that if Einar had had anything to say he would have hoiked it out before now. I wondered if Hild had laid some seidr on him that kept his lips fastened on the matter – but he stirred like a man coming out of a sleep.

'We will get there,' he said, so softly that those at the back had to have it repeated to them. 'Then what?' He looked around us, challengingly. 'We get there and do what? Knock on the door and ask politely if we can have the hospitality of this dead hov? Some ale and meat and, oh, by the way, all the silver we can hold? What if there is no door, no way in – how do we make one?'

He wiped his mouth, reached for a skin and filled his horn, which was held between his knees, for the ground was too baked hard to stand it upright.

'More to the point,' he added, slashing us all with that black stare, 'how do you carry it away? In our shirts? Stuff it down our boots, or in our hats?'

'True enough,' Bagnose said cheerfully. 'There's a mountain of silver. We'll need a few big boots for that.'

They chuckled and Einar explained, 'We need rope and hoes and mattocks and carts to carry all of that – and to take the silver away in. And ponies to haul the carts. Not oxen, for they are too slow.'

There was silence while we all chewed on that and how to go about it. In the end, of course, Bersi put it to Einar.

'We wait,' he said. No one liked that answer.

'For what?' demanded Ketil Crow. 'We can take all those things—'

'And get how far – a mile? Two?' growled Illugi, shaking his head. 'Those horsemen move fast and charge hard.'

'Shouldn't have thrown so many apple cores at them,' offered Skarti, his lumpy face a nightmare in the red fire-glow. No one laughed much at that, remembering the horsemen, their armour and lances and bows.

'Wait for what then?' demanded Valknut sullenly, pitching a dung chip into the fire. 'I'm sick of gods-cursed cowhides and glue.'

'Better that than a ladder up those walls,' said a voice from further in, a deep growl I recognised as a Novgorod Slav called Eindridi. There were a few growls of assent at that.

'We wait until we get hungrier than this,' Einar declared quietly. 'Until the animals are being slaughtered and salted because there isn't enough good grass for them around here. Until the saddles of those grain-fed horses go in a notch or two.'

Everyone stared blankly, bewildered. But I knew what he was making them think. Gods, he was clever and cold as the edge of winter, right enough.

'Forage parties,' said Illugi triumphantly. 'Good reasons for being away from here with carts and horses and gear.'

'Right enough,' agreed Bersi and chuckled. 'Now there's deep-minded.'

I kept my counsel, for I had already seen forage parties going out, a collection of carts and horses, with thralls and women for the labouring and lance-armed cavalry for the muscle. Never foot warriors of the *druzhina*, though.

There was only one way, I realised, for *varjazi* like us to be away from all others, on the steppe with carts and horses and no questions asked, out of deference to our own rituals.

And some of us would have to die first.

'Forage parties. Deep thinking, right enough,' agreed Steinthor and tipped his ale horn empty. 'Now give us a riddle, Bagnose, and brighten up the evening.'

And, as Bagnose screwed up his face and worked one out in his head, Einar met my stare across the fire, knew what I was thinking, dared me to speak it.

'I am a strange creature, for I satisfy women, grow very tall and erect in bed, am hairy underneath and, now and then, a brave daughter of some fellow dares to hold me, grips my reddish skin, robs me of my head and puts me in her pantry. She remembers the meeting, her eyes moisten—' Bagnose intoned.

'An onion,' roared someone from the back. 'Heard that one when I was still crawling . . .'

Eventually, Einar dropped his eyes, but I ached with too much tension to claim a triumph.

THIRTEEN

U p close, the dazzling walls of the White Castle were a disappointing tan and yellow, pocked with the scabs of hurled rocks and scored with lashes of black where fireballs had gored.

Merlons had crumbled, giving it the gap-toothed grin of a crone at whose feet was a litter of smashed tiles: Turk pictures of horses and men that looked like runes to us. *Tamgas*, they called them, and our battering stones had ripped them away.

The plain before the city seethed like an anthill. Horsemen thundered, lance-tips glittering through the huge pall of dust that hazed everything to a golden fog.

I sweated and longed for a drink. My eyes stung from the dust and it gritted in every crease under the armour and my helmet, even in the corners of my mouth, turning to mud with my spittle.

To my left was Bersi, shield lying against his knees, tying a leather thong round the fourth of his red braids, trembling from fever fits. To my right, Wryneck stuck the finger of one gnarled hand up his nose and dug out a plug of dust and snot, which he wiped absently on his breeks.

I saw the glassy white of old scars on the back of his hand, the mark of seasoned warriors everywhere – the marks that were still raw and new on my own – since hands were almost always cut in fights, even friendly ones.

Behind us came the screeching groan of a giant with belly-ache. It went on and on and ended with a clunk. Then there was a sudden blast of heat and I shrank my head down into my neck, seeing that others were doing the same.

A pause. A huge blast of hot air and a deep booming thump: the great engine heaved a fireball over our heads, a streak of orange-red, trailing oily black smoke through the golden haze. I never saw or heard where it landed.

I saw a woman and child moving through the Oathsworn ranks, carrying yokes of clay water pitchers into which the men dipped, then drank gratefully. The woman smiled at Bersi, who grinned back through the fat, rolling globules of sweat on his face and said something in her ear that earned him a thump on the shoulder. But as she moved on, she was still smiling.

A horseman, bare-armed and wearing a leather helmet, trotted up to where Einar stood, a silhouette in the dust-gloom.

'Shit,' muttered Wryneck and I tensed, sensing his unease.

The horseman and Einar exchanged words, then the man galloped off and Einar said something to Valknut.

The Raven Banner went up so that everyone could see it. Then it dipped twice, three times in quick succession, the signal to move forward.

There was a sick feeling in the pit of my stomach, a cold-ness that reached to my groin and shrank it to the kernel of a nut. I was in the front rank: the Lost. Behind was another mailed rank and behind that two ranks of unarmoured men with long spears. A fifth rank contained Bagnose, Steinthor and every other man who knew which end of a bow was which.

Twenty men wide, five ranks deep, the Oathsworn tramped through the haze to war.

I had no idea who was to our left or right – or if anyone was. I knew our job was to protect this engine, now thrust close to the walls, which loomed now and then through the swirl of dust and smoke.

'Are we attacking?' I asked Wryneck and he grunted, hefting his shield to a more comfortable position.

'Nah, they are coming at us, I am thinking,' he replied, blinking sweat from his eyes.

The Raven Banner swung side to side. I had forgotten what that meant, but no one moved so I stayed where I was, too. Then I saw bowmen and realised Einar had called them out to skirmish in front of us.

Engines thumped and whooshed, men shrieked and cried in the unseen haze, horses galloped back and forth. Horns blared somewhere. A block of spear-armed men jogged diagonally across our front, heading to our rear. Ours? Khazar? Attacking? Running? I was licking cracked lips and looking wildly left and right when Wryneck nudged me.

'Don't try to eat it, Orm Bear Slayer,' he growled. 'If they come up our arse, there is nothing you can do now to prevent it. If it happens, we will deal with it, but there's no sense in chewing on it. That way, you not only end up with men up your arse, but you have ruined all this perfectly quiet time.'

Perfectly quiet? Horns blasted again. Horsemen cantered up and past us. I saw one . . . then another . . . and another turn in the saddle, nock arrows and let fly behind them.

'Get ready,' said Bersi, hunching his shoulders.

'Shield!' roared Einar. A pause. 'Wall!'

The shields came up with a single great clash of overlap. My right hand slammed the crosspiece of my sword hard against the join with my neighbour and we were now locked. Einar and Valknut turned and moved to one end, rather than force a way through us.

Arrows hissed out of the murk, skittering along the raw, tramped earth, slapping weakly off a shield here and there.

273

Bersi was shaking, the sweat rolling off him and mixing with the dust to turn his back and underarms to mud.

Our bowmen scampered back, trying to make for the ends of our line. Those who couldn't pitched their bows over our heads and dived for our feet, wriggling like eels between our boots.

The ground trembled. More horsemen appeared, swirling like sparrows when they saw us. They looked no different to our own: men on horses with bows, fur-clad helmets, tan cloaks, white tunics. They shrieked from black-bearded faces, loosed a straggle of arrows and wheeled away, back into their own dust.

We stood. Wryneck reached over his locked shield, swept his sword down and sheared off the shaft of an arrow I had not even seen or heard. I swallowed the hot lump in my throat, but it stuck and choked me.

The ground shook and thunder rolled somewhere.

'Spears,' Einar called and they came hissing past my ear, sticking beyond us, a hedge of points.

'F-fucker,' stammered Bersi, his teeth clattering. 'Nearly had m-m-my f-f-fucking ear then.'

The ground danced; the thunder resolved to a rolling drum of noise. The dust seethed, figures loomed and the Khazar horse crashed out of the gloom.

They were unsure where we were, moving too slowly and too late to speed up when they spotted us. They were a sally force to wreck the siege engines and were out to hit hard and run, but the sight of a hundred-odd men, mailed, with the obvious red cloaks of a *druzhina* and the grim faces of seasoned warriors, made them haul on reins.

The spear-points did the rest. That hedge wasn't for them. They came to a halt, rank upon rank crashing into each other, ruining their formation.

Our archers sailed arrows at them from flanks and over our heads, which clattered on them but did little harm.

274

Then they lumbered round, cursing and shrieking, and moved off like some giant, frustrated beast, back into the mirk.

Someone cheered and we all took it up, pounding sword on shield and offering deep 'hooms' of taunt to them until the dust choked us.

We stayed there for another hour, eating the dry steppe until we were spitting mud, sweltering and baking, locked in the shieldwall, until someone remembered and sent word to stand down.

Weary, we tramped back to our scraps of cloth awnings and tents near the river – anything that gave shade – and dropped, gulping water the women and children brought, too choked and hot and tired to think of food. The whining insect clouds plunged on us at once.

'That was well done,' beamed Skarti, clattering helmet and shield down. 'We saw them off and no one got a scratch. A good day for the Oathsworn of Einar.'

A few agreed with grunts; most were too tired to say anything. We swatted flies when we had the energy and Skarti lost his good humour, maddened by them. 'What did they eat before we came?' he demanded, slapping furiously. Like all of us, he was covered in the red weals of their bites.

'A pity Skapti never made it this far,' growled Kvasir from the dark of a makeshift lean-to. 'They could have eaten him all day and left us alone.'

Women slithered between us as the sun died, lighting pitfires and hooking cauldrons on their chains and tripods over them. The smell of woodsmoke made my heart ache for remembered fires and the eye-sting of it was a small price to pay for the disappearance of the insects.

Gradually, as the heat seeped out of the ground, the Oathsworn moved closer to the fires, found fresh energy and started to weave themselves back together. I knew they were recovered when Finn Horsehead hunkered down beside me and shoved a coin into my face. 'What's this, young Orm? You know coins like ostlers know horses.'

'He knows horses like ostlers know horses,' Ketil Crow reminded him and Finn acknowledged it with a wave as I looked at the coin.

It was gold, from the Great City, called in Greek *nomisma* and in Latin a *solidus*. It had the heads of Constantine VII and Romanus I, for the Greeks who called themselves Romans nearly always had two rulers, foolish though that was.

'Makes you wonder why they have lasted so long,' growled Eindridi.

'They have big walls,' Valknut pointed out.

'Apart from their big walls,' argued Eindridi, 'which can be scaled.'

'Lots of warriors,' mused Bagnose. 'Who are not sometime farmers, but warriors all the time.'

'Just so,' admitted Eindridi. 'Apart from the walls and the warriors.'

'These,' I said, tossing the coin so that it caught the fire-light, turning red and yellow-gold, end over end, and locking all their gazes, like a snake on a rabbit.

Finn snatched it out of the air and the cave of his fist broke the spell. He scowled at them.

'Aye,' sighed Eindridi. 'Coins like that would do it, right enough.'

'Is it any good then?' demanded Finn. 'I had it off a dead man out there, but I have never seen stamped gold before.'

'It's a full-weight,' I told him, 'worth twelve of their silver *milaresia*, which is about the same in Arab *dirham*. The Great City mints gold coins and the only other ones who do that are the Arabs of Serkland. You can tell the difference because the Serkland coins have no little people on them, only squiggles of writing.'

'Just so,' breathed Finn, while the others craned to see. He held it between finger and thumb, turning it this way and that.

'Is the treasure of Atil like this?' demanded Wryneck and I missed the bite of his voice and the fact that this was more for the shadowed figure of Einar than me.

'No,' I said scornfully. 'You are lucky, Finn, because this coin was minted about ten years ago. The ones of the new Emperor, Nicephorus, are identical, but gold-lighter by one-twelfth and traders are wary of them. You won't get any of them in a hoard from the age of the Volsungs. No gold at all, probably, only silver.

'In truth,' I ploughed on, 'silver *milaresia* are always full weight and pure, but getting rarer these days. The hoard of Atil will be pure, for that is the Volsung treasure that Sigurd took from the dragon Fafnir.

'Of course,' I blundered on, airing my skills, 'pure is a relative term, since it is also cursed—'

I stopped, realising the mire I had stepped into with both feet. There was silence, broken only by the distant droning hum of the army, the soft mutter of women, the crackle and hiss of fire and cauldron.

'Odin's balls, young Orm,' declared Finn admiringly. 'You are the one for business, right enough.'

Across in the shadows, made deeper by the fire's light, I suddenly saw the gleam of Einar's eyes, watching me as Finn showed his marvellous prize to the others and the stare went on and on until the arrival of one of the Greek priests broke the spell.

These priests, invited by Sviatoslav to cater to the spiritual needs of his prized Greek engineers, missed no chance to spread the Christ doctrine, determined to bring the whole of the Rus to their god.

This one, black-bearded and simply robed, introduced himself as Theotokios and had brought a flask of wine, for he knew how to win his way to the fires of the Norse. Wine was a rare treat and we welcomed him, as we had others of his kind, and proceeded to drink his gift and ignore his attempts to convert us.

After we had eaten, as the women were clearing up, Finn pulled one on to his lap and she, being a thrall and having no say in it, gave in to him after a token squeal or two. Certainly having Finn's greasy beard wiped over her face and his fingers in her secret places was preferable to slogging down to the river and washing out pots. Just.

Theotokios made a noise in his throat and Finn looked up from what he was doing, which involved hooking a breast out of the shift the woman wore and popping it in his mouth. 'What are you looking at?' he growled and Theotokios replied – in Greek, which Finn didn't understand.

I had picked up enough of it to tell him Theotokios was concerned for his sinful soul. Finn laughed and shook his head. 'That's the problem with Christ-followers,' he said. 'Everything is a sin, it seems to me, if you are tempted. Yet how is it a sin if you can't help yourself? The more beautiful a woman is, the less you can help yourself, so the less of a sin it is, says I.'

I was impressed by this – but Spittle wasn't. He grabbed the woman next to him and pulled her down beside him, grinning as she fought and cursed.

'Nonsense,' he growled. 'As usual, Finn Horsearse, you have the wrong grasp of the Christ way of things. You will enjoy having your beautiful woman and so that is a sin. Me, on the other hand—' He broke off and jerked the woman forward into the fireglow. She was short, red-faced with anger and pig-eyed with hate, which a squint did not help. Those who liked them fat might have found pleasure in her. 'I won't get much enjoyment out of this,' Spittle declared mournfully, 'so it won't be a sin. In fact, now that I see her clearly, I'll hardly have sinned at all. I may even get to this Christ Valholl, Heaven, on the strength of what I do next.'

278

Theotokios clearly had more Norse than I thought, for he had followed this and shook his head sorrowfully. 'The way to Heaven is through self-denial,' he intoned sonorously and the laughter brought heads round from neighbouring fires.

'I prefer a prettier road,' yelled Finn and set to work finding it. Kvasir Spittle, with another mournful look at his catch, let her scramble up and away, amid the laughter and jeers of the others.

'I do not feel up to being saved for Christ tonight,' he growled. 'Perhaps our Orm will do it for me, for I hear that he can hump a pile of shavings on a wooden floor.'

And that brought more laughter and a thump or two on my back. Across the fire, my father raised his ale horn in toast and, for a brief spark of a moment, I was one with them, this hard family, so that even the weight of Einar's eyes was almost a caress.

But that night, Bersi died raving, burned to a husk by fever.

By the end of the week, the corpses were piling up so fast Sviatoslav ordered them burned, had camps moved – and launched an all-out attack, presumably before his army melted like rendered grease into the steppe.

And that pimpled boy, Yaropolk, curse his memory, demanded the honour of leading the assault with his *druzhina*.

Us.

He was splendid with us; nothing was too good the night before and he brought ale and soft-skinned, doe-eyed women to our campfires, offered wine and choice food – well, by then, any food without worm in it – and the priests of our choice to cater for our spiritual needs.

But those who weren't shaking and dribbling evil bile were too knotted to eat and too shrunk with fear to attack the women, while the priests were too busy trying to keep the sick alive until morning to be bothered by those wanting simple comfort.

Nor was the friendly reminder that the garrison of Sarkel

numbered no more than a thousand any help. Even with all the able-bodied in their city added in, their forces were outnumbered ten to one. That was supposed to make us feel better, but most of us were depressed by the news that so few could hold off so many.

I saw, to my amazement, that Martin was moving among the fires, scowling and uncomfortable about it, but sent by his master Oleg to help the Christ-men of his brother's *druzhina*.

'I thought you'd be safe in Kiev,' I said to him in that red-glow night and saw his white smile in the dark beyond the fire.

'There are God's chosen among you heathens still,' he said, 'and they cry out for succour.'

'And you are the only Christ priest of your kind here,' Valknut pointed out grimly, having a sharp grasp of the religious realities. 'If you did not come, then the Greek Christ priests would score another victory, eh?'

'There is only one true God,' Martin pointed out, kneeling to place a pot on the fire and stir it. Then he stiffened as Einar loomed out of the darkness, Hild a dark presence at his side. She crouched like a hound at his feet, staring at Martin and smiling, her head tilted as if she was sniffing him.

'Is it safe, priest?' she demanded and he regarded her with narrowed eyes, knowing what she meant.

'Safe from you,' he answered levelly and I couldn't help but admire him, since I did not even dare look her in the eyes these days.

She smiled her fey smile and cocked her head like a bird. 'I may reclaim that stick of mine one day, priest.'

Martin rose, smoothed his ratty brown robes and picked up the pot from the fire. Then he made the sign of the cross at her and she laughed as he moved into the darkness.

Einar, fish-belly pale, knelt by the fire and heated his hands, for it was cold now – that gods-cursed steppe baked all day and then froze at night, so that Bersi had once woken up with his red-gold braids iced to the ground.

Bersi, who was now ash and memory.

'We should run for it tonight,' my father declared morosely from where he sat at my side. I glanced at him, since it was the first time he had shown any sign of such things. But Einar didn't even bother to reply – it was too late to do that now and I think my father had known it even as he spoke.

So, huddled together and wrapped in cloaks against the cold, we sat and stared at the fire, listening to the shift and stamp and murmur of the vast camp, fiddling with straps and honing the serrated edges of blades, too tense to sleep.

'After your mother died,' my father said suddenly, as the sky began to grey out of the night black, 'her father, old Stammkel, whom they called Refr, Fox, on account of his cunning, wanted the farm back. It came as Gudrid's dowry, see, so he had claim on it after she died.'

He was silent for a long time and I was breath-locked with this. I felt I was hovering on the edge of something, as if trying to persuade a sheep back from the edge of a cliff, where one sudden movement would make it shy and plunge over.

'Of course, so did I,' he said eventually. 'And so did you, though you were barely getting to your feet at the time and were wet-nursed by a good thrall.'

'What happened?' I asked, driven to make a movement, however reckless, when the silence that followed became too harsh to bear.

He stirred. 'He took it to a Thing for judgement. He had many to speak for him and I had no one.'

'What of Gudleif? Or Bjarni? Or Gunnar Raudi, even?' I demanded, astonished that none of those had helped. My father laughed softly.

'Gudleif and Bjarni would not speak against Stammkel. Not big-balls Stammkel, he who roared and bellowed. Not

281

even after he came back from his raid on Dyfflin, which they they went on. Some six hundred men went and four hundred of those never came back and the whole sorry episode nearly ruined Stammkel, which was why he wanted the farm in the first place.' He paused and shrugged, scrubbing his face. 'I think Gudleif and Bjarni felt they could not stand in Stammkel's way, having in some way failed him in the raid.'

'They only got back because of Gunnar Raudi,' I said, remembering what Halldis had told me. 'Didn't he help you?'

My father shifted, as if something dug him in the ribs. 'Ah,' he said, gentle as a sighing breeze into the night. 'Gunnar Raudi. He was away so long everyone thought him and the others dead . . .'

He stopped for a long moment, then: 'Did you know that Gudrid Stammkelsdottir had hair the colour of yellow corn and could tuck it in the belt round her waist?' He shook his head with the bright memory of it. 'Gold she was. Gold and glowing and slender as a wheatstalk – and everyone wanted her. But she came to me in the end. Came to me when her father came hirpling back from Dyfflin with his balls shrunk to walnuts and too many lives laid at his door.'

He stirred and heaved a long sigh. 'Narrow in the waist she was – and too narrow in the hip, as it turned out. But she wanted me and Stammkel had to give up a farm which he could not afford to do and still keep the partitions from going up in his hall.'

There was silence again.

'What of Gunnar Raudi?' I asked and my father stared at the fire for a moment longer.

'Gunnar spoke for me at the Thing and judgement was given in my favour,' he said, all in one swift sentence and I blinked at that, for I had expected a different tale entirely. Which was stupid of me, for I remember my father telling me he had sold the farm when he fostered me on Gudleif.

282

Still, I was thinking, this could not be the end of it and said so.

'No,' agreed my father, 'it was not. Stammkel hated Gunnar Raudi before this and, after that, tore his beard out over it and made it known he would have his farm, one way or the other. He hired two known hard men, Ospak and Styrmir, who claimed to be berserkers. Then he sent them round with two thralls to deal with me.'

He stirred a log back into the fire with his foot and watched the embers swirl like red flies in the dark.

'Why did Stammkel hate Gunnar Raudi so much?' I asked and he shot me a sideways glance.

'No matter,' he answered. 'So these men came to the hov this night, as they had announced they would, all four of them and well armed and me with only myself to face them.'

Wide-eyed, I waited and, when nothing came, I demanded, 'What happened?'

'I died, of course,' he said and grinned as I blinked, then realised he had led me into the oldest and worst joke in saga-telling, which is just what a father does to his child at some point. I grinned back at him, my heart leaping with the warmth of it.

'In fact,' he went on, 'I would have done just that, save that Gunnar Raudi swaggers up, as was his way, and winks at me as he passes me. "Hello, lads," he says to these four. "No need for this, for Rurik here has decided to quit this place."

'Which was news to me and must have sounded strange to them, looking at me standing there with a seax in one hand and a wood axe in the other and the look of a man not about to quit anything.'

He shook his head and chuckled. 'A deep thinker was Gunnar. "Listen, lads," he says. "We'll drink on it and part friends and you can tell Stammkel to turn up the day after tomorrow, for then this place will be empty." And he winks at me again and walks all four of them into the hall of my hov and sits them down, calling for ale and food.'

'What did you do?' I demanded and he shrugged.

'What else? I followed them in and sat down with them and we drank until it ran down our noses. After a long while, Gunnar Raudi gets up and announces he is off for a piss and goes outside. After a bit longer, we all remember he went and laugh at him, thinking he had probably fallen in the privy.

'But I had seen him wink on the way out, so I say to Ospak to go find him and he is drunk enough to do just that. After a while longer, of course, Ospak never comes back either and I mention this and put my head on my arms and pretend to sleep.

'So Styrmir gets up and goes out and the two thralls carry on drinking and laughing at me snoring, so that when Gunnar Raudi steps in, his blade all red and dripping, they piss themselves all over my floor.

'And that was that,' my father said. 'Gunnar tells the two thralls to carry the bodies of Ospak and Styrmir back to Stammkel and tell him to give up any claims on the farm. "The heads," he says, "I will keep and stick on poles, to watch out for more of Stammkel's foolishness." Which he did.'

He stopped and squeezed his eyes shut, then rubbed them, for he had been staring into the embers too long. 'By the time all this had been done you were toddling around and causing trouble and, though I was left alone after that, I had no stomach for it, so I sold the place and went over to Gudleif with you.'

He looked at me, eyes watering from the staring so that they made my heart thunder, for the moistness was as like tears as not. 'I always meant to return,' he said. 'But I knew you would be safe with Gunnar. More so with him than me.'

I wanted to ask more, but he clapped a hand on my shoulder and levered himself to his feet, then patted me gently a couple of times, as you would a horse or a dog, and moved off into the dark, leaving me with the fire and my thoughts whirling like the sparks.

At some point, I fell asleep and dreamed, though. Or thought I did. Or stepped into the fetch world, that half-lit Other.

I was in Dengizik's tomb again, alone, in a blue dark, like a night with a shrouded moon. The lines of soldiers, dead but still with eyes that followed me, were sitting patiently and Hild sat at the foot of the throne, chained to it by the neck.

I took a step to her and the soldiers shifted. I took another and they rose, with a hissing rustle like insect wings.

Then I ran and they surged on me, a blinding mass like bats, like a blizzard of dust and fury with no more substance than memory.

And, suddenly, I was there, looking into the great white-rimmed pools of Hild's eyes, while she smiled up at me. My arm rose and fell, the sword in it chopping the withered hand from Dengizik, which held Hild's neck chain.

It fell, slowly, slowly, tumbling, shredding scraps of flayed skin, dusty bone.

Then I was awake, by the fire, staring into the limpid eyes of Hild, who sat astride me, her face inches from mine. Her mouth worked, twisting this way and that; sounds tore from her in a rippling, wheezing hiss: 'Don't . . . go . . . with us. Live . . .'

Limpid eyes, dewed with . . . tears? I watched them expand, to where the black ate all the white, saw the hands which cupped my face claw like talons, felt her quiver and then, with a sickening liquid surge, rise up over me and step away, into the darkness.

I breathed. I know I did, because I heard it, ragged and thundering in my ears. There was no other sound for a moment, then all the noise of the world crashed back and I blinked at the camp murmur, the hiss of dung-chips on the fire, my father's groan and stir, Skarti's fluttering fart.

I sat up, looked wildly around, but everything was as it should be – and yet nothing was. Had it happened? Had I dozed and woken in my dream? Did I dream still?

All the rest of that night I wondered, staring into the glowing embers until my eyeballs seared.

There were horns and drums sounding, like ships lost in a golden fog. Under our feet the steppe had crumbled, crusted over and was kicked to dust again, hanging in the air, gritting our eyeballs, scorching tongue and nose and throat.

The acrid stink of horses hung in that dust as they sluiced nervous piss and moved to our flanks, ghosts in the murk, to make sure the assault wasn't smacked by a counter-foray from the once-white city.

This time there were just sixty-two of us, half with their teeth clamped tight because otherwise they'd chip or crack them with the fever's jaw-quaking chatter. Twenty more lay under awnings back at a new camp, amid the hundreds of other sick gathered in one place so that what aid there was could be more easily given. Not that there was much . . . they lay and shook and died in pools of their own loosened bowels.

But we stood and waited, while fire and death occupied the space between us and the ravaged city. In the yellow shroud of dust, five dark towers moved, like the fingers of a hand, while archers rushed forward in pairs, one holding a pavise of reeds, the other shooting, then ducking under to reload.

There were hoots and screeches and shrieks and, through it all, the high, thin scream of horses dying, a sound which, to me, seemed worst of all.

I leaned on my shield, on one knee, watching, almost detached from it. Skarti, shivering, was glass-eyed and shit dribbled down one leg, but he didn't seem to notice. The smell of that and dust and oil on steel – that was battle and any component part of it reaching my nostrils later in my life would bring my head sharply up, like a chariot horse of the Blues when it hears the roar of the crowd.

A block of sweating men heaved and strained, some in front and some behind, moving the tower foot by slow foot towards the walls, from which rained death, unseen in the murk.

Unseen but felt. Like some giant snail, the block of men round the tower left a slick, viscous trail of blood and sprawled bodies behind, felled by arrows, fist-sized stones fired from small engines and large spears fired from bigger engines.

There was a bird, amazingly. It flitted out of the dust and perched briefly on the shaft of one of the hedgehog maze of arrows sticking from the assault tower, then whirred off again, gone in an eyeblink.

Then a flock of small boys appeared, darting out of the saffron haze with bunches of arrows: they got silver for every twenty they recovered. A dog was with them, limp-running on three legs, then four, then three again. The boys plunged on, laughing, panting, sneezing, carefree dancers on the edge of the abyss.

I laughed, too, at the sheer incongruity of it. Skarti heard it and his lumpy head came up, tight-mouthed. He shook it, saw what made me chuckle and managed a savage grin. He was holding himself to prevent the shakes – even his hair looked clenched – yet he leaned forward and spoke.

'S-s-see many s-s-strange things in b-b-battle,' he managed. 'B-b-birds, b-b-beasts, w-w-women, d-dogs. S-s-saw a s-s-stag once, r-run between two armies.' Then he shut one eye, which fluttered as he did so, and placed a quivering finger alongside his nose in a grotesque parody of the knowing look. 'B-but you n-n-never see a c-c-cat on a battlefield,' he finished portentously and, drained, sank back to lean on his shield.

Mounted couriers galloped to and fro. A man on foot spilled out of the shimmer, looked wildly around and spotted the Raven Banner.

He stumbled towards Einar, his tunic streaked with dark sweat patches and worse, spoke quickly, pointed, waved his hands furiously and then, done, slumped down, his legs buckling. Einar began to pace, slowly, up and down.

I realised, eventually, that he was counting. On five hundred of my count, he stopped, signalled to Valknut and the Raven Banner went up, then bobbed three times.

The Oathsworn lurched upright and moved at a walk, then broke into a jog. Skarti weaved and staggered with me and I slowed to let him keep up as he clattered into me and almost fell, caught my shoulder, muttered an apology.

In a loose bunch, shields up, we headed into that sulphurous maw, shrinking ourselves as small as possible and wishing we were anywhere else. I caught sight of others, equally thick with dust, trotting forward in small groups, their own banners up. My father appeared from the crowd, raised his sword briefly in salute, then was gone again. I loped on and the arrows arrived.

The sagas will tell you of arrows like rain, like sleet. Not so. They come in flurries, in flocks, like birds. You see a brief flicker in the air and then they hit with a drum-roll smack.

I had three in my shield almost at the same time, the shu-shu-shunk of them making me stagger. Another whicked past my head; Skarti went down, gurgling, drowning in his own blood. Another hit his thigh as he rolled.

I half stopped, wanting to turn to help him, but dared not expose my back. Another bird-flicker through the dust and a man to my right yelled, hirpled a few steps, then started hopping, his injured leg held up, the shaft through the calf from one side to the other.

'Ah, fuck,' he yelled, then fell over. 'Fuckfuckfuck.'

A dark shape loomed: our assault tower, now hard against

the scabbed wall. Close up, that white wall was a yellowed fang, rough and pitted, the base littered with rag-bag corpses in dust-tanned white, stained ominously black and clumped on the shards of picture tiles torn from the walls.

Fireflies sparkled in the dust and I stared at them until they whunked into the earth and the tower. One sizzled past me; someone behind screamed and Eindridi staggered out of the pack of men squeezing up the lower entrance, waving his arms wildly, a shaft sticking from his neck and his hair on fire.

'Help me. Tyr help me . . .' But he reeled off into the dust before anyone, man or god, could lay a hand on him.

Fire-arrows smacked the tower. It smouldered already and the haulers were trying to keep the cowhides wet with frantic licks of water from wooden buckets, but the heat was drying them out almost as fast. Inside, men struggled up ladders in a dripping rain of mud, sliding and cursing and sweating.

I waited, shuffling forward with the rest, breathing ragged and still hunched, though the tower offered shelter from the arrows. Almost. The man in front of me – not one of the Oathsworn – half turned to say something to the man next to him and his head jerked with a sudden high clang. He dropped, twitching and I saw there was a huge dent in his helmet and the blood was pouring from his nose.

I pushed past him. Something slammed into the timber nearest me and, unable to go further in the queue, I ended up staring at the round, pebble-sized lead shot embedded there. I swallowed and looked back at the felled man, who was thrashing now, his back arched off the ground and blood coming out of his ears and nose and even streaking down his cheeks from his eyes, like tears.

There was a flurry of movement ahead. I was almost on the ladder when the whole tower shook and, just as I was putting my foot on the first rung, a body plunged to the ground with a clatter of iron and breaking bones.

The tower lurched again, then embers and chunks of burning timber rained down through the muddy drips. Another body crashed down, then several more and people above me were scrambling back down the ladder. I took the full weight of a man on me, scrambling, kicking.

He stepped on me and another one would have done the same if I hadn't lashed out and sent him spinning, which let me scramble back out, away from the tower, which had suddenly gone crazy. The ladder had tilted.

No, not the ladder. The whole tower. As I scrambled away on all fours, losing my shield in the process, the assault tower toppled like a falling tree. The top half was on fire; it had then been hooked with grapples from the wall and hauled over sideways.

It fell with a great bell of a crash and a blast of choking air, thick with dust and smoke. Flaming debris spun and whirled in it, like the end of the world.

I found my shield, got up and stumbled backwards over half-seen figures on the ground, caught my boot and fell over one on to another and lay on it, panting for breath. I levered up, felt stickiness under my hand and heard the clang of steel.

It made no sense – had they sallied? I got up on one knee, looked at the body and blinked. Steinkel. My cousin, last seen being dragged out of Martin's company, scowling and sullen.

Now he lay on his back with dust in his glazed eyes and entrails oozing from between the shattered rings of his fine mail. And something dark and gibbering rose in me. Gudleif's sons.

Fresh clangs, a grunt, a series of triumphant shrieks and, for the first time, I saw the figures nearby, hazed silhouettes in the gold. One crumpled as I watched, the other hacking with frantic blows, each one heralded by a grunt.

I rose and moved, half blurred in my head, and saw the horror of it; saw the fear that had been rising in me, shapeless and screaming, given truth.

Bjorn turned from hacking my father to bloody ruin, his mouth slack, his eyes wild. He saw me and snarled, but his voice came out too high-pitched. 'You. Now it is complete.'

My father. I wanted to brush him aside, not to be bothered by his idiot raving and his quarrel, to get to the side of that bloody, leaking thing that had been my father.

But Bjorn was there and his sword was up, thick, fat blood runnels sliding down the blade. My father's blood. His face was still young, round with puppy fat, but the mouth was twisted in fear and hatred.

I stepped back in my mind and saw, for a flashing second, through his eyes, what faced him: his age, but leaner, axe-faced and wiry with new muscle, bulked unnaturally at the shoulder by oar and sword, blasted brown by sun and wind.

He was too young and soft, this boy, for trying to exact bloodprice – but he and his brother had hacked my father down.

I went for him then and I don't remember much of it, save that, for the first time, I had no fear. Perhaps that was what Pinleg had found, that disregard for death or harm in the pursuit of something desperate. Maybe *berserk* was different, but I tasted something of it then, in the dancing golden dust in front of the White Castle.

How did the fight go? A good skald would have made much of it, but all I know is that when I blinked back into the Now of it, Bjorn was laid out on his back with his head all bloody and one ankle almost severed.

I saw that blood was dripping from a cut on my forearm, that my shield was slashed and tattered and that I had lost the last two fingers of my left hand.

My father was still alive when I knelt by him, but only just, and I had nothing to offer, not even water and certainly not help. I knelt there, my hands waving uselessly because I couldn't even work out where to start in the slick gore of what he had been. All I did was drip blood and snot-tears on him and I have always remembered, with shame, how useless I was then.

He grinned at me, his teeth stained red. 'Dead, are they?'

I nodded, trapped in silence, hands fluttering.

'Good. Fucks – should have known they'd never leave it alone. Got one – that silly little arse, Steinkel. Had no sword-sense at all. Should both have stayed away. That fucking Christ priest . . .'

He would have spat, but had no fire left to do it. Blood worked into froth at the corners of his mouth and he was gargling when he spoke. He looked at me, still grinning. 'Bad business. That fu-fucking bear. You look like your mother.'

Again I couldn't say anything and the tears were splashing muddily on his shoulder.

'Good woman. Loved her after a fashion and she me, I am thinking. Never had a chance to grow.'

He coughed up more blood and I patted aimlessly, help-lessly.

'Lies,' he said. 'For good reasons. We each had our true loves. Mine rode the whale road, swift and sure. With a good sail on it I could cut a day . . . off any . . . journey anywhere. Find my way by the stars to the end of the world.'

He spasmed; the grin froze. 'You are my pride, though.' His eyes went glassy and he hissed, one hand grasping me by the wrist: 'But not my son. Her true love was Gunnar . . .'

And he went across the rainbow bridge, while the world spun and crashed and roared like the sea and all my thoughts were dust.

I would have stayed there, but some others passing dragged me away and dropped me safely out of arrow range, beside the huge engines with their Lebanese cedar throwing arms and sweating Greek engineers.

They loaded and fired, loaded and fired, for the assault had failed dismally and the only way into the city now was to pound the walls to rubble. Some of them, seeing the state

I was in, gave me water and bound my wounds up with only slightly dirty rags, while I sat and let them, solid as a stump on the outside. Inside, I was . . . disconnected, like sea-rotted mail, falling link by link.

Not my father. Gunnar her true love. Stammkel hated Gunnar. The new links locked and riveted themselves into place and, though it was patchy, the shape of it was there.

My mother, already carrying me and knowing it, brings herself to my father . . . no, to Rurik, I realised. To Rurik, who marries her and gets a farm for his old age, he thinks, taking someone else's son with it. Someone thought dead until he turns up, like a ghost at the feast.

Gunnar. No wonder he had stayed at Bjornshafen and no one dared say anything of it. No wonder, too, that Gudleif had to be sleekit about trying to do away with me, for he must have known.

And Gunnar had stayed with Einar because I was there – had died for being a father and kept it all to himself to the grave. I wept for that, splashing muddy tears down my face, for all the things we would not now say to each other, for all the remembered things that now made sense.

Gunnar Raudi. Swaggering, bracken-haired hard man, a sea-raider who had more in him for fathering than Rurik, who had wanted a farm and peace. Somehow, in a Loki joke, they had swapped lives.

Eventually, the dullness lifted and the tears stopped. I thought of him lying out there, dead in the dust and unclaimed. I couldn't let that happen, so I went to find the Oathsworn.

I found a man I knew, Flosi, who had been my oarmate on the old *Elk* and he greeted me with a weary wave. 'Thought you were gone,' he said, jerking a grimy thumb behind him. 'The rest are over yonder – Illugi is taking a tally. I've been sent to fetch food and water for us.'

He stood there, grinning madly, his hair a wild tangle and

his beard stiff with matted blood and all the same tawny yellow from the dust. His eyes showed white and red-rimmed from the crusted scab of his face but he had no colour in anything he wore, just a coating of that dust. It came to me, then, that I looked no different – save for the tear-tracks, which he did his best to ignore.

Nor did any of the others, slumped in slack-mouthed exhaustion round the remains of what had been our camp, trampled by horsemen at some point, our flimsy shelters scattered. Illugi and Einar were finding out who lived, and who did not.

I was greeted with a raise of the hand, or a nod. Einar, blood streaked in his hair, turned and grinned a lopsided smirk, then jerked his head at Illugi. 'Better mark him off the dead roll,' he said.

'Leave the mark,' I replied, heaving up a slack skin of tepid water. I sluiced it over my head, then drank some. It was foul.

'Fair enough,' said Wryneck. 'You look more dead than alive – and you just used all the water we had left, so some of us might kill you anyway.'

'Leave the mark,' I repeated, 'but tally it to my father.'

'Aah,' groaned Wryneck. 'Old Rurik? Gone?'

'A loss we will feel sorely,' Einar added sorrowfully, 'when we have the wind at our back and a fair sea. How will we find a course now?'

'Any course will do,' I snarled, 'on the whale road.'

Einar nodded and tried to pat my shoulder as if I was merely overwrought; I glared at him through the streaked crust of my face. Illugi stepped forward, just one pace into that space heating up between us.

'Anyone else you saw go down?' he asked.

I blinked away from Einar, into the ravaged creases of Illugi's worn face, made deeper by the dust caked in them. 'Skarti,' I said. 'Took an arrow.'

'In the throat,' agreed Valknut, cross-legged. He was trying to comb the matted tangle of his hair and beard. He looked up, eyes blank, his voice full of wonder. 'He drowned. I heard him drown in the middle of all the dust.'

'I saw Eindridi,' muttered Ketil Crow. 'At least I think it was him, for I could not see his face. His head was on fire.'

'A fire-arrow took him in the neck,' agreed Wryneck. 'I saw him get it, but he ran off before anyone could help.'

'We have to recover our dead,' I said and others growled. Einar nodded, looked round us all, then squinted at the dust. No one mentioned wounded. By now there would be no wounded, for anyone who couldn't make it back off that field would have had their throats cut by looters. From our own side, most likely.

'Wait for this to settle, else you will be blundering around achieving nothing,' Einar said. 'Food and water will arrive for us. Rest, regain strength and then honour the dead.'

It made too much sense to oppose, so that's what we did, all through the settling haze of that golden day, while the great engines thumped and the sick and injured moaned and screamed.

The rations arrived, were prepared by women, some of whom were genuinely weeping for men who were lost. For once, we had more than enough to eat, since they had given rations for more than a hundred and there were, by Illugi's final tally, forty-three of us fit enough to eat.

The dust never quite went away, but cleared enough for us to see the sun begin to die in streaks of gold and purple on a distant horizon, so we went out, naked to the waist in the shimmering heat, shoving the cart that rations had come in.

Until it became too dark to see, we loaded the bodies of those we recognised on to the cart and trundled them back to a place by the river, where the women keened and cleaned them as best they could, even though the entire Don was tinged pink and the twilight insects came in stinging clouds.

I found Rurik, untouched by the hordes of plundering boys, no longer after arrows but out to rob the dead. Skarti, however, had been stripped, his body white under the soft golden layer of dust.

We prised him from a crusted pool of his own blood, thick with gorged insects, and the arrow in his throat came out with a soft suck of sound and a gobbet of red. The one in his thigh wouldn't come out at all, so I had to saw the shaft short, an awkward job with my bound hand.

All the while I could feel the eyes on me from the cart, the dead eyes of the man I had known as my father, and the storm in me rolled and swelled, for I was angry at him for having kept the secret so long, so that I did not even have my real father. Sad as a wolf-howl for him, too, that he had borne it all this long.

Skarti's pox-ravaged head lolled sideways as I closed his eyes, hearing his voice say: 'But you never see a cat on a battlefield,' and we placed him on the cart, too.

We also laid out Eindridi – well, we were reasonably sure it was him, from the shield and weapons he bore, but even his own mother would not have known the blackened, peeling thing that had been his face.

We found Hrut, who knew more riddles than Bagnose, and Kol Otryggsson, who could carve out delicate, swirling patterns in leather with an awl, and Isleif from Aldeigjuborg and Rorik, the half-Slav from Kiev, who had come up to Holmgard for the season and joined us there, had hardly been with us long enough for anything to be known about him.

Then there was Ranvaik Sleekstone-eye, one of the old Oathsworn, his odd-coloured eyes closed for ever, the centre of his face punched bloody by one of those lead pebbles.

And more, each ragdoll body a new keening for the women, another stone in the heart of us all.

Einar and Valknut looked at Ranvaik's corpse, blank-faced and wordless. Ketil Crow, almost tenderly, wiped the crusted mess from the dead face. There were, I knew, no more than a handful of the original Oathsworn left, the ones who had once sailed from where the bergs calved off in floating mountains to the lands where sand was drifted by the wind into a parody of the ocean.

Flosi came back for the cart eventually, eyeing with distaste the smear of fluids streaking it, for our bread and meat had to be piled there. Grumbling, he headed down to the river to clean it out, muttering that he wished he had known all this before he had taken that binding oath.

And, on the way, he flung back carelessly at Einar: 'A new lot have arrived from up north, well-mailed and -armed Danes. Maybe you can tempt fresh men from them. Their leader is talking to Sviatoslav. Walks with a bad limp, calls himself Starkad.'

FOURTEEN

A wind snaked out of the north and drove a thin spray of grit and dust against me, whipping my cloak so hard I stumbled sideways. It was driving against our shield side and a few had decided to walk with the things up as shelter.

My arm was too sore for that, the pain throbbing out from the missing fingers all the way up to my elbow, so I had hauled up the cloak round my head and hunched into it, wondering whether my ankle hurt more than my hand, or if I had miasmic rot in the stumps of my fingers. I remembered the bee-keeper from Uppsala and his arm, blackening as he raved into the long night.

Up ahead strode Einar, alongside the jolting cart where Hild sat, cross-legged, swathed and veiled in his fine red cloak.

When he had heard Flosi's news, Einar had stopped in his tracks and the matted yellow dust on his face had not hidden how he had paled. Ketil Crow had hawked and spat and said, 'Loki's hairy arse.' Illugi had just looked sick with weariness.

Then Einar shook himself – physically, like a dog, so that the dust came off him like water – and growled, 'Time for us to go, then, I am thinking.'

'Do we have enough dead yet?' I snarled back at him and he whirled, taking a step towards me. I think he expected me to back from him, remembering the steel of his fingers round my neck, but I was savage for it, wanted it more than my life, even though the thought flashed through me that I was dead.

'Enough for what?' asked a bemused Wryneck, with his tic-twitch.

Einar stopped, forced a grin and shrugged. 'Our Bear Slayer has lost his father,' he declared, for all to hear, 'and it is not surprising a little of his mind has gone with him.' He turned to Wryneck. 'Look after him, old one, while I arrange for the proper rites for our fallen.'

Then he looked round the rest of us, raising his voice so all could hear. 'Wash. Dress in your finest, for these are your oath-brothers and deserve it.'

So we all straggled out, searching for our scattered belongings from where the horsemen had dragged them, then went down to the river and cleaned ourselves and our clothes, as much as we could in that pink-tinged, mud-tainted flow.

But the Don was wide here and swallowed all our filth. By the time Ketil Crow and Einar came back, with thralls leading a dozen carts, each with two solid wheels and a stringy pony, we were, if not shining, more fitting than we had been before.

But I did it only for Rurik. I wanted to spit in Einar's eye.

We took the bodies north into the steppe as the twilight grew, far out from where the city smouldered, until the fires of our own camp were distant enough for some to be uneasy about getting back. Of course, I knew we weren't going back.

In the half-dark, thralls dug out a great boat-shaped pit in the black earth and placed the bodies in it, for there wasn't enough wood left for a pyre after all the great burnings we'd already had.

It was a dark and silent affair, of hissing wind and the grunts of the thralls as they dug the earth with chopping sounds. Nearby, like a great storm crow, Hild squatted in her dark dress, knees up at her ears, hands clasped in her lap, presiding over it like some idol.

I folded Rurik's hands on his chest over the hilt of his sword and silently asked the All-Father to guide him. Then the thralls filled the pit in with furious, nervous energy, as the dark came down and they grew ever more fearful.

They were right to be afraid. Maybe one or two suspected, but most were scared of the wrong people for, after they had unloaded the head-sized white stones we had begged or stolen from the Greek engineers and placed them as a border round the grave, Ketil Crow had them all seized.

Illugi Godi led the chanting prayers as, one by one, their throats were slit and they were laid out in a circle, head towards the mound, feet away. Hild stirred then, as the iron stink of blood swirled on the steppe wind and unfolded herself.

'Are we done here?' she rasped and heads turned angrily to her, only to be silenced by the cold stare they had in return.

It was a hasty excuse, half-ashamed in the dark, for a proper burial in the old way, with fire and dignity, but I made my own peace with Rurik then, for I thought it unlikely I would be back here – or that the scavengers would leave much. But all were safely across Bifrost, the rainbow bridge.

Afterwards, Einar told them what he planned: to strike out north and east, round the city, then back to the river beyond it and on down to the greatest wealth of silver they had ever seen.

Thirty agreed at once and eight thereafter, reluctant and muttering about every hand being against them.

'Did you think such a prize was to be had lightly?' Einar demanded, as much to all of us as to them.

'No,' answered one of those who still refused – baptised

Christ-followers to a man, I noted. 'I did not think to have to pay my soul as the price.'

'Your soul?' snarled Ketil Crow. 'What is this? The after-life in Christ-Valholl? If so, it seems a poor place, full of poor people and gods who scorn a hard arm.'

The man, a Dane from Hedeby called Aslaf, was not fazed by Ketil Crow and merely shrugged, since he had no gold-browed argument and Christ hung on him like a new tunic, still creased and scratchy here and there.

For all that, he and his three oarmates would not give in and stood their ground, shuffling their feet and keeping a wary eye and a hand on a hilt.

'You swore an oath,' Illugi reminded them and Aslaf glanced at him, uneasy now that this door had opened. But he had courage, this Dane, and pushed it a little wider.

'Not made to the One God we follow,' he countered defi-antly, then licked his lips and stared hard at Einar. 'Anyway, I am not the first to break that old oath. I will not follow a madwoman into the Grass Sea in search of a tale for children.'

The words hung in the air with the flutter and whine of insects and the gutter of new torches in the rising wind.

'Nithing turds,' Ketil Crow growled, waving a dismissive hand. 'I hate fucking Christ-men; they are not even worth killing.'

Hild laughed, high and crazed and cracked like a bell, and half of those who had already agreed to go almost changed their minds there and then, I saw. I was one.

For a moment I thought Aslaf would ruin it all, for his eyes narrowed and I could feel him flush from where I stood. If he fought, he would die, that was certain.

Then he relaxed, took two or three steps backwards, insult-ingly, until he was beyond range of a backstab, whirled and trotted into the night, back to the sprawling fires of the camp. With a brief wild look at each other, the other three did the same.

'If Yaropolk doesn't kill him,' Einar growled to the uneasy stirrings around him, 'then Sviatoslav will. If Starkad doesn't get to them first, that is.'

The men round him growled with bare-toothed, savage delight at that, the fate these oath-breakers deserved. But it was the wolf-grin of the desperate.

There wasn't much left now to bind us. Not oath, certainly – like a badly built hov, the roofbeams of which were splitting. For some, the lure of the hoard was still enough. For most it was the sick realisation that, unsteady as it was, the shrinking band of Oathsworn was the safest place to be for the moment.

And for me? There was only one reason I was going now. A son cannot leave his murdered father without taking revenge.

We moved out through the darkness, keeping the fires to our back until they disappeared. Then we turned east, with Steinthor questing ahead and Bagnose to our shield side.

Now the men knew of the plan, a few were cursing that they had left this or that behind, thinking they'd return. Short Eldgrim and Kvasir were the most loud and furious, since they'd bought a concubine between them and spent almost all they had on her only to have left her behind.

Most were as *varjazi* always had been. They wore all they possessed, carrying wealth in boot or under armpit. If you could not leave something behind in an eyeblink, you were a fool.

By dawn, the wind had risen to a snake-hiss and we trundled across short grass peeking from between stones, over endless, rolling hills, cut with steep-gulleyed streams, some dust-dry, some trickling with water and almost choked with eager growth.

It was well named, this Grass Sea, a great, undulating vastness unmarked as an ocean. When the city had shrunk behind us to a scab on the distant horizon, Einar put the wind at our back and headed us to the river. Now and then he spoke softly with Hild, but she made not a sound and no one wanted to go near her, not even me, for the Other rose off her like a sweat-stink and made the hairs on your arms stand up.

We spotted the first dust, whipped away like smoke on a sighing wind, as we tramped tiredly up to another of the steep gulleys, which those Novgorod Slavs among us called *balkas*. They were annoying, for the shelter let scrub and stunted trees spring up and the carts had to be manhandled over them. Even the tough little ponies were tiring.

Einar decided to rest for a while in one and wait for Steinthor and Bagnose to come back in. Sheltered from the wind, with water and some kindling, we got a couple of fires going and those with the skill for it boiled up meat into a gruel and made flatbread on a griddle.

Bagnose came in, loping like a weary dog, laid his bow and quiver down and took a swig from a horn that was offered. Then he made a face and spat. 'Water, you arses!'

The men chuckled; Bagnose was a lift to the spirits, the one man who really did thumb his nose at the gods and never questioned that what he was doing was the way things should be. The whale road was as natural to him – and Steinthor – as if they were a pair of the great beasts it was named after.

He grabbed a bowl, hauled out a horn spoon from inside his tunic and sucked gruel into his mouth, chewing gobbets of tough gristle, spitting sideways. We all waited until he had finished, then Einar asked, 'Well, Geir Bagnose?'

Bagnose wiped his glistening beard, stuffed flatbread in, washed it down with another swig of water and sighed, then belched. 'Twenty, perhaps thirty horsemen, those little ones on little ponies. Moving north to east, circling us.'

'Enemy?' asked a voice and Bagnose snorted.

'Arse! Every horseman is our enemy now.'

'Those turds on their dog-horses are not fighters,' said Flosi

303

with a sneer and a spit. 'You can fight them off armed with a bladder on a stick.'

Bagnose shook his head sorrowfully. 'Tell me more when they shoot you full of arrows from a distance,' he growled. 'They'll make you look like a hedgepig, then cut off your little bladder on a stick and shove it in your flapping mouth.'

More chuckles and Flosi acknowledged that they were, it had to be said, nasty with their little bows. But all of us had begged, stolen, bought – or, in my case, inherited – the thick underkirtle for mail. It made movement even harder, but kept the arrows off unless the little nithings got to close range, or you had Loki luck. I wore my father close to my skin and there was some comfort in that.

'Steinthor in yet?' asked Bagnose. Ketil Crow shook his head and Bagnose frowned, then shrugged and held out his wooden bowl for a refill. 'Have you heard this one, lads? Stop me if you have. I flee the deep earth, there is no place for me on the ground, nor any part of the poles . . .'

His voice covered me like a blanket and I drifted off to it before I heard the answer – but I knew it already and it was apt enough. I lay watching the clouds scud in the wind until my eyes closed and I dozed until kicked awake. We moved out.

Two miles further on we found Steinthor. His head, at least, stuck on a short spear, straggled hair and beard matted with blood. A great black bird hopped off it, wiping its beak with quick sideways flicks and completely unconcerned.

Illugi Godi made a quick, chanting prayer, but Sighvat, whom we called Deep-minded and whose mother had been the same, gave a snort of scorn.

'That's a crow, a big hoodie,' he said. 'Any minute it will fly off, widdershins, not sunwise.'

As if in response, the bird flapped off to the left, sluggish with Steinthor's eyes.

Sighvat felt our stares and looked at us, bemused. 'What? All crows are left-handed.'

'Crows don't have hands,' Ketil Crow replied, staring at Steinthor's flesh-flaked head.

'Nothing to do with these,' snapped Sighvat, holding up his hands. 'It's all here,' he went on and tapped his head. 'Why do you think you are called Ketil Crow?'

And that was true enough. Ketil Crow was corrie-fisted, a left-hander and a fearsomely difficult man to fight.

Bagnose, however, said nothing at all, just stood by that head looking wildly round for the rest of the body. We all spread out and looked, too, but found nothing and it was my thought that he had been killed elsewhere and the head carried to where we could not fail to find it, as a warning.

Illugi Godi and Bagnose lifted the grisly thing off the spear and put it in a hole we dug. We mounded earth over it but, like the bigger mound we'd left far behind, I had a notion that scavengers would dig it up before we'd gone too far.

It was a poor thing for the likes of Steinthor and, for days afterwards, I kept hearing his voice telling the story of finding me with the white bear, in that other world where I had once been a boy whose biggest adventure was finding a gull's nest with four eggs.

That done, we moved on, reaching the river as darkness fell, but Bagnose was not asked to go scouting again. That night, as we huddled round the small fire, eaten by the crushing dark, we knew there would be no more riddles or saga tales from the dark, hunched figure who sat and stared, not at the flames, but into the darkness.

Even whales die on the whale road.

The endless rolling steppe affects your mind, paring away thoughts until there is little more left than the desire to put one foot in front of the other. At one point I had the sick, dizzying feeling that I wasn't walking forward at all, but that the whole steppe was moving backwards.

I even stopped, to see if it carried me backwards and, when it seemed to do just that, as everyone kept on moving, I cried out with fear and dropped to my knees. It was Wryneck, coming up behind me, who grabbed me by the back of my mail and hauled me upright. As my feet stumbled forward I snapped out of it and turned to gasp my thanks.

The flicker of movement silenced everyone, making all heads turn. Hild, in one strange, fluid movement, stood, the red cloak falling from her. She leaped from the cart and strode forward in her bruise-blue dress, long dark hair whipping in that endless, soughing wind.

We all stared. She strode forward for another dozen paces, then stopped. One arm rose slowly and pointed. 'There,' she said. And we looked. And saw only the endless steppe.

'A magic, invisible mountain, is it?' growled Flosi. No one else spoke, but we moved forward to where Hild stood – giving her a wide berth, I noticed, as if she smelled bad.

And we gaped, the shock of realisation coming to us as the steppe fell away into another *balka*, a big one, dust-dry and spilling out in a steep-sided canyon. Not a mountain. A pit. They had dug a pit into the steppe, a vast thing, big as a city, then mounded the middle of it back up in the shape of a great steppe lord's tent, but still below the original ground level.

'They diverted the stream,' Einar marvelled after we had moved down further. 'To hide the entrance, they turned a river across it. This was once . . . a lake, a great pool, with water flowing in there' – he pointed – 'and running out there to the Don.'

Everyone marvelled, save Illugi. The godi had not said much of anything other than muttered chants. Once, in the night, I had seen him by the fire casting his rune bones and muttering to himself and thought then that he was growing as dark as Hild in some ways.

306

'Atil's howe,' breathed Valknut.

'If this one is to be believed,' growled Ketil Crow, moving past him to where Hild squatted. She smiled beautifully up at him and he scowled. 'Cunt to jawline,' he reminded her and moved on.

Einar took us in a scramble down the *balka*, where it led like a road straight to a cleft in the brooding mound.

Hild, silent and hugged to herself, raised one pale hand and pointed at the stones on either side of it, fat stones as tall as a man, ones you would not be ashamed to rune and set up on a hill in memory. But these, though pocked and scarred, were unmarked; however, Illugi looked at them suspiciously.

'The door,' declared Einar with his wolf-grin, his crow-hair flapping in the breeze. 'We can set up camp here and start digging at first light.'

Men found fresh energy, unloaded gear and supplies and rubbed their hands with glee. Round the fire that night there was banter and talk of what they would do with all that silver. There was no doubting it now, for we had all seen the marvel of it.

Ketil Crow and Einar said nothing at all, but sat with their own dreams whirling in their heads. I doubted if they shared the same ones, though.

Atil's howe. A mountain of treasure. She had known after all, it seemed, and the realisation of that made me shiver – for how could she have led us so unerringly to this unmarked, unknown place? How could anyone have done that and still be like the rest of us?

I watched her sitting upright in front of those two stones and that cleft, which was like the dark invite of a woman's body. Her hair floated in the wind, a dark snake-crown, and, even with her back to us all, she exuded something that made the fear rise in you like old mead fumes. She sat there all night, was still there in the morning, she had not moved.

Did not move, until the horsemen swept on us.

Einar had split us, sensibly enough. There were those to guard and we wore all our gear, while those digging had stripped to the waist and were hacking away at the earth. A cart was being broken up, so that the wood could be used as shoring, for we had no clear idea of how much we'd have to dig to break in.

The drumming of hooves brought all heads up. The diggers ran for the cover of the carts; those on guard hefted their weapons. Of the twenty, about half knew how to use a bow and were nocking arrows. But they also had mail and fat padded arms, all of which made drawing and loosing accurately a nightmare.

The horsemen swept down the *balka* in a cloud of dust, without any shouts or cries. They skidded at full tilt down the slopes we had taken ages to traverse, shooting arrows as they came.

I heard them thud into the earth around me. One hissed over my head. Another smacked my shield boss with a clang and dropped to the ground.

They were true steppe warriors, these, all sheepskins and wool hats and active as cats on those horses. They didn't so much ride them as climb all over them, shooting their little arrows until they got close, then whipping out their light swords, darting them like snake-tongues at us from the other side of the horse, and swooping away before we could strike.

They swirled and whooped and vanished and appeared again in the dust until we were dizzy with it, whirling our heavy swords and axes at nothing.

A figure stepped out of our ranks into the dust.

'Hold!' yelled Einar. 'Don't let them drag you out into their killing ground.'

But it was Bagnose and he was past caring. He nocked, took aim, shot and a man pitched off. Walking forward, he nocked, took aim, shot and another horseman shrieked.

They saw him then and the arrows hissed. He took two full in the chest, staggering him. But he walked forward, nocked, took aim . . .

He had no mail, no padding, for he was an archer who took pride in it and never missed, wanted nothing to tangle his flights or string.

But Bagnose was already dead, though his legs and heart didn't know it and he was still roaring something when he fell.

We ignored Einar and went after him, of course – it was Bagnose, after all – charging into the dust, screaming. But by then the horsemen had thundered off and all we could do was drag back the corpse, studded with arrows.

'Like a hedgepig,' said Flosi mournfully. Out on the slope of the *balka*, though, six corpses lay, each killed with a single shot.

'What was he shouting?' asked Valknut, who had been one of the diggers.

'He wasn't shouting,' answered Einar softly. 'He was making verses. On his own death. A good song, but only he knows it.'

'Odin's balls,' Valknut growled, shaking his head. 'The cost of seeing them off was high.'

'A test?' Ketil Crow hazarded, wiping his streaming face. 'To see how good we are?'

'Now they know,' spat Wryneck with a brief twitch. 'Six for one.'

'Let's hope the price is too high for them,' I offered.

Of course, it wasn't. But they waited until the next day to try to wipe us out.

We dug feverishly, well into the night, taking it in turns to stand guard or swing a pick, so that no one got any real rest. Valknut and Illugi Godi did their own digging, another boat-grave for the animals to dig up, while Hild sat and watched us, perched on a wagon-trace with her knees at her chin. She reminded everyone of a carrion crow.

It was Valknut who speared the first of the treasure, with the very last hack of a mattock, dragging earth back out of the hole we had made between the stones.

He held up what he had found, scraping the dirt off and, in the red glow of a torch, something gleamed. He spat, polished it and the flash of silver shone. We all gawped.

Einar took it from him, turning it this way and that. 'A bowl,' he hazarded. 'Or a plate, flattened and bent. Good workmanship, though.'

'It's silver, right enough,' breathed Valknut and would have gone back in, save that the stretch he had cleared out needed roof supports and it was too dark to see properly to put them in. The tunnel we had dug was six foot long, three high and leaking loose dirt like water because we were using wood sparingly; we needed all the carts to carry our haul away in.

All night long the men turned that bent semi-circle of age-black silver to and fro, cleaned it, marvelled at it, discovered the delicate border of leaves and fruit, birds in flight and even bees, all embossed in the silver in perfect little portraits.

Sighvat studied it with interest and said, 'Those are the dreams of birds.'

'You and your birds,' growled Valknut. 'What do they dream of?'

'Songs, mostly,' Sighvat replied seriously, then wagged a finger at Valknut. 'If we scorn the wisdom of birds and beasts, we fool only ourselves.'

'What wisdom?' asked Wryneck, curious now, while he smoothed the notched edge of his sword back to sharpness in a comforting, rhythmic rasp of whetstone.

'Well,' said Sighvat, considering. 'Bees know when fire is coming and will swarm. Hornets and wasps know the very tree that Thor will hurl his hammer at. And a frog is better at being a frog than a man.'

We chuckled at that, but Sighvat merely shrugged and said, 'Could you live naked in a pool all winter and survive?'

'What else?' demanded Wryneck, for this was decent compensation for the sad lack of Bagnose's wit.

'My mother could speak with birds and some beasts,' said Sighvat, 'but never could teach it to me. She told me hedgepigs and wasps will not spy for anyone, but woodpeckers and starlings can be persuaded to tell what they know. And most hawks hate autumn.'

'Why?' demanded Einar, suddenly interested. 'I have hunted a hawk in autumn, but it never does well and I have always wondered why that is.'

'You should have had someone like my old mum ask it,' Sighvat replied. 'But it is simple enough. Here is a bird that hangs in the air, looking for the least little movement on the ground, which is its supper. And there are thousands of blowing leaves.'

Einar stroked his moustaches thoughtfully and nodded.

Valknut waved a dismissive hand, adding: 'That's just . . . sense.'

'You did not know it,' Sivhgat pointed out and Valknut fumed, having no answer to that.

'And,' I said, half dreamily, 'you never see a cat on a battle-field.'

There was amazed silence for a moment, then Sighvat grinned. 'Exactly – you know a thing or two, young Orm.'

'All I know is that this' – Valknut held up the battered silver – 'is a sign that riches lie in that hill.'

'Just so,' declared Einar with a slight smile, 'and here's something for you to think on. Riches are like horse shit.'

We looked at each other. Some shrugged; no one could understand it and more than a few, never having heard him do it before, were not sure if Einar was making a joke.

Einar grinned. 'They stink when they are in a heap in someone else's patch, but make everything fruitful when spread about.'

And we laughed and felt almost like the old brotherhood,

311

sitting by the fire, fretting for light so we could get back to digging.

But when morning did come, we had hardly blown life back into the fire embers, barely had time for a stretch and a fart, before the horsemen appeared on the steppe above the *balka* and everyone sprinted for weapons and armour.

FIFTEEN

This time, they were heavy horse, men in armour, with spears held low or overarm, with maces and cased bows and curved swords. They carried silver discs on poles that told us they were Khazars.

There was a pause then as we struggled into padding and mail, nocked arrows, hefted swords. Up on the lip of the steppe, two men talked . . . argued, in fact, waving arms. Wryneck chuckled. 'They don't like it one bit,' he said. 'The light horse can get down fast and hard, but we can see them off and even shelter from their arrows. Those big men aren't so happy, for they will not have as easy a time coming down as we did.'

'You have the right of it, old one,' agreed Einar. 'No speed, no shock – and charging into all this guddle underfoot.' He waved one hand at the carts and gear and earth spill and I moved closer to it.

So it proved. The big men left their big horses and came down at us on foot, slithering unsteadily in their great, ankle-lapping armour of little plates like metal leaves, with round hide-covered shields and sabres and maces. Some snapped off their great lances to use as spears on foot.

No shieldwall. This time it was hack and slash and survive.

Illugi, his godi staff discarded in favour of a shield and axe, took a rushing charge at the stand and locked himself in a fierce grapple with the first of these armoured oxen to hit us. Einar and Ketil Crow moved fluidly as a killing pair; metal clanged on metal, curses and blood sprayed.

One came at me, eyes dark and fierce under his helmet rim, his teeth startling white in the bush of a black beard. He stabbed at my thigh and I blocked it, knocking the weapon sideways with my shield. He reversed the stroke with incredible speed, lunging at my head and I had to throw myself back as the point flicked like a snake tongue almost in my eye.

He darted in again. I half dropped, slashed, felt my sword bite and recoil from that armour. His point flicked out again; I blocked and hacked again to no purpose other than chipping metal leaves off him.

Something whirled next to me; the man shrieked and dropped. Wryneck popped up like some mad puppet, rammed his sword straight through the open front of the screaming man's helmet and yelled, 'Too many to go dancing with them, young Orm. Cut the feet from the fucks.'

I remembered, then, Gunnar Raudi's lessons back in Bjornshafen: any way you can. Teeth, fists, elbows – aim for the feet and ankles. My father, teaching me how to survive . . .

There were too many. I had three on me, one with a spear, two flanking him with shields as guards. My breath was ragged; my whole arm throbbed from blows on the shield. The spearman waded in chopping in a cross-pattern, which was lucky for me. It let me know these men had no idea how to fight on foot.

I slapped the iron blade point away with a sweep of the sword, stepped, spun up inside it, rammed the shield against his armoured carapace and slammed the fat pommel of Bjarni's old sword into his face.

I knew where they all were, as if I could see it. I spun out of that, weightless it seemed to me, went into a crouch and scythed round, taking a second one just above the ankles, feeling the blade bite, hearing him howl.

The spearman was on his back now, so I leaped up, landed both feet and drove the air from him as I hurled myself at the third man, who was snarling and swinging his sabre furiously.

The blow hooked up under my shield and slammed into my ribs so hard I felt them bend. Then I hit him hard, felt the searing agony of pain in my shield-arm as we collided, falling together like two steel trees.

I rolled right, over the sword-arm, came up in a half-crouch, shield up. My left arm was pure fire now, but I hacked viciously with the sword as he struggled like a trapped beetle in his heavy armour. It swept up under the nasal of his helmet, took his nose off in a flick of blood, ripped the helmet half off his head and left him yowling and scrabbling away from me.

I sliced again, seeing the spearman wallowing back to his feet, felt the blade shear down into muscle and bone, through Noseless's neck.

The spearman was up, dragging out his sabre and I had no shield-arm, just a mass of fiery pain with a dead weight dragging it. I lunged forward as Black Beard's sabre cleared the sheath, hacked forward, backstroked and he squealed, the sabre flying away, hand still attached.

I was on one knee, sucking air. One was dead, one was rolling around with blood seeping from his boot, one was howling with the stump of a right hand.

And Einar was coming at me, dust spurting under his boots.

He had lost his shield and helmet and his hair was flying like a black net. He had also lost his sword and gained one of their cavalry sabres, the great lazy S-curve of it pointing at me as he roared forward.

I couldn't get my left arm to move. He came hurtling at me and all I could think to do was snarl back at him and slash.

The blow took him hard in the side. I saw rings explode, the straw of his padded jerkin puffed out, then blood sprayed and he shrieked, the sabre curving over my shoulder.

Taking the cavalryman coming up behind me straight in the face.

He hit, we fell together in a grunting heap of dust and blood, spilled apart, lay there. My shield straps broke – mercifully – and I rolled free of it and got up, left arm dangling.

Einar struggled up, grinned at me with bloody teeth, collected his sabre from the face of the man who had been about to kill me and hirpled off, half-bent.

I stared as the dust swirled. Men groaned, yelled. Valknut moved wearily over, finished off the one whose leg I had all but severed – the other one was gone – then walked a few paces forward and raised both arms. 'Any more? Have you any more, you pox-eaten holes?'

I hoped they hadn't, but there were some ragged cheers. With my breath thundering in my ears I looked at the cavalry-man with the punched-in face. Had Einar saved me? Had he tried to kill me there and was his luck so bad he had actually stopped me from being killed?

I didn't know; I couldn't be sure. But I had hurt him. Ketil Crow was with him, helping him off with his mail. Others, Illugi among them, were moving among the bodies, looking for dead and wounded.

Wryneck lay up against a wagon wheel, pinned to the ground like a hunted boar, thick blood welling round the point where the lance had sliced into the rings and mail and through him to the steppe.

I couldn't speak as I knelt by him. He felt it, opened his eyes with difficulty and grinned, spilling blood all over his white beard. 'She said I'd never get old *and* rich,' he said and died.

'Are you hurt bad?' I heard and turned to see Valknut looking at me. I stood up, weaving, and he steadied me, looking me over.

'This needs sewing,' he said with a chuckle, flicking the dangling rings round rents in the mail. My ribs, I knew, were bruised, but not cut. The pain in my hand was beginning to subside, too, and I realised I had got off lightly.

So did Valknut, who slapped me on one shoulder and looked at the dead men nearby. 'Not bad,' he said. 'Three in one – but that fourth would have had you if it hadn't been for Einar.'

And he strode off, sword round both shoulders, as if coming off a practice field. Over by the fire, Einar was naked to the waist, grim-faced and white as milk, while Illugi picked rings out of his flesh and heated up a knife.

I saw him force Einar to drink and, an hour later, I could already smell the garlic from his severed gut from where I stood, but Einar gave a little shake of his head when Illugi came to him and put his tunic back on.

Hild crouched nearby, watching like a buzzard waiting for prey to die.

Eight were dead, almost all the others wounded and two of those had soup wounds, which Ketil Crow dealt with. Sixteen enemy corpses were left where they lay, though they were stripped naked. The horsemen had disappeared.

An hour after the battle, half of those still fit started to shore up the tunnel and recommenced digging, those too hurt to dig tended the wounded and prepared food. At noon, I handed Einar a bowl of meat and bread and our eyes met.

He was so pale the veins on his hands were blue ropes, but his eyes locked with mine and were still black and steady and I was first to look away, still unsure whether he had been trying to kill me or save me.

When I collected the bowl again, it was still full, the food congealed. Einar looked asleep, head on his chest, face hidden by the matted wings of his hair, but his hands looked so white I thought, for a second, that I could see through them.

All that day I wondered about him, while the heat grew brassy and the corpses swelled and began to blacken and stink.

'We shall have to get out of here soon,' muttered Kvasir. 'If not, we will get sick and die.'

They called him Spittle as a joke, after the wise man made from the saliva of the gods, because there were stones with more sense than Kvasir. But it is possible that he had made his first-ever joke, since most of us were sick or dying already. Kvasir himself had an infection in one eye that leaked pus: if a cure wasn't found, he would go blind in it.

I wasn't even sure of my own state. The bindings round my lost fingers were filthy and stained, my ankle ached and, once I had peeled the tattered mail and padding off, my ribs were looking anything but healthy under the tunic.

'Looks like Bifrost,' said Finn Horsehead. It was a measure of how bad things were, for he never said much at the best of times. 'It will have more colours than the rainbow bridge by morning, I am thinking. Does that hurt?'

It did and I slapped his hand away and told him to leave off prodding it. I could feel it grate when I moved and worried that I had broken a rib or more.

'We are so cursed that we will soon come to envy the dead,' answered Short Eldgrim morosely.

We still called him Short Eldgrim, even though the reason for it – another Eldgrim, nicknamed Long – was under the mound of earth nearby. Short Eldgrim, slashed badly about the face and hands, didn't look like he would be long in lying next to him.

'You old woman,' answered a man called Arnod, though he made a sign against the evil eye with the one arm that was still good. The other was strapped to his side with two wooden spars on either side, badly smashed by one of the cavalrymen's maces.

'I would like to see my old woman,' Finn muttered and everyone glanced at him, stunned by this display of affection. He saw it and scowled. 'She owes me money.'

I sat by the fire, whose flames twisted and flattened in the rising wind and listened to them talk, as if they had no injuries worth speaking of, about what they might find inside that gods-cursed howe.

They had everything in there, from Odin's magic ring, Draupnir, to the Mead of Poetry, brewed from blood and honey.

Then Short Eldgrim, hunched and grumbling and in pain from the carvings on his face and hands, moodily pointed out that, if we were descending into the realm of saga tales, there was every chance we'd find Hati, the wolf who chases and tries to devour the moon, or even Nidhogg, the corpse-devouring dragon.

In the distance came a rumbling on the rising wind. As the twilight grew and the wind moaned down the *balka*, Valknut came up to where we all huddled round the fire, watching the blue-white flashes light up the sky in the distance, listening to the rumbling wheels of Thor's goat-pulled chariot.

He held up a guttering torch, whose flames were nearly flat in the wind. 'We have broken into the howe of Attila,' he said, 'and Hild has gone inside.'

There was a mad scramble from the fire then, a scrabble of eager men heading for the tunnel until they were brought up short by the grim figure of Ketil Crow, standing light on the balls of his feet, his sword, saw-edged with nicks, swinging in one hand.

'Best if only a few go in,' Einar said, moving slowly, half-hunched to one side. His face seemed to have shrunk and had a greenish tinge, the eyes sunk so deep that his face already looked like a corpse. There was a huge seep of blood from his bandaged side. 'The tunnel isn't all that wide, or safe. Ketil Crow, me, Illugi, Sig – Orm, you are fit, I am thinking, so you will go. The rest remain.'

'Prepare the carts, lads,' Ketil Crow added with a grin. 'We will be hauling out a fortune soon.'

That mollified them but it didn't take much – while the lure of plundering a huge hoard of silver was strong, the fear of Nidhogg or worse was stronger. Best, I could see them all reason, to let someone else find out the dangers. There was plenty of opportunity for plunder later.

The dawn horizon flashed and roared behind me as I ducked into the tunnel. I was the last man, almost on all fours, wincing at my various pains and carrying only my sword. Ahead, Einar's arse was barely visible and I could hear him grunt and pant. Up front, Ketil Crow, Valknut and Illugi Godi struggled to keep torch flames from their faces and still avoid elbowing all the shaky timber uprights.

Earth trickled down my neck – a run of it, like thick water, spilled over the back of my hand as I brushed the roof. Something dug into my knee: metal. I dug it out, made out a dull gleam, held it close, saw the wink of silver.

Now that I looked, I could see other lumps of dull, age-black metal. We had dug straight through a wall of silver objects and earth.

I crawled on, feeling my other hand slap into something sticky and, when I brought it close to my face, smelled the iron tang of fresh blood. Einar, leaking like a sprung bucket, slithered along the tunnel and, suddenly, stood upright.

I followed, scrambling out into the howe of Attila.

I had had no idea what we would find, even from the start. A cave, I had imagined, with neat piles of gleaming treasure, like all the sagas seemed to have. Hopefully with no coiled dragon.

But this was no cave. Even in the light of the torches, held high by Ketil Crow, Sigtrygg and Illugi, you could see that his people had done Attila proud.

The howe was the size of a small town, though I only had that impression from the great vault of the roof. The floor was flagged with stone; the roof, which should have been dirt, was a vague, arched shape in the darkness, its great wooden beams socketed into solid stone pillars and, though crusted with age, still firm.

At one end of this flagstoned square was a huge throne, a magnificent edifice of wood and gleaming silver raised high above the flagged level, with a pile of bright, brocaded robes in red and green and blue lying at the foot of it.

And all around, everywhere, piled to the roof, gleaming here and there, were blackened shapes, ominous and flickering in the torch shadows, a great tumble of forms, like buildings, strange and slanted, holding the gods knew what.

Each arm of that throne was as large as a table and, fastened to one, I saw with a sudden leap to my throat, was a skeleton, held at the neck and wrists by short, thick black chains embedded in the base.

I knew it was a woman, though there was nothing there to let me know that. Naked, she had been chained to the throne of the dead Attila. I knew who she was: Ildico, his bride of one night. The dream rushed back to me, of Hild and the collar of silver.

Ketil Crow saw none of this, just the pile of robes at the foot of the throne and he knew what that meant. His scream of rage should have echoed. Instead, it was sucked dead by that place. 'The sword. She has taken the sword!'

He rushed forward and raked his own blade in the robes. Yellowed bones and insects spilled out from the bright, curling gold embroidered dragons on it. A skull rolled, part of what was left of Attila, who had been on that throne until flung from it by Hild, tearing free the sword he had held in his lap for centuries.

With a curse, Ketil Crow flung himself at the dark, bulked shapes, searching for her and yelling curses. Things clattered and fell and he screamed wildly and hurled bits of black metal backwards. He wanted that sword, as badly as Einar wanted the gifthrone.

Einar was now moving like an old man, bent and shuffling. I watched him give a choking, bitter half-laugh and hirple weakly forward, then slowly and painfully climb on to the great silver chair, where he slumped, laughing blood on to his moustaches.

I scarcely noticed, or heard Illugi Godi's muttered chanting. I had just realised, for the first time, what the building-sized shapes really were.

Age-blackened silver. The sheer extent of it sucked breath and reason right out of me. Acres of it, piled high to the roof, round the throne, beyond the throne, the riches of a dozen kingdoms, the craft of a thousand smiths.

Jewelled fans, I saw, with silver feathers. A miniature of a castle gleamed, sparkling with gemstone flags. A silver ship reared out of a sea of coins, with ropes and stays of silver wire. A shirt of mail, each ring silver, every small rivet gold. Anklets and brooches and rings and tumbled pots on tumbled pots of coins, spilling like waterfalls.

For the first – and only – time, I discovered the silver-lust that so grips a man he loses his reason. I was, on that day, infected and cured of it for ever. I grabbed Illugi's torch from him and I doubt if he noticed.

I fell on my knees, picked something up. A cup, slightly flattened on one side, with stem and embossing. I picked up another, then another, until I was scrabbling in the piles, heedless of the hurts. A silver pin stabbed me: I stuck it in my tunic. A silver-hilted dagger drew blood on my palm: I stuck it in my belt.

There were rings and armrings, which we still call ringmoney. Plates, shields, helmets, brooches, bowls, ewers, bracelets, necklaces, earrings and coins, thousands of coins. There were knuckledusters of gold and daggers of silver with jewelled hilts.

They were everywhere, piled high, forced together until cups flattened and thrones bent, a fortune, all in silver, wrenched from the world by Attila and his armies, a fitting panoply for the greatest of great steppe kings.

It was the scream that wrenched me out of it, my tunic stuffed, my boots full, my arms laden with a bowl the size of a bath.

'Burning ice, biting flame,' Illugi said. 'That is how life began, in the south, in Muspell, where it seethes and shines and no man can look on it.'

In the flickering torchlight, I suppose, all that cold silver, bouncing with flame, could have reminded him of Muspell, the land of molten ice and shining flame where life was first created. At the time I thought his mind had gone. I am still not sure what was right.

The scream came again, then Ketil Crow slid down a hill, stumbling in an avalanche of coin, cursing and shrieking. He had lost his sword and there was blood on his mouth. He hit the flagstones and fell, scrambled up, fell again and tried to crawl to the exit.

Valknut went to him, but he was already sliding out of this world, bleeding in slowing gouts and spilling blue-pink coils from the rip in his stomach that went from groin to throat. Cunt to jawline.

His eyes chilled us. They were livid with fear and he was so gibbering with it that he couldn't speak, his mouth moving like a fish until it stopped and he died.

I stood up and moved, shedding rings and cups and a fork with two tines. I let the huge bowl clatter and Valknut whirled, searching the darkness.

'Einar . . . ?' I asked, but there was silence.

I moved to where he sat, like the jarl he had always striven to be, surrounded by all the wealth of the world, on the throne of a ring-giver. He looked like spume on a wave, as if a breath would blow him away.

'Was it worth it?' I demanded of him and the sunken eyes flicked open, the pale face rose a little. One strand of black hair stuck to his cold-sweated cheek like a scar and his grin was as pale as the torc he wore, that mark of his status.

He grinned and touched it, that thick, braided ring of silver, shredded and lopsided where gift-sections had been hacked off.

'You . . . may have . . . to learn . . . for yourself,' he said, with that wolf-snarl of his. 'The weight of a jarl torc like this.'

It was the smile that finished it. I had seen it before, just as he'd reached the back of Gunnar Raudi in Dengizik's tomb.

'Before you die,' I said. 'I have a message.'

His head wobbled as he raised it to look at me. I took Bjarni's sword and rammed it hard in him, so that he folded round it and gasped.

'From Gunnar,' I said to the fade in his black eyes. 'My father.'

Valknut wiped his mouth with the back of one hand, glanced wildly at me, then at Illugi. Then he heaved in a great suck of air and stepped forward, sword up, staring into the darkness. 'I am here. Come ahead, if you think you are hard enough to fight me. I am Odin's chosen. Let him deal with me as he pleases, for I am not afraid to die.'

There was a black chuckle, a rustling, insect-wing of a thing and something shaded detached itself from the dark and came down the silver mountain in a clatter of riches.

'Freyja,' said Illugi, his mouth open in awe. Truth to tell, it certainly wasn't Hild and could easily have been Freyja the sister of Yngvi, foremost of the Vanir, the old gods. Freyja, the Queen of Witches, shapechanger, teacher of the dark seidr magic.

324

'Hild . . .' I managed and she turned at that, hair draped half over her face in black tangles, the delicate S-curve of the sabre in both hands, her dark dress shredded. A wind blew up the tunnel and into the howe, then, snaking her hair back from a mask of a face.

'Not . . . Hild,' she said, in that lost voice. 'We Volsung say it as Ildico.'

Ildico, the bride sent to Attila, who had died on his wedding night to her, rumour said by her hand, in vengeance for Attila's betrayal of the Volsung. They had chained her to his throne for all eternity, naked and alive.

I believed then that her fetch called to the bloodline to come and free her, made powerful by that double-damned runesword and what it was made from. Whatever the right of it, the girl I had known as Hild was gone. What she was now was something to run from, screaming, as Ketil Crow had done.

Valknut gave a howl. Witch or no witch, Valknut knew how to die and he hurled himself at her, swinging, frothing, screaming on Odin for help.

Behind me, Illugi was also calling to the All-Father and the wind hissed round the howe as if in answer, guttering torches, flaring shadows everywhere, bringing the clean, cold smell of rain.

Valknut would have kippered her if things had been normal, but they weren't normal. He swung, she parried, did it again and again until he backed off to get his breath.

'Help me,' he grated. I blinked away from Einar's dead stare and hauled my sword out of him. It came with a slight suck and a groan of air, as if he was alive, and that made me step back a pace. But he was gone across Bifrost, for sure.

So I stepped to Valknut's side, still uneasy. It was Hild, after all. Illugi Godi came up on Valknut's right.

It wasn't Hild. Those eyes were just all blackness now and

the smell of rot was on her. We all tasted it, saw what we saw – and I was so scared that I felt the piss wash hot down my leg.

Illugi rapped his staff and uttered some commanding phrase, looked down at the splash it made, then up, while she blocked Valknut's rush and moved sideways as if she floated, sinking the sword-point straight in Illugi's slow-spreading smile.

He fell away, choking. I lashed at her and she turned the blade slightly to meet it. There was a high ting of sound and my sword halved just above the hilt, the main part spinning into the darkness. Now, it seemed, I had the gods' answer for my having stolen it in the first place.

Valknut hacked down, reversed, hacked back. Each time it was met with a delicate parry. I stood there and gawped at the ruin of Bjarni's blade and the only thing that I could think was that he was going to be really annoyed about that.

Then I staggered away, fell over Ketil Crow and sprawled backwards at the foot of the throne, scrabbling in the heavy silk, dragon-embroidered robes that had draped Attila's corpse. Bones crunched and scattered and I dropped the useless sword, which was so perfectly broken it barely had a jagged edge.

Valknut, panting and gasping, backed away, unable to sustain his attacks. Illugi was writhing and choking to death in his own blood as it splashed on the floor. I wondered why he had smiled . . .

Splashing. I was wet through and not because I had pissed myself. The floor was wet. The floor was wet . . . ?

Valknut started to launch himself again, but she swung, he deflected and his sword shattered into three and the pieces flew off, clattering into the dark. Before he could even curse, she whicked the sabre left and right and left and blood flew, an arm circled lazily and then Valknut folded from the waist,

326

his bottom half falling backwards and gore spraying every-where.

Wet. The floor was wet because water was sliding greasily up the tunnel, thick with slurry and mud. And I remembered us arriving here, and Einar's marvelling voice: 'To hide the entrance, they turned a river across it. This was once . . . a lake, a great pool, with water flowing in there and running out there to the Don.'

Illugi had smiled because he'd had an answer from the gods and, as usual, it was a Loki joke. Not once a lake. Always a lake when it rained – as it had done far to the north all night.

She came to me then, scarcely making splash or a ripple as she stepped, her hair wild, her eyes as black as I realised her heart now was. She had known this would happen all along, I remembered, had pleaded with me to stay away.

'Hild . . .' I said. I begged, if truth is being told here. I remembered, with a bright flash, how she had looked just like a fine princess, once, with a fine prince by her side. We ate meat on wooden skewers, drank honey mead on a perfect day.

This was not her, though. Not this avenging Valkyrie, sword up, moving with sickening speed, fluid as shadow. She laughed, high and fierce with triumph and . . . what? Revenge, for all that had been done to her, to her mother and all her kin before? Or, if she was truly fetch-hagged, for being Ildico, chained and left to a slow death?

She only had to whirl that rune blade and I was done, with nothing under my hand . . . but something hard.

A hilt it felt like, but not Bjarni's ruined sword. This was round and perfect and slid into my palm.

I flicked it out, a reflex more than anything. It was a hilt and on it a blade, as curved and true as the one she wielded and they rang like bells.

She howled like a wounded wolf, tried again and again

327

and each time my blade held. The water was round my ankles now and I scrabbled back; she flailed wildly, slashed, shrieked and each time I parried, until the hall rang like a Christ temple on a feast day.

Two swords. Each bell-clear tang of sound as they struck drove the surety of it into me. Two swords. I saw them lying across Dengizik's dead lap. His father had had them, too – all great steppe lords had them: the mark of their lordship.

The Volsung smiths had made two swords, not one, as gifts for Attila: she had one and I had the other. Ridill and Hrotti the saga tales called them, part of Sigurd's cursed Fanir treasure. I did not stop to wonder which one was clenched in my fist.

I darted for the tunnel and she was too late to prevent it. I backed up it, feeling the water surge round my boots; she followed, still swinging and stabbing. Two roof supports shattered under her blows. She wailed and hurled forward as the earth poured in.

I last saw her as nothing but a snarl in a pale face, her mouth like a red wound, the sword thrusting still as the earth piled up with a soft, sighing rush of sound.

I almost laughed with the sheer relief of it. Until the water in the tunnel, unable to go anywhere else, surged up and I was sucked in the muddy slush of it.

I wriggled and splashed. The tunnel was full now and I saw earth silting through it, knew it was filling the whole tunnel, knew I was almost as trapped as she.

I went mad then, a little. I fought, grunting, jabbing with the sword to get through. I was choking; there was nothing in that tunnel but slurry now – then a last, quicksand moment of resistance and I was out, neck deep, pulling in air in great maddened whoops.

The *balka* was a surging mass of tan slurry, pouring down, spilling out and round the mound to make the lake, filthy brown with mud and rolling with old corpses. Soon it would swallow the mound itself, drown it until the next drought.

Someone yelled as I struggled to the steep sides, where the crumbling earth calved like bergs off a mountain of ice. I should have floated, but didn't. I was drowning in greed.

Frantically, I hauled my belt off, let my tunic fly free and everything in it that was dragging me down. Brooches, rings, coins: all vanished. I could not get my boots off, they were pulling me down . . . but still I held on to the sabre.

'Orm! Orm!'

The voice came from above. Short Eldgrim's face appeared, a length of rope slithered like a wet snake and I stuck the sabre in my mouth and grabbed it. Willing hands hauled me and I never even felt the pain in my ruined left hand until long afterwards.

I lay on the edge of the dawn-smeared steppe, which crumbled even as we stood there, so they dragged me away again. Eventually, gasping, I sat up. I couldn't believe I was alive and neither could they.

'Everyone else?' asked Kvasir.

I shook my head.

'Einar too?' said Sighvat.

I nodded. The muddy lake swirled and gurgled. I thought of them all under it, wondered if the tunnel was so blocked it would keep the chamber from filling . . . remembered her open mouth and the hate in her eyes.

Not that it mattered. No one was getting in now. The treasure was buried once more, safe under the lake, as had been intended by those who had brought Attila here.

And I laughed, then, thinking of a time when . . . if . . . others ever came back here, did what we had done and dug through to Attila's throne when drought bared it once more.

They'd find Einar on that throne, not Attila, think him the great lord, wonder at his riches and how he died.

That's if they had time, for I had the idea that Hild's fetch would haunt that hall a long time, thanks to her runespelled sword.

I never wanted to go back there.

The others looked at me laughing and I got up, winced, and stood for a moment.

'Well,' said Short Eldgrim, holding up the battered plate of silver, with its embossed rim of little fruits and bees and birds. 'Looks like this is the only hoard of silver we will see this day.'

'Or any day,' agreed Kvasir. He sounded almost relieved.

Short Eldgrim turned it over in his hands and then tossed it back in the waters, an offering to the tortured fetches of Einar and the others.

No one protested.

'Sigurd's cursed silver,' muttered Finn.

'Right enough,' agreed Short Eldgrim.

I hoped not – but no one suggested I throw the sabre back, so I stayed quiet.

They had rescued three ponies and some supplies and a dozen men, those fit enough actually to run for it. All the rest had died, were rolling and tumbling in the maelstrom of muddy water.

There was no rain that day, so we made a fire and I watched what was left of them huddle round it, beyond my hearing, talking. I knew what they were doing and, with a black despair, what I would do when they came to me, their secret whisperings done. I did not care about that: I had my own secret.

It was done simply enough the next day. It had rained then, just when I thought we couldn't be more miserable and I was sitting in it, enduring, when Kvasir came to me and hunkered down where I sat tracing the runes along the sabre's shining, watered blade. Ridill or Hrotti, I wondered.

'Scrubbed up well, that sticker,' he grunted, cautiously probing his red eye, which now leaked green pus and was blind, I knew, from the way he cocked his head.

The rest of them had sabres, too, stripped from cavalrymen who had attacked us, but no one thought much of them – a pig-sticker, too light and pointed for men who fought with the double slashing edge. None were like this one, but if any of the others noticed that, they bit down on it and stayed silent.

I turned the blade in the pearl light of the wet day and agreed it had scrubbed up well, knowing that it was as different from the other sabres we had as night from day.

Eventually, Kvasir cleared his throat and said, 'So, will you lead us then, now that Einar has gone?'

So it was done, despite the fact that the youngest of them was older than me by a decade. I was Orm the White-bear Slayer, who had survived the howe of Attila.

I was sick with it, though. We stood in the hissing wind of that bare steppe and I sacrificed a hare on a rock, as I had seen Illugi do an age ago on the beach at Birka – and it was a sacrifice, for getting the thing was hard enough, let alone not eating it.

Then we looked at each other across the acrid fur-burning stink and nodded and spoke the words together.

'*We swear to be brothers to each other, bone, blood and steel. On Gungnir, Odin's spear, we swear, may he curse us to the Nine Realms and beyond if we break this faith, one to another.*'

A hard oath to swear. To break it now, I would have to become a Christ-follower in Constantinople, or find some fool to take my place – and who could replace the jarl without killing him first?

But I was young and dared to think I could spit in All-Father's one eye.

My first jarl test came when horsemen thundered up to us on the steppe, as we squelched miserably towards the Don. They were a cautious, fur-clad, flat-nosed, fierce-looking bunch of Kipchak dogs who had never seen our like before – which was our good luck.

They stopped some way beyond long arrow-shot and considered us. Their bows were uncased, but no arrows were nocked, which gave me hope.

'They could shoot us down like sheep in a pen,' Kvasir said, his voice tight, his shield up.

'But they have not,' I answered and jerked my downy chin at the rider who had broken away from them and was ambling his scraggy pony towards us, his hands up and clear of his body.

'They want to talk,' Finn Horsehead said. 'Maybe we can frighten them into letting us pass without a fight.'

I looked at him; he was serious. I looked at the rest of them, this tattered band of grim men, prepared to fight and die. I shook my head, half in sorrow at their thick heads, half in sorrow for what I realised, even then, was passing.

'There is another way, I am thinking,' I said, pulling off my boots and spilling out the ringmoney, the brooches, the coins that would have pulled me down but for Short Eldgrim's rope. My secret.

They gaped, circle-mouthed. I grinned back at them.

'Now we trade,' I said.

EPILOGUE

In the light of the dancing lantern, guttering fish-oil smoke that was whipped away by the wind, only their eyes gleamed as they hunkered down out of the spray at one end of the ship.

I felt those eyes like brands but tried to ignore them, concentrating on the Greek captain and staring at him in turn, until he felt the burn of my eyes and whirled on his men, barking angry and pointless orders in his unease.

He had taken us aboard in two minds, that captain, caught between greed and fear. On the one hand, we had paid him well and stacked all our weapons – save mine – and that reassured him.

On the other, he knew what we were, suspected we were deserters from the Rus army at Sarkel and knew that, even armed with just eating knives and horn spoons, we might try to take his ship.

Finn suggested as much, hissing it in my ear, and they waited for my signal, huddled and miserable. I would not give it, for I was not about to risk my life for a filthy little coastal fish-trader like this.

Sarkel had fallen, the captain told us, trying to judge our reaction to that news. No one blinked much at it – what was

333

Sarkel now to us? We had no ship and were crushed with loss. We could not set foot in the Rus lands now, so the only safe place was the Great City, where we had no prospects.

Well, that last was not quite true and Kvasir voiced it for all. He hunched himself up by my side, the wind whipping the greasy tangles of his hair. 'You have the right of it, Trader,' he growled, ducking as the spray lashed us. 'This is not the ship for us.'

'Just so,' Finn echoed. 'What we need is a solid *knarr*. Or one of those Greek *dromon* ships.'

'A big-bellied one,' agreed Short Eldgrim, picking a scab on his face. 'That can carry a lot. There are many in Miklagard.'

'And some more good men,' offered Sighvat. 'Good Norsemen or Slavs, not afraid of a hard oath.'

And they grinned like wolves, yellow-fanged in the dark, so that my stomach turned over.

I knew why they needed all this, and were looking to me to come up with a deep-minded plan to get it. I sat in the salt-slick wind, feeling the bite of it, the damp seeping through the stained wool of my tunic and the despair settling on me like morning haar in a fjord.

It was what they did – what they were. The fear they had felt just weeks before had eased, leaving only the lure of what was still out there to be found. You could not be a Northman, have the knowledge of a mountain of silver and simply leave it there.

They had not seen what I had seen and none of my horror tales of Hild's fetch would keep them from going back.

We were still on the whale road and, in the wind that keened and thrummed the ropes, I swore I could hear Odin laugh.

A NOTE ON THE HISTORY

The Whale Road is set in and around the year 965AD, an era when the line of kings in Norway and Denmark is confidently set out by historians and, for the same era, the nation that would end up as Sweden is generally marked as 'chaos and confusion', with not even the names of the protagonists known for certain.

More confidently, the history of several hundred years earlier does record that Attila died on the night of his wedding to Ildico, who was found beside the bloody corpse the next day. No one knows where he is actually interred, though the Hungarians make the loudest claim for it, at the same time as repudiating that the Hun part of their name has anything to do with that barbarous tribe. I prefer the idea of his being interred out on the open steppe, but that is pure invention on my part.

He did have a famous battle-winning sword and both he and it seemed to have been interchangeably called The Scourge of God – but who made it, its twin and what they were made from is also my own invention.

The Volsungs are real – well, more real. They figure in the classic Saga of the Volsungs – no one has yet confidently identified who they actually were – composed anonymously between 1200 and 1270, almost certainly in Iceland and probably using all the stories, in prose and poetry, which had been handed down about the Volsungs and Gjukungs.

In it, the whole relationship with Attila the Hun, tributes of treasure and more is an integral part of the story. Elements of that and other Icelandic *eddas* went on to become the basis for Wagner's epic *Ring Cycle* and, later, Tolkien's *Lord of the Rings*.

Birka and the other trading ports along the Baltic all suffered from the lack of eastern silver around this time, but Birka suffered most of all and, by 972AD was all but gone from history. Gotland, until then a seasonal fair, picked up the trade and now some of the richest archaeological finds of Dark Age silver come from that island.

The rise of the Rus into a nation at this time is fascinating. The Norse, the Slavs, the strange Khazars and all the steppe tribes swirled in the huge cauldron of central Russia, slowly being moulded into an empire, first by Sviatoslav, then Vladimir and finally, Yaroslav, the Wise, who re-fashioned Kiev in the image of Byzantium, laid the foundations for a new Kremlin and built the famous Golden Gates, as well as the Saint Sophia cathedral.

Finally, there are the *varjazi*, the Rus name for those bands of Norse warriors hiring themselves out for pay. They had carved out the kingdoms of the Norse, but now those kingdoms had no use for them – they were busy making themselves into nations and the sea raiders of the past were now interlopers to be fought off.

Even their gods were under threat from the rise of Christianity and only the growing rift between the Greek church of Byzantium and the western worship of Rome seemed to slow the process. The final schism between those two churches came in the 11th century, but arrived too late to prevent the demise of the Aesir gods of the north. Stubbornly, the *varjazi* fought on until only their name was left – the Greek rendering of it was *Varangii* and the famed Varangian Guard of the Byzantine emperors was composed of 6000 originals sent by Vladimir to Byzantium only some 20 years after the events of this story.

Less than a hundred years later the ranks of this elite Viking guard were almost all filled by Saxons from England, fleeing after Hastings, having been defeated, ironically, by the Normans – the Vikings who had settled in France.

The so-called Dark Age was coming to an end. Those who imagine this meant civilisation coming out of a long, dark tunnel of barbarism, where beleaguered souls huddled round fires in skins, bemoaning the loss of a good Roman bath and waiting desperately for someone to reinvent underfloor heating, should consider that the Norse, at this time, traded, raided and settled from Iceland to Russia, from Orkney to Jerusalem. Byzantium, at this time, was a city of more than a million people when Paris was a collection of huts with a few thousand – and the Norse attacked both with equal arrogant confidence.

Finally, this is a saga, to be read round a fire against the lurking dark. Any errors or omissions I claim as my own – but don't let it spoil the tale.

ACKNOWLEDGEMENTS

Top of the list of people who made this book a reality are the Oathsworn – all the crew of Glasgow Vikings (www.glasgowvikings.co.uk) who, wittingly and unwittingly, have ended up sailing on the *Fjord Elk* through these pages. Thanks a lot Colin, Aeneus, Jill, Eric the Tight, Gail, Helen, Presto and others too numerous to mention – and a huge shout to Boj, Einar the Black himself and the best swordsmith around (www.armourclass.co.uk).

There are even more Norse around than that and much of what has been uncovered, discovered and recovered in this book is down to The Vikings re-enactment group (www.vikingsonline.org.uk) who are unstinting in their efforts to bring the authentic flavour of Viking, Saxon, Norman and Celtic life back to the 21st century, including drinking entire communities dry.

None of which would matter if James Gill, my agent at PFD, had not spotted the potential in this – full marks to him and to Susan Watt, my editor at HarperCollins, who took the unruly band of Oathsworn, trimmed their hair, blew their noses and pointed them in the right direction of a proper saga. She and the rest of the HarperCollins team are brilliant.

A big thanks, too, to all those on the Khazaria Fiction group who gave of their time and expertise to make sure I got that part right, especially Kevin Brook, author of *The Jews Of Khazaria*. Also to Norm Finkelshteyn, whose own website on The Red Kaganate is a wealth of treasured info on the steppe tribe (www.geocities.com/kaganate).

Lastly – thanks to Largs, my home town and the place where the Vikings were finally kicked out of the UK by the Scots in 1263. So surprised were the Largonians at this victory that they have been waiting for them to return ever since and are so apologetic they have created an entire tourist industry round them, just to say sorry. I know – for ten days every year, I am part of it, at the annual Viking Festival and that is what inspired my interest.

GLOSSARY OF NAMES

ALDEIGJUBORG – Starya Ladoga, a town near the eventual site of St Petersburg and a trading port at the entrance to the first of the rivers leading south into Russia.

BIRKA – Main trading port of the Baltic in the 9th and 10th centuries, it was also noted for being the site of the first Christian congregation in Sweden, founded by Angskar (see Hammaburg, below). After 972AD, Birka vanished from historical record - it is thought that a combination of silting harbours and a failure in the flow of silver from the east killed it off. Gotland, further east, rose in its stead.

BJORNSHAFEN – Orm's home – fictional, it is based on archaeological evidence in many farm sites, such as Ribblehead in Yorkshire.

DYFFLIN – 'Dubh Linn' (Black Pool) was established in the 10th century and became a favoured trading place for the Norse.

GARDARIKI – Norse name for early Russia, the kingdoms of Novgorod and Kiev. Usually translated as 'kingdom of cities'.

HAMMABURG – Early name for Hamburg, seat of Bishop Angskar, whose missionary zeal drove Christian priests out to convert the north. In reply, Vikings sacked the place in 845AD and the bishop barely escaped with his life.

HEDEBY – One of the best-known centres for commerce and industry, situated at the bottom of the Danish peninsula of Jutland; the territory at that time was part of Denmark but it now belongs to Germany. This thriving 'town on the heather', was destroyed in 1066 and no longer exists.

HOLMGARD – 'Island town', the Viking name for Novgorod, which was originally the chief town of Gardariki (see above) until the capture of Kiev, further south.

ITIL – Capital of the Khazarian Empire - moved to this city in 750AD from Balanjar – Itil was also the Khazar name for the Volga River. Destroyed circa 965/66AD by Sviatoslav of Kiev.

JORSALIR – Jerusalem – in the 10th century, it was the city of the People of the Book – Jews, Muslims and Christians – and, despite warfare outside it, maintained a religious peace inside. The baptised Norse, newest and most-travelled pilgrims, made a point of visiting it.

JORVIK – The pre-eminent city of Norse Britain from 866AD, better known as York.

KHAZAR KHANATE - The Khazar empire extended (8th–10th centuries) from the northern shores of the Black Sea and the Caspian Sea to the Urals and as far westward as Kiev. In the 8th century this essentially Turkic people adopted Judaism.

KONUGARD – Kiev – 'city of the king'. Eventual capital of the Rus/Slav kingdoms which became modern Russia, the city was established by Turkic tribes and 'liberated' by Swedish Vikings Askold and Dir, traditionally in the year 860AD.

LANGABARDALAND – Norse name for Italy, which was gradually transmuted into 'Lombardy'.

MIKLAGARD – Constantinople, also known as 'the great city'. The place to be in the 9th and 10th centuries, the Big Apple of its age and capital of the Byzantine Empire.

NORVASUND – The Straits of Gibraltar.

SARKEL – Byzantine-engineered fortress of the Khazars on the Don river, which controlled the trade routes to the east so successfully that the Rus of Kiev eventually decided that it had to be captured.

SERKLAND – Baghdad. Also the generic name for the Middle East (so called because, it seemed to the Norse, the people there only ever wore underwear - a 'serk' or white undershirt).

SKIRRINGSAAL – Once a Norse Baltic seasonal trade fair, called 'Kaupang' by foreigners - a Viking joke, since that's what they told them it was called when asked. Kaupang simply means 'a market'.